# *THE SECRETS OF TIME TRAVEL*

## A Novel

## James J. Warchol

# DEDICATION

For my dear parents, Bernice and Lee, who enabled me to have such an amazing life. They introduced me to so many wonderful experiences and adventures through the years—some of which inspired parts of this novel. They filled my life with love, happiness, and great memories. And although "Pop" has moved on to be with our Lord in Heaven, he's still with us in our hearts.

And for my wonderful wife Carmen, the greatest encourager I've ever known. Her incredible love brightens the world and continually helps me become a better man. She is truly a gift from the Lord and I thank Him often for blessing us with such an amazing marriage.

# ACKNOWLEDGMENTS

I would like to extend my heartfelt thanks to:

Almighty God the Father, God the Son Jesus, and God the Holy Spirit—to You I extend praise and thanks from the deepest parts of my heart. Without You, all is meaningless, but with You, life is utterly amazing. Your inspiration fueled my mind and spirit every step of the way.

Tom Bird for helping me fulfill my dream of being an author.

Paul D. McCarthy for sharing his wisdom and insight that ensured this novel would be at its highest level.

Ramajon for his tireless support and for being a searcher who loves to find.

Denise Cassino for her amazing energy and can-do attitude.

# CONTENTS

# PART I:

## *The Long Quest Continues*

# Chapter 1
## Monday, 4:00 p.m.
## Many Years from Now

Alton Reed struggled up the mountain, his legs aching from the strain of the climb. His heart sank as he came upon a group of blackened trees. He took in the sour smell of charred wood dampened by recent rain as he drew closer to the trees and scrutinized each one. The damage indicated lightning strikes, but not in a random fashion. The evidence clearly showed a designed pattern. He shifted his gaze downward and sighed. Time was short.

His tension eased for a moment as he felt a fresh breeze against his face, blowing away the stench of parched trees. He smelled the crisp, pine-scented air and glanced at the breathtaking blue sky, decorated with puffs of white.

"Oh God," prayed Alton, "thank you for the beauty of Your amazing earth. I hate to see it scarred."

He massaged his forehead as the tension crept back in. He tilted his head back to try to suck in more air but being in the high Rockies of Colorado was taking its toll.

"Mighty God, will this quest ever end? Three hard years of study and searching caves, but still no scroll." He reached his arms to the sky, his fingers straining toward the heavens. "I know it's out there. But I'm just so ... tired. I know I'm only forty-four years old, but I feel like I'm eighty." He lowered his arms as his head sagged. "Please help us."

He plodded forward, stumbling on a root and nearly losing his footing. Pain shot up his legs as he scrambled to avoid a fall. Disaster averted, he plopped onto a rock to catch his breath and think for a bit. He knew the tree damage was another sign of Sivvius's growing, more focused power. His ability to control nature in such a precise way was outright scary. But far worse than the power was what it really meant at the core. Alton's logical and scientific mind had concluded that using such power was part of Sivvius's plan to rule the entire earth. The fact that millions would be led down a path toward eternal damnation broke Alton's heart far more than the destruction of the earth's beauty.

He looked back down the trail and saw his ever-faithful friend in the journey, Walter Briggs, approaching. Alton could see he was exhausted. "God, I hope I haven't pushed him too hard. How much more can he take?"

Alton raked his swollen fingers through his long, frazzled hair and attempted to smooth out the wrinkles in his white button-down shirt. He always wore a dress shirt, even when hiking, since he felt like attire that was more formal helped him think better. His hair, however, felt too ordered after the raking, so he messed it up a little. He loved neatness and order, but his hair was another matter altogether. Wild hair seemed to inspire out-of-the-box thinking. He focused on slowing down his breathing and attempted to look composed for his fellow Council member.

He watched as his rail-thin friend trudged up to him, wiping the sweat from his glistening, mostly-bald head. When Walter reached Alton, he unfastened his backpack's hip belt and pushed the pack off his shoulders, letting it slam to the ground. He trudged over to Alton, grimacing as he bent to sit by him on the rock. Walter looked nervous as usual, abruptly shifting his gaze back and forth as he scanned the area. The trials of the past three years had taken their toll. He did his usual routine of checking that the two compasses were still in his left pocket, and the trail map was still in his right pocket. He never used the compasses or the map, but Alton knew the presence of older technologies helped to lessen Walter's stress level. He knew Walter loved discovering new things, but also knew he found comfort in the simple things, and in the things of the past.

Alton contained a chuckle as Walter checked the notch his pants belt was on, undid the belt, inspected the notch, squeezed his stomach a few times, and finally fastened the belt again after unsuccessfully trying to achieve the next-tighter notch. After a few more tries, he settled on the looser notch position, and let out a loud, halting sigh. Alton rested a hand upon Walter's shoulder.

"How are you feeling, my friend?"

Walter paused for a few seconds, gasping for air. "Fat and tired."

"I know it's been brutal. But we're getting close."

"I want to believe that, Alton. But this whole thing is starting to feel like a lost cause."

Walter paused again, still panting. After a few moments, he was able to eke out a few more words.

"I can taste the disappointment but I can't spit it out."

"Hang in there. Today could be the day we find the scroll."

Yet even as Alton heard his own words of confidence, a memory of a terrible day filled his mind. It was a day he hated to remember, yet a day that still haunted him. So many years ago, when he was just a boy. He could see the smoldering oak, his favorite tree. He could hear the crackling bark, smell the pungent odor of burning leaves, taste the thick presence of gasoline in the air. But far worse was the haunting memory of the evil laugh of his long-lost friend as he watched Alton cry.

"Alton, are you thinking about him again?"

"I can't help it. I saw more burned trees today. A tight cluster. Very controlled hit. How can I forget what he's done … what he's doing?"

"Just what we need. More attacks."

"Many more. And we're only seeing a glimpse of what he's doing, almost as if he's toying with us. I heard on the news a few days ago about strange weather phenomena across the nation—devastating stuff. His range of weather control has increased dramatically. And you know what that means."

"Yes. People are scared and will do just about anything to be protected."

"That's right. Even to the point of giving their souls over to his evil cause."

Alton's mind kept churning as they got off the rock and continued onward. The need to find the scroll was imminent. He knew the scientific breakthroughs contained in the scroll would reveal how they could stop Sivvius. His heart ached more each day, knowing so many were turning their backs to God and their hearts toward Sivvius, and ultimately Satan. And he knew God's heart was breaking seeing so many of His beloved creations turning away from Him.

"Hey, Alton. Let's take another break. My legs are burning, my back's aching, and my head's pounding. This high-altitude climbing is killing me."

Walter struggled up to Alton and bent over, panting like a parched dog.

"I just don't know what I'm going to do about all this extra weight I'm carrying."

"We really don't have that much in our packs, Walter. You know our years of practice have taught us to pack light. We have just the right mix of spelunking and technical research gear."

"Surely you know I'm talking about the weight around my middle."

"How many times must I tell you you're thin as a rail? If anything, you ought to put on a few pounds. You know your weight is at least ten pounds lower than the recommended weight for your height."

Alton watched his wiry friend squeeze the sides of his stomach and shake his head in disgust.

"You're just trying to make me feel better. I don't trust scales any more than I trust those new fat-blast pocket pens. I can't let this paunch get the better of me. What would Ingrid say? Oh, how I miss her."

Alton tried to think of a way to steer the conversation in a better direction before Walter spun himself into a web of tangled thoughts.

"Why don't we try to—"

Alton snapped his mouth shut as he felt a cool breeze waft across his face. His eyes darted back and forth but saw no indications; there were no rock outcroppings, no crevices, no signs of any kind. Yet the breeze wafted across his face again. It smelled musty, like an old cellar on a cool fall day. He had smelled it many times before. His pulse quickened.

"Walter, do you feel it? Do you smell it?"

"Smell what? I'm too tired and fat to smell right now."

Alton kept scanning the area, straining to see where the odor might be coming from. Then it caught his eye.

"Look ahead on the trail. Do you see a strange sight by that boulder?"

"Not really. Just a big rock."

"Look closer. See how barren it is on its left side?"

Walter stared for a while, the scowl on his face menacing. Then the scowl faded. He let go of his stomach. And he stood.

"I see three more boulders off to the left."

"Precisely. And look between the three and the one."

"Looks ... looks like a void."

"Yes. And the one and the three. The three and the one. One on the right of the void and three on the left. Just as foretold. I can't believe what I'm seeing. This must be a dream. This could be the one!"

"It's possible, Alton. But we thought it was the right cave so many times before."

"But none with the one and the three so precisely configured. This really could be it. Let's go!"

As they approached, Alton noticed that the three boulders on the left of the void were each the height of a yardstick times two and twice as wide as they were high. And the one on the right was half the size of each of the three. It was exactly as the secret Einstein text had described.

As Walter broke into a run toward the void, Alton felt pins and needles race down his spine.

"Stop!"

Walter jerked his head around and stuttered to a clumsy stop.

"What is it?"

"Something's not quite right."

"Why?"

"I'm not sure yet, but we have to proceed with caution. As much as we need to go full steam ahead, we must ponder this before we move any closer. All must be right. A mistake now could derail our progress. Let us ponder and pray while we dance, just to be safe."

"Are you sure? Do we really *have* to do another dance?"

"We must do this the right way. We can't ignore what I'm sensing. You know to gain the deepest knowledge and insight we must dance, and we must combine the motion with pondering and prayer."

"But this dance stuff just reminds me how out of shape I am. And even though I love the pondering and praying, I struggle sometimes with the logic of the dancing. It frustrates me that I can't prove how it works with any formula. No matter how much I analyze it and try to wrap some science around it, I just can't seem to make sense of it."

"Just remember the benefits. You know when we combine motion with the pondering and prayer we always seem to end up discovering the most amazing things. It paves the way for God to send His wisdom. So let's start. We can't waste precious time!"

Walter looked back to the boulders, then over at Alton. His gaze drifted toward the ground as he let out a long, steady sigh.

"Of course you're right. It does work somehow."

Walter walked back to Alton and faced him. They bowed their heads, breathed in deeply, and began the dance. It really was more like a series of elegant poses than a dance. An arm outstretched to the sky. A head bowed toward a knee. A leg pulled behind the body. The only sounds were clothes rubbing against bodies and deep breathing. At the end of the dance, they turned toward each other and locked eyes. No words. No expressions. Alton blew out the tension as the need for a quick answer nagged at him. Then he felt a slight movement of his right eye. He didn't force it to happen. It just happened. He noticed that Walter noticed. He saw the expression on Walter's face intensify as he focused his stare into Alton's right eye. Alton watched Walter watching him. He waited. Again, he felt the eye movement. A squinting. Just the right eye. Squinting ever so slightly. He felt it squinting. He sensed a thought.

"What is it?" asked Walter.

"My heart burns within me to throw caution to the wind and run to the void. I know we can't waste precious time but … something … there is still something. I just don't feel at peace yet."

"This is really depressing me, Alton. I have this awful feeling you're going to say we must dance some more."

"Yes, we must dance a bit more, and pray. Let us pray and open our minds to receive God's wisdom."

9

Alton was amazed just how far Walter's head could sag when he was trying to make his point, but Alton could spend no more time debating.

"We must do this. Millions of souls are at stake. We have to get past ourselves, and we have to do it now."

Walter let out one of the longest sighs Alton had ever heard, but he gave in and got in position. The poses were more elegant and refined this time, the breathing more controlled. As Alton prayed not only for himself, but also for Walter to receive wisdom, he noticed Walter's expression changing. He was receiving something as they danced.

"How do you feel?" asked Alton as he stopped his dancing. "Do you sense a deep peace?"

Walter stopped his dancing and looked into Alton's eyes. "Yes. I feel an amazingly deep peace."

"Excellent. This peace is from God. I sense we will face something awful in short order, but we must move past our fear. God's perfect love drives out all fear, and He is with us. We needed these few moments to draw near to Him before we pressed on."

"I agree. We can never have too much help from God."

"Then to the edge, my friend … to the edge."

# Chapter 2
## Monday, 4:45 p.m.

"Alton, this must be the right cave," said Walter, as they inched toward the opening. "This is all that is left in my life that gives me hope of ever finding Ingrid. Even though it's been decades, I can still picture her. I'll never forget that day by the tree in the schoolyard when I finally mustered the courage to talk to her. Such a sweet voice ... such sparkling eyes ... such an intoxicating laugh. It was a dream come true that day. I knew we were meant to be together. If the class bell hadn't rung, I think we would have talked for hours. I never knew it would be my last chance before summer break. I couldn't wait for summer to end so I could see her again ... only to find out her family had moved out of state. If only I had gotten her number. If only I had told her of my feelings—"

"I know," interrupted Alton, as he patted him on the back. "I ache with you. I see such sadness in you at times. I know how much she means to you. I will help you find her. The scroll will help us find her."

"You're a good man, Alton. I know your passion is to save millions from eternal agony, and I know you're under unbelievable time pressure, yet you so often stop everything to listen to my Ingrid lamentations ... even though you've probably heard them a thousand times."

"You are my dear friend. You will always be my dear friend and I will always make time for you. It is my joy to help you and encourage you. And together, we will encourage so many others as we spread God's love and truth. Science introduces us to truth but God fulfills it. God's love and wisdom bring a real understanding of the truth, and amazing levels of peace and joy about the truth. We cannot let Sivvius continue to lead people toward what is false."

As they drew closer, Alton felt his body tingling, as if a puff of fear had just drifted by. They reached the edge of the cave opening and stopped. Alton tapped his right eyebrow twice, activating the tiny chip beneath his skin that revealed key atmospheric and dimensional details in a heads-up display. Alton's heart raced as he scanned the area. The temperature of the air was as foretold. The wind direction: precisely as it should be. The boulders: of the correct size and alignment. The dimensions of the opening: exact. All was as Einstein's old secret book said it should be—Alton had memorized the details. His thoughts drifted briefly to the amazing day he'd first found the book in an obscure bookstore overseen by such an eccentric old fellow. What he read then was so unusual for Einstein, yet interlaced with such flawless logic and formulaic proof. It clearly showed his style. Now, the unusual parts, those more like musings, were coming to life right before his eyes. His wild anticipation, however, was mixed with a trace of fear.

"Alton?"

"Sorry. Just thinking. Hard to believe we're here."

The cool air blew across his cheeks and through his clothes. The musty smell filled his nostrils—a smell he loved, a smell he craved. They peered in together, seeing nothing but darkness. They stared. Neither spoke. It was hard to tell what was within, hard to tell if it was just a small chamber or a vast cave.

Alton felt his body tingling again. It was sharp and focused this time, and now he knew for sure ... not from God. He sensed something terrible. Something evil. Dread pulsed through his mind. He stood straight and gasped.

"What is it, Alton?" asked Walter. "Do you see something?"

"It's not what I see, Walter. It's what I sense."

"You don't mean—"

"Yes. I do mean. I sense Sivvius. And in a way more terrifying than ever before."

Alton felt the tingling transform into a hailstorm raging through his body. And then he heard it—subtle laughter seeping out of the cave. A laugh he knew all too well. He felt bile rising from his stomach. He felt it in his throat. He looked at Walter and knew he heard the taunting laughter too.

"Not the laugh again," groaned Walter.

"Yes, it is the dreaded laugh again. No matter how many times I hear it, I'm still chilled to the bone each time. There is always such pride in his laughter. It is laughter gone bad. Yet it seems worse this time. Something strange about it I cannot quite describe. Subtle, yet strong."

"Yes, you fool. I am stronger, you feeble-minded, decrepit wretch of a man."

Alton's blood ran cold as he heard the familiar voice seep out from the cave. A voice so filled with evil, hatred, and mockery of all things good that it permeated his blood vessels, veins, and arteries. The laughter had chilled his bones, and now the voice felt like it was weaving its evil essence through his bloodstream. It felt like a wave of putrid sewage laced with acid, rushing, pulsing, pounding through his body. He'd heard it so many times before, but this time it seemed even more evil. Just like the laugh.

"Tell me Alton, why are you here?"

Alton could not find words. His face flushed and he felt sweat on his body, causing his shirt to stick to his back, even in the midst of the cool breeze that blew across his body as he stood at the lip of the cave. The musty smell he loved so much was mixed with a rancid odor, like milk gone bad. His mind raced as fear pulsed through his body. Fear greater than ever before. Not just fear of Sivvius's evil, but fear that Sivvius had found the scroll before them. The agonizing, debilitating fear felt physical and heavy, weighing him down and causing his upper body to sag.

"Well, Alton? Can't you even speak?"

"I ... I ... I can—"

"You can what? Make a fool of yourself? This I already know. But don't worry about your foolishness. It's only because you're so proud. You think you're God's gift to the world. Get off your pedestal."

"Sivvius, any pride I have is in God's greatness. He truly is mighty. And loving. And He still calls to you."

"You still trying to turn me to your side? You still think there's hope for me? How many times have I told you you're wasting your time? Now shut up. I don't want to waste another second talking about God. What I want to do more than anything right now is cause you pain."

Alton felt a piercing pain fill him, as if every extremity of his body was about to explode. Even though he could barely keep his eyes open, he forced himself to, just so he could watch his fingers. It felt like they were about to burst open at the tips. He had endured pain from Sivvius so many times before, but this was a new level. This was an unbearable surge of gut-wrenching, mind-numbing pain. He dropped to his knees and cried out for God to help him. He managed to turn his head just enough to notice that Walter had passed out on the ground.

"Please stop hurting Walter," whimpered Alton as he fought to maintain consciousness.

\*   \*   \*

Sivvius crouched low in the dark cave. His scarred flesh was covered in sweat and grime and glistened in the subtle light from above. He'd been searching for hours, digging feverishly into the moist, mucky sludge on the cave floor. Excavating tools of all varieties were scattered around him, along with a lab coat, chemical-analysis apparatus, and cave sketches. If he could find what Alton and his pathetic friends were seeking before they did, there is no way they could stop him from achieving his goals. But his search was yet again proving to be fruitless. He slammed his hard hat on the ground in frustration, causing the headlamp to flicker.

He prayed quietly, coughing a bit. "Oh my mighty friends from beyond, help me stop Alton from finding what he seeks. Help me find it first."

Sivvius rubbed his right cheek and felt the deformed skin, the pockmarks left from the burns of so long ago. He rubbed a finger across his lips. The plastic surgery had helped some, but they weren't really lips any more. They were too thin, and there was no texture. He felt as if he was rubbing the surface of a disposable plastic dinner plate. And how he hated to touch his nose. It felt like the snout of a pig, with openings far too large and exposed. At least he could hide the leathery skin on his shoulders and back under his flannel shirt, but his face was exposed to the world. How he missed the days of his youth when he often heard the girls in his school talking about how cute he was. But that was decades ago and now only a torturous memory that would never leave him.

He ripped his hand away from his face, looked up at the cave opening, and yelled out to Alton.

"Suffer, you fool! Suffer again for what you've done to me!"

Sivvius sent out another wave of pain. A smile grew on his face as he heard Alton whimpering. He waited, enjoying Alton's suffering. And then hated himself for enjoying it. He struggled with feelings of what might be madness, but pushed the thoughts deep into himself. He must stay focused. Time was short. He had to keep ahead of Alton in the search for the scroll. He put his hard hat back on and continued scanning as he moved toward the other cave entrance.

\* \* \*

Alton continued to kneel by the cave opening. The waves of pain Sivvius sent sapped his strength, making it nearly impossible for him to stand. He was only starting to catch his breath when he felt a drastic change in the air pressure. He felt like he was at the bottom of a deep pool, with his ears aching from the pressure. Then he saw what he could only attempt to describe as the sky dipping to the ground. He saw the ground bend inward as the sky pushed down upon it. It was like a tornado funnel but fixed in place with no motion. And the color was so strange. Partly gray, but mostly like a clear blue sky. Alton could not stop staring, filled with utter fascination at what he was seeing. He eventually managed to stand again, driven by his need to investigate the strange sight. He struggled over to check on Walter first and was relieved when he saw that he was starting to revive.

"Are you okay, Walter?"

"I think … I think … so. I'm dazed. I need to rest. What did he do to me? What did he do to you? Are you okay, Alton?"

"I'm better now. It was intense, what he did today. It was the most pain I've ever felt. He's getting even stronger."

"Yes, I think you're right … but … but … sorry Alton … I must shut my eyes … must rest … must … rest."

Alton turned his head back and saw the sky still pressing into the ground. He was flabbergasted. How could he be seeing what he was seeing? He walked closer to investigate, but as he drew near, he felt his head start to tingle and noticed the hair on his arms standing on end. The space around him filled with flashes of lightning. Peals of thunder and the sound of splintering trees assaulted his ears. He felt as if he was bathing in electricity. He fell flat to the ground. His throat burned as he strained to suck in the scorched air. He curled himself into a ball, closing his eyes tight, knowing it was a feeble attempt at trying to protect his body from the brutal assault.

"Oh God, help me! Please let it stop!"

Almost as quickly as it had started, the assault of weather stopped. He opened his eyes and saw huge branches strewn all over the ground, and all he could hear was the crackling of trees as they roasted in the aftermath of the lightning strikes. He coughed, and rubbed his burning eyes to take in the magnitude of the devastation. There had to have been thousands of lightning strikes into the focused area.

"Walter, are you all right?"

"Barely, Alton. I can't believe this."

"Nor can I. This is beyond comprehension. So much destruction, so quickly. Sivvius's control of the weather is so focused now. His powers have reached a new high. We've seen many of his weather attacks, but this one was so precise, so lethal. I'm exhausted from these relentless and ever-growing attacks. I know he's honing his great knowledge of physics and chemistry to enable him to have such control of the lightning, but it's more than just science at this point. Surely the hellish forces he prays to are giving him supernatural help."

"How can we possibly stand against this, Alton? His power is just too great. First, pain like never before, then this precise control of lightning."

"I know it seems impossible to stand against it. Yet we *must* stand, Walter. We *will* stand. But not alone. Only with God's help. He is our only hope against such power."

Alton walked away from Walter and looked over the damage. It was unbelievable destruction, and he was still amazed at how it happened so fast. He hated what he saw. He hated the death of such beauty, he hated the smell of ended life, and he hated the evil that was behind it all. But more than anything, his heart ached for those who were being deceived into joining Sivvius's evil cause.

"Alton?"

Alton looked over at Walter who was now sitting up, looking better.

"Yes, my friend."

"Do you think he found the scroll?"

Alton walked back to Walter and spoke in a whisper.

"I don't know, Walter. Every other time he just left his telltale sign by the cave openings, just to taunt us: just to let us know that yet again he was ahead of us. His friends from beyond somehow always managed to lead him to the caves before us, although never to the one that actually contained the scroll. Yet this time he was still here. I'm afraid it can only mean one thing, and I can't bear to think upon that one thing. If this is finally the right cave, but Sivvius has already found the scroll in it … if he has taken it … oh Walter, I can't allow myself to ponder this option."

"Surely he hasn't found it. How could he know?" Walter whispered.

"I don't know for sure. Maybe his friends from beyond were finally right. All I can hope is that he just wanted to remain in the cave to strike fear into us by showing an even greater display of his power."

"Do you still sense him?"

Alton closed his eyes and focused his thoughts for a few moments, reaching out to God for help, listening with his spirit for God's still small voice.

"I don't think so." He walked back to the cave opening and peered inside, focusing his thoughts again.

"I don't sense him right now. And I don't sense ... them. I can sense their lingering presence, but I think it's only that. Still, it's hard to know for sure. Sometimes they seem able to block me from sensing them. At least the pain and the weather attack have both subsided. Let us hope he has left empty-handed, off to search for another cave. Let us hope his search here was futile and yet the scroll waits for us within, hidden from his evil mind. Let us hope God Almighty has prevented him from finding the scroll. What we find could change all that science holds to be true. It could be the very thing that can help me conquer my ancient foe, and ensure we'll always be able to enjoy a beautiful flower and a gentle breeze. It could be the very thing that will help us do God's great work and stop Sivvius from drawing more souls to his evil cause."

"Let us look then," said Walter.

"Yes. Let us look."

"And let us hope," said Walter, a subtle smile forming on his face.

"Yes. Let us hope. But first, let us pray. Come kneel with me. We may be scientists, but without God's insight, what we know of science is but a taste of its depths."

They knelt together, bowed their heads, and prayed silently. In his mind, Alton cried out to God, seeking His blessing and guidance. He felt peace. He opened his eyes and peered into the cave.

He tried his best to block his fear that Sivvius had already found the scroll. He hoped beyond all hope Sivvius had not found the secret sign that would lead to the scroll's location. He looked deep into the cave, squinting to help his focus.

Alton looked so intently for so long that his vision blurred. He rubbed his eyes and tried to refocus. Cupping his hands around the outer edges of his eyes, he blocked out as much light as possible. He scanned up and down each side of the cave, but still saw nothing. He took a deep breath, and let out a long sigh. He thought for certain he would see the sign. If what they sought was in the cave, they should be able to see the sign from the cave opening with only natural light seeping in. Einstein's secret book had been very clear about that.

Alton closed his eyes and prayed softly. "What have we done wrong, God? How can there be no sign? All is as it should be. This has to be the cave. Oh God, please let us see the sign."

Alton kept his eyes closed, continuing his prayer, now in silence. He suddenly felt an overwhelming sense of confidence. He slowly opened his eyes, and sensed a brief glimmer. It wasn't that he saw a glimmer; he just felt it. Somehow, his mind knew there was something in the cave reflecting light, yet his eyes had not fully registered the reality of it.

He stared at the spot where he felt the glimmer was coming from, and his eyes eventually agreed with his mind. Something was reflecting light near the right side of the cave. He shielded his eyes more and focused on the spot. Then he saw them. Stalactites from above and stalagmites from below, grown over time to meet each other, forming majestic columns. The deposits that had formed the columns contained elements that caused the gentle glimmer as the subtle light from above struck the surface.

The alignment of the columns was just as the Einstein text had detailed. The closest one to the cave opening was about the length of two men away from the right wall, the next one farther into the cave was a man and a half away from the right wall, and the farthest of the three was about the length of a man away from the right wall.

This has to be the sign, he thought. This *is* the sign. Thank you God!

Alton didn't want to break his stare, but sensed that Walter was looking at him. He snuck a quick glance at him and saw despair on his face.

"I see nothing, Alton. And in this posture it really accentuates the feel of the annoying girth around my middle."

Alton stared into Walter's eyes and remained silent. When he noticed Walter was starting to look uncomfortable, he finally spoke.

"It is there, my friend."

"What? Where? I see nothing!"

"It is there."

"Show me! Where? Are you sure?"

Alton sat there, mesmerized. He felt a tear slide down his cheek; he was filled with an overwhelming sense of peace and joy.

"Yes, Walter. I've seen the sign. For three years we've struggled and searched and cried and hurt. All the pain … now worth it. That which will help us save the earth and stop Sivvius is nearly in our grasp. Let us continue to hope Sivvius did not know of the sign. Let us hope he had no way of knowing."

"I can't believe it, Alton! We've really found it? Let's go in. Let's go in the cave right now!"

"Wait," Alton said as he placed a hand upon Walter's shoulder. "Remember the Council."

"But you're our leader. Can you not venture in and advise the Council of our findings later?"

"I desire more than anything to venture in right now. It takes all my strength to hold myself back. But we must wait."

"Why?"

"After what Sivvius just did, it is not wise to be separated. We must prepare, and we must act as one. Even with time so short, we must take the time to do this."

"But Alton—" Walter paused and looked at Alton. After a few moments, he let out a sigh. "I suppose you're right. We must wait for the rest of the Council. But where are they?"

"I'm ashamed to say it, but I'm not certain. In my feverish pace to press on, I let them slip behind."

Alton gazed down the trail, straining his eyes, seeing nothing.

"I'm getting a bit worried, Walter. I hope Sivvius hasn't waged an attack on them without us being there. I hope—"

Alton heard a familiar voice, and the tension drained from his body. Then he saw them come into view.

"C'mon, laddie. Let's pick up the pace. You're slowin' up the whole train. We're embarrassingly behind Alton and Walter."

"I'm trying," said Michael. "I'm pushing as hard as I can."

"Well, tryin' isn't good enough! Push! Push!"

"Angus!" yelled Alton.

Angus jerked his head up toward Alton. "Aye! Alton! Sorry we're so far behind. This laddie here is holdin' up the whole show. And the blasted heads-up display of this blasted GPS implant keeps fadin' in and out. You'd think by now they'd have the bugs worked out. It's a wonder we've not lost you for good."

"You won't believe what we've found," said Alton. "Come quickly and gather 'round."

When the five other Council members got to Alton and Walter, all Alton could hear was packs dropping to the ground, groans, gasps, and sighs of relief. A couple of packs burst open, spewing rope, harnesses, picks, and even some of the sensitive technical gear.

"Be careful, you wild bunch of laddies! That's the last thing we need is to have some of our scientific gear dashed on a rock. You're so slow with your hikin' but so fast when it comes time to take a break!"

Angus looked past Alton when he reached his side. He pushed up on his toes, purposely flexing his stout calf muscles as he peered forward. He smoothed his long, wiry hair back, doing so in such a way as to achieve maximum bicep flex.

"What have you got there, laddie? Looks like we've found another hole in the ground?"

"Yes, Angus. That we have. But this is like none other." He reached out his hands and waved the others in. "Let us gather, my friends. This is a time of great rejoicing, for I have seen the sign! But let us first prepare for a time of meditation and prayer before we plan the entrance into our destiny. Let us seek God's wisdom, and let us draw together in unity and purpose."

The Council members let out hoots of excitement, and Alton's heart leapt as they exchanged bear hugs and handshakes. He loved to see his fellow scientists smiling and laughing. He cherished the moment. After searching so many caves, they had finally found the sign. He felt like he was dreaming.

After the rejoicing simmered down, Alton motioned for them to sit in a circle and enter into the time of prayer, meditation, and subtle motion activities. He knew how critical it was for this time. They needed God's protection, and they needed to be unified and strong. They must be prepared for what was ahead of them. He watched with approval as they entered their meditation poses.

# Chapter 3
# Three Years Earlier

Alton breathed in the intoxicating odor of ancient texts as he walked into his favorite bookstore. It wasn't just the smell of the old paper that made it so special, but also knowing there was such incredible scientific wisdom and knowledge contained in the books. It was as if the words themselves emitted the captivating aroma.

The store specialized in scientific books. Books from the greatest and most well known scientists of all time filled the shelves, yet there were also numerous obscure texts written by unknown authors. Some days he would just roam around the store, pick out a text from a scientist he had never heard of before, and delve into a new world for a day. But the writings of Einstein were his favorites and he was always looking for something new from him.

As he walked deeper into the store, he took it all in: the aged wood paneling, the squeaky hardwood floors, the dim lighting, the deep silence—they all worked to create a magical getaway from the outside world. And the quirky owner, Mandrake, added to the perfect ambience. Quirky, but amazing—possibly the greatest scientist Alton had ever met. He sat far in the back in his partially hidden alcove, hunched over his desk, glasses at the tip of his nose, reading. Always reading.

The only time Alton would hear him was when he came across a particular theory or proof that really amazed him. The response was always the same—sudden, soft sucking in of air, followed by a mumbled word: "Razintazin." Alton didn't know the meaning of the word, and was quite sure it probably *had* no meaning. But he loved the days he would hear the word, for on those days, the old man would call out to Alton to sit and reason with him regarding his latest find.

Alton walked to one of the racks near the back of the store, one where he had found some very unusual writings before. He looked along the shelf at eye level and spotted a book with some wonderful markings along its spine. He pulled it down and looked more closely to identify the author. Zinitar Nucleus, he read. What an amazing name, thought Alton. As he looked at the title, it piqued his interest: 'A Practical Guide to Transforming Anti-matter into Matter'. This cannot be possible, mused Alton. This I must read.

Alton found his favorite chair, the one with the permanently formed indentations that fit him perfectly. It was his chair, at least as far as he was concerned. He plopped down, anxious to delve into this intriguing book. At first, he was fascinated by Zinitar's ideas, but the farther into the book he read, the more he realized Zinitar was way off base. His proofs that anti-matter could be transformed into matter were weak and sketchy. He rested the book on his lap and sighed. He longed for something new and life changing. He longed to find something that would revolutionize science. He tried to keep reading Zinitar's work, hoping something would jump out at him, but he struggled to keep his eyelids from drooping.

"Razintazin!"

Alton jolted awake as he heard his favorite word. He jumped up and trotted to the end of the aisle. As Alton peeked around the corner, he could just make out the look on Mandrake's face. He appeared to be glowing as he gazed at the ceiling, deep in thought. Then he snapped his face back down to the book, his nose almost touching the page, resuming a feverish assault upon the text. Alton's heart was beating fast, in hopes that the old man—the great scientist—would call to him today. He craved something deep, something unusual, something new.

But Mandrake said nothing, and as Alton glanced at his watch he realized it was time for him to leave. He liked to eat dinner early so he wouldn't feel bloated and sleepy during his time of evening study. He liked to spend his evenings at home, poring over scientific journals, trying to find something new. As he walked toward the door, his mind focused on only one thing—the voice of Mandrake asking him to come reason with him.

As he neared the door, he slowed. He looked back and saw Mandrake, still fixated on the book. Alton stared at him, hoping for the call. But there was none. Alton reached the door, grasped the handle, and shook it vigorously. He looked back at Mandrake, but still nothing. Alton cleared his throat and coughed a few times. Still no reaction. He yanked open the door, letting it slam on the wall behind it. Still, Mandrake's eyes stayed fixated on the book.

Alton's shoulders sagged after one more throat-clearing, coughing session brought no reaction. He stepped over the threshold of the door—

"Razintazin! Razintazin!"

Alton froze. In his years of coming to this incredible store, he never, ever heard Mandrake utter a double Razintazin. Never.

Mandrake's head snapped up from the text.

"Alton!"

"Sorry, Mandrake … I … I did not mean to disturb you. I know I have been unusually loud today."

"No, my boy. You have not disturbed me. I have heard nothing since I started reading this text. Come, sit with me for a bit and let us reason together. Let me show you what I have found."

Alton scurried to Mandrake and peered over his shoulder. Mandrake slowly lifted the book so Alton could see the title on the spine. His heart jumped when he saw the title ... and then he stopped breathing when he saw the author's name.

"Oh my God," said Alton. "It can't be! How can this be? I have never heard of this work before. And I know all of Einstein's works!"

"Yes, Alton. I too know all of his works. And this one ... well this one I have never seen. That is, until today."

"Mandrake," said Alton as he gazed upon the text, "it is handwritten!"

"Yes, Alton. A text of Einstein's never seen before, and written in his own hand. Look, my friend."

Alton gently took the text into his hands and studied the writing. He had studied handwritten letters and notes from Einstein to other colleagues before—writings that had become available to the general public. He knew the handwriting of Einstein well, and this looked precisely like his cursive style. And it was written in German, just like Einstein's other works.

"I assure you the text is his, my dear friend and fellow scientist, Alton. Not only the handwriting, but the style and the content are clearly Einsteinian."

"If there is anyone I fully trust, it is you, Mandrake. Your word alone is enough. You are not only the greatest scientist I have ever known, but also a man with integrity beyond any other."

"Your words are most kind, my dear friend Alton. I assure you, the feeling is mutual. Our discussions are the highlight of my life. Now sit, my friend. Let us read together."

They took turns reading the text aloud and discussing. The reading and discussing continued well into the night. As the night ended with the morning sun peeking through the front door, Alton closed the book and turned to Mandrake.

"I'm utterly amazed at what we have read, Mandrake."

"As am I, Alton. I am amazed that this book has somehow fallen into our hands. A secret Einstein text—handwritten at that! And now, Alton, I give it to you. It is my gift to you. I see the fire it brings to your heart and mind, and I have this strong feeling that it was meant for you."

Alton paused for a few moments, staring at the book.

"Mandrake, I'm deeply touched by your gift. I thank you with all my heart. I'm amazed by the mystery of this book as well. The more I ponder it, the more I believe it was God's will for us to find this secret text. I do not fully understand it, but I believe it was God's will for the text to appear in this store. I believe it was God's will for you to find it and show it to me. I know God has a great purpose for me. I will study this book further and seek God's will. Today I will embark on a great quest: I will find what this book speaks of. This very day, a new and exciting chapter of my life begins. Would you like to join me, Mandrake?"

"I am flattered by your offer, Alton, and I would join you if I could. But I am much too old. Besides, my adventure is here amongst my books. Just know you will be in my thoughts and prayers each day. I will miss you."

"Thank you, Mandrake. I will miss you as well. I pray that God will bless you every day of your life."

\* \* \*

Alton sat in a quaint coffee shop, sipping the coffee of the day. He was taking it easy for a few days after enduring three hard months searching the Rocky Mountains referenced in the Einstein text. He was reading an article about the few still-remaining contradictions between quantum physics and general relativity. He gazed into the heavens, pondering about dark matter, dark energy, negative energy, and closed timelike curves. After a few moments, he reached into his pack and pulled out the Einstein text.

"Thank you God, for not letting Sivvius get the book. I do believe this book truly is from Einstein. I know his writings, Lord. I know these are his words. But this scroll he speaks of. In a cave in the Rockies—a single cave among thousands! I can't find the cave alone, I can't find the scroll alone, and fighting Sivvius alone is much too difficult. He is getting stronger, and I sense the evil around him growing. And Lord, finding out that Sivvius is actually my long-lost boyhood friend Eddie gone bad ... oh Lord ... it's just too much for me to handle. I can't believe he secretly spent all these years plotting against me, and against You. Even though he just revealed himself to me three months ago, it seems like I've been struggling against him for years. I need help, Lord. I need another scientist to help me in this great quest. Please let this be the day I find another."

After praying for a few more minutes, Alton wiped his moist eyes and looked at the book in his lap. Just as he opened the text, he heard a man loudly shout, "Aha!" Alton lifted his eyes, and noticed a man sitting a couple of tables away, engrossed in a book. Alton couldn't quite place it, but other than the loud "Aha!" there was something unique about the man. Something Alton sensed about him, although he was not sure what it was. Just something. Alton shook his head and focused back on the text.

Try as he might, he couldn't seem to absorb what he read, and glanced back over at the man. He felt the sense again, even stronger this time.

"Okay, God. What is going on here? Are you trying to tell me something?" Just as Alton asked, he felt chills through his body. Good chills. The man stood up, dropped some money on the table, and walked off. Alton reached into his wallet to get a few dollars to pay for his coffee and scone. He noticed the smallest bill he had was a fifty.

The man was nearly out of sight.

Alton looked for a waiter but saw none available. He scanned his wallet again. No fives, no tens, not even a twenty. No waiter. Man almost gone.

He slapped down the fifty and scurried after the man, who rounded a corner and slipped out of Alton's sight. Alton picked up his pace and rounded the corner, but the man was still out of sight. He looked around frantically. Out of the corner of his eye, he spotted the man in a nearby park, gazing up toward the sky. He breathed a sigh of relief and hurried over to the man.

"Simply amazing," said Alton, as he also gazed at the sky.

"What was that?" asked the man next to him.

"Oh, sorry … I was just thinking … out loud it appears."

"That's quite all right. Tell me … what is so amazing to you?"

"I'm just amazed at the intricacies of God's creation," said Alton.

"I am amazed as well. God's knowledge is so far beyond ours. And I so much enjoy studying the things of science to get at least a little more understanding of God's amazing creation."

"Oh? Are you a scientist?" asked Alton.

"As a matter of fact, yes. I have a passion for the things of science. And you? What is it you do?"

"I am a scientist as well. The name's Alton. Alton Reed."

"It's nice to meet you, Alton. My name is Walter. Walter Briggs."

"Well, I must say, Walter, it is most definitely an honor to meet you. It is always a pleasure to speak with a fellow scientist, especially one who appreciates the wonders of God and His creation. Tell me, if you don't mind, what is your main field of interest?"

"Time travel."

"Did you say time travel?"

"Yes. I'm fascinated with the concept of time travel. In fact, I'm currently doing a study of the old VCR technology."

"Please, tell me more."

"Well, I was studying magnetism and its effects on space-time a few days ago. As I was running a list of magnetic devices through my mind, the old VCR technology popped into my thoughts. As you may know, magnetism was used in the recording process. And if you deeply ponder the functioning of the VCR, with its main purpose being the recording of programs for later viewing, you can't help but be struck by the thought that you are enabling viewing of a past occurrence in the future."

Alton turned his full attention to Walter.

"Go on … please."

"Think about it. We record a show, and then when we watch it later, we are truly watching the past. We have brought the past to the present. We have indirectly traveled in time to the past."

"That is intriguing, Walter. I had never pondered it quite that way."

"Don't feel bad about that, Alton. Most have not."

"But tell me Walter. What about photographs—or even old paintings? What about history books? These tell of the past as well. These, in essence, bring the past to the present."

"Yes, yes, this is true in a sense, Alton. But in my experiments, I discovered that there are changes to space-time when the VCR is fast-forwarded or rewound. Time in and around a VCR moves slightly slower or faster than time at a

James J. Warchol

distance. Granted the differences are almost negligible, and almost impossible to measure. Yet the differences are there."

"How did you measure the differences, Walter?"

"I designed a special time-mapping device that can measure time alterations to the trillionth of a second. The device also measures magnetic field changes. The VCR causes both time changes and magnetic field changes."

"Walter, I'm absolutely amazed by your analysis. I'm fascinated with time travel as well, and have done many of my own experiments. Although I have invented many things over the years, my inventions have not been associated with time travel. I long to master the art of time travel one day, but I fear I have reached my intellectual limits. I have actually reached my limits in many areas of science. Attaining my many degrees has taught me much, and helped me with my inventions, yet I wish to go much deeper. I know that with the help of other scientists who have the passion for discovery I have, I can achieve great new heights. I would love to study with you the deep things of science, physics, and time travel. Perhaps together we could unlock the mysteries of the universe."

"I'm most pleased and quite humbled by your offer, Alton. I too feel as if I have reached my limits. I feel I have touched on many deep concepts, but I know there is more. Much more. I know there must be deeper truths out there. Truths beyond what I have learned in the universities, and what I have discovered on my own. I hardly know you, but I sense a strong intellectual bond with you. I accept your offer for the two of us to study the deep things of science."

"Excellent, my new friend! But there is something I must tell you, for if I do not, you will discover it on your own one day and wish to accompany me no longer."

"Please tell me. I'm certain that whatever it is, it will not shock me. I've seen much in my lifetime."

"It goes back quite far. Quite far indeed. Actually, it started when I was but a boy. I had a very close friend as a boy, and we had wonderful times together, doing the things young boys do. We were adventurers and explorers, and life was so simple and free. But my young friend changed, partly due to his father, and partly due to me, or at least so he believes. There was a particular day … a terrible day … a day that he will never forget, and a day that was a turning point in his life. He became evil, and sadly, he funneled the hatred that consumed him toward me. Unbeknownst to me, since that day so many years ago, he has been secretly plotting against me, and against God. After all these years of not seeing him, he confronted me about three months ago. He is terribly evil now … and terribly powerful. And his focus in life is to stop me."

"Stop you from what, Alton?"

"I do not want to overwhelm you, Walter, but for now, suffice it to say, the earth is in grave danger. The souls of millions are in grave danger. I'm on a great quest not only for scientific discovery, but also to protect the world from this terrible evil—"

Alton stopped short. He could see the look of confusion on Walter's face. He could see the look of skepticism. Walter remained quiet. Alton reached into his backpack.

"I assure you, Walter, I have not lost my mind. I assure you what I speak of is truth. Here, let me show you something. Do you follow the works of Einstein?"

Walter's face softened. "Oh yes, Alton. I'm a great admirer of Einstein's work. Such a fan that I spent years studying German so I could read his works in the original language."

"As am I, Walter. I have read nearly all of his works. Yet this one I had never read or even seen before until three months ago. Do you recognize it?"

Walter took the book from Alton and gazed at its cover. Alton noticed a new interest on his face.

"No, Alton. I most definitely do not recognize it. Are you certain this is his work?"

"Absolutely, Walter. I know Einstein's writing style very well, and this is most definitely one of his works."

"A most interesting title: 'Seeking Time'."

"Yes, Walter. It is interesting. Yet what is contained within is even more interesting."

"Hmmm. 'Seeking Time.' This could mean many things, Alton. It could be Einstein's musings on time management, or it could be much more."

"Believe me, my friend, it is much more. Much, much more. It has inspired me to enter into an epic quest. A quest to find what Einstein speaks of in the book."

"What is it he speaks of?"

"Why don't we sit on that bench over there by the pond, and you can read his work yourself. It is not long, so you should be able to do at least a first-pass reading in a couple of hours. I have my journals with me, so I can study those while you're reading. When you finish, let me know if you would like to come with me—or not. But please, know that the evil man I spoke to you about is real. And know that should you decide to join me in my quest, it will not be easy. In fact, it will likely be the most difficult thing you have ever done, or will ever do. But also know that it will be the greatest thing you will ever do."

Walter looked deeply into Alton's eyes. Alton sensed Walter was wondering if he could really trust him. Wondering if he was sane.

"Very well, my friend. Your talk of trying to save the world is a bit much for me, but let me see what Einstein has written. I very much want to see what is in this book that has affected you so. And Einstein! I can't believe this book of his is in my hands. It is a book I have never seen, and never heard of. I am deeply intrigued."

"Excellent, Walter. All I ask is for you to give it a chance. Read for yourself and decide. Decide if I'm on track with what I say, or, as I'm sure you're wondering, if I have lost my mind."

They walked to the bench and sat down. Walter looked at the cover for a few moments, sliding his fingers along the surface. He opened the book and let his eyes feast upon the text.

\*　\*　\*

Alton was just finishing reading an article about gravity manipulation when he heard Walter clear his throat. Alton looked at him, and saw him closing the book. He noticed his forehead was crinkled, and his eyes were staring straight ahead. He just sat there, quiet, staring.

"Tell me Alton ... you say you have been searching for what Einstein mentions in this text?"

"Yes, Walter. For three hard months I have searched."

"Where?"

"In the Rocky Mountains."

"In the caves?"

"Yes, in the caves."

"Have you found anything yet?"

"Not yet. It is too much for me to do alone. I need help in the quest. I need help against the evil one."

Walter was silent again. He looked back down at the book cover, mouthing the word "Einstein." He looked over at Alton.

"I'm not sure about this evil one you speak of, Alton. I'm not sure of the evil one Einstein speaks of. But I will join you. How can I not, after reading Einstein's incredible words? How can a scientist like me not be intrigued and drawn to find what the book speaks of? Yes, I will join you. Let us seek together."

"Yes, Walter! Let us seek together ... and let us find."

# Chapter 4
## Monday, 5:15 p.m.

After a few minutes, Alton opened his eyes and gazed fondly at each of his colleagues in science: Walter, Angus, Michael, Patrick, Letter A and Letter B. Such an odd collection of scientists, some wildly unique even in name, yet each wise beyond measure. They had spent about a year together as The Council of Seven, searching, praying, laboring, and preparing for this moment. I'm so blessed to have such wonderful friends and fellow scientists, he thought. So strong in science and yet such a faith in God at the same time. Thank you God, that our study of science fully supports our faith in You. He sensed the peace. He sensed the unity.

"It is time," announced Alton.

Alton watched them moving out of their meditation poses, eyes opening, heads lifting, subtle motion activities tapering off.

"We have gathered, we have prayed, and we have prepared our minds," said Alton. "I have seen the sign. Finally, this appears to be the right cave. The time is right. The time is now. Let us venture in. Let us touch that which we have sought."

Alton stood first and walked to the cave opening. He peered in again. As he looked, all he could hear was the sound of his own breathing. It was as if the birds, the squirrels, the insects, and the very wind itself all stopped moving and breathing, waiting for this magnificent event to occur.

He walked around the edge of the cave entrance, looking in from various angles, his body tense with anticipation and a bit of fear. Fear had seeped into his mind as he began to worry that the sign wouldn't be there—that he had imagined it. Perhaps he just thought he had seen it earlier. Just because he had dreamed of, longed for, and talked about this moment for so long. Just because it *must* be there.

The others gathered near the opening, waiting silently.

Alton peered over the edge again, eyes darting back and forth, searching for the sign. He saw nothing, and his heart sank. He focused on the area where he had last seen it but still nothing. He was sure he had seen it before. He squinted and cupped his hands around his eyes again to block out as much light as possible.

Finally, something caught his attention. He gazed intensely, letting his eyes adjust to the darkness. He breathed a massive sigh of relief as the columns came into view again. They were really there. But had Sivvius already found the scroll? And if he had, would he have been able to decipher it?

"Okay, my friends. This is it. Time for me to enter!"

They all jumped into action, pitching in to get Alton ready for the descent. Apart from the Letter brothers nearly knocking Alton into the cave as they rushed over to install his harness, the preparation was highly efficient. With rope and harness secure, they eased Alton into the cave opening.

Darkness enveloped Alton as they lowered him. He felt as if he were being compressed, with flesh pushing against muscle. His mind was a battlefield, with excitement and fear warring against each other. It was so hard to believe that his feet would soon touch the floor of the cave that hopefully contained the object of his dreams.

It was hard to distinguish much because his eyes were still adjusting to the darkness. He looked to where he had last seen the sign, afraid again that it wouldn't be there. But it was. He could see the glimmer as the light reflected off the three columns. But the cave floor still seemed so far below. He focused every fiber of his being on straining his toes downward to feel them touch the surface.

Time seemed to slow to a snail's pace. He felt his body being lowered, but did not feel like he was getting any closer to the bottom. "Oh my God, does this cave really have a bottom? Why haven't I reached it yet? Is this a trap? Oh God—"

Alton's feet touched the ground. It felt squishy but stable. He breathed a massive sigh of relief and a prayer of thanksgiving to God.

"I'm down!" he yelled to the Council members. "Wait above while I move toward the sign. And pray for protection and wisdom!"

Alton removed the harness and gazed toward the columns. He felt a sense of reality again. As he walked closer, their beauty mesmerized him. The way they had flowed together, bottom to top, top to bottom. It was amazing. And the colors were glorious. Shimmering, glistening hues, brought to life by the tiny bit of light seeping into the cave.

As he inched toward the sign, he left his headlamp off, recalling from the Einstein text that artificial light should not be used at this point. He saw how the colors formed an intricate pattern that subtly converged and narrowed into a thin line that appeared to point back to the cave opening.

He looked back along the direction of the line formed by the converged colors, studying the cave floor. He saw no indications of digging, no holes, no piles of mud or dirt or rock. Perhaps Sivvius really had not found the scroll. But the light was dim and he couldn't see much. He walked back toward the cave opening, studying the cave floor as he walked. A footprint? He was sure he saw a footprint. Then another. Then he noticed a hole with a heap of mud at its side.

He walked to the hole, and saw many footprints and further signs of digging. When he knelt to examine the hole, his heart raced when he noticed just how extensive the digging had been. There were numerous holes and piles of dirt and muck everywhere.

"Sivvius has been hard at work, Lord," he said. "Somehow he and his friends from beyond must have sensed the scroll was in the cave. I hope with all that is within me Sivvius hasn't found it." Anxious to do something, he took off his pack, rummaged around, and found the pick. He dropped to his knees and started digging his own hole.

He dug feverishly with the pick and his bare hands, slinging mud everywhere. He dug until he got through the muddy mess and the pick scraped on hard dirt and rock. The sweat dripped down his forehead and into his eyes, even in the chill of the cave. He moved to a different spot and dug another hole, then another, and another. He moved back to the first hole and hammered the pick like a maniac, breaking up dirt and rock. His heart raced, sweat poured down his cheeks, and he gasped for air. When he could hammer no more, he collapsed onto the muddy ground, exhausted.

He heard a commotion from outside the cave, and Walter's voice echoed off the walls.

"Alton, are you okay? Angus is getting really impatient up here."

"I'm fine," yelled Alton. "I'm still investigating."

"Nothing yet, Alton?" yelled Walter.

"Not yet. I'll let you know as soon as I find something."

When Alton heard the commotion tapering off, he resumed his investigation. He crawled from hole to hole, checking each one, digging and groping until there was no strength left in his body and his fingers ached. Yet he found nothing. He collapsed onto the ground again.

Sivvius must have found it, he thought. He found it, he took it, and now he's gone. All our searching and hoping, wasted.

He sat there, covered in mud and sweat, gazing around hopelessly. "O God," he whispered, "how could this happen? We've searched for so long. You've always been with me. You led me on this quest. You showed me the miracle when I was a boy. You showed me my purpose: to be Your warrior, to protect Your creation, to help Your people, to stop the evil one. Why is there nothing now? How could it not be here? Has Sivvius found it? Has he found it before me? Oh God, show me if it's here. Show me where it is."

Alton stopped his prayer and listened. He listened with his spirit. He sensed nothing at first. He cleared his mind of all distracting thoughts, and he waited. Then, after a long time of silence, he felt peace, a sense that all would be well.

He gazed around the cave, thinking about how to find the right place to dig. He looked back at the columns, becoming even more convinced he was digging in the correct place. The converged light had pointed this way, but even the way the columns were aligned seemed to point to the place where he was digging, along the line where Sivvius had dug. Alton looked up and saw nothing unusual at first, but eventually noticed six small stalactites protruding from the ceiling. Another indication this could be the spot. First the line of direction from the converged colors and alignment of the columns, and now the stalactites above, possibly marking the exact spot. But he didn't recall anything in the Einstein text about the six. He knew he was missing something.

Then he recalled something from the Einstein text about a doubling that would deceive and yet not deceive. He hadn't understood before, but now he did. The doubling could be in reference to the six stalactites being twice the number of the columns. The deception—maybe the six could be a deception to some, yet not to others. Not to him. The six were meant to deceive. To make others think the scroll was near them!

He heard commotion from outside again.

"Alton! Anything yet?" yelled Walter.

"I might be onto something, Walter! But I must focus. I must concentrate. We must have quiet and peace. Please meditate and pray. I'll let you know as soon as I find something."

As the commotion subsided, Alton studied the six again, looking for a pattern, something that would give a further clue. Then he noticed it. They appeared to be arranged in groups of two. Groups of two, he thought. Groups of two.

He ran back to the three columns and studied them. They all looked the same. He studied the second column very closely, noticing nothing unusual. He saw no unique patterns, indentations, or marks on it. Surely the stalactites in groups of two have some significance, he thought. I thought for sure they could in some way be referencing the second column. He pictured the six stalactites in his mind again, and it hit him. He ran back to the six and stared up at them again. He was right. The middle two jutted out closer to the adjacent wall.

He ran back to the second column, nearly stumbling on the way. He knew now it wasn't something he needed to find on the column itself, but rather something the column was pointing to. He stood by the column, facing the same cave wall the two center stalactites on the ceiling had pointed toward. The wall was glistening with dampness, shimmering in the subtle light. It was beautiful. But that was all it was. He looked back and forth along it, but noticed nothing unusual. He stared until his eyes ached.

"God, what am I missing?" he cried out.

He cleared his mind, reached out to God with his spirit, and waited. A word began nibbling at his brain ... per ... persepec ... perspective.

"Perspective?" mumbled Alton.

He felt a rush of adrenaline as the clarity came. He lowered himself to the ground and sat against the second column, still facing the wall. Something caught his attention. More than just beauty. Something directly ahead, right in his line of sight. It was something strange, hard to pinpoint. It just felt different. He noticed it out of his peripheral vision only when he looked slightly away from the spot. It seemed like that section of the wall had a slight variation in color. When he looked right at it, he could barely perceive it. It could be easily missed, especially if light was shined directly upon it. He had to strain to notice the aberration.

He inched up to the wall on his hands and knees, keeping his eyes fixed on the spot. When he reached the wall, he touched the cold, damp surface. It felt good. It felt refreshing, hopeful. He pulled out the pick again and chipped away at the surface. Chunks of mud and soft rock fell away. It was rather easy to make progress, and before he knew it, he had dug about a foot into the wall.

He reached into the hole and started clearing out the debris. After a few minutes of that, he was about to start picking again when one of his fingers touched something that felt odd, somewhat rubbery. He pressed his finger harder against the substance, and it felt as if he was pressing on an orange. He groped around the area and confirmed there was some type of object embedded in the mud and soft rock. His mind was spinning as he dug away more debris and mud with his fingers, pawing it out into the cave. As he did so, he felt a boundary along the left edge of the rubbery object. He pawed and picked at a feverish pace, trying to discern all the boundaries. He was eventually able to feel a left and right side and place his fingers on the sides. He pushed the object back and forth with his fingers, trying to loosen it from the cave's hold. His heart was racing so rapidly he had trouble breathing. He was eventually able to pull the object out a bit and rest his palms against its sides. He squeezed a little tighter, being careful not to press too hard, and pulled some more. The object started a steady slide outward and before he knew it, the rubbery mass, about the size of a shoebox, pulled free from the cave's grip and rested in his hands. He could not believe what he was seeing.

He rose from his knees and went back to the column, resting his back against it as he sat gazing upon the object. "My God, this could be it," he prayed. "It's in my hands: I hold the dream in my hands. Thank you for showing me the way."

He caressed the rubbery mass. He knew this was only the covering, the protection. He reached up to his hard hat and flicked on the headlamp, shining the light on the object. He grabbed the pick again and gently pierced the surface, easing the pick inward. He was very careful, slowly hooking it into the substance and pulling outward. A chunk tore free. He put his hands into the opening and began peeling the rubbery covering away. Then he saw a glimmer. He ripped the rest of the coating away, his caution gone.

In his hands remained a small, silvery box. He felt its cool, smooth surface against his fingertips. It felt wonderful and magical. He gazed upon it, unable to grasp the reality that it was really in his hands. All he could do was sit—and weep. The tears streamed down his face. His chest heaved with emotion. The longer he sat and the more he caressed the object, the more he realized it was real. He did not wake from a dream, clutching his pillow. He had found it. God had helped him find it. He entered into a prayer of thanksgiving.

# Chapter 5
# Two Years Earlier

Alton and Walter had spent a year together searching more caves, studying the things of science and making more discoveries. They especially loved to discuss time-travel theories and spent many long nights pondering the possibilities. Those were grand times, but hard times as well: Walter learned of the reality of Sivvius as he and Alton struggled against the unrelenting attacks.

They eventually reached a point where Alton felt like things were stagnating. They had done all they could do. They needed more help. They needed other scientists to help them in their studies and aid them in their battles against Sivvius. It was getting far too hard to stand against Sivvius, and each day Alton felt more worried that Sivvius would find the scroll before they did. And each day he agonized over Sivvius's destruction of the earth. Their focus shifted toward finding others to join them but the process dragged on for months.

"I don't know, Alton. We've been searching for a long time and still haven't found any possible candidates to join us. Seems like most of the scientists and intellects we have spoken with just can't grasp our theories. We have spoken to nearly all of my colleagues here in Denver."

"Yes, you're right, Walter. I think many turn the other way when they hear our talk of Sivvius. But we must trust God. He will show us the right ones, just as He brought the two of us together."

"Of course, Alton. I'm sure you are right—Alton, do you smell that?"

"I was just about to say something, Walter. What delightful smells! Smells like fresh-baked bread … and pizza. Oh, how I love pizza! There must be an Italian restaurant near here … yes … yes … up ahead, Walter. I see it just ahead. I'm famished. Let's call it a day and enjoy a nice dinner."

"Sounds wonderful, Alton."

They entered a quaint Italian restaurant. The lights were dim, and there were jars of peppers and dry pasta arranged attractively on shelves. Photographs of celebrities lined the walls, and as they walked toward the host, Alton noticed some photos of men he was sure must be Mafioso, each with his arm around an elderly man—probably the owner. He noticed some other photos that looked like scenes of Italy. Smells of homemade breads and pastas and life-changing sauces filled Alton's mind and titillated his senses. He knew this was going to be a wonderful celebration for his taste buds.

The host seated the two of them at a table near the back of the restaurant. The restaurant was full and Alton felt lucky to have gotten a table so quickly. As he glanced around at the other tables near them, he was drawn to a small, dimly lit corner booth, almost within arm's length. He saw two men deep in conversation, faces close, arms and hands gesticulating. They seemed oblivious to the chatter of the other customers that filled the restaurant.

He couldn't help but stare, since he felt as if he was watching a scene from the old classic Godfather movie. Even though Alton wasn't even born when the movie was filmed, his father was a fan and had a copy in their movie collection. Alton's favorite actors in the movie were Al Pacino and Marlon Brando, and he was amazed how the two men in the corner booth resembled them so strongly. The man who looked like Al Pacino had the same type of nose and jet-black hair, and the man with a strong resemblance to Marlon Brando had the same type of sagging jowls. As Alton listened, he managed to catch their names. The one who looked and even sounded like Marlon Brando was Patrick, and the one who looked like Al Pacino was Michael. Alton was mesmerized by their conversation as he listened. He noticed Walter was fixated on them as well.

"You know, Patrick, I sure have fond memories of a special day many years ago."

"Really, my friend?"

"Yes—I will never forget it."

"Tell me of this great day."

"It was a day filled with some of the greatest joy in eating I've ever experienced."

"Tell me more, Michael."

"Have you ever tried chocolate-stuffed flounder?"

"Not chocolate-stuffed, no, but I've experimented with many other types of stuffing."

"But never chocolate-stuffed?"

"Never."

"So what type of stuffing is your favorite?"

"I enjoy the Tabasco-infused, pepper-stringed liver."

"Really?"

"Oh, yes. It's absolutely wonderful."

"How do you prepare it?"

"Well, let me tell you, Michael. I dip the liver slabs into a vat of raspberry coating, which is a mix of raspberry preserves, dill weed, and mustard. Then I inject Tabasco sauce into the center of the slabs, you know, to give the whole thing a little zing. Next, I cut the slabs into thin sheets, and sew them on the edges with pepper string. I leave a small opening in the sheet pocket, which I fill with liquid garlic, cloves, and lemon-pepper seasoning. Once I sew the opening with pepper string, I baste the final product for seven days over warmish coals."

"That sounds wonderful! But how do you keep everything from leaking out through the sew joints?"

"Oh, I forgot to tell you that. I make a paste out of a mixture of pure Vermont maple syrup and a mild food epoxy—another great invention, by the way. I boil the solution for twelve hours, then plop in the fillets and let them soak for two days. This seals the entire sew line. But enough about my idea. Tell me more about your chocolate-stuffed flounder."

"Well, one day I was studying the impact of heat and light upon a magnetic plasma I had invented, when the experiment yielded a doubling of the magnetic intensity of the plasma at a certain light intensity and heat level. The doubling concept, although exciting to me regarding the implications to magnetic-field control, was even more exciting as I thought of it in relation to my chocolate-stuffed flounder. You see—"

Alton knew they had stumbled upon the Godfather of food and his right-hand man. The two men went on for quite some time about how the magnetic plasma study and other studies influenced many of their food concoctions. He was fascinated by their scientific discussions, and how they related science with food. The more he listened, the more he realized they were far more than lovers of food; they were lovers of science—and extremely intelligent. He was amazed at their analyses. So amazed, he began to wonder if the two of them might be meant to join them in their quest.

And he just loved to watch Patrick talk. He was so serious as he spoke of food—the look of intensity upon his face as if he was planning a major hit upon a rival Mafia family member, the hand movements and arm motions displaying his passion for the topic. He truly was the Godfather of food. Alton finally built up the courage to interrupt their conversation.

"Excuse me, gentlemen, I hate to interrupt, but I could not help but overhear your conversation. I'm impressed by your deep scientific analysis of food. Please tell me, if you don't mind, how you have come across such incredible knowledge."

Alton thought that perhaps he had made a huge mistake. Patrick stared him down, his eyes squinting, his jowls sagging, not a word out of his mouth. Alton saw him look at Michael, and as they whispered quietly to each other, he imagined them planning how to make sure he would never talk again.

"We have discussed your proposition," said Patrick.

Alton waited for more but heard nothing as Patrick continued to stare at him. Alton felt sweat forming on his forehead. He was about to cry out that he was so sorry for interrupting them, when Patrick broke the silence.

"And we need to know a little more about the two of you before we can further consider your offer. If we like what we hear, and we perhaps decide to disclose to you the sources of our knowledge, then maybe someday you can do a little something for us in return."

"Walter," Alton whispered into his ear, "I think maybe they really are Mafia. But how can we not pursue these two? Just in this short observation, I can tell they would be of massive benefit to us. Their analytical ability and scientific background are most impressive. And I sense so strongly that God has led us to them. We've searched the caves for months without success, and Sivvius rages on. I believe they must join us ... Mafia or not."

"I agree, Alton," Walter whispered back. "We need their help."

Alton spoke of their great quest to save the earth and make incredible scientific discoveries. As he spoke, he noticed that Patrick and Michael seemed to soften and develop looks of interest. They eventually invited Alton and Walter to join them at their table. Alton learned just how intelligent they were, and that they were multi-degreed scientists who spent many years engaged in deep scientific studies. Over the past couple of years, they had focused their studies in the area of food and nutrition since they were convinced that food was the building block of the greatest thought possible. He also learned that Michael had a passion for navigation and travel directing.

Alton began to salivate as he imagined how much their analytical and navigation abilities could help them. He told them of the Einstein book, and the quest for the scroll. He even spoke to them of Sivvius, and his plans to make the earth desolate and draw millions of souls to evil. Alton spoke with passion about the power of God, and how he believed God was with them in this quest ... protecting them ... helping them.

Walter vouched for Alton and spoke of the attacks from Sivvius, explaining how his attempts to hurt them and try to stop them were a clear indication that they must find the scroll soon. He said that with their help, chances of finding the scroll more quickly would be much better. Walter also spoke of his deep love for science and his own inventions. He and Alton poured it on thickly, doing all they could to interest them.

Alton sensed it was time to wrap up the marketing campaign, and capped it off with mention of the strong possibility of discovery of new and exciting types of food if they were to join them. When he finished speaking, Patrick sat motionless, staring into Alton's eyes.

Patrick eventually asked for a few moments to consult with Michael. The two whispered for a while again, and Alton could swear they were speaking in Italian. After a few minutes of whispering and hand waving, Patrick turned back toward Alton.

"We are intrigued by what you and Walter speak of, Alton, especially your talk of Einstein and his secret book. And your talk of this Sivvius is fascinating—scary, but fascinating. What you tell us of your growing ability to sense an evil presence around Sivvius also intrigues us. We would like to learn more about this. And we can also see your deep trust in God. This is very reassuring to us, since we share in your love of God.

"But this decision is difficult. We are entrenched here in this community. Granted, we have no wives or children to worry about leaving, but that is only because we've devoted our lives and our time to the study of science, and now of food. We've done most of our studies here, and we love this town. We love the people—"

"Yes, Alton," said Michael, "we are devoted to our food club. It's an excellent group of food intellects that we've bonded quite deeply with. We are not just about creating food with great taste—we are into the design of new spices, into the analysis of the chemical building blocks of the various foods, even into the history of the origin of the foods. I spend much time doing virtual travel research for our club."

Patrick pulled Michael to his side. The whispering began again. Alton was certain it was Italian. Patrick turned back to Alton.

"Yes, Alton, most difficult to leave. Yet we can't stop talking about this Einstein book you have found. We are fascinated. And this scroll you speak of ... how can we not be enticed?"

"And your discoveries, Alton," said Michael. "You have spoken to us of inventions that baffle our minds. We can see that both you and Walter are amazing scientists—"

"And to have the chance to study with such great scientists," said Patrick, "could be an opportunity we may never have again."

The two of them turned away again, resuming their whispering in Italian. The whispering turned to loud discussion as the hand gestures reached new levels of intensity. One particularly wild wave resulted in accidental connection with the lip of their breadbasket, sending garlic rolls high into the air and nearly into a woman's soup bowl at an adjacent table.

Alton watched with deep joy, chuckling at their antics. He loved these two men already. He saw their passion. He sensed good in them, and a pure love of science. He prayed with all his might that God would put it in their hearts to join them. As he watched, he noticed the hand waving slowing, the loud discussion softening. Then, silence. Patrick slowly turned so he was looking straight into Alton's eyes.

"We have considered your offer and have decided to join you in your great quest."

Alton nearly jumped in the air as he felt his heart leap for joy. They all shook hands, and there were even some hugs. Patrick poured glasses of good red wine for all of them.

"Let us toast our newfound friendships," said Patrick.

As the glasses clinked and they made their toasts, Alton's mind was racing with thoughts of what they would investigate next. But he knew they needed to form an official Council first. He had been thinking about and planning for this day for months. Alton raised his glass to make a very special toast.

"My colleagues in science. Today is a great day, a day that marks the beginning of an incredible future of discovery and revelation. We are a perfect mix of skills and abilities. And as we have talked today, I have come to realize we are of like mind and purpose. We all burn for the things of science. We all are driven to discover new and incredible things. And we all love the wonders of God's earth, and desire to protect it and the people upon it. Today, as we toast, we are officially establishing ourselves as The Council of Four. As an official Council, we will have a better sense of mission and identity. We must also have official titles. Do you all agree it is wise to establish such a Council?"

They nodded their heads in agreement as they clinked their glasses together.

"I not only agree," said Walter. "I also recommend our first action as The Council of Four should be to establish you as the President."

"Here, here," said Patrick.

"I agree," said Michael.

"I am deeply honored by your desire for me to be leader. I receive this honor with humility and serious commitment. I shall do everything in my power to lead us in the best manner possible. As my first act as President, I recommend you, Walter, as Vice President of the Council. Do you concur with my recommendation, Patrick and Michael?"

The two of them whispered again for a few moments.

"We absolutely concur, Alton," said Patrick. "We have come to know Walter well during this meal, and it's clear to us he's an amazing man with not only a wonderful passion for the things of science, but also a man of deep compassion for others. He will make an excellent Vice President."

"Most excellent!" said Alton. "As for you, Patrick, I recommend you to be Chief Dietician and Meal Planner for the Council. You are a natural for this position. Your talk of food, meal planning, consumption, and analysis of the various aspects and nutritional benefits of food is amazing. Do you all agree with this recommendation?"

Intense head nods and glass clinks confirmed the recommendation.

"Finally, Michael. I recommend you first as Apprentice Dietician to Patrick. I can clearly see your passion for all things of food makes you an excellent assistant to Patrick in this area. Secondly, I would like to recommend you as Travel Director for the Council. I see not only your incredible passion for food, but also your passion for virtual travel. You can take this virtual travel passion, and translate it into real travel planning and directing as we move forward in our quest. Do you all concur with my recommendations?"

Again, there were head nods and clinking glasses.

"Then it is official! We are now The Council of Four. Let us begin our quest to discover incredible new things of science, and to find the mysterious scroll of which Einstein speaks. And let us fight the good fight for the sake of the earth and for the sake of the people God has placed upon it!"

The glasses clinked again, and the discussion flowed freely. They spent the rest of the day in the restaurant, planning their future. Alton felt an indescribable peace and a strong sense of God's presence. He knew God was pleased with the formation of the Council. He knew God had brought them together. He knew God would be with them in their quest.

# Chapter 6
# Monday, 6:00 p.m.

Sivvius sat in a dark recess, watching Alton. He had decided to stay in the cave when he had heard the others gathering around the opening. He sensed he should wait, just to be sure he had not missed something in his search of the cave. Now the light from Alton's headlamp allowed Sivvius to see his head bowed in prayer. And the box in his hands. This was disastrous. Total failure after so long. He had hoped this day would never come. His plans to draw all souls to his side and rule as supreme leader of the world were grinding to a halt.

He whispered a prayer to his friends from beyond. "My friends, I searched this cave all day. The cave you led me to. Just like you led me to all the ones before this, yet this one with the greatest promise of discovery. I'm always so amazed at how you help me, how you answer my prayers with strong impressions in my mind. For so many years you've helped me, helped me build my hate, my power. Even given me my new name. You're all I need. But how was Alton able to find the box before me? How could this have happened?"

It seems impossible that Alton could have found the box on his own, he thought. Could Alton really have received help from God? Does this mean there really could be a God? He hated this thought. He felt debilitating fear knowing that Alton had found the box. He knew there was some type of scroll inside. His friends from beyond had whispered it in his mind. It was a scroll that could be a huge problem for Sivvius, a scroll that could enable the Council to bring his plan to a dead stop. Perhaps he should just run over to Alton and kill him. He should be able to overpower him, to smash the life from his body. But he couldn't do it. Something was stopping him, deep within himself. Something always stopped him, and he knew what it was.

"My friends from beyond," he prayed softly, "will the day ever come when I can fully purge the final remnants of good from deep inside me? Will the day ever come when I will be able to lash out and tear the life away from Alton? Please help me. Please help me to become pure evil for you."

Sivvius sat there, staring at Alton, a sick feeling growing in his stomach as he witnessed Alton's joy.

"Oh, my friends. What should I do? I want to kill him. Yet I can't. He has the box. He will soon be a major threat."

Sivvius bowed his head and waited for inspiration from his friends. He reached out with his thoughts. He waited for impressions to fill his mind and reveal to him what to do next. He felt the presence of his friends, their power, their hatred: he liked it. He knew what he needed to do.

*     *     *

Alton's prayer of thanksgiving was interrupted when he heard Angus shouting from outside the cave.

"C'mon, Alton! I can't stand it another minute! What's goin' on down there?"

Alton could hardly wait to get back to the surface and show his colleagues the box. They must enter into motion together and prepare for the opening of the box. He ran to the harness beneath the cave opening and yelled up.

"It's beyond comprehension, but I have the box in my hands right now! Get ready to pull me up! Just give me a moment to reattach the harness."

As Alton was reaching down to grab the harness, he felt a sudden chill course through his body. A chill of fear. A terrible sensation of deep evil came over him. It was strong and focused. And close. It was not just Sivvius he sensed: the friends from beyond were with him. He sensed their demonic presence growing. He couldn't see them, but he knew they were there, and he knew they were frighteningly powerful. He frantically groped for the harness.

\* \* \*

Sivvius felt rage pulse through his mind as he lunged at Alton, tackling him with all his strength, ripping the box from his grip. He jumped to his feet, the box held high above his head.

"Ha! You stupid fool! How easy it was! You see my power? You have lost your box! It is mine! How easy! How could you be so—"

Sivvius felt massive pain rush into his hands. The pain was a mix of fire and ice. When he tried to move his fingers, pain raced up his arms. It felt like all his fingers were broken. He felt the fire and ice moving through his shoulders and into his head. His thoughts blurred. His vision faded. His tongue felt like an old leather shoe. He felt his body withering, collapsing to the ground. He dropped the box.

Sivvius sat there stunned, nearly unable to think. He barely heard the Council members yelling from above as his mind raced with agony. The pain eventually started to subside and his vision was clearing. He could swallow again, and his tongue felt nearly normal. He heard Alton assuring the others he was okay. Sivvius reached out to his friends from beyond.

"Oh, my friends," he whispered. "Why? Why can't I even touch the box?"

"Sivvius," said Alton as he picked up the box, "don't you know God does not want evil to have this box? Don't you know it's your evil that keeps you from what is contained within? Repent, Sivvius. Turn to God. Turn away from your friends from beyond."

Sivvius looked up at Alton. He saw the expression of love and compassion on Alton's face. He hated it.

"I don't need your God, Alton. How many times must I tell you? What has He ever done for me? Has He given me the power I have? Has He given me the mighty army I have on this earth? Has He given me anything? Would He ever give me what I really wanted? No! My friends have given me the dreams of my heart."

"And yet I have the box, Sivvius. Your friends could not give it to you. Don't you see now that God is much more powerful than your friends?"

Sivvius's face contorted with rage. He looked at the box and felt despair and frustration wash through his body and mind. He couldn't speak. He struggled up from the ground, his head spinning.

"Sivvius, do you actually think your friends from beyond are really friends? Do you really think demons can be your friends? Do you think they have your best interests in mind? Do you think they care about you? And when you die, do you think your so-called friends will welcome you with open arms?

"Think upon the eternal consequences. Must I remind you *again* what you're risking? Don't make the Judas mistake! Don't wait until it's too late to repent. If you don't turn away from your evil life and your demonic friends, you face eternal damnation. And you will see then that they are not friends. They will have you as their pawn: you will be their toy and their slave for all of eternity. You will be in agonizing, debilitating pain in the pit of Hell for all of time. Any sense of control and power you have now will be utterly gone."

"Oh, just shut up, Alton. You're a fool—"

"No! You're the fool! Think, Sivvius! Think of your life now. Can you honestly tell me you're happy? Think how you used to feel when we were young. Remember the joy, the laughter, the innocence. Remember how much fun we had together as boys! Can you not remember how you used to be— how you played, and how you laughed in a good way? Can't you remember how we discovered and loved the things of science together? Think back and remember how it felt. Remember how God's love felt. Don't let what happened in the past cause you to be so hateful. Come pray with me. God can forgive anything: He can forgive you, even now. He waits for you with love. You can gain your life back and be on the road to Heaven. You can receive blessings from God far beyond anything you could ever receive from your deceptive friends. Choose now to turn to Him."

Sivvius cringed with pain as he stood up. "I'm sick and tired of your preaching, Alton. Will you never relent? I've already made my choice."

"Which just shows God's love all the more! He didn't stop you from making the choice you did, because He loves us enough to give us our own free will. God doesn't want robots for friends. He loves you, and longs for you to love Him. But He will never force you. God is truly a gentleman."

Sivvius looked deep into Alton's eyes. Then he looked at the box.

"I despise you, Alton. And I despise your God."

Sivvius turned and walked deep into the cave again. His mind was spinning so much that he soon collapsed onto the cold cave floor, exhausted from the emotional roller coaster. Alton's words tore at his heart, and he hated that they did. He closed his eyes and forced the confusing thoughts from his mind. He needed his friends.

"My friends, help me. Purge my mind of Alton's foolish words, and help me to stop him. I can't kill him. I can't get the box. Help me. Help me, as your General of evil, to ratchet up the war against good. Let the epic battle against good launch to new heights. Let there be exponential growth in conversion of souls to our cause. Help me to become pure evil, so I will be all I must be to ensure the victory will be ours and I will be supreme ruler of the world."

Sivvius stopped his prayer. The words felt hollow. He could pray no more. He was drained of hope, drained of confidence. Being unable to obtain the box was a massive blow to his mind and heart.

\* \* \*

"Alton, hurry up and attach the harness! We need to get you up now!" barked Angus.

Alton stood for a moment, looking at the box, pondering. God had just done an amazing thing. It was as if God had used the evil in Sivvius against him. Somehow the evil in Sivvius couldn't come into physical contact with that which was destined for good.

Even though Sivvius had left him, Alton still felt his presence, and he sensed the lingering presence of demons. Surely, the miracle of the protection of the box must have had an impact on Sivvius.

"Lord Jesus, I thank you for the miracle of the protection of the box. I know it must be Sivvius's evil that keeps him from it. You have saved it for good, and you have protected it for your cause. Lord, I still sense there is a bit of good left in Sivvius … something that can be touched with love … brought out. Please, Jesus, show Sivvius your love. I still hold on to hope for him. A hope that he will turn to You."

Alton looked up at the cave opening again, and then at the glorious box in his hands.

"My God, I still can't believe it," he whispered. "The object of our epic quest is finally in my hands! The key to winning the war against evil could be in this box. The key to the greatest scientific discoveries of all time could be with me. Right here. And right now. I can't wait to share this glorious moment with my dear friends."

# Chapter 7
# One Year Earlier

The Council of Four had spent a year together seeking the scroll and struggling against Sivvius, as he did all he could to ensure they would not find the scroll first. Michael and Patrick got first-hand experience of the terribly evil man and his ever-increasing weather-control ability, his pain-sending techniques, and his ability to win souls for his evil army.

They tried everything to stop Sivvius: prayer sessions, preaching to him about God, distraction strategies, and even physical attempts. But he raged on. Yet Alton refused to accept the possibility that Sivvius would one day win the war and rule his desolated earth, making a mockery of all the one true God had made. He promised to himself and to God that he would never let such a thing happen.

Even though they grew in good and strength and unity as they fought evil together, the more Alton prayed to God for wisdom, the more he sensed they needed additional Council members. The number seven constantly ran through his mind, and he began to feel they would ultimately become The Council of Seven.

One day the four of them walked into a bookstore, to do some research about the Rocky Mountains. The sense within Alton that this would be the day God would bring others to them was stronger than ever. Alton watched as Walter approached an employee.

"Excuse me, young man," said Walter. "May we pull these books off the shelves and throw them on the floor so that we may wallow in them?"

"What was that?"

"I said, may we pull these books off the shelves and onto the floor so we may wallow in them?"

"Sir, why in the world would you want to pull these books off the shelves and throw them all over the floor?"

"As I said twice already ... to wallow in them."

"What do you mean by wallow in them?"

"It is quite obvious, young one. Have you never wallowed in books before?"

"I'm sorry, sir, but I don't even know what wallow means."

"Oh poor, dear boy. Have you never wallowed?"

"I'm afraid not sir. Especially since I don't even know what wallowing is."

"To wallow is to lie down with the books and let your body touch them and feel them. To read one book as you are surrounded by others. It is to be consumed with words, to be immersed in knowledge, to have it all around you."

"I just don't get it, sir."

"I am so sorry for you, young one. You work in this place of knowledge and yet you do not appreciate what is right before you?"

"I like the magazines."

Alton saw the look of disgust on Walter's face.

"Young one ... you ... oh ... never mind. I hope that someday you will understand the deeper truths of life. For now, can you at least get us some books about the Rocky Mountains?"

"Now, that I think I can help you with. In fact, I might even be able to do better than books if you really want to know about the Rockies."

"How so?" asked Walter.

"There's a guy who lives in a cabin not too far from here who is supposed to be some kind of expert or something. I heard my boss talking about him, said he was out there for some type of physical training and the guy couldn't stop talking about the Rockies. I think his name is Ingus or something like that."

Alton's heart was racing. An expert on the Rockies. This could be the break they needed. In fact, it could be more than just a break.

"We must see this man," said Alton. "Do you know his address?"

"No, but I'm sure my boss does. Give me a few seconds."

\* \* \*

The four of them left the bookstore and took a cab to the address the employee gave them. Alton was impressed when they arrived. The cabin was nestled in a beautiful patch of forest, surrounded by huge pines. The air was fresh and invigorating. The grounds around the cabin were meticulously maintained. The landscaping beds were void of weeds, the chopped-wood pile was stacked in perfect order and uniformity, and the shrubs in front were trimmed so tightly there was not a stray leaf or twig to be seen. The front porch was in excellent condition with the wood flooring looking as if it had just been stained and varnished. The cabin itself was made of real logs, and the design was impressive. The dramatic entry with huge arched windows reminded Alton of some of the cabins he had seen in log-cabin magazines.

As Alton peered through one of the windows, he noticed the main room of the cabin had hardly any furniture. There was really no room for it, due to the extensive collection of exercise equipment: a treadmill, two exercise bicycles, an elliptical machine, a series of complicated weight machines, various-sized exercise balls, and an array of free weights.

"You like it?"

Alton spun around, startled. He was about to reply, but Walter jumped in first.

"Oh yes, it's quite interesting. Are you—?"

"Am I who?"

"Are you Sean Connery's son?"

"Don't be daft, laddie."

"But you look just like him! And you even sound like him—just like in the old James Bond movies."

"Does that make me his son, then?"

"Well, no, but—you're sure you're not his son?"

"I said I'm not, so I'm not. Now quit wastin' my time."

"Excuse me, sir," said Alton. "I hate to interrupt, but I would like to introduce myself."

"Well then, introduce yourself! Don't make me stand here and wait while you waste time explainin' what you would like to do, or what you are goin' to do. Just do it, man!"

"Yes, of course. My name is Alton."

"Nice to meet you, Alton. I'm Angus."

"Why so much exercise equipment?"

"It's for my trade of physical therapy and personal trainin'."

"So far out here in the boonies?"

"Aye. I receive clients from all over the world. I'm quite well known for my physical therapy techniques and also for my uncanny sense of humor."

Walter jumped back into the conversation.

"This physical therapy you teach, do you specialize in any one area?"

"I love to work with people who are way out of shape, just like you."

"Way out of shape?"

"That's what I said. But don't be sad. Let the teeth show. Let out some air!"

"What?"

"You must admit you're rather gaunt lookin'. Are you still alive?"

"Very funny."

"Thank you."

"Anyway, let me ask you—"

"I know—you want to ask me about an exercise plan. It's a good thing, too. My God, man, you look awful. I've just the thing in mind for you. I think what we need to do is start you out with some weight trainin'. You look like you have absolutely no muscle on your frame. I'm not sure you're even alive. I'll need to push you hard, possibly even into heart-attack mode."

"Heart-attack mode?"

"Aye. I've studied the functioning of the heart durin' my years as a scientist. Minor heart attacks are actually quite beneficial. I encourage my patients to look past the immediate pain of a heart attack and strive to induce multiple attacks. The heart is a muscle just like any other, and can be strengthened by tearin' it down and buildin' it back up. And let me tell you, muscle mass really does improve the mind's thinkin' ability."

"What was that you said?" asked Alton.

"Which part?"

"The part about the thinking ability."

"Aye, it's definitely true that muscle mass improves the mind's thinkin' ability. I like to call it the mass-to-brain ratio. I did a thesis on this when I was finishin' up one of my degrees."

Alton's heart leapt. This was more than he had expected. He hadn't even begun talking about the Rockies, and already he sensed something special about Angus. He sensed that they had met him for much more than a talk about the Rockies. His innovative ideas about health and improved thinking ability, along with his physical prowess, could be of great benefit to the Council.

"Tell us Angus, what do you know about the Rock—"

"Oh Lord! It's time to go!"

"Go where?" asked Alton.

"I need to go golfin'."

"Oh, you're a golfer?"

"I've never golfed in my life," said Angus.

"Why so intent on going right now?"

"It just feels right. I've been thinkin' about tryin' it for years, and now is as good a time as any!"

"But let me ask you," said Alton, "what do you know about the Rocky Mountains?"

Angus gazed into the distance, silent for a few moments. "Aye, the Rockies ... I do love 'em so. I know 'em like I made 'em. I hate to be prideful, but I'm the world's greatest expert on the Rocky Mountains. What do you need to know?"

"Well, we've been exploring some caves there, trying to find something that might be of interest to you. But we are having a most difficult time finding the right cave. Do you know the caves?"

"Do I know the caves, laddie? You ask me if I know the caves? Of course I know the caves. I have 'em mapped out."

"How many have you explored?"

"That depends on what you mean by explored. I have a huge map on which I've put dots where the caves are supposed to be."

"Supposed to be?" asked Walter.

"Aye."

"You mean you've never seen them?"

"You got it, man. You may be gaunt, but your brain still works some."

"So how do you know where they are?" asked Alton.

"It's called the Internet. Didn't you see the laptop when you looked through the window? Oh wait—I think I left it in stealth mode so you couldn't have seen it."

"So you've never really seen the caves."

"Nope. Never got the chance. But I'd love to go. Always wanted to get out that way."

Alton wasn't quite sure what to say.

"Why all this interest in the Rockies?" asked Angus.

"We are on a great quest."

"What're you lookin' for ... some muscles for your friend there?"

Angus arched his head backward and let out a bellowing laugh.

"Very funny, Angus," said Walter. "Our quest is to find a mysterious scroll mentioned in an obscure Einstein text. We are on a quest to find this scroll and to save the earth from desolation and from a terrible man drawing souls to evil."

"Laddie ... what have you been smokin'? Now I know why you look so gaunt. It's that wacky tobacci you been suckin' on—I bet you took full advantage of it bein' legal in Colorado since 2014. My God, man, you really need my help."

"Seriously, Angus," said Alton. "We're on a great quest. It is real. It is vital. It ... here ... tell you what ... have you studied any of Einstein's work?"

"Of course. He's one of my favorite scientists. When I'm not studyin' the Rockies, or trainin' a client, you can find me with my nose in one of his texts."

Alton looked deep into Angus's eyes. He could tell he was serious.

"One of my degrees is in physics. I studied Einstein's theories then, and I study 'em now. I've done many experiments over the years based on his theories, and have made some great discoveries. You might've seen one or two of 'em when you were lookin' into my home. Did you notice the stack of dumbbells?"

"I think I recall seeing them," said Alton.

"Well, they're more than just dumbbells. I designed 'em such that a lighter weight has the same effect as a heavier one. For example, if you were doin' arm curls with one of my twenty-pound dumbbells ... oh wait, I take that back ... for your friend there, imagine you were doin' arm curls with a five-pound dumbbell. Based on the way I've designed the angle of the ends, combined with the magnetic optical matrix I've built into the bar, utilizin' wisdom from Einstein's theories, the five-pound weight would truly feel like a five-pound weight to you, yet it would have the effect of a twenty-pound weight! Can you believe it! Imagine the possibilities."

"That is quite amazing."

"Aye. I may look like no more than a perfect physical specimen of the ultimate human male, true, but I'm a scientist as well. It's just that I use most of what I learn to help others get fit."

Alton was excited. The more he analyzed Angus, the more he sensed it was his destiny to join the Council. He pulled off his backpack, reached in, and gently slid out the Einstein text.

"Here, Angus. Take a look at this."

Alton watched the smirk fade from Angus's face as he read the title.

"Oh my God, laddie. I've never heard of this book. I've read all of Einstein's works. Studied German for years so I could read the original versions. But not this. Are you certain it's from him?"

"Without doubt, Angus. Check out page ten."

Angus rifled through the pages until he got to page ten. He stood speechless, eyes scanning the page. He turned it and kept reading. About a minute later he flipped back to page ten and read some more. He closed the book and looked at the cover again. He raised his face and gazed into Alton's eyes.

"My God, man," said Angus, his voice soft.

"Come with us, Angus," said Alton. "Join us in our quest to save the earth and fight the evil one. I sense very strongly that you are meant to join us. Your deep scientific knowledge will be of great benefit, and we could use a trainer such as you, to help us in the difficulties we have yet to face. And your knowledge of the Rockies should help us find the scroll. Beyond all this, we are scientists as you are. We can explore the deep things of science together. We can invent new things together. We can show you so much of what we've already learned."

Alton waited anxiously for an answer.

"Well, I must say your offer is tempting. And I am gettin' antsy. I haven't been on a trip for a few months now—so many clients here, you know." He looked down at his left hand. "And it *is* just me. I mean, no wife or kids. They're uh ... well, they're uh ... well they're no longer here ... I mean alive ... I mean ... they're gone. It would do me good to get away."

"Sorry to hear about your family, Angus."

"Aye. But the wife was a good clip while she was alive, let me tell you! Tough old crow. She could put most men to shame when it came to exercise. And my boys ... what a handful they were. But what a joy! Aye, I miss 'em, but, what can you do. Got to keep livin'. I know my wife would give me a good swift kick in the shin if she knew I was wastin' time mopin'. So I accept your offer! It's about time I finally made it to the Rockies in the flesh! Before we go, though, how 'bout we head to the golf course?"

"Sure, Angus. It would do us all good to take a break."

"Got to take care of a couple things before we go. Most importantly, got to make sure my dogs are cared for while I'm gone."

"You have dogs?" asked Michael.

"Of course not!"

"But you just said you did!"

"I did?"

"Yes, you did."

"No, I couldn't have."

"Well, you did."

"I know!"

"Then why did you say you couldn't have?"

"Just because you wasted my time by askin' me if I had dogs after I already said I did. I just hate havin' my time wasted, laddie. I can see you will need some work."

Michael kept his mouth shut.

"Jake, come here!" shouted Angus.

Alton watched as a group of huskies came running toward them. It was a gorgeous pack of ten dogs. They looked strong, had beautiful coats, and were bursting with energy.

"Amazing how they all followed Jake, the lead dog," said Alton.

"Oh no, laddie. They're not followin' the first dog. They're all named Jake. It makes it so much easier for me since most of the time when I need the dogs I need 'em all together. It's easier to remember one name rather than ten."

"But what if you only want to call one of them?" asked Walter.

"Are you daft, laddie? All I need to do is lock 'em all up except for one of 'em, and then call that one."

"But then you have to go to the dogs and lock them up, which kind of defeats the whole benefit of being able to call from a distance, doesn't it?"

"You think far too much laddie. I can tell you have some issues. You must learn to live! Don't over-analyze everything. Just enjoy! I can see I'm goin' to have to do a lot of work with you. Now hang on a second. I'll be right back."

Angus walked about fifty yards away from his house, toward another cabin.

"Hey, Jake!" he yelled.

The pack of huskies ran over to where Angus was standing.

"I wonder why he called the dogs over there?" asked Michael.

"I don't know," said Alton.

"Jake!" he yelled again. The dogs were jumping up and down and pushing against Angus with their paws.

"Why does he keep calling them, Alton? They're right there with him. Are you sure he's okay?"

"Hey Jake, it's me. You there?"

Alton heard a door slam open and saw an old man standing on the threshold of the cabin next door to Angus's cabin.

"What is it, Angus? What in the dag-shackles do you want? I'm right in the middle of my favorite show."

"Oh, you mean reruns of The Golden Girls? Or was it The Partridge Family reruns? I always forget which show is your favorite."

"Very funny, you crazy jackrabbit. What do you want, anyway?"

"I was hopin' you could do me a favor, old Jakie boy."

"First you pull me from my show, then you make fun of my show, then you ask for a favor? You dig-jibbled crate of rotten horse apples. If I didn't have this broken arm I'd come over there right now and show you a thing or two."

Angus walked toward his neighbor's house. The Council members followed him to get a better look at what was going on.

"Oh c'mon now. You know I'm just kiddin'! Besides, don't forget I let you have that last trainin' session for free."

"Yeah, yeah, I remember."

Angus got up to the doorstep and they shook hands hard.

"Good to see you, Jake."

The huskies came running toward Angus, jumping all over him and Jake, some of them bounding into Jake's house.

"What in the dag-nab is goin' on, Angus? Get these blasted dogs out of here."

"Actually, that favor I was talkin' about? Well … it kind of involves the dogs."

"Oh, come on, Angus. More work on your kennels? You know I can't keep them here! I just don't have the room."

"No, no, I don't need you to keep 'em here. We can keep 'em at my place. I just need you to feed 'em and make sure the trainer gets out here every week. I know you need some extra money, and this could be some steady income for you for a while."

"So, where are you goin'?"

"On a quest!"

"A quest? What in tarnation are you talking about now? Always something up your sleeve."

"It's a long story, but I may be gone for a while. Can you do it?"

"I can keep 'em at your place?"

"Aye."

"And the pay will be for as long as you're gone?"

"Absolutely. I'll give you a year's pay up front, and you can keep it even if I'm back in a month."

"Well, I can't turn that down. Sure. Count on it. The Jakes will be fine. I'll see to it."

"Thanks, Jake. I'm goin' to take the Jakes with me for the rest of the day, before we head out of town. I'll bring 'em back to the kennel before we leave. I'll pay you then."

"Sounds good."

"Jake!" yelled Angus.

"WHAT?" asked Jake. "I'm right here. What do you want now?"

"Sorry, Jake. I'm just callin' the dogs."

"I wish you'd never named those blasted things after me! Now, get out of here!"

"See you 'round, Jake."

He walked up to the Council members, the Jakes by his side. Walter was snickering.

"What's so funny, laddie?"

"Nothing."

"Well then, shut your yap. Are we ready, Alton?"

"Ready when you are, Angus. What about the dogs?"

"Oh, I'm just takin' them with us for the day. Give me some time to say my goodbyes, you know? So, let's head to the golf course before it gets too late."

Walter looked at the dogs, and Alton could tell he wanted to say something about Angus bringing them to a golf course, but he held his tongue.

*   *   *

As they walked to the course, Alton marveled at what a unique fellow Angus was. Such a wry sense of humor. Such a cocky disposition. Such pride in his physique. And the Jakes. Alton loved the whole Jake incident. He noticed Angus had rolled up his sleeves and was flexing his triceps every so often. He also noticed his occasional mock-yawns, clearly designed to allow him to flex and display his biceps. Alton couldn't help but chuckle. He was so glad they had found him.

As soon as they got to the course, Angus led them right to the pro shop.

"Hey fellas, hang on just a minute," said the shop pro. "Those dogs aren't allowed in here!"

"Got somethin' against dogs, laddie?"

The pro decided it was better to let it go as he received Angus's power stare.

"Do you have a tee time?"

"Tee time?"

"Oh, boy—yeah, tee time. You must have a tee time to get on the course. You can't just walk on to your heart's content, especially on a weekend!"

"So tell me then, laddie, what could our tee time be? If you could squeeze us in, we could give you some of our knowledge in exchange for this courtesy."

"You really are something."

"Why thank you, laddie."

"Listen here ... oh, never mind. Look, why don't you go out to the driving range and hit some balls. Bring your dogs out there with you. There are some spots at the end of the range where you can be far away from other people. I'll let you know if we get an opening on the course."

"That sounds excellent. Are the balls and the clubs out there for us?"

"Do you mean to tell me you don't have clubs?"

"Are we supposed to?"

"It's a good idea, especially if you want something to hit the balls with! But you're in luck since we have rentals available."

"Can we rent one set and share it amongst ourselves?"

"I suppose this would be okay for the driving range, but definitely not for the course. Now please, just take this set, go to the range, and take these crazy dogs with you."

"All right, laddie. But only because we want to."

"Whatever. Please just go."

When they got to the range, Alton watched Angus grab a club and plop a ball on the grass. He chuckled as he listened to Angus's interpretation of the proper golf swing.

"Now, it seems very simple to me. The book I read said to relax, keep the knees bent slightly, not grip the club too tightly, start the backswing slowly and smoothly, extend the club along the target line on the backswing, let the body rotate, keep the left arm fairly straight, keep the eyes on the ball, keep the head fairly still, shift the weight to the right side on the backswing, cock the wrists as the backswing is made, turn the shoulders fully, then start the downswing slowly, drop the club into some sort of slot, transfer the weight to the other side of the body, turn the hips, release the wrists, extend the arms through the ball, keep the left wrist from bendin' at impact point, avoid somethin' called a chicken wing, aim down the target line, keep the club from goin' outside the swing plane, and stay balanced when the swing is complete."

"And that's supposed to be simple?" asked Walter.

"Of course, laddie. Very simple indeed, although I've only mentioned about one thousandth of the number of items to remember in a golf swing. But we can start with this simple set of thoughts and see how it goes."

Alton laughed to himself as he watched Angus setting up his body for the first swing attempt. His knees were drastically bent, his head sticking way up in the air, arms in a strange contorted position, legs excessively far apart. As he moved through the motions of the swing, it looked to Alton like someone being shot to death by a barrage of machine-gun fire. The swing was not a short event either. Angus went through at least twenty different moves, iterations, and spasms throughout the backswing. But then an amazing thing happened. As Angus struck the ball, there was a loud, thunderous noise from the impact, followed by a whooshing sound as the ball cut through the air. The ball launched so far, it was lost from Alton's sight.

Alton was amazed. He pleaded with Angus to show the others how to do what he had done. He was even more amazed that within just a few minutes, Angus managed to teach all of them to do exactly that. All of them were launching ball after ball off the grass and out of sight. Perfect shot after perfect shot, all thanks to Angus. Alton rejoiced as he witnessed even more confirmation that Angus was going to be an excellent addition to their group. He was not only sharp and talented, but a great teacher as well. And the best part, thought Alton, was that Angus helped him to laugh.

# Chapter 8
## Monday, 6:15 p.m.

Alton set the box down, keeping his eyes fixed on it as he secured the harness to his body. Once secured, he grasped the box again and clutched it against his chest.

"Okay, I'm ready. Please be careful as you haul me up—"

Alton's feet jerked off the ground, nearly causing him to drop the box. He held it tighter to his chest as they hauled. About half way up, he started swaying back and forth, and feared they might lose control of the rope.

"Be careful!" he yelled. "I nearly dropped the box!"

Alton heard some heated discussion from above, with Angus's voice dominating. He could picture the scene, with Angus reprimanding the five other scientists for being so careless. He couldn't help but smile as he imagined the intense look on Angus's face: the narrowed eyes, the pursed lips, the ears somehow pinned back like an angry dog. Fortunately, Angus's tactics must have worked, and the swaying subsided. Alton leaned his head back and watched the light from the opening get closer and brighter. When he reached the lip, they hauled him out and helped him remove the harness. The object was pressed against Alton's chest, locked in a human vice-grip. It glistened and reflected the light from the sun as Alton's chest heaved.

"I can't believe it's here!" Walter cried out.

"It truly is," said Alton. He paused for a few seconds to catch his breath as he gazed upon the find. "The object is with us. Our quest of sacrifice and shattered hopes has not been in vain. But let us not rush carelessly into our analysis. It's vital we engage in motion to prepare our minds to look upon the contents within. Let us engage in the dance of stones. This stream by the cave appears to have numerous stones of adequate size and shape."

"Alton, did Sivvius hurt you?"

"Thank God, no, Walter."

"Did he try to kill you again, Alton?"

"I'm sure he wanted to. But he focused on trying to take the box from me."

"What happened? Why did he not succeed?"

"Glory be to God. Sivvius had the box. He took it from me. It was in his hands. But I saw the agony on his face as he held it. I saw him in so much pain he couldn't maintain his hold on it. He is just too evil. He has so much evil within him, I don't think he can be in contact with something destined for good. It's like the box is protected in some way by the powers of heaven!"

The others stood there, mesmerized, staring at Alton. Alton could tell they were amazed at what he had told them. Even Angus was speechless.

Angus finally broke the silence. "Well, I'm glad to hear the scum dog got some pain of his own. I'm sick and tired of his attacks on us. I hope he fills up with so much pain that he dies in agony."

"Many times I've wished for him to die as well, Angus. But I feel awful every time I do. He still has good deep within. But let us discuss this again later. The box is with us! Let us begin the dance of stones now, and marry it with your intense prayers. We must prepare our minds to see what is inside the box. But we must move forward quickly. I'm sure Sivvius is seeking his demonic friends right now to find a way to wrest this from us."

"Aye, Alton! C'mon laddies, let's do it!"

Alton watched as they gathered by the stream and analyzed the situation. There were no protests, no complaints. He knew they all understood the need for a motion activity before analyzing what Alton had found. The dance of stones, as they called it, consisted of stepping or jumping from stone to stone within a stream. They must stay focused. They must continue moving along the stones at a steady pace. It was one of the riskier motion activities, but also one of the most effective.

Alton watched as his friends started the dance. It looked quite silly, he had to admit. Sometimes in his mind, he questioned the motion activities they did, yet he knew that somehow they worked. He couldn't explain it fully, this power of the motion. It just seemed to stimulate thought so well. He felt like it was something with which God had blessed them. He thought about the incredible connection between the body and the mind. How when they took care of and exercised their bodies, their minds became more clear and receptive to great ideas. Besides, he just loved to watch them engage in motion. He chuckled to himself and tried to hide a smile as he saw Angus making sure the others clearly saw his strength. At the start of each step, he would enter into a bicep-flexing pose as he prepared to launch to the next rock. At the end of each step, he would extend his arms for balance, flexing his triceps as he steadied himself.

"Well, Alton—are you goin' to join us or just watch? Bein' in your 40's is no excuse for avoidin' the dance … we're all in our 40's and doin' just fine!"

"I'm coming, Angus," said Alton with a laugh. "I've just been having such fun watching your great athletic ability."

"Ahhh, yes, it's true I'm quite the manly man, but come on in and give me a run for my money!"

Alton rummaged in his pack, found his poncho, wrapped it tightly around the box, and sealed the open edges with duct tape. Then he secured it tightly to his chest. Any risk of the box getting wet or lost had to be zero. Even with all the protection, he stayed near the edge of the stream, and did only very small hops onto large and stable rocks. He paused for a moment, amazed at the physical prowess of Angus as he moved from stone to stone with such apparent ease. Even the smaller stones didn't faze him. They were lucky to have Angus as their physical trainer. But Walter had to focus intently before each move, analyzing the next position, the length of the move, the apparent steadiness of the next stone. Every so often Alton would catch Angus looking at Walter, beaming a large grin his way, with a clenched jaw and proud, nodding head.

He paused for a moment to watch the Letter brothers as they were deciding which stone to jump to next. Alton was so glad they had decided to join the Council and bring it to its final number of seven scientists. He never ceased to be amazed by how well they worked together in the motion activities and how their cross-talking discussions brought such deep insights to the Council. They glanced at Alton, and he felt as if their intense eyes and tight facial expressions were emitting analytical thought waves. They shifted their eyes back to the stones and Alton listened with joy as they began their cross-talking.

"Looks risky," said A.

"Risky, but not too risky," said B.

"Risky enough," said A.

"Risky but doable," said B.

"Doable but risky," said A.

"Worth the risk," said B.

"Maybe worth the risk," said A.

"Worth the risk," said B.

"Maybe find another stone," said A.

"This is the stone," said B.

"Risky," said A.

"Worth the risk." Said B.

"Let's do it," said A.

"Let's do it," said B.

Alton noticed Patrick examining some moss on one of the stones. Surely, he must be considering how he could use the moss for a nice soup or possibly for an unusual salad complement, he thought. I wonder if he ever stops thinking of food. Actually, I hope not, since he certainly makes our stomachs happy and our minds energized for thought.

As Michael came near, Alton noticed him gazing into the distance, and then scribbling something on a notepad. We sure are fortunate to have him with us, Alton thought. His passion for navigation amazes me. Even when he leads us in completely the wrong direction—which he so often does—somehow we always stumble across something of significance.

They continued their dance until Alton felt the time was right. He stopped his motion and gestured for the others to do the same.

"It is time. I sense that our thoughts are at their peak. Let us venture out and gather around the box."

They followed Alton's command and scurried out of the stream. Alton unfastened the protected box from his chest, and freed it from the poncho. As he gazed at the beautiful, silvery surface, the others gathered closely around him.

"Who shall be the one to open our great find?"

"Of course it must be you, Alton," said Walter. "You are our leader. You are the reason we are here now. Without your determination and unwavering commitment, this box would not be before us now. Do you all agree?"

All of them nodded their heads in agreement.

"Thank you Walter. I am honored to be the one."

Alton's hands gently moved across the surface. It was hard to contain his excitement as thoughts of incredible discoveries of deep knowledge raced through his mind. His hands trembled as he searched for a way in. He could barely breathe as his fingers touched the clasp. He could almost sense the knowledge that must be contained within. If what they had foreseen were true, what was within would radically alter many scientific proofs and formulas.

He pulled on the clasp, half expecting it to be locked tight. Yet he was surprised as it sprang open with ease when he pressed his fingers against it. He began to lift the top of the box, afraid to peer inside. He wondered if the scroll would really be there, or if the box would be empty. He continued to open the lid, peering in out of the corner of his left eye. He thought he saw the edge of a scroll, and then thought it might not be. He closed the lid as his heart raced so fast that he couldn't even think. He felt as if all the blood was draining from his head.

Alton grasped the lid again and inched it upward. As he peered in, he began to see something. There was definitely something in the box. He threw open the lid, caution gone as the emotions of a lifetime seemed to flow through his hand in one instantaneous moment.

There was silence. Alton felt strange. Not quite happy, yet not quite sad either.

"Well?" asked Angus. "What do you see, laddie?"

"I'm afraid I don't see a scroll, but I do see another box—a smaller box."

"Another box? Are you daft?" Angus chuckled.

"No, my friend. I'm not daft. There truly is another box inside."

Alton's fingers moved across the exterior of the second box. The material, the temperature, the smooth surface—much like the first box. Yet he found no clasp. There was no apparent way in, no lock, no latch, no opening of any kind. His fingers moved more frantically along the surfaces of the box, but it felt completely smooth. He lifted the second box out of the first, and ran his fingers over the bottom. Smooth, no clasp. No apparent way in from the bottom, either.

"It appears to be a solid box with no way in!" said Alton.

"There must be a way in," barked Angus.

"May I hold it, Alton? May I feel its texture upon my fingers?" asked Walter.

"Please do. Perhaps you will find the way in."

As Alton was slowly handing the box to Walter, not quite fully letting go, he saw the expression on Walter's face change. It was as if light was radiating from his face. Alton felt a tingling sensation pass through his fingers and race up his arms.

"Walter, do you feel it?"

"Yes, Alton! It feels like electricity pulsing through me. What's going on?"

The box started to vibrate, giving off a subtle humming sound.

"Alton! What's happening?"

"I don't know. The tingling sensation is getting more intense. And the humming is growing. Quickly, let me place it on the ground. There could be some protection mechanism built into it. Perhaps the warmth of our touch has started some reaction."

Walter let go as Alton placed the box on the ground. The humming ceased.

"What happened, Alton? I felt tingling, but no pain."

"I'm not sure, but there is either a protection mechanism, or it could be something else. Something very intriguing."

"What, Alton? What could be so intriguing?"

"It's about you, Walter."

"Me?"

"Yes, you. When I was holding the inner box, there was no tingling, no humming. It was only when *you* touched the inner box that the tingling sensation began."

"What are you saying?"

"I'm not sure yet, but for some reason, you may be the one who has to open the box. Perhaps what we heard and felt was the box responding to your touch, preparing to open. There could be some connection with you. This is most interesting. We must be very careful. We must be sure what it is that we are to do next. We can take no chances of damaging the box or what we hope it contains.

"My friends, let us gather, and let us pray."

# Chapter 9
# One Year Earlier

Alton couldn't stop watching his friends as they continued launching golf balls out of sight. As he stood there, mesmerized, reflecting on Angus's amazing ability to teach them how to swing a golf club so perfectly, two men approached Alton.

"Excuse us, sir," said one of the men, "but we could not help but notice your tremendous skills on this range. Are you professionals?"

Alton was intrigued; the two men looked exactly the same. He had never seen twins that were so perfectly identical: the small, thin noses, with a slight upturn at the tip, the perfectly aligned, bright white teeth, the thin angular faces, the gangly, tall bodies, each the same height. Even their hairstyles were identical—light brown in color, neatly cropped around the ears, flat and tight on the top. He was eventually able to stop staring and speak up.

"Oh no. We are simple beginners here on the range, following that which our good friend Angus has taught us."

"Ahhh. And where did he gain this ability?"

"From a book."

"You mean to tell us he learned to hit so well from a book? And that he showed you just now and you learned so quickly?"

"Absolutely. Many things can be learned from a book. Or from a friend."

"Well, that is amazing! We've been working on our swings for years, and have never come anywhere near your level of achievement."

"Well, thank you so much for your kind words. Who might you be anyway?"

"We are A and B."

"Your names are A and B?"

"That is correct."

"Are these your full names or just nicknames?"

"Actually, these are the names given to us by our parents."

"Your names at birth?"

"Close," said A. "You see, my father just loved the name Steven, and wanted to name both of us Steven. Yet even with much pleading, my father could not convince my mother to give us the exact same name. Fortunately, she did eventually bend and agree to one of us being Steven and one being Stephen. It was just close enough to keep my father happy, yet different enough for our parents to be able to tell us apart. Or so they thought. Unfortunately, during the first few months of our lives, they often confused us with each other, since our names were just too similar.

"Since my mother was getting discouraged about the situation, my father, knowing my mother's passion for teaching the alphabet to her elementary-school students, eventually came up with the idea of re-naming us as letters of the alphabet. To his surprise and delight, she was more excited about the idea than he could have ever hoped. He immediately proposed the names of Y and Z, but she had a friend who had named her hamster Y. She was concerned this could be terribly embarrassing one day if our friends ever found out one of us had a hamster's name. She insisted on naming us A and B, to protect us completely from potential embarrassment. She worried that if she named one of us S or T or perhaps even P, someone may forget the name one day, and think to themselves that they knew the name was close to the end of the alphabet, and that perhaps it was Y. Then she just knew this person would call her son Y. Of course her son would have already found out Y was a hamster's name. So she knew her son would then hate her for the rest of his life for giving him a name so close to the end of the alphabet. So that is why she gave us the names A and B. Much to our father's disapproval, I might add, since he so loved the names Y and Z."

"But B is a good name for me," said B.

"And A is a good name for me," said A.

"B is good," said B.

"A is good," said A.

"A is good," said B.

"Thank you," said A. "B is good."

"Thank you," said B.

"A good, B good," said A.

"A good, B good," said B.

"So it is settled," said A.

"So it is settled," said B.

"And yet to be A and B or B and A or A or B and B or A—"

Alton was fascinated by the two as they went on and on with their analytical naming discussion. He decided he wanted to get to know them better, so he considered inviting them to join the Council in a round of golf. Something about the two really struck Alton. He sensed something strong in his spirit about them. He knew he had just met them, but his mind raced as he wondered if God had brought them to him. He wondered if they would be the final two that would bring their number to seven. To find three in one day, first Angus and now Letter A and Letter B, would be utterly amazing, he thought. Oh Lord, please let this be the day, he prayed silently. Please put it in their hearts to join us. Please let this be the day we become seven. This must be the day. We are in dire need of help.

"Excuse me for interrupting, A and B, but I wonder if you would like to join us in a round of golf. It would be an excellent opportunity for us to get to know each other better, and you may also have the opportunity to receive some wonderful swing instruction from Angus."

"This is a very tempting offer," said A. "I think this could be a good thing. What do you think, B?"

"Join?" asked B.

"Join," said A.

"Join now?" asked B.

"Join now," said A.

"Let us join now," said B.

"You concur with the joining?" asked A.

"I concur," said B.

"Let us join," said A.

"Let us join," said B.

"It is settled," said A.

"It is settled," said B.

"Outstanding!" said Alton. "Well, Angus. What do you say? Off to the course?"

"Aye, Alton. An excellent idea."

"Council members ... let us head to the course!"

Angus led them to the first tee. The other six, along with the pack of Jakes, followed. As they gathered around the first tee, Angus stepped up to the tee box and teed up his ball. The people waiting in line started complaining about them skipping ahead, and having such a large group, with all the yapping dogs. They started getting more vocal, and some of the words they used were not pleasant.

"Settle down, laddies," said Angus. "Let us show you what the game of golf is all about."

Before anyone could stop him, Angus launched a perfect shot down the fairway, far out of sight and probably the longest tee shot ever seen by any of them. As the crowd stood mesmerized, A and B stepped up to the tee and consulted with Angus for a few moments. After a few instructions from Angus, they swung together, simultaneously hitting two perfect shots, right down the center of the fairway and out of sight. Applause broke forth from the crowd. The others followed suit, with Alton hitting last.

As Alton prepared to swing, he was a little nervous, but focused on what Angus had taught him. He launched the ball down the fairway and out of sight just as the others had. Applause rang out again. It was as if the crowd thought they might be celebrities or some type of entertainment group.

As they played, Alton watched A and B closely. The more he watched them and listened to their deep analytical discussions, and heard of their many scientific discoveries and inventions, the more he sensed there was indeed something very special about them. He felt even more strongly they were meant to join the Council. Oh, Lord, he prayed silently, I ask you again: please let this be the day we become seven.

He walked over to them as they were engaged in another deep discussion in a bunker.

"Two and four," said A.

"Yes, two and four," said B.

"Hit two inches before the ball," said A.

"And four inches after," said B.

"Two and four," said A.

"Two and four," said B.

"Let the sand launch the ball from the trap," said A.

"The sand," said B.

"It is the sand that does the work," said A.

"It is the sand," said B.

Alton watched Letter B move his feet around in the sand, getting his stance properly settled. He swung his club through the sand and the ball popped out smoothly, landed a foot from the pin and rolled to the edge of the cup.

"Perfect," said A.

"Excellent," said B.

"Excellent," said A.

"Perfect," said B.

They entered into a new discussion about their last invention, the inflatable laptop, when Alton heard yelling from the fairway behind them.

"What's goin' on up there, laddies? Quit playin' in the sand and get your backsides out of the way. We haven't got all day, you know! Jake's gettin' hungry!"

Alton let out a hearty laugh as he watched the Jakes jump all over Angus after he mentioned their name.

"Sorry," yelled A as he and B stepped out of the trap. "Feel free to hit on up."

"Excuse me, A and B," said Alton as he stepped away from the trap with them. "I hesitate to interrupt your discussion, but I have a very important question I would like to ask you."

"Please ask," said A.

"Yes, please ask," said B.

"Would you like to join us on our quest to find great scientific discoveries and save the earth from desolation?"

Alton explained further about the history of the quest, the Einstein book, and the battle against Sivvius, as he waited for Angus and the others to get up to the green.

"That does sound massively intriguing," said A. "We are scientists who love the earth and the study of its wonders. That is why we love golf so much, since God gives us so many opportunities to study nature as we play. Yet we are tired of playing this same golf course every day. We may be ready for a change. What do you think, B?"

"I agree it does sound intriguing, A. What do you think?"

"Well, as I said, I think it sounds intriguing," said A.

"Yes, that is what I have just said also," said B.

"But I said it first," said A.

"Yes, but I said it last. And the last shall be first," said B.

"But if you are the first by being the last, and I am the first by being the first, then we are both first, which cannot be true in the truest sense of the word, or words, depending upon how much you like to speak," said A.

"Yes, I see your point ... and yet I don't," said B. "However, I think I see it more than I do not see it. Now I'm not sure what to do about what I'm thinking. If I'm thinking I see it and yet I may not see it, then you could be truly first or not and I could be truly first or not, or we could be simultaneously first or not. Now I'm confused, but not fully confused. Actually, I'm intrigued. Now that I think about it, do I even want to be first? If not, then I should be last. But if by being last, I become first, by my own declaration, then I'm forced to be first in every regard, whether I want to or not. I want to be last! I want to be last! But then I'm first! What shall I do?" asked B.

"My brother, become last, and therefore become first, yet be first with me so we share in the firstness, and you need not shoulder the burden alone. We can be first and possibly even last together," said A.

"Yes! This brings me peace," said B. "Let us be first or last together. But what of this quest Alton has mentioned?"

"It would be hard to leave our science club," said A.

"And what of our model railroad club?" said B.

"Yes, what of the model railroad club?" said A.

"Many wonderful colleagues in both," said B.

"Indeed," said A.

"To leave will be tough," said B.

"To leave will be tough," said A.

"But no wives to leave," said B.

"No wives, no children," said A.

"Never any time for that," said B.

"Never any time for that," said A.

"Never could find women who would put up with our endless discussions about science," said B.

"Or our obsession with it," said A.

"Couldn't expect to," said B.

"Couldn't expect to," said A.

The conversation paused for just a moment. Alton saw his chance and was about to speak but didn't act fast enough.

"No way to expect to," said B.

"Just no way," said A

"Shall we join?" asked B.

"Let us join," said A.

"Join the quest," said B.

"Join the quest," said A.

"Save the earth," said B.

"Save the earth," said A.

Another brief pause. Alton jumped in.

"Gentlemen—"

"But just to be sure," said B, "let us have a meeting to determine if the time is right. But let us have meeting Two first, just to decide if we should have meeting One.

"Excellent thought, my brother. But shouldn't we first have a meeting Three to discuss plans for meeting Two?" asked A.

"I like your idea, my brother, but perhaps we really need a meeting Four first, just to come up with a solid agenda for meeting Three," said B.

"Ahhh, yes. I had not thought of this. A meeting Four would be most useful, that is, after meeting Five," said A.

Alton listened as the discussion about the meetings continued for some time. When it got to discussing the possibility of meeting Fifteen, they paused, and whispered to each other for a few moments. Then Letter A looked to Alton.

"Alton," said A, "we have realized during the time of discussion about potentially having multiple meetings, the discussion itself is that which has cemented our decision. The meetings are not required. We would be honored to join you in your great quest."

"Yes, to join," said B.

"To join," said A.

"We shall join," they said in unison.

Alton's face lit up as a huge smile spread across it.

"Excellent! A and B, you are now bequeathed with the official title of Senior Analysts for the Council. You will bless our number with many great insights and revelations. Of this, I am certain. Do you officially accept this indoctrination as Senior Analysts for the Council?"

"Most definitely," said A.

"Without doubt," said B.

"Without doubt," said A.

"Most definitely," said B.

"Absolutely," they said in unison.

"Thank God, laddies! Now we can finally get back to the game!" yelled Angus, who was already waiting on the next tee box.

Alton's heart was racing. He trotted over to Angus.

"Angus, you said earlier you would like to join us in our quest. Do you confirm this day that you would like to officially become a member of our Council?"

"Aye, Alton. I give my allegiance to the Council."

"Then I now bequeath you with the official title of Physical Therapist and Trainer for the Council. Your physical skills, along with your teaching abilities, make you an excellent addition to our number. I'm confident that in your official role, you will help us achieve new levels of physical endurance. This endurance will help us develop deeper mental insight as we use the physical strength we gain to increase motion and gain knowledge. Do you officially accept this indoctrination as Physical Therapist and Trainer for the Council?"

"Aye, Alton. It'll give me deep satisfaction to teach you what I know."

"Excellent," said Alton as his face beamed.

"But let's play more golf first!"

Alton walked alone while they played the next few holes— he was deep in prayer. As they reached the 18th green, he ran to the center and looked back at the others. He raised his arms into the air and proclaimed with a loud voice:

"Today is an epic day. The gathering of the elect is complete. I have been praying much about this, and strongly sense and believe that God desires for our final number to be seven. We are the perfect mix of skills and abilities. To add more to our number would cause excessive overlap of skills, leading to petty jealousies and ineffective thought. To have fewer would leave a gap in our skill mix. I feel a peace about our number of seven. It is a peace that passes all human understanding. We are now officially The Council of Seven. Our quest will now commence with an intensity like never before."

They all yelled out their satisfaction with Alton's announcements. They shook hands and hugged each other. Alton felt a peace and a joy in his heart beyond anything he had felt before.

"Let us gather into the circle of approval," said Alton.

Alton explained the circle of approval to those who had never experienced it, then had them huddle in a circle to start the process. Their heads were bowed, with each right hand raised high, and each right palm open and facing the sky. Then the right hand of each man came down and rested upon the forehead of the man to his right. Finally, the right hand slid slowly downward with the fingers gently closing the eyes of the contacted man. After a few moments, hands were lifted, eyes were opened, necks were craned backwards and each let out a yell of victory. Then they broke the circle, shook hands and hugged.

As the rejoicing was dying down, Alton gathered them in a circle again and instructed them to put their arms around each other's shoulders.

"We have completed our ceremony. We have agreed with each other that we are now The Council of Seven. Now, let us give thanks to God, and entrust ourselves and our quest to Him."

They bowed their heads as Alton prayed.

"Lord Jesus, we give this Council of Seven to you. We entrust our lives and our mission to you. Guide us and protect us. Help us work together as one in your cause. Help us stop Sivvius, and end his warped campaign of winning souls for evil. Help us save the earth from desolation, and fill the world with your love."

Alton felt chills through his body, and a deep, thick sense of a divine presence all around them. He knew God was pleased with The Council of Seven, and he knew God was with them.

\* \* \*

After they brought the Jakes back for Jake to take care of, the Council members set off on their quest. They spent a year together making amazing discoveries and inventing many new things. They explored numerous caves in search of the scroll, and continually stood against Sivvius and his plans of world destruction and domination. Times were tough, and each day was filled with a strong sense of urgency, but they worked well together as The Council of Seven.

# Chapter 10
## Monday, 7:15 p.m.

The time of prayer drew to a close and Alton looked around the circle at the other six scientists.

"I feel great peace from God that we will find a way into the box. I think Walter may be the key."

Alton picked up the box and moved toward Walter.

"Walter, I give the box to you. I believe it's your destiny to be the one to find the way in."

Walter's hands trembled as he took the box. It felt wonderful in his hands, as if it was meant to be there. The tingling feeling flowed through his fingers again as he caressed the surface. He heard the gentle hum as well. The tingling started growing and the humming intensified.

"Alton, the tingling is happening again."

"I hear the humming as well, Walter."

"I'm not sure if I should keep holding it. The tingling is getting more intense!"

"Aw, shut up laddie," barked Angus. "Take it like a man. Shut your yap and take the pain!"

The humming grew so loud it was all Walter could hear. The tingling was racing up and down his arms.

"Alton!" he yelled, "I'm not sure I can hold on!"

"Hang on, Walter," Alton yelled back. "I do not sense danger. Believe that destiny is yours today. Believe you are meant to be the one to reveal the contents. Believe you are the one to open the box."

Just as the word *open* rolled off Alton's tongue, the box opened with a subtle clicking sound. All by itself. It opened only a bit, just enough for Walter to be able to glimpse the dark interior. It appeared that one of the ends of the box had slid partly open.

Walter stood motionless, speechless. The tingling and humming had stopped. He had found no latch. He had found no lock. He had found no way in. Yet it opened. Perhaps the way his fingers pressed upon the surface? Perhaps a certain spot he pressed just a little more with one of his fingers? Possibly due to the warmth of his hands upon the box? He knew not.

Walter did not hear a sound from the others. He could tell they were just as mesmerized as he was. He tried to make out what was inside. He gazed into the box with one eye, a myriad of emotions flooding his mind. Alton placed a hand upon Walter's shoulder.

"Reach in, my friend," said Alton. "The honor is yours."

"But you should be the one."

"Thank you, Walter, but I give the honor to you. Again I say to you that it's your destiny this day."

Walter could not speak. Alton's words touched his heart. Allowing him to be the first one to touch the scroll? If it was there, that is. Oh God, it must be there, he thought. If it's not, I will never find my beloved Ingrid. In his mind, he held a great debate with himself. Finally, he could not hold back any longer.

He grasped the edge of the side that had slid open; it was easy to pull it open further. When there was enough room for his entire hand, he carefully reached in. He was afraid to look, afraid he might see nothing inside. Or even worse, that he might see only dust, the remains of a once-great scroll. But his fingers felt something tangible, something with substance and form. And it was not the hard metal of the box. It felt softer, and it felt wonderful. It felt like parchment. And it smelled as parchment should, just like other parchments he had studied.

He continued to caress the material and noticed it was in a tubular form. It was a scroll! It was definitely a scroll. He could not believe it. Sivvius had not stolen it after all, he thought. It felt well preserved, which gave him peace. It had not worn away into dust. He gently pulled out the scroll and studied it. It was about two inches in diameter in its rolled-up form, and its length was nearly twelve inches.

He noticed a seal in the middle of the length, secured to a red ribbon, and gazed upon it with wonder. It appeared to be a wax seal, although reinforced in some way, as if there was metal melded in with it. He gently grasped the seal to see if it might pull away from the ribbon and scroll without damaging the scroll itself, but it wouldn't budge. Then he placed one of his fingers under the edge and tried to pry it loose. But it wouldn't move. When he tried to slide the ribbon off the scroll it would not budge, either. He looked up and noticed the others staring at him with looks of wonder. Except for Angus. It was impossible not to notice his impatience.

"Aw, c'mon laddie," bellowed Angus. "Hurry up and break the seal, you string bean. I can't stand it another second. Let's see what we got here!"

Walter, without thinking much about it, ran to Angus, kicked him in the shin, and put a hand over his mouth.

"Be quiet you crazy man! Let us continue in silence, that we may fully appreciate this wonder of wonders."

Angus choked out some words between Walter's fingers: "Got—to know—whaaat—is—on—the scro—laddie."

"Angus, please be quiet for now," said Alton in an ever-so-gentle way.

Walter was relieved that Alton's words seemed to calm Angus down. There was complete silence again, and Walter's fingers continued to test the seal, attempting to find a way to remove it. As he rested his thumb upon the seal, he heard a strange noise, like an ocean wave crashing upon the shoreline, as one would hear it from a distance. Then the seal released its hold upon the scroll and fell to the ground. He stared in amazement.

As soon as he caught his breath, he grasped the ribbon and it easily slid off. He gently unrolled the scroll, his heart pounding. He saw handwritten text upon the parchment. The coded text was beautiful, and strangely familiar. He could not believe what he was seeing. It was almost too much to bear. He looked up at the others.

"I recognize the writing," said Walter, his voice shaking. "As you know, I've studied many ancient languages. It has been a passion of mine. I also studied numerous forms of code. The more complex and difficult, the more enjoyable. One day I had been walking my cats along our usual route—"

"C'mon laddie! Get to the point! We don't want to hear about your blasted cats!"

"Please, Angus, let me finish. It's vital you hear this story."

"Well, speed it up then, man."

"Anyway," continued Walter, "I had been walking my cats along our usual route when one of them got spooked by a dog and somehow managed to slip out of his collar and sprint away. I was barely able to keep him in my sights as I chased after him but it turned out all right, since he ended up running right back to the house. As I approached the oak tree in my front yard where he loved to take refuge, I saw a man stooped by my front door. As I walked closer to get a better view, a branch cracked beneath my foot and he spun around and stared at me. He stood there motionless for quite some time, just staring into my eyes. His look did not frighten me, since it felt like a look of interest. He seemed to be probing my eyes, analyzing me. When he finally spoke, all he said was for me to study it, as he looked down at his feet. Then he stepped off the porch and walked away across my lawn.

"I ran to the door and saw a document there with my name on it. As I leafed through it, I saw that it was filled with a coded writing I had never seen before. I had deciphered hundreds of the very best codes ever devised throughout history, yet this one appeared to be unlike any other. There were sections of explanations in English here and there, but they appeared to be very complex. I was utterly fascinated by what I saw and was anxious to delve deeper. I looked up to ask the man who he was but he was gone. I never did find out who he was or where he went.

"I spent the next few days holed up in my home, studying the document. The more I studied, the more fascinated I became. It was a detailed study of a code I had never seen the likes of before. As I compared it to other codes I had studied, I confirmed its uniqueness. It was far more complex and intricate. To this day, I've studied it and painstakingly learned how to interpret it. And tried to determine why it was given to me.

"Now I know why. Now the day has come. The most challenging code I have ever studied and tried to master appears to be very similar to the code used in the scroll I hold in my hands this very moment. The man knew we would find this scroll, and he knew I would be the one to decipher it."

"That is incredible my friend!" said Alton. "This truly is destiny. Please, begin the deciphering!"

Walter felt the parchment upon his fingertips again. That which would help him find Ingrid and win her heart was in his hands. He rolled the scroll open and looked in detail at the words on the first page. He ran through the deciphering process in his mind as he read the first sentence. Letter rearrangement, reverse-sequence counting, hidden repetition scheme analysis, substitution analysis, frequency analysis—he used all of these techniques and more as he read. But it was more difficult than he anticipated. The coding was more complex, with subtle nuances bringing him to dead ends every time he thought he was getting close. He heard a rustling sound, and glancing up he saw Angus drilling into him with his penetrating stare.

"Come on laddie! I thought you knew this code. Are you goin' to tell us what it says or keep it to yourself?"

"Sorry, but it's amazingly intricate. Subtle nuances shift the flow along multiple possible interpretation lines. Some schemes loop me right back to the starting point. One path cancels another only to re-establish it in a varied form. My mind is spinning."

"Well quit talkin' then and get back to it!"

Walter pressed on, straining his mind, reaching beyond his normal limits of analysis, trying many variations of interpretation. Much time passed without success. He heard a heavy sigh from Angus.

"I can't take it another minute! Why don't you let Alton take a look. Or try somethin' different."

Alton walked up to Walter and rested a hand on his shoulder.

"Why don't we leave Walter alone for a while so he can concentrate? Let's go get dinner ready."

Walter breathed a sigh of relief almost as loud as Angus's sigh of agitation, watched the others trudge away, and dove back into his analysis. He analyzed right through Alton placing a plate of food by his side, through Angus yelling out occasionally for a progress report, through his eyelids growing heavier by the moment, and through a few head bobs. As the head bobs were getting more frequent, he saw Alton approaching.

"Time to sleep. You need to give your mind a rest and start fresh in the morning. Let us retire early and rise with the sun."

Walter saw the others nod their heads in agreement, and even though he could tell they were not happy about the situation, one by one they approached him, patted his shoulder and gave him reassuring smiles. Even Angus touched him gently. It gave him peace and helped him to drift off into sleep.

# PART II:

## *A Taste of Time*

# Chapter 11
## Tuesday, 6:00 a.m.

At dawn, when the others were still sleeping, Walter snapped awake. After a few moments of getting reoriented, he felt the box under his arm and quickly reached in to make sure the scroll was still there. The feel of the parchment brought a flash of anticipation into his mind. He kept quiet, because he wanted to see the scroll again ... alone this time, without interruption.

He removed the scroll from the box and carefully rolled it open, letting his eyes move toward the first few words. He moved through his interpretation process again, and it seemed to flow a bit more clearly. He began to notice something very interesting. One of the apparent dead-ends that re-routed him back to the beginning of a section brought a slight variation of the pacing. He thought about pacing more, working through a few more dead-ends and re-routes. It started to gel. With the correct pacing of analysis, multiple diagnostics were merging to bring some symbols into logical sequencing. Using the new pacing technique, he focused on the title. And there it was. The jumble of words seemed to jump from the page with order. And what he read stopped him cold. He couldn't move. He couldn't blink. He could not break his stare from the coded letters. What he saw would change science forever. A simple title. But an extremely profound one:

### *The Secrets of Time Travel*

It was truly that which they had sought for so long. The title was exactly what it was supposed to be, what Alton had

James J. Warchol

told them it must be. He felt tears welling in his eyes and he wiped them away. He took a deep breath, let it out, and gazed back upon the scroll. His mind raced with anticipation and excitement. He glanced over at the others and confirmed they were still sleeping. Surely a little while longer on his own couldn't hurt.

He read the title a few more times to get it completely clear in his mind what the deciphering process was. It made perfect sense. The coding was extremely elegant once understood. He shifted his eyes to the first paragraph and was amazed how quickly he could read the first few words: "This scroll was written for ..." His heart raced. He read on.

"This scroll was written for you, Walter. The words contained herein will enable you to change the very fabric of time. Do not be afraid. Know that what you learn will shatter the laws of physics many hold as eternal truths. Science as you know it will never be the same. You and your friends will live out and experience the truths of this scroll. For you are the ones who must save the earth, and pave the way for the salvation of many souls.

"For centuries, scientists have discussed, analyzed, theorized, and imagined so many ways to travel in time, but not one has ever mastered this coveted feat. Yet I say, and you will see in this scroll, the secrets to time travel are not about developing complex and expensive modes of travel to approach the speed of light, or utilizing gravitational fields, or traveling through worm holes. Not to say these approaches will not work. It is just that they would be difficult and costly. What I will show you is much simpler. It has to do with mass.

"I speak of the mass that signifies the weight of an object. All objects have mass. Some are heavy and some are light. Some have incredible mass, like the earth or the sun. But why do so many things have completely different masses? Why

108

must this be? There must be some significance to this. There must be something we can learn.

"What is it we can learn? Let me first say that it is about correlation. Each object has its own mass, yet the mass is not independent of all other things. It relates to other things. Specifically, it relates to time. Even more specifically, time equals mass, both directly and inversely. Ponder this! Do you grasp this? Do you understand? TIME EQUALS MASS!

"Let me tell you more. Since time equals mass, when time passes, even though it appears to be gone, and in the past, as we say, it is not actually gone. Since the mass remains, there is still something there. If time did not equal mass, once time passed, time would be gone. But time does equal mass, as I will show, and therefore time can never go away and be in the past.

"Mass is never destroyed, although it may be transformed, or reduced to its smallest components such as molecules and atoms. For example, if a log burns in a fire, the mass of the log, in its original form, decreases, and therefore one might think that as the log-mass decreases, present time becomes past time, and would appear on the surface to be gone. Yet I say that although the original form of the log is gone, ashes remain, and therefore mass remains. Furthermore, the log released vapors as it burned, and these vapors contain a small amount of mass. Therefore, the mass of the log never completely goes away, and therefore time can never completely go away. However, I tell you many deep things. Things that one needs to take time to ponder. So please, take some time to enter into deep thought before you read further."

Walter set down the scroll and closed his eyes. He could not believe what he just read. It was incredible, it was wonderful, it was beyond comprehension, and it caused his heart to beat at such a pace that he thought he might die of exhilaration. He had read something that probably no one else in all of time had ever read. And even more amazing, it was addressed personally to him. He could not get his mind around that fact. How could it be? Why was he singled out? He was in such a state of exultation as he pondered this, he felt as if he could leap into the air and fly.

He considered whether he should tell the others what he had read; he didn't feel prepared to share just yet. But as he pondered this, he knew deep in his heart of hearts he must tell them. He knew he must share these amazing words and the wondrous mystery of the scroll being addressed to him. Perhaps they can help me to understand how this is possible, and what it means, he thought.

"Time equals mass," he whispered to himself. "Time equals mass! TIME EQUALS MASS!" This is unbelievable, he thought. The ground he was sitting on was actually time itself? Could it really be true? It was so perplexing yet so exhilarating! He must tell the others, but first he would ponder on his own for a while, just to cherish this moment of the beginning of new scientific truths. He would think about how this truth might enable him to find Ingrid, and to win her love. He settled into a comfortable position and pondered.

# Chapter 12
# Tuesday, 6:15 a.m.

Sivvius had exited the cave from another opening but stayed hidden under a rock outcropping not far from Walter. He had moved as far back under the ledge as he could, where it was the most barren, the darkest. He agonized within himself as he watched Walter reading the scroll. The others were still asleep, but they would awaken soon, and hear the contents of the scroll for themselves. Sivvius couldn't believe they had gotten so far. They had found the silver box, the scroll within, and even a way to release the seal. It had all happened so fast. Anger and desperation pulsed within his brain. A sense of urgency raced through him. He felt his own insanity welling up again, and fought to maintain a measure of control. He knew he must disrupt them, stop their momentum, shatter their peace and unity.

He looked at Alton lying on the ground, chest gently rising and falling, resting in peaceful slumber. Probably dreaming about his great find, he thought.

"He has brought them all so far," he whispered in prayer to his friends. "I've watched him build his Council but I never thought he would get this far. He has brought them all together, he has inspired them, and he has even taught them about his God and prayer. How I hate to think of the unity they have gained. How I hate to think of the knowledge and the power they have gained. How I hate to see them with the scroll. How could this have happened? How have I let this happen? Why could I not stop them from finding the scroll? I feel like such a failure.

"I feel compelled to lunge at Walter and steal the scroll from him. Yet I can't forget the agony I felt when I tried to steal the box from Alton. I'm still weak from that encounter. I'm afraid to try again. Surely the scroll will have the same effect on me. Maybe even worse. Oh my friends, I'm in such agony. I feel so helpless. I hate this feeling. It's not me."

Sivvius's head ached and his stomach tightened. He felt like someone's hand was inside his body, squishing his internal organs together. He flushed with rage as he continued to think about Alton's relationship with God and the Council members. Sweat mixed with the caked cave mud on his arms, forming a slimy goo. He tried to wipe it off but ended up massaging it into his pores. He bowed his head and reached out to his friends from beyond once more. He prayed silently, placing his fear and frustration before them; he asked for their help.

He sat and waited, concentrating, listening. Fear crept in again as he imagined the knowledge Walter must be gaining. Why couldn't he allay the fear? He squeezed his eyes tight and centered all his thoughts on hearing his friends. He shut out everything around him and waited.

A softness. He felt a softness in his mind, almost like a hand gently massaging within his head. He felt the fear subsiding. His frustration began to drift away. He felt a breeze blow across his face, and then he felt it pushing itself through his skull and into his mind. Slowly at first, he felt something building there … getting bigger, stronger. Not just one voice but three: and yet one. It was his friends from beyond. They were trying to speak to him. It was not so much words he heard, but impressions. Thoughts were being placed in his mind, thoughts he did not yet comprehend. But he could feel them rumbling in his head. How he loved it when his friends spoke with him this way.

Sivvius felt a sudden rush fill his mind. His thoughts spun like a whirlwind. He couldn't decipher them. He couldn't understand them. Then the whirlwind slowed as the thoughts began to center. He felt a focus building in his mind. He felt a word, then another. He tasted them, the two words. They grew thick on his tongue. They filled his mind and his body. Just two words: knowledge destruction.

He felt a clear direction, knowing exactly what to do. His heart raced with joy as he anticipated what was about to happen. He couldn't believe this new power of knowledge destruction his friends had given him. Surely greater than any other they had ever given him. How he would love this.

He closed his eyes and focused. He felt something building in his mind, filling his head with a sense of unbelievable power. It felt as if his skull was expanding as energy pushed outward from his brain.

"We will bring them to their knees with this lethal wave of knowledge-destroying power," he prayed. "They will be so concerned with stopping this mighty attack that they will be unable to read the scroll! We will keep them from the secrets of the scroll. My friends from beyond, you have blessed me in a mighty way this day!"

He looked at the slumbering Council members. He knew what he had to do. The energy filled his mind to overflowing. He felt waves of energy seeping out of his head and through his hair. He felt electrical charges dancing on his face. His toes and fingers tingled. He let the energy build and intensify until he could hold it in no longer. He stared at the Council members with burning eyes and sent out a rush of invisible energy toward them. He felt it blow out of his head. It felt incredible. It felt so powerful. He felt so powerful. The epic battle was about to shift in his favor again.

\*   \*   \*

Alton stirred from his sleep and saw Walter hunched over the scroll. He stood to run over to him, but saw him drop the scroll, lift his head and stare blankly into space. His mouth hung open, silent. It was a strange sight. He didn't look like himself. "My God," said Alton, "what is going on—"

Suddenly, Alton felt a blast of air against his head and in a split-second felt like the air was rushing through his mind. He sensed a strong evil presence, thick in the air. A wave of fear rushed into his mind. He didn't know what was happening, but he knew it was from Sivvius. He waited for pain, but felt none. He knew Sivvius was doing something, but couldn't place it. He felt his mind drifting, his focus slipping away. Then it felt like little fingers were inside his head, picking at his brain, probing. A sense of loss came to him. He was not sure of the specifics … just a sense of loss.

"Walter! Are you okay?"

"I don't …"

"Walter, what's wrong? What's happen—"

Alton couldn't think of how to finish the word. "Happen … happ … what is the word, Lord? What's going on? What is this strange new attack? Lord, I … Lord … what was I thinking?"

Alton looked at the others and noticed the confusion on their faces.

"Get up, qui … qui … fast! Get up fast! Come here to me and let's gath … gath … let's crowd together!"

They gathered around Alton. Alton knew it was time to use the special dance they had been working on. He had feared Sivvius would be unleashing a new weapon upon them at any moment, so they had been preparing this dance as a defense.

"Sivvius is doing something to our minds. I sense loss. He has some new awful and terr … terr … bad weapon. We must do the emergency dance we've been working on: the dance of defense. Please follow my lead. Oh, Lord, protect us from Sivvius, and bless this new dance."

Alton started with his arms hanging at his sides, and then lifted his hands to about elbow height, facing his palms upward. With hands in position, he lifted his right leg until his right thigh was parallel to the ground, with the lower portion of his leg staying perpendicular to the ground. He watched as the others also moved into position, some struggling to maintain balance.

"Focus. Concentrate on maintaining your balance, and be sure to keep your palms facing upward, symbolizing your openness to receive from God. The Lord is showing me that Sivvius's new weapon is knowledge destruction. His friends from beyond have given him a new power to destr ... destr ... well ... remove knowledge from our minds. We must stop this right now before he does deep damage. Let us join in a song of praise and prepare for the stomp."

They sang together as they fine-tuned their positioning and strained to hold their right legs rigid and poised, preparing for the stomp. When they looked as ready as they could be, Alton yelled out the command.

"Council members ... STOMP!"

They each slammed their right foot to the ground, causing a loud THWUMP sound.

"Sivvius, we stomp on your power just as God stomps upon the head of the serpent. We stand as one against you, with God at our side."

Alton felt the strange sensations in his mind subsiding. It felt as if the fingers in his head were slipping away.

"And again ... lift and STOMP!"

Another THWUMP filled the air.

"Pray for protection, pray for strength. Clear your minds. Now—one more STOMP."

They stomped one last time, and then bowed their heads in prayer. Alton felt great peace. His mind was at rest. He sensed good around them—a powerful goodness protecting them from further harm. Yet, he knew he had lost some knowledge. He was thinking of a formula he had studied just a few days earlier, and could remember no details. He had known it perfectly, yet now it was gone. It had happened so fast. This new power of Sivvius's was far more dangerous than pain.

"My friends, do you feel all right?"

He watched them nod their heads as they expressed relief and thankfulness that this very strange attack was over. As they talked, each relayed certain items of knowledge they had lost. Alton motioned for them to be silent.

"Let us be thankful to God the dance He has given us has worked. Let us be thankful God has come to our aid quickly. We've lost some knowledge, but for now, we are safe. We must work on enhancing our dance and perhaps even developing others, so we may be protected against future attacks from this devastating new power. God has shown me in my mind this is like a warfare dance. It is our act of faith in God, and as we act in faith, He responds. I see now that motion is also one of the keys to unleashing God's action!"

\* \* \*

"I did not think it possible," chuckled Sivvius as he approached Alton. "But it's true. You are even more foolish today than you were yesterday! Your dance … how can I help but laugh? If you only knew how ridiculous you all looked. Do you realize how silly Alton makes you look? Do you think this dance really does anything for you? Do you really think God does anything for you? How many times must I tell you that you are wasting your time with God?"

Sivvius saw the scroll beside the tree, unprotected. How could he let the chance pass when it was right there taunting him? He knew he had to try. He pushed his fear aside and hoped the scroll would not affect him like the box had.

"You can't stop me. I'm far more powerful than any of you, and my friends from beyond are far more powerful than your God. You continue fighting a losing battle."

They stood paralyzed with fear, silent. Even Angus's mouth remained closed.

Sivvius darted to the tree and grabbed the scroll. As he turned to run, fire and ice raced up his arms, even more intensely than when he had tried to steal the box from Alton. He dropped to his knees in agony as he felt the scroll sliding out of his hand.

He watched in disbelief as it rolled on the ground toward the Council members. It was a steady, continuous roll; and there was no wind. It rolled right up against the feet of Walter, who bent down, picked it up, and looked at Sivvius. Sivvius hated the look. It was a look of smugness. A look of power. And yet, the look had a softness to it: pity. He looked at Alton and saw even more than pity: he saw compassion. The goodness, the pity, the compassion. They brought a sick feeling to his stomach. He rose to his feet.

"You are all fools! The scroll is a waste of time, anyway! Don't you see I'm so much more powerful than you are? Don't you see you have already failed? So many souls are with me. The earth will be ours soon."

"Sivvius, the desperation is clear in your voice," said Alton. "Your power is nothing. See how easily God has stopped it today?"

Sivvius felt a rush of discouragement. His attempt to get the scroll ended in embarrassment, and the latest attack he was so confident about was quelled so quickly. But his mind was filling with a sense of his friends again. They were preparing him for an immediate attack of a completely different sort. As a word formed in his mind, he felt power rising from within. His discouragement transformed into a firestorm of excitement and anticipation. The word gelled in his mind and brought a massive smile to his face. His cackling laugh seeped through the air as he walked closer to the Council members.

"You think your silly dance has stopped my new power? You think God has stopped my power? You are idiots. I've had all I can take of you! See just how great my power is!"

Sivvius began waving his arms in the air, slow small circular gyrations at first, near his face. Then the circular motions grew into a larger arc, as his arms rose higher. The intensity of the gyrations grew, the form of the motion becoming intricate and creative, arms and hands waving and flowing in an eerie pattern. Sivvius's eyes blazed as a cackling laugh erupted from his lungs and a deranged look consumed his face. He fought to maintain a sense of sanity.

\* \* \*

Alton felt the ground beneath him shifting, sliding. He had a hard time maintaining his balance. He heard cracks forming all around him, getting louder, their frequency growing. He heard the others yelling for help as the ground around them cracked as well. A circle of cracks formed around Alton, and the earth around him pulled away. He was left standing on a small circle of earth, about five feet in diameter. The gap all around him was huge, and its depth was vast. There was no way to jump across and get off the small circle of land on which he stood. Any attempt would clearly end in a fall to his death. He watched helplessly as the gaps formed around his friends, and soon each was stranded on his own small circle of land. They were completely isolated from one another. Alton's heart sank.

\*   \*   \*

"You see?" yelled Sivvius. "You see my power! Now you are not one. I have inflicted isolation upon you. I leave you as a disjointed band of fools. I leave you to watch each other slowly starve and die, separated from one another, unable to join your hands in prayer."

Sivvius walked off into the woods, far away from the Council members. He found a large rock and sat down, panting, exhausted. His mind was overloaded with a barrage of thoughts and emotions. "My friends, how did they stop the knowledge-destroying power so quickly? Somehow this dance of theirs did something. Somehow God must have helped them again. But I know some of their knowledge was destroyed. I know I can use this power again. Help me to grow in ability to use this power more effectively ... that is, if I even need to use it again. It may be enough that they are on the pedestals."

Sivvius sat for a few moments, thinking. He felt a disturbing sense of unease and emptiness. For some reason he could not rejoice about the power to isolate the Council members from one another. His uneasiness grew into a fear that raced through his mind. He couldn't understand the fear, couldn't figure out where it was coming from or why. His thoughts drifted back to the Council members. He pictured them sitting on their isolated pedestals of land, helpless. He imagined them being there for days, starving, suffering, eventually dying. Now he knew why he felt the fear. If there is a God, would He allow this? And what if He did? What will happen to me then? What price would I pay for what I've done to them? What if they *are* God's elect? What price would I pay for killing them?

"Ahhhh! I hate this!" he yelled to no one. "I hate this trace of good in me that won't let me kill them and move on!"

He jumped off the rock and walked back to them. He watched them sitting helplessly on their small circles of land, yelling to each other, trying to figure out what to do. He knew there was nothing they could do. He knew it was up to him. He held their lives in his hands. It could be over in just a few days. No more Council to worry about. He stood there for a long time, silent, thinking.

And then he lifted his hands in the air and engaged in his wild gyrations again. The land around the many circles started shaking, then moving. Slowly the land flowed together, the distinct circles gone. He watched in disgust as the Council members embraced each other, rejoicing. He walked back into the woods, shoulders sagging, feeling like a complete failure. He found the large rock and climbed back on it.

"Oh, my friends. Forgive me. I cannot let them die. This agonizing trace of good left in me just won't let me do it. Please, my friends, take it from me! I know you must be tired of me asking, but I'm desperate over this. Please root out the last remnants of good in me. Take away my conscience. Let me be pure evil for you so I can kill them off, finish the battle, and be master of the world. Help me."

He sat there, waiting. He focused more than before, imagining his friends purging him of any traces of good. He knew it had to happen now; he knew he was almost out of time.

Yet he felt nothing, sensed nothing from his friends. Again it was confirmed: he was the one who had to root the final good out of himself. It was up to him.

He lifted his head, realizing his only hope was to press on in his evil cause. He had to throw himself one hundred percent into evil, his every action being for the cause of evil. He must fight any good thought that seeped into his mind. He must take every thought captive to the obedience of Satan. It was up to him to purge the final traces of good from deep within himself.

*   *   *

Sivvius walked for nearly a mile to the rendezvous point. They were waiting for him, and as he approached, they stood at attention and saluted. The salutes were strong and abrupt, each man slamming a fist onto his chest and then thrusting his arm outward rigidly.

"General Sivvius," they roared in unison.

"Your reports," said Sivvius.

"My sector has had great success over the past week, General. Nearly 40,000 souls converted to our evil cause. And all are in our crash-training course as we speak. The latest weather attacks have been amazingly effective, and the people still think it is God who is against them. They are turning to our cause with wild abandon."

"Excellent, Captain Marcus."

"We have had great success in our sector as well, General. Over 30,000 conversions with many from the upper classes. We have over 5,000 in advanced mental warfare training."

"Good work, Captain Tirellius. Both of you will be rewarded. We must step up our conversion rate now. We are on the verge of final victory. But the enemy is strong. The enemy has something now that is of grave danger to us. We must complete our mission within a few days. Let all your leaders know it is time for the final phase, the final push for souls. I will be advising the other Captains as well. We are on the verge of complete and total victory. We are on the verge of world domination. Press on with all that is within you."

"Yes, General!" they barked as they saluted again and stormed off to fulfill their duties.

Sivvius stood alone, staring at nothing: silent.

\* \* \*

As they sat together, discussing what had happened, Alton gestured for them to be silent.

"My dear friends, we have been spared."

"Yes, Alton! God has saved us!" yelled Walter.

"Walter. Let me tell you something."

He paused, waiting for complete silence.

"God saved us from complete knowledge destruction. But do you know that it was not He who rejoined the land?"

"What?" said Angus. "What're you sayin'? What do you mean God didn't rejoin the land? Did you do it, Alton?"

"Oh no, Angus, not I. I do not have that type of power. But Sivvius does."

"Sivvius? Come on, Alton. Why would he rejoin the land? He had us right where he wanted us! He's the one who separated it. Why would he rejoin it?"

"He had to."

"What do you mean he had to?" asked Walter.

"It's the small measure of good left in him. I know it. I sense it. It was what drove him to rejoin the land. He could not bear for us to die. The good in him will not let him kill us. God knows this. God didn't join the land because He knew that

Sivvius had to be the one to do it. It's all part of the process that allows good to stay alive in Sivvius."

"C'mon, Alton! How can there still be good in that shank wedge of a scum dog. That freak can't know what good is."

"Then how could he save us from death, Angus? Why would he? There is no reason, unless it's the small good in him that compels him. He knows we are a major threat. Now with the scroll in our possession, the scales in our epic battle are about to shift our way. He may be in the lead now, with his army growing at exponential rates, and the new and unbelievable powers from his friends at his disposal. But with the scroll, our gift from God, the tides are about to turn. Don't you think he senses this? And yet he can't stop us. He can't kill us, and he can't even touch the scroll. The good left in him keeps us alive. And do you know why the good is still there?"

"Because of our prayers," said Walter. "You have told us many times Alton. We are the only reason there is still any good left in him."

"Precisely. And it's vital that I remind you again today. We draw very close to the end of our battle. The good must remain in him, for if it doesn't, he *will* kill all of us. And then he will win. We must step up our prayers, filling them with love and compassion toward Sivvius. We must never give up on him. There is still hope that he will turn back to God, as long as he doesn't become pure evil and let his heart turn perfectly hard and cold. If he returns to God, his example will open the door of repentance for the throngs of people already deceived by his lies, and the recruiting of millions more for his evil cause will be stopped."

"Yes, Alton, I've learned to love with this kind of love, thanks to your teachings," said Walter. "It's not easy. Sometimes I hate it. Sometimes I hate to love. That sounds so awful as I say it, but it's how I feel. Sometimes, it's so hard to love Sivvius."

"Yes, my dear friend. Very hard. But you have grown much. As have all of you. It is God's will for us: to love our enemies. Even the worst of the worst can repent."

"Aye," said Angus. "Aye. But I think it's harder for me than most. I must be honest; I still hate him to the core sometimes … okay, most of the time."

"And I appreciate your honesty, Angus. But I've seen you grow in this area as well. Do not beat yourself up over your struggle. Just keep asking God for how to love as He loves. He never gives up on people. That is why He has waited for so long to return. He wants as many as possible to come to Him, simply because of His love for us and His desire to be with us."

"Aye, Alton … aye."

The Letter brothers looked at each other.

"Love," said A.

"Love," said B.

Alton waited for more from the Letters, but they were done. It was the shortest cross-talking session he had ever heard. And yet the most powerful.

"Yes, A and B … love."

Alton sensed a wonderful divine presence around them. There was a peace so thick in the air he could almost taste it.

"Let us pray."

# Chapter 13
## Tuesday, 8:15 a.m.

"What time is it?" asked Alton when the prayer ended.

Walter ran the question through his mind repeatedly: what time is it? He began to think about what this really meant. Couldn't one ask what mass is it? Oh, it's the ground I'm sitting on, he thought he could say. How bizarre! How could he respond to a question about what time it is with the description of the ground?

"I may know, Alton, yet I can't be sure," said Walter.

"What do you mean?"

"Well, in a sense, yes, but in another sense no."

"Are you certain you're feeling okay?"

"It's complicated, Alton."

"Now you have me worried, Walter. Has Sivvius's knowledge-destruction attack ripped that deeply into your mind?"

"Please do not worry Alton. It's true that the knowledge destruction has robbed me of precious knowledge; even a recent revelation I had about how to modify gravity fields with a ball-point pen has slipped from my mind, but—".

"Yes, Walter," interrupted Alton, "I've had similar loss; I can't even recall the quark composition of clotrons. And no matter how hard I've tried, I've been unable to retrieve the lost knowledge ... it appears to be permanent loss. We need a new dance to restore our lost knowledge. I've been formulating some ideas, and I shall lead us into this new dance just as soon as I have it developed. The dance of defense is somewhat effective in shielding against the knowledge-destruction attacks, but even as we work on it and perfect it, it will not be able to restore lost knowledge. We'll definitely need a new dance to reverse the effects of knowledge loss. I can't bear the thought of any of us losing more knowledge. We need everything within our minds to stand against Sivvius—"

"Aye, Alton," spouted Angus. "It's bad enough I can't recall the formula for my ultra-high protein drink, and my muscle-blastin' theory is but a name with no content—"

"You think you guys have it bad?" asked Patrick. "One of my favorite manicotti recipes is gone from my mind ... just like it was never there. I can't believe—"

"Please!" yelled Walter. "My comments about time have nothing to do with knowledge destruction. It's just that ... well ... I have started deciphering the scroll."

Walter saw a look of wonder flow across Alton's face.

"What is it you have seen? Tell us!"

"It is amazing. And fascinating. And it will change all we hold dear to our hearts within science! And there is one more thing ... something I can't wrap my mind around. The scroll ... it was written for me."

"For you, Walter?"

"Yes, Alton. The very first sentence says that the scroll was written for me! I'm not sure how this is possible; I'm not sure what it means."

"This is most interesting—and amazing," said Alton. "Yet I'm not entirely shocked. It makes sense. You were the only one who could open the second box. And Sivvius couldn't even hold on to the first one. My sense has been strong that the scroll was meant for you to decipher. As to the details of exactly why and how, this is a mystery. How could it be that the writer of the scroll would know you would ever touch it? And why were you chosen to study the very code you would need to decipher the scroll this day? Mystery ... all mystery. All I can say is that all things work together for good. It is, in some way, all part of God's plan. And the mystery of it all is most exhilarating!

"Now, tell us, my friend. Tell us what the words of the scroll say!"

Walter pondered the question. How could he answer? he wondered. He had seen so much, so much more than he could absorb. He needed to focus.

"Before I do, can we engage in motion, Alton? What I've read so far is so intense that we must ponder through motion before I can utter a word to you about what I've read. Besides, part way through the scroll, the writer was adamant about me entering into deep thought before I read farther. What better way to enter into deep thought than to engage in motion?"

"Yes. I agree a time of motion is vital right now. How about group ballet?"

"Outstanding idea, Alton."

"Council members … unite! It's time for motion. We must engage before we can hear what it is that Walter has learned. Let us engage in group ballet."

They rushed into a circle, joined hands and looked up to the sky. They were silent for a few moments and then lifted upon their toes. Walter peeked over at Angus and could see his look of skepticism. He knew how Angus hated this type of motion. He could see him glancing all around as if he was afraid someone might see them doing such an unmanly act. Yet to Walter, this was a beautiful display of minor motion, actually a form of pre-motion as they called it. A subtle motion, leading to one that is much more intense. There had been many previous debates among them regarding the need for pre-motion. Walter held to the belief that pre-motion, although not as effective as full motion, was a necessary precursor. Often when they engaged in full motion, he would do a quick pre-motion in his own way. Things such as a slow wrist flex or a gentle sigh were often a part of Walter's pre-motion routine.

Walter knew Angus thought pre-motion was a waste of time. He had told Walter more than once he didn't believe pre-motion was required, since he felt full motion was just as effective without it, and far more manly. Even though Walter never stated that pre-motion was better or even at the same level of full motion, he believed that full motion could *never* be as effective without a pre-motion activity. He and Angus would sometimes debate this for hours and he could see by the look on Angus's face that another debate was about to begin.

"This calf-flexin' pre-motion is a waste of time."

"Oh be quiet, Angus. You know we believe it to be essential."

"No Walter. YOU believe it to be essential. No one else does."

"That is not true Angus. Many of us believe in the pre."

"Oh, the pre, the pre, the pre. I'm sick and tired of hearin' of the pre. Why must we go on and on and on about the pre, laddie?"

"It's because without the pre, there is no true full or post motion. Without the pre, it's as if we live in a state of only partially fulfilled motion. Think of it this way, Angus. When you brush your teeth, you put the toothpaste on the brush first. And think of drinking a glass of milk ... you must pour the milk before you can drink it. These are forms of pre-motion. Without these pre-motions, the final motion would be less effective or even impossible! With the milk, what is there to drink if one had not first poured? How could one argue with such flawless logic?"

"Oh, it's easy for me, laddie. I just know you're wrong because I know I'm right."

"That's a ridiculous answer! Can't we just enjoy the pre-motion? If it bothers you Angus, just don't think about it. Just pretend you are stretching your calves. Why must you bash the pre? What good does that serve?"

"It serves to make me feel better, laddie."

"Angus!" Alton interrupted. "Let us not forget why we are engaging in motion in the first place. Do you not crave the knowledge from the scroll?"

Walter looked at Angus and noticed that he appeared to soften. It was amazing how Alton could have such an impact.

"Perhaps you're right Alton. We must remember our mission. Please forgive my intense bashin' of the pre-motion. It's hard for me to do the pre with enthusiasm, but I'll do my best, for the sake of the scroll."

"Yes, for the sake of the scroll, Angus."

"Lord bless us in the dance," prayed Alton softly as he flexed his calves.

They followed Alton's lead and extended their calves again, rising upon their toes. Walter noticed the agonized look on Angus's face as he tried to keep a good attitude about the pre. Walter loved to see the others poised in extension; he felt a need to dance a wild, reckless ballet. His calves burned with anticipation as he watched Alton, waiting for his signal to let the full motion begin. Many seconds passed—Alton appeared to be holding the pre for longer than usual, perhaps to push them to a new level of preparation. Finally, he released the command:

"Council members ... DANCE!"

At Alton's command, the dance began. It was a radical ballet. Certainly, there was never a ballet of this nature ever in the history of humankind, thought Walter. He watched Angus walk aggressively in a circular pattern, stopping every few seconds to look at his arms as he flexed his biceps, then his triceps, grunting as he squeezed his arms as tight as he could. The closest he got to anything resembling classic ballet was a brief reaching of his arms above his head, hands touching at the peak but quickly followed by hands forming into fists and another flexing of arm muscles. Michael and Patrick jumped up and down, entering into brief but majestic poses each time they left the ground—arms flailing to the sides, legs angling backwards, necks craning. Alton's body flowed with an amazing motion, seemingly unfettered by the limitations of his physical body—more like advanced martial arts than formal ballet. It was quite a sight, and Walter knew the pre-motion had helped them achieve this level of intensity. He entered into the dance with joy.

After nearly five minutes, they stopped and sprawled face down on the ground. A whisper emanated from Alton's mouth that sounded to Walter like, "Ruh rime zoo zead tu koll inz oww!"

"What was that Alton?" asked Walter. "I couldn't quite make that out."

Alton rolled onto his back and yelled into the sky, "The time to read the scroll is NOW!"

Walter immediately stood up and ran to the scroll. He could hardly wait another moment to read more. He carefully picked it up, and brought it to where the others were waiting. His heart was pounding as he prepared to speak.

He turned to Alton and then gazed upon the others. He could see the anticipation on their faces. He could sense their burning desire to hear the translation of the code.

"The title at the top of the first page is the exact sequence of words it's supposed to be. My translation of the code is precise and completely accurate. The title is: THE SECRETS OF TIME TRAVEL."

Walter watched Alton fall to his knees, bow his head, and lift his hands to the sky. He watched the others as their faces filled with joy and amazement. All were at a loss for words, even Angus. As he continued, he could see the tears welling in all their eyes, even those of Angus.

"My dear friends and fellow scientists, this is truly the scroll we have longed to find. It is the title exactly as foretold. What you are about to hear from the scroll will change you forever. You will never again look at anything as you used to. Every time you look at your watch, you will begin to ponder deep things. Every time you look at a tree, or a rock, or a flower, you will begin to ponder deep things. Every time you study formulas and equations, your minds will again ponder what I'm about to tell you.

"The scroll gives us a new formula that alters all we hold true in physics. It gives us a relationship that is beyond comprehension or understanding. I'm anxious to read more in the scroll to see the proof of the equation, but let me tell you what I've seen so far. In the shell of a nut, what the scroll reveals to us is that time equals mass!"

There was complete silence among them ... for a long time.

"Did you say that the scroll says time equals mass?" whispered Michael. "Did I hear you right?"

"Yes, you did my friend. Time equals mass."

"How can that be? Do you realize the implications of such a truth? That is, if it is in fact a truth."

"I have only begun to realize. As I'm sure is the case with all of you. For one thing it means that all of you are sitting or lying not only on the mass of the ground right now, but you are also sitting or lying on time itself!"

"This is mind-boggling—how can this be?" asked Alton. "How do we know this is truth? What is the author's proof? And what are the implications? If this is true, life as we know it has just been radically altered. In fact, all that we believe about time travel will be thrown into the trash bin if this equation is true. Let us hear more. Let us hear the proofs!"

"Yes, let us hear! Let us hear!" they all shouted.

"Very well. The scroll says that scientists for centuries have discussed, analyzed, theorized, and imagined so many possible ways to travel in time, but none ever did it. It also says that the key to time travel is not about approaching the speed of light, or utilizing gravitational fields, or traveling through wormholes. It's much simpler. It mentions that it all has to do with mass. It mentions that all objects have mass, some more, some less. The scroll asks why so many things have such completely different masses, and postulates that there must be some significance to that. Then the scroll talks about correlation—but wait, let me just pick up where I left off with my reading."

Walter picked up the scroll again, rolled it open, and began reading slowly as he deciphered. "So you see it is about correlation. The correlation between time and mass. One tangible, the other not. Yet both become tangible and non-tangible simultaneously as they integrate with each other. How do we know time equals mass? How do we prove this? The proofs are not complex. Actually, they are quite simple.

"Just remember that although the proofs are simple, and may even appear silly to you, with simplicity comes power. A simple truth can be more powerful than the most complex formula. Do not think there must be complexity to bring truth.

"So, then … the proofs. First, think of this: as a man gets older, he gets fatter. That is all there is to this first proof. Did I not tell you it was simple? This shows an infallible positive relationship between time and mass. As time increases so does mass.

"Proof number two is next. It is based on an inverse relationship. Are you ready? As one writes with a pencil, the mass of the pencil decreases. Therefore as time increases, mass decreases. This proves that mass and time are also proportional inversely. Even though they are not necessarily equal in the positive sense of simultaneous increase, they are dissimilar in a similar sense. This might be a little confusing, but one day you can read my paper titled 'The Similarity of Dissimilarity'. It should help you get a much clearer understanding.

"Proof number three brings it all together. It is in the relationship of proofs one and two. Proof three states that since proof one shows a positive relationship between time and mass, and proof two shows an inverse relationship, then the two proofs together cause a negation effect, thereby creating a neutrality between time and mass. Through a neutral relationship, time and mass are in essence equal.

"Simple! Three proofs of positive relationship, inverse relationship, and neutral relationship. No matter how you look at it, and in fact the more you think about it, time truly equals mass.

"The real question though is not about the proof of my equation of time equals mass, but rather what will you do with this information now that you have it? What will you do about the fact that your left foot is time itself? What will you say now when someone asks you what time it is? Will you respond by saying 50.3 grams? Moreover, what can you change, now that you know this? I am here to tell you that as you learn more, you will begin to see how even time travel itself is a simple thing. Understanding the implications of the fact that time equals mass will enable you to travel in time just as easily as you put on a sock or wash your hands. And I will teach you how to do this; I will teach you how to travel in time."

Walter paused, unable to read farther. He felt so overwhelmed by what he had read that he could not find the strength to open his mouth. The others were silent. They had found the scroll and heard the words, thought Walter. The words they had sought to hear for so long. The words were so simple, yet so complex in their simplicity!

Walter's thoughts drifted to Ingrid. Was she still alive? She has to be, he thought. That one day by the tree in the schoolyard had been the day he had spoken to the woman of his destiny. He knew she was the one for him; he had waited a lifetime to see her again.

Now the means was in his grasp. He would have to ponder much more about what he had read in the scroll, but he was already considering how the formula of time = mass might help him find her. Perhaps the formula would enable him to travel back in time to that day in the schoolyard. He could find his younger self, and tell him to express his feelings toward Ingrid and get her phone number before she was gone forever. He would tell him not to let the day end without kissing her sweet lips. She would know when they kissed that they were meant for each other.

He could feel the fire in his heart. He would win her love: the scroll would show him the way.

\* \* \*

Alton gazed upon the scroll in Walter's hands. How incredible it was. He still could not believe they had found it. They had heard truths that would radically alter the current teachings of science and physics. Time equals mass! I can't believe it, he thought. It's beyond my comprehension. I'm on fire with a storm of mental activity. My synapses won't stop firing. The electrical impulses in my brain are so strong that I can almost feel them leaving my head! And the thought that time travel is a simple thing—it's so hard to believe this could be true.

Alton gazed in awe as he pondered, noticing that a gentle breeze was caressing the leaves of a nearby tree. He loved to watch them flutter, showing their life. The wind, the trees, the flowers—they were all alive: all from God. How magnificent God's creation is, he thought. What a beautiful and magical testimony to His creative power. He felt a tear trickle down his face. He felt such peace, such oneness with what God had made, such oneness with God. He did not sense Sivvius; he did not feel fear. He began to believe they could stop his evil plans, that they could stop him from destroying the beauty of the earth, that they could stop him from deceiving more souls. Somehow, the information in the scroll would help them.

But it was about more than just stopping him. It was about Sivvius returning to God; it seemed more feasible now that they had found the scroll. Alton felt chills run down his spine as he imagined Sivvius softening, turning away from his deceptive life, walking away from his friends from beyond and reaching out to God. And even becoming Alton's friend again. He had to hold back the tears as he pondered this. He missed his old friend.

He looked at Walter and noticed he was about to begin reading again. He could hardly wait.

# Chapter 14
## Tuesday, 9:00 a.m.

"I think I can continue," said Walter. "I'm so overwhelmed by what I've read; I thought I might never be able to speak again. But the desire to know more drives me. Let me see ... where was I ... let's see, yes ... time travel ... yes ... the three proofs that time equals mass ... the proof of my ... what can you really change now that you know this ... ahhhh yes here we go ... Understanding the true implications of the fact that time equals mass will enable you to travel in time just as easily as you put on a sock or wash your hands. Okay, here is more."

"Time travel is not a distant possibility. It is not far from reality. It is reality. It is within your reach. All you need do is grasp it, as I will show you. You will learn how your perceptions of time and mass are so shallow. You will see that you are not limited by the apparent distances from one place to another. I will help you to open your minds to a new way of thinking, to a new way of living. But more cannot be revealed in this scroll. You must find the rest in another place. There is a hint for you. Find the hint and you shall know where to go next."

Walter stopped reading and stared at the scroll.

"That is all there is?" gasped Alton. "Are you sure there is no more?"

"There is no more for us, Alton. Of that I am certain."

"Oh dear, oh dear, oh dear. Walter, I do not think I can accept that there is no more. Are you sure?"

"Yes, Alton. Again I tell you there is no more for us."

"But what do we do next? How do we find more? Where is the hint?"

"I don't know!"

"It must be somewhere in the scroll! Did you not see it anywhere? What about at the end?"

Walter rolled the scroll to the end and looked. He stared for quite some time.

"There is nothing more for us Alton."

"I can't believe this, Walter. The hint must be there. Any ideas anyone?"

"Ziti!" yelled Patrick.

"What are you doin' laddie? Thinkin' about eatin' now? We're supposed to be thinkin' about the hint!"

"No, no ... although I'll admit that it was a thought about food that inspired me. Fresh, tender ziti. Cooked just right ... not too soft ... not too hard ... just the right amount of sauce. Wonderful, glorious little tubes of pasta—"

"C'mon, laddie! Get to the point!"

"Yes ... sorry. Anyway, the ziti made me think of the word tube, and then the word grew and grew in my mind. It's so strong now. It must have some significance."

"Keep pondering," said Alton. "What is the tube? Where is the tube? Let your thoughts flow."

Alton noticed Letter A raise his eyebrows.

"Do you have something, Letter A?"

"Tube," said Letter A.

Letter B ran over to Letter A and stood by his side.

"Tube," said Letter B.

"Tube near us?" said Letter A.

"Could be near us," said Letter B.

"Where?" said Letter A.

"Where?" said Letter B.

"Near us," said Letter A.

"Must be close," said Letter B.

"Has to be close," said Letter A.

"What's close?" said Letter B.

"Tube is close," said Letter A.

"Very close," said Letter B.

"Scroll!" shouted Letter A.

"Scroll?" said Letter B.

"The scroll is a tube!" shouted Letter A.

"The scroll is a tube," said Letter B.

"The hint is in the tube," said Letter A.

"The scroll is the tube," said Letter B.

"The hint is in the scroll," said Letter A.

The Letter brothers paused.

"What do you mean, the hint's in the scroll, you pair of Letter-laddies? Walter has already read the scroll! There was no hint!"

"Roll it," said A.

"Roll it up," said B.

"Look at it while it's rolled up," said A.

"Keep it rolled, look on through," said B.

"Look on through," said A.

Alton looked at A and B, confirming they were done cross-talking.

"I think the Letters may be on to something," said Alton. "The hint may not be in the coded text, but maybe somehow seen when the scroll is looked at in a different way. Walter, check out the scroll in its tubular form."

Walter picked up the rolled-up scroll, and peered into its center from one end. Then he looked through the other end. Alton noticed no sign of revelation in his expression.

"I see nothing."

"Keep looking Walter," said Alton. "There must be a hint."

"I still see nothing. I'm looking and looking and looking … nothing."

"Try something different. Try—"

"Wait! I see something. I see something within the scroll core! I was about to give up, but as I tried other innovative ways to view the scroll, as I spun it between my hands, I noticed some words beginning to appear on the inner wall of the scroll. Here ... let me keep spinning to see what the words are. I see ... Ad ... Adir ... Adir ... Adiron ... I see the word Adirondack."

Alton watched Walter close his eyes tight, apparently straining to focus his mind. Then he opened one eye and looked into the scroll again, as he spun it steadily.

"Yes, Alton ... I see Adirondack," said Walter.

"What else, Walter? I know of the Adirondacks."

"Let me see, In ... yes, something with In ... In ... Inset. Something like inset. Wait ... no ... not set ... it's let ... yes ... let ... Inlet. It says Inlet."

"Inlet?" shouted Alton. "I know of Inlet! It's a small town in the Adirondack Park area of Upstate New York. It's a beautiful little town. So we are supposed to go to Inlet?"

"I'm not sure yet, Alton. Could be, but ... let's see ... there is more. I see ... hmmm ... looks like rock ... and looks like point ... rock point."

"Rock Point? Could it be Rocky Point?" asked Alton.

"Let's see ... Rock ... Rocky ... yes! Rocky Point, Alton! How did you know?"

"I know of Rocky Point. It's a beautiful resort in the Inlet area. What else, Walter? Does it show anything else?"

"Well, it looks like just one more thing ... looks like wood ... wood something ... wood ... wood is ... wood islan ... ah! Wood island. It says wood island!"

"What is wood island?"

"I don't know, Alton. It just says wood island."

"Wood island ... wood island ... what could that be?" murmured Alton.

"Beats me Alton," said Walter.

"You are certain there is no more?"

"That's it."

"Well, it sounds to me like we need to go to the Rocky Point resort near Inlet in the Adirondack Park of Upstate New York! I don't know about this wood island comment, but I know about Rocky Point. We can ask some people there if maybe there is an island near there called Wood Island. We must go now! Let's hike back down to the trailhead and head to the Denver airport. Michael, why don't you lead the way today? After all, you are our Travel Director!"

"Nothing would please me more, Alton. Follow me!"

Alton felt the intensity in his step as he followed Michael down the trail. They had discovered the hint. First the scroll, and now a hint. He could hardly believe their good fortune. He looked at some flowers along the path, and felt a sense of wonder and delight. He breathed in their wonderful aroma. Perhaps they would stop the desolation of the earth after all. Perhaps they really could help stop millions of souls from being led to eternal damnation. Things were looking up.

# Chapter 15
# Tuesday, 3:00 p.m.

Michael rushed to the American Airlines ticket counter inside the Denver airport, and began telling the agent what they needed. Alton was busy with the others, double-checking luggage and verifying they had not left anything in the rental car. After a few minutes, Alton and Angus stepped up to the counter to see how things were going.

"Okay then, sir," said the agent. "I think we have the itinerary set for you and your six friends. We have you with only one change of planes, and ultimately ending up in Seattle, Washington."

"Perfect!" said Michael.

"Seattle!" barked Angus. "What are you doin', laddie?"

"Well, we had trouble booking the Syracuse, New York trip, so I had her set it up for a flight into Seattle instead."

"Why?" asked Angus, bringing his nose right up to Michael's face.

"Well, it's the seating. I couldn't get us seats that were together for the first flight into Charlotte, North Carolina, or the final leg into Syracuse, but the flights to Seattle have plenty of availability. We can take a cab from Seattle to Syracuse."

"Michael?"

"Yes, I know, Angus. You don't need to express your gratitude. I knew you would be pleased that I got us seats together."

"Michael?"

"Yes, Angus?"

"Do you know where Seattle is?"

"Of course, Angus. It's in the North."

"Where in the North?"

"Oh, just up there in the North. I don't need the details. As long as we're far north, it can't be too far to New York. From what I recall, I think Washington and New York are right near each other. It should be a short drive."

"Michael," said Angus, his face turning the color of a strawberry, "don't you realize there's a huge difference between the state of Washington, and Washington, DC?"

"What do you mean?"

"Michael! Washington DC is in the Northeast, but the state of Washington is in the Northwest, and Seattle is in the state of Washington!"

"That's ridiculous, Angus. They're the same thing! How can they be so far apart? I'm worried about you. I think you need some rest."

"That's it! You shank wedge—I've had all I can take of you—"

Alton, doing his best to hold back laughter, had to intervene as Angus was about to do some awful things to poor Michael.

"Now, Angus, let's not get carried away. After all, the bookings are not finalized yet. I can see how someone could confuse the two Washingtons—"

"But he's not a little boy, Alton! He's a grown man. Don't you think he should know by now that Washington DC is different from the state of Washington? After all, he's our Travel Director!" Angus cocked his arm, getting ready to release his frustration on Michael.

"Angus, please relax. It looks like the others could use your help with some of the luggage over there. Look at the mess they've made."

Angus glanced over and saw the mess all over the floor and chairs. "My God, man. Sometimes I can't believe this group.

Do I have to do everything? Patrick, get your hands off my ankle weights. And Walter, what are you doin' with my jump rope? Let's get this mess straightened out!"

Alton watched as Angus trotted over to the others and ranted on and on about the need to achieve some semblance of organization.

"Okay, Michael, let's try again. Let's book the trip to Syracuse. It's okay if we can't all sit together. Miss, can you get all seven of us into Syracuse today?"

"You're sure it's okay if I can't get you all together?"

"That's fine, miss. Uh, Michael, why don't you finish the seat selections? We'll be back shortly to give you our information. I've got to get over to the group. It looks like Angus is about to lose it again."

They finally got their luggage straightened out, and finished checking in at the counter. After they got through security, hit the bathrooms, bought some gum, and found their gate, it was just about time to board. Alton noticed that Angus was not looking well.

"You all right, Angus?"

"Aye, Alton ... aye . The little runt over there reminded me of one of my boys ..."

"Oh, yes, Angus. Still hurts after all these years, doesn't it? Do you want to talk about it?"

"Well, I miss 'em Alton. Sometimes I really miss 'em. Wouldn't have been so bad if I could've at least had a chance to say goodbye. The accident was so sudden. Aye ... I miss 'em. But, got to go on livin'. Got to keep on fightin'! Aye."

Alton put a hand on Angus's shoulder and gave him a reassuring squeeze. "Any time you need to talk, I'm here for you Angus. I mean that."

"Thanks, Alton. I'll be all right. Just need to keep busy—"

"Ladies and Gentlemen, we are about to start boarding our flight. Please have your boarding passes, cell phones, or finger chips ready."

When it came time for them to board, Alton noticed Angus checking with everyone he saw to confirm this first flight was headed to Charlotte. He apparently still had no faith in Michael. After the fifth confirmation, he appeared to be satisfied all was as it should be.

When Angus reached his seat, he stuffed his carry-on into the overhead bin and whispered to Alton, "All I've got to say, Alton, is that I'm glad I'm on this side. Look over there."

Alton looked to the other side of the aisle and noticed two huge men, one in the aisle seat and one in the window seat. There was only a sliver of space left in the center seat. Alton looked up at the seat number, then snapped his eyes to his ticket, breathing a huge sigh of relief when he realized it was not his seat.

"I see what you mean, Angus," whispered Alton. "I feel sorry for whoever gets stuck there."

"Aye … literally, Alton!"

They laughed together as Angus moved into his row. "Excuse me, young lady, I think I have the middle seat here between you and … is that your sister?"

"Yes sir, we're twins."

"Well it's nice to meet you lassies. So glad I'm here and not between those giants across the aisle. I'm not even sure one of *you* could fit over there!"

Just as Angus settled into his seat, someone reached across the girl in the aisle and tapped him on the shoulder. He looked up and saw an elderly woman staring down at him.

"Excuse me, sir. I believe one of you is in my seat. Are you sure you and your daughters are in the right seats? I believe I have the middle seat on this side."

"Oh, they're not my daughters. Say, lassies, are you sure you're in the right seats?"

The woman in the row in front of them lifted up in her seat and turned toward them.

"Sir, I would kindly ask you to stop harassing my girls. Of course they are in the right seats. Here, look at their tickets."

Angus glanced at the tickets and confirmed they were in the right row.

"Looks fine to me," he said to the elderly woman. "Are you sure you read your ticket right? You're probably in the row across the aisle." He pointed between the two huge men.

"No, no. This is my row right here. Look at my ticket!"

Angus breathed a loud sigh as he glanced at the ticket. He appeared to be poised to argue, but then paused. He leaned his head closer, inspecting the ticket with great care. He sat silent.

"See? Now stop being such a troublemaker. My goodness, what is this world coming to? First you badger these young girls and then you treat me as if I'm some kind of deranged old woman. You should be ashamed of yourself."

Angus reached into his pocket and pulled out his ticket. He looked at it, then snapped his head up and looked at the seat marker across the aisle. He snapped his head back down to the ticket, then back up to the seat marker. His face flushed red.

"Michael, I'm goin' to kill you!"

"Sir! Please! What is wrong with you? Do I need to get a flight attendant over here—"

"Uh, sorry. It's just that there's been some kind of mix-up here. They appear to have put me in the wrong seat—"

The intercom system crackled to life. "Ladies and Gentleman, we have a full flight today, and need you to get your luggage loaded into the overhead bins quickly. You will need to put some items under the seats in front of you if the bins are full. Please get settled in your seats quickly, as we are

145

running a bit behind schedule and want to ensure we get you to your destination as quickly as possible. The pilot thinks we may be able to make up a bit of time, but we need to get going."

Angus squirmed his way out of the seat and attempted to move toward the front of the plane to get his seat changed, but there was nowhere to go. The aisle was filled with people hurrying to their seats.

"Sir, please sit back down," said the elderly woman. "You are holding up everyone. I have to meet my granddaughter and I cannot be late. Please stop being so selfish. You are not the only one on the plane, you know."

Hey lassies, said Angus, ignoring the old woman, "would one of you like to switch with me? Look how fun it would be to sit over on the other side. Look at the big men. Aren't they neat?"

The little girls started screaming. "Mommy! Mommy! This man is trying to hurt us!"

The mother snapped her head around and yelled at Angus, "Leave my girls alone before I call for the flight attendants to haul you off this plane. Please, just sit down, and stop thinking only of yourself."

"Really, sir. What is wrong with you?" said the elderly woman.

Angus looked at all the people jammed in the aisle waiting for him to sit.

"Ladies and Gentlemen, I ask you again to please get seated as quickly as possible. Please do not hold up the flow by standing in the middle of the aisle and blocking traffic."

Angus looked at the two huge men, then down the aisle again, then back to the giants. He saw the flight attendant at the front of the plane glaring at him. He had no choice.

"Excuse me, sir," he said to the man on the aisle, "would you mind sittin' by your friend so I can take the aisle seat? I'll lean toward the aisle as much as possible durin' the flight to give you plenty of room."

"He's not my friend."

"What was that?"

"I said he's not my friend. I don't even know him. What is wrong with you, anyway? First you harass the young girls, then the elderly woman, and now me? What are you saying? That just because we're both large men we must know each other?"

"But I don't think I can fit in the middle. I can hardly see the seat!"

"That is your problem little man, not mine."

"Please," said the flight attendant over the intercom, "will the gentleman in the aisle holding up traffic, please take his seat!"

Alton noticed that everyone on the plane was glaring at Angus.

"Angus, please take your seat. There is no alternative."

Angus stared at Alton for a moment, then began inching his way toward the center seat. It took him a few seconds to contort himself enough so he could squeeze into it. Once he finally sat, his bottom didn't quite reach the fabric of the seat. He was wedged between the two men, suspended just above the seat bottom.

Both men were heavy breathers, and each time they breathed, their sweaty bodies pushed against Angus. One of them kept snorting—he either had a bad cold or bad allergies. Alton knew that when they landed, he would need to whisk Michael far away from Angus.

Alton found his window seat and gazed out of the plane as they departed from the Denver airport. He enjoyed watching the land beneath them as they ascended. Alton never got tired of flying. He loved the unique perspective it gave him, being so far above and beyond everything. It was a small taste of the perspective God must have, he thought. Everything so distant and small to Him, and yet such strong love for each individual person. Each, even though small, was huge in God's heart.

As he watched the cars below getting smaller and the trees shrinking to small clumps, something struck him. A strange pattern. A brown pattern. Many missing trees. The higher they got, the more he noticed. Much of the land near the mountains was barren. Where there should be lush green, all was brown and depressing. As they rose even higher, the vastness of the desolation caused his heart to sink. "Lord Jesus," he whispered, "I can't believe what I'm seeing. Sivvius is much further along than I realized. So many people must be in complete despair. So many souls must be turning to Sivvius and his evil army. Oh dear God, help us. Help us to stop this terrible reality before it spreads throughout the entire earth!"

\* \* \*

As they were coming out of the bathroom in the Syracuse airport, Walter was finally starting to relax. The flight to Charlotte was fairly smooth but they had encountered quite a bit of turbulence on the flight from Charlotte to Syracuse.

Walter asked a man standing by the water fountain where the rental-car counter was.

"Who have we here?" asked the man, as his eyes grew wide. "Don't be alarmed by the wind! Why do you worry about the wind? It does not chase you. It is of itself. It just blows. Do not run from it! Why do you run from it? Can't you see it? No, you can't. So does it matter?"

Walter tilted his head and squinted his eyes.

"But it is the thought that brings the wind. Don't you see? The wind and the thoughts work together! Think like the wind, and the wind will think like you. Did you realize that? Did you know that the wind thinks? But do I care? No, but yes."

The man ran away, arms flailing, as if the wind was pushing him.

"That was quite the strange lad," snickered Angus.

"Yeah ... let's get out of here," said Michael.

As they continued walking, another man approached. To Walter, he looked to be the same man, except for the beard.

"Hello, Gentlemen. I hear that you need some assistance. How may I help you?"

"Thank you, sir, but we are fine. We are in a rush to get to our rental car."

"You know, now that you mention it, I think what I think just to have thought a thought. Think about it! Think about the wind!"

The man started to look agitated.

"No, stop it! You are wrong about the thinking!" the man screamed to himself.

"No I'm not wrong! Think the thought about the wind. The wind is the thought. The thought is the wind."

"No, no, no! Do not say another word!" the man continued to yell at himself. "Hey! Just where do you think you're going?"

The man moved slowly away, but in such a strange contorted way. One leg pulling one way, the other pulling the other way.

"Stop pulling me! Let go of me!"

"No I will not. You will come with me!"

"No way. Let go!"

"The wind! The wind!"

"Oh stop with the wind!"

"Think of the wind. See it? See it?"

The man moved in front of Walter, his disposition changing. He stood still and calm.

"I am really quite sane. My many personalities come in handy for serving the Captain. He's a good man, the Captain. He helped a bunch of us. Things were pretty bad ... no food ... no water ... storm after storm ... lots of wind ... fires. The city I flew in from today was totally barren, but Captain took care of us. He helped us. He showed us how God had turned His back on us. He showed us the truth. And he told us nearly 100,000 accepted the way of Sivvius just last week at the ceremony I attended! It was a magnificent event! The bending of our knees, the reading of the words that gave our allegiance to Sivvius and to his special friends ... just amazing! Now we have all the food and water we need. And here I am, with all kinds of voices in my head to help me. In fact, I hear them again now."

Walter noticed the man's expression changing again.

"Oh, and the wind! The wind! A chasing after the wind. Think about the wind! Chase it! Chase it! No! Run away from it! Don't think about it! Just chase it! Or run from it! Run wherever you want, as long as it is toward Sivvius!"

The man ran back down the hall.

"Let's go NOW," said Alton.

\* \* \*

Alton led them away at a feverish pace, trying his best to hide his concern. It was not the man's apparent insanity that bothered him, but rather the mention of Sivvius and the many that had turned to him. And the voices in the man's head. He knew they were the voices of demons—demons that were subject to the mighty friends from beyond that ruled Sivvius. It was clear to Alton this was a fairly new recruit, still subject to wild, personality-shifting episodes. But Alton also knew the man would eventually grow more controlled, steadier, and more dangerous in the battle against good. And he was just one of many. "Oh God, please help us," he prayed as he ratcheted up the pace another notch.

# Chapter 16
# Wednesday, 8:00 a.m.

Walter wondered if they would ever get to Inlet. A good night's sleep in the hotel in Syracuse had been a Godsend, and the early-morning drive to the Adirondacks had been filled with gorgeous scenery, but he was anxious to find the place the scroll hint had identified. He was feeling burned out on the Letter brothers' discussions about their old science club and model railroad-club friends, and fidgeted as he suffered through yet another talk. At least when they were in full cross-talk mode the conversation was quicker, but their lag-talk mode was agonizing.

"Yes, yes," said A. "I remember the old shay locomotive Jasper had. What a beauty. He detailed that bad boy to the n'th degree."

"Yes," said B. "And the weathering he did to it blew me away. So realistic. Sometimes I would look at it and feel like I was back in the time when the real thing was made."

"Me too," said A. "And Jasper … man do I miss the old boy. He really helped us figure out some prototypical features for our layout."

"He was amazing," said B. "Of course, spending the weekends camped out by the train yard really helped him."

"True, true," said A. "He was a radical when it came to model railroading. He would do anything to learn something we could incorporate into our club layout."

"I miss our science club friends also," said B.

"Me too," said A. "Like Randall, with his off-the-wall theories about how our eating habits affect the earth's gravitational field."

"Or Simeon, with his underwater hairdryer experiments," said B.

"Yes ... I do miss them all," said A.

"Me too," said B.

"Me too," said A.

When the lag-talking stopped, Walter relaxed. He rolled down his window and breathed in the fresh mountain air as he gazed upon the magnificent scenery. He was just starting to drift into a nap when the others got into a huge debate about one of the lakes they had passed. Michael kept insisting it was called Thirteenth Lake, but the others seemed to recall it being Third Lake. The debate dragged on until Angus gave one of his heart-stopping glares and yelled out for silence. His outburst was quickly followed by wonderful news from Alton.

"Here we are!" said Alton. "Rocky Point!"

Walter looked out the window with great anticipation as Alton slowed the van and flicked on the right blinker. Alton pulled into the entrance, and as he did, Walter's heart leapt. It was a beautiful development of quaint town homes with green metal roofs and beautiful wood siding, nestled at various points into the surrounding woods. As they drove a little farther, Walter saw a huge lake toward the back of the development. He could make out mountains in the distance, surrounding the lake. They were magical and mesmerizing, drawing his mind to another place of thought—a place of wonder and peace. He imagined a day when he would bring Ingrid here. He pictured them sitting by the lake, holding hands and cuddling, lost in the joy of each other.

\* \* \*

"Here we are!" said Alton. "We've found the Rocky Point the scroll mentioned. Isn't this amazing? Now we just need to figure out what to do next. Let's park the van and walk to the lake. Maybe there will be some signs about the Wood Island that was referenced in the scroll hint."

They came upon the water's edge and Alton thought he was going to pass out. It was intoxicating: the rolling mountains surrounding the massive lake, the gentle ripples on the crystal-clear water, the refreshing air tossing his hair to and fro.

"I don't see any signs," said Angus. "What do we do now?"

"Just keep looking, Angus," said Alton. "There has to be something about Wood Island."

They walked all around the shoreline, over near the tennis courts, and along the trail that weaved through the woods near the water's edge. But they found nothing.

"Hey, Alton," shouted Walter. "Look at this beautiful gazebo! Come on out!"

Alton looked across the water and saw Walter standing on a lovely gazebo, waving to him. Alton found the walkway that led to the gazebo, and ventured out. He loved the walkway. It was rather narrow, cutting a swath across the water. The wooden handrails were smooth to the touch, wonderfully designed. He could hear the gentle splashing of the ripples upon the walkway's base. As he neared the gazebo, he noticed the huge stone fireplace with a chimney that reached high into the sky. He stepped onto the gazebo and saw the massive hearth of the fireplace, and the intricate stonework. He saw Walter sitting in one of the Adirondack chairs on the deck. He strolled over and plopped into the chair beside him. They sat for a few minutes, silent, taking it all in.

"Alton, this is unbelievable."

"Yes, Walter … magical."

After a few more minutes, Alton forced himself out of his trance and thought about the hint again. He looked around the gazebo for any signs or plaques about islands. He could see some islands out on the lake, and wondered which one might be Wood Island.

"Well, Walter, we haven't seen any signs for a Wood Island, but it looks like we have a few to choose from out there. Why don't we head to the office here and see if one of the folks knows where this island is."

"Good idea, Alton. But could we sit just a tad longer?"

"Of course, Walter. I think that is a splendid idea."

They sat silent for a few more minutes. Alton felt more at peace than he had felt in a long time. All the pressures of the quest and worry about Sivvius drifted from his mind. He dwelled only on the gorgeous scene around him and the intoxicating feel and smell of the fresh, cool mountain air.

He jolted when he heard a ruckus back on land, near the entry point of the gazebo walkway. Alton heard Angus ranting.

"Get outta here, you devil dog, before I make you regret you were ever born. I'll—"

Alton heard a crack, like wood upon wood. Then silence. He spun around to see what was happening when he heard heavy footsteps on the walkway. Someone was approaching fast.

"What's going on, Alton?" asked Walter.

"I don't know, but I don't hear Angus yelling any more. Maybe he's coming out here."

"It's NOT him, foolish one," said Sivvius, his cackling laugh assaulting the peaceful aura around them. "He's taking a nap right now. Might have a bit of a headache when he wakes up. So, where's the Wood Island?"

"What are you talking about, Sivvius?" asked Alton, as he felt chills of fear racing through his body. He had been so at peace, he had let his guard down. He couldn't believe he had let Sivvius catch them like this. No prayer preparation, and Council members scattered all around the area, divided. They were completely vulnerable. Two sheep, separated from the herd, face to face with the most evil man on the face of the earth.

"You know exactly what I'm talking about, Alton. I know of your Wood Island hint. So which island is it? I've been looking all over this place for a clue. Even spoke with the people in the office. They don't know anything. They've never heard of it. So ... tell me which one it is. I know you know."

"We really don't know," said Alton, not sure what to do. He started praying silently, asking for God's help and protection.

"Alton. Let me give you something. Just a little reminder."

Sivvius raised his hands high into the air and stood there for a moment. He mumbled something, then rushed his hands downward, pointing them at Alton and Walter.

Alton fell to his knees as Sivvius sent the pain wave.

"Come on, Alton. Just tell me. Which island is it?"

"I ... told you ... Sivvius ... I ... don't ... know."

"Have it your way. I'm not going to stand here all day and bring you pain. There's just no time. You force my hand."

Alton watched as Sivvius's face tightened and his eyes squinted, strained. Sivvius squeezed his hands into fists, the knuckles turning white.

\* \* \*

Troubling thoughts raced through Sivvius's mind. Thoughts he hated. He would never admit it to Alton, but he did have doubts. Fear of eternal hell nibbled, even gnawed, at his mind like a mad dog that had clamped its jaws onto his brain ... chewing ... chewing. He feared the eternal consequences of what he was doing to the Council members. So much pain he had already brought upon them, and now, he was about to use a power again that was so destructive, so lethal, it was hard to imagine God would allow him to keep using it.

He did the best he could to force the fear and feelings of insanity from his mind, and strained to take all his thoughts captive to the obedience of evil. He was so close to victory. So close to world domination. He couldn't stop now. The end draweth nigh, he thought. My Captains are reporting mind-boggling conversion rates. Surely I will rule this earth. And my friends will protect me. "Help me, my friends. Help me to stop the Council members from finding the next scroll."

He focused all his energy on the knowledge-destruction power. He reached out to his friends. He felt power pulsing through his body, filling his hands. It was so strong he couldn't contain it. He felt energy seeping out between his fingers. He threw his hands outwards, splaying his fingers open, as if he were flicking water on Alton and Walter.

\* \* \*

Alton felt a wave of air, pushing through his head. It was not painful, but he recognized the feeling. He knew it was the knowledge-destruction power. He felt the fingers inside his head. It was happening so fast, and they were not prepared. He glanced at Walter, hoping the two of them could attempt a quick dance of defense, but Walter was sprawled on the ground, still in pain from the pain wave. Alton scrunched his eyes shut and silently cried out to God from deep within his mind. Oh God, protect us, show us what to do. He felt fingers picking at his brain. Oh God, don't let Sivvius destroy more knowledge. Show me, God … what should we do?

"I can tell you're praying, Alton. Don't waste your time. The longer you wait, the more knowledge you will lose. Just tell me which island it is and I'll let you go from my grip of destruction."

Alton kept reaching out to God in his mind. Something came to him.

"I tell you, Sivvius, I don't know—" As Alton denied knowing, he let his eyes subtly glance at the island closest to the Gazebo. He was certain to be extremely subtle, only glancing for a moment. "I just don't know, Sivvius."

"HA! You fool, Alton. You just told me. Now, time for you to take a nap."

Sivvius sent another pain wave, and Alton's thoughts swam in a pool of agony as he lost his balance. Pain stabbed at his knees when they hit the deck. As he rolled on his side, so he could massage his aching knees, he saw Sivvius storm off onto the walkway. Relieved that he was gone but not sure what to do next, he kept rubbing his knees while he rested his head upon the deck. Even though it had brought such pain to his knees, he couldn't help but appreciate the beautiful wood that formed the deck. Such a rich color, such a wonderful texture. He suddenly understood.

"Alton, I ... I can hardly move," said Walter. My head feels fried and my body is a wreck. I can't take many more of Sivvius's attacks. Why did he leave? What happened?"

"God answered my prayer. He showed me how to steer Sivvius off track. We should see him heading out to the island soon. But even more important, Walter," whispered Alton only after he confirmed Sivvius was out of hearing range, "is that I understand the hint. I know exactly what it meant. But for now, just lie there. Keep looking helpless. I'll do the same. Just look miserable. Let's just wait."

Alton watched Sivvius as he tried to find a boat. He saw him struggle with a couple craft that were securely locked to the dock, but eventually he found a canoe that was only roped to a pole. He watched him push off from the dock and paddle like a maniac toward the island. Sivvius glanced back once, let out a cackle, and forged full-speed-ahead. He was so fixated on the goal ahead of him that he didn't look back again.

"Okay, Walter. We must move quickly. First, let me get Angus and the others. I need to make sure everyone is okay."

As Alton ran toward the walkway, he saw Angus already coming toward him, rubbing his head. He also noticed the Letter brothers nearing the far end of the walkway, with Michael and Patrick close behind.

"Angus, quickly. Come quickly!" Alton was going to yell to the others as well, but didn't want to take a chance of alerting Sivvius. He waved his hand intensely, motioning for them to gather at the gazebo. As soon as they all arrived, he told them about Sivvius taking the bait and heading out to the island. A huge smile filled his face.

"I understand the hint. The wood island? This is it! We are standing on it. This wooden gazebo is the wood island. I know it. I sense it. There must be a clue here somewhere ... something. Spread out and check the area. But watch out for Sivvius. If you see him looking back, just sit still as if you are gazing at him with despair. He will thrive on that."

They scurried around, looking for some type of clue. Angus was checking the floorboards, apparently looking for writing or etching on the wood. The Letter brothers were looking at the wood handrails and along the outer edge of the platform. Patrick was looking inside the fireplace and around the hearth. Michael was checking the stones that made up the body of the fireplace. Walter started helping Angus check the floorboards. Alton watched Sivvius paddling feverishly toward his goal, still not glancing back. There was no talk. Everyone was fully absorbed in trying to find a clue. Nearly ten minutes passed, and Alton could see that Sivvius was getting close to the island.

"Alton!"

"What is it, Michael?"

"I think I've found something on one of these stones on the side here. Look … it's etched in … it says: To the Peak."

They gathered around Michael.

"To the Peak?" asked Angus. "That could mean anything, laddie! That could be any peak. Anyone could've written that."

"But look at the arrow. It's pointing up."

"Well, of course you nut-wedge. All peaks are up!"

"But look up the side here. Doesn't it look like there is some etching on one of the higher stones?"

Angus squinted his eyes as he looked up.

"Oh maybe a bit, laddie. Probably just some drunken kids doin' some mountain-style graffiti."

"Wait a minute, Angus," said Alton as he looked upward as well. "That etching is probably twice as high as you are tall, and you're fairly tall. It would have taken some ingenuity to get up there. I'm not saying it couldn't have been done by some graffiti-loving kids, but it seems a little too involved to me. It would have been nearly impossible for them to do it even if one climbed on another's shoulders. And would they have brought a ladder out here? Doesn't seem likely to me. Let's check this out."

"All right, Alton," said Angus. "Move on over, Michael. Let me brace myself here. Okay, c'mon Walter, climb on my back. Might as well be you since you're so portly—if you fall, you'll bounce."

Alton saw the scowl on Walter's face as he squeezed the sides of his stomach. Angus knew just how to mess with Walter's obsession over his imagined fatness. Walter reached to his right upper arm and massaged the flesh.

"Aw, come on, you pork shank! Quit playin' with your lard and jump on."

Walter let out a long sigh as he checked his other arm. He shook his head, apparently trying to reset his thoughts. He jumped hard onto Angus's back, almost knocking him over.

"Easy, laddie! Are you tryin' to crush me?"

Angus steadied himself and extended up as the others supported him. "Oh God," said Walter. "I don't believe it."

"What, Walter? What do you see?" asked Alton.

"The etching. It's the same code that was in the first scroll. I don't believe it. Let me see ... it says ... hmmm ... it says ... what you must ... what you must do ... what you must do is ... is ... go ... go ... to ... the peak. Yes, that's it! It says that what you must do is go to the peak."

"Go to the peak?" grunted Angus. "We already saw somethin' about the peak. How does that help?"

"Wait ... there is more. Here is a long string of symbols to the right. Let's see ... it says to think of a car. Yes, think of a car. And it also says to ... to ... think of a truck. And let's see ... think of ... think of ... a bicycle. Okay, that is it. It says to think of a car, a truck, and a bicycle."

"That's it?" asked Alton.

"I think that's it," said Walter. "Give me just a couple more minutes to be certain."

A minute passed with no commentary.

"Aww, c'mon laddie! Hurry up! Your weight is more than even I can bear."

"Okay," said Walter. "Almost done checking. Okay ... there is no more for us. Just the hint about the car, truck, and bicycle."

"What the heck kind of hint was that?" barked Angus. "How are we supposed to do anything with that ridiculous hint?"

"Wait. Be patient, Angus," said Alton. "We must ponder. Let us leave here. We need to get as far away from Sivvius as possible. He's on the island now, and he will be back with a vengeance when he finds nothing. Let's jog to the minivan to stimulate our thoughts."

As they jogged, Alton glanced back, taking the incredible beauty in one last time. He hoped with all that was in him he would be able to come back to this place one day soon—and under less stressful circumstances. They reached the van and piled in.

"Okay," said Alton as he cranked up the van and sped off toward the exit. "Think! What is the significance of a car, a truck, and a bicycle?"

"They are all forms of transportation," said Walter.

"And they are also items that have a steering mechanism," added Michael.

"What about the fact that they all have brakes?" chimed in Patrick.

"Good thoughts one and all. But what is the significance? Transportation, steering, brakes. What could these have to do with a peak?"

"How about thinking of a place where there is a lot of transportation? Maybe the peak is near a city?"

"Good, Letter A. A good thought. Is that it? Could it be that this peak is near a big city?"

"Could be. But there are so many cities with mountains not too far away. It would be tough to narrow it down," said Letter B.

"True, Letter B. Do you have another thought?"

"I'm just trying to think of what else these items have in common. What are we missing? I do not see how brakes would help us. Or steering mechanisms. There has to be more. What else do they have in common?"

"Ah! My great Letter brother B! You have inspired me again as your dear friend and brother A. What about tires? They all have tires."

"Or what about wheels, they all have wheels too, my A brother."

"Good thinking A & B!" said Alton. "Tires and wheels. But what does this do for us? How do tires and wheels have anything to do with a peak?"

"What about word association?" asked Michael. "I often think of many types of supporting foods when I'm preparing a meal. I think of a main course, say boiled veal shanks. Then I brainstorm to determine other foods that might go well with the main course that have part of the main-course word in their structure."

"Yes, Michael! Excellent thinking," said Patrick. "For example, boiled is within the description of a main course. We would then ask, what else would be good boiled."

"Exactly, Patrick. Like boiled okra, boiled peas, boiled corn, boiled beans, etc. It's the word association that makes my meal creations fun. So why not try that here?"

"I agree," said Patrick. "We should think of peaks or mountains that contain the words we've identified as similar between cars, trucks, and bikes."

"Yes, Patrick. Word association. It works!" said Michael.

"I think you may be on to something," said Alton. "Okay, then, we have brakes, we have transportation, we have tires, and we have wheels. Does anyone know of any mountains that contain these words? Think of where you have hiked in the past. Think of Colorado. Think of Seattle. Think. Think. Think."

"Or think of New Mexico! New Mexico is the place! I think I know the mountain. I really think I know the mountain!" Michael was bouncing in his seat. "I was researching elevation changes one day, as I was preparing to do a study on the effect elevation change has on hair density. I was studying the highest peaks in each state, and remember now the name of the highest peak in New Mexico. What do you think it is?"

"I have no idea."

"Well I do, Alton. It's Wheeler Peak, in the Taos area. Wheeler Peak contains the common word of wheel. This must be where we are to go!"

"But how can we be sure? There could be many other mountains that might have a word common between a car, truck, and bike," said Angus. "How can we know Wheeler Peak is the right place? New Mexico is a long way from here. And Sivvius is upon us. We can't afford to waste time."

"We need to do the line dance," said Alton. "Let's pull off the road here—it looks like a parking area—maybe there's a trailhead here. We must do this quickly. Sivvius won't stay on the island for long.

"Just to refresh your minds," said Alton, "we all need to line up next to each other with a few feet between each of us and start our synchronized dance. I'll be on the right end and Angus will be on the left since we're the most familiar with the dance. We will lead as we do the dance—just follow our lead as the line moves left or right. Angus's study of Texas culture comes in handy here, so watch him especially closely. Lord, bless the line."

Angus kicked off the dance, moving to the left as he clapped his hands and flexed his triceps. Alton led them back to the right, did another clap, and kicked his left foot forward. Then Angus led them forward, adding in a series of aggressive claps and shouts, along with some bicep flexing. The others followed Angus and Alton as best they could but it was one of the most unique line dances ever attempted. Alton saw the look of pride on Angus's face, certain that Angus felt it was the best Texas-style line dance ever done.

After a few minutes of stepping, sliding, kicking, flexing, and twirling, Alton motioned for them to stop. He paused for a few moments, catching his breath. He felt a deep peace, and out from his mouth emerged a word, launching forth as if it had a mind of its own: "Wheeler." The others looked toward Alton and one by one uttered the word Wheeler.

"My friends, we have the confirmation we've sought. The line dance has done its job. There was so much intense confirmation that Wheeler Peak is where we must go that my mind flushed of all thoughts except for that one. Let us head off to New Mexico, but first let us bow in prayer.

"Lord Jesus, bless us as we travel. Keep us safe. Protect us from future attacks from Sivvius. Protect our minds from his destructive powers. Lord, we praise You and thank You for Your love and Your protection."

Alton was silent for a few moments as he pondered what he knew was coming. It would not be long before the final battle against Sivvius would occur. He wondered what it would be like. He knew the demons would not physically attack him or his colleagues; he knew that for whatever reason, boundaries had been set in place. They could only go so far. But he knew they worked powerfully through Sivvius. He had allowed them to. He deeply feared what they would do through Sivvius in the final battle.

He also wondered if Sivvius's evil organization would be directly involved. He hoped not, but he knew they needed to be prepared for the worst. He knew they couldn't physically stop Sivvius, and he was quite sure they would not be able to physically stop the Captains either, if they were present. He also knew there was no way they could directly fight the demons. It would take prayer. It would take much prayer. It would take massive intervention from God. They needed to be ready for the day that was coming. They would need to be unified in prayer and in devotion to God. God would be their only hope on that day.

\*   \*   \*

As they drove toward the airport, Walter thought about what else he had seen on the rocks. He had not lied to the others when they asked if there was more, he simply told them there was no more for *us*. And that was true—there was no more for the group, at least in Walter's mind. He was the only one who could interpret the markings, so surely some things must be meant just for him—at least for now.

The brief clue he interpreted as: camping store—huge white ash—trunk—canister—tt key, intrigued him: especially the tt key part. Was tt key to mean time-travel key? Would there be some kind of key in the trunk of the tree? He wanted to see it before anyone else did, just to be able to think about how it might help him find Ingrid.

# Chapter 17
## Wednesday, 5:30 p.m.

Walter was relieved that their flight into Albuquerque was uneventful and that he was able to get in some nap time. The line dance had worn him out. Michael had made absolutely certain Angus was not in the dreaded center seat again, and had even managed to get him into first class. With Angus happy, commotion on the plane was kept to a minimum. Their ride in the rental van toward Taos had also been peaceful, allowing Walter plenty of time to think about the hints at Rocky Point. He noticed a sign for Taos, and sat up tall in his seat, looking for a camping store.

"Well, we've made it to Taos," said Alton. "Let us find Wheeler Peak and begin our ascent!"

When they came upon a camping store, Walter convinced them they needed to get some supplies and directions as well. A few minutes after entering the store and browsing around, Walter snuck out and looked around the area for a huge white ash tree. He didn't see one in front of the store, or anywhere nearby, so he walked around to the back. He saw it right away. A huge white ash with a massive trunk.

Heart pounding, Walter ran to the tree and inspected its trunk. He saw no gaps or openings in the front, so he walked around it, rubbing his hand on the surface. His fingers caught on something in the back. He felt a slight gap in the bark. He found a small flat rock and wedged it into the gap. As he pried outward, a chunk of bark pulled away from the trunk. He was able to get his fingers on the exposed lip, and pull the chunk out of the tree. There was plenty of room for him to reach his hand in, and as he did so, he felt a cold metal cylinder. When he pulled it out, he noticed a lid that looked as if it was screwed on. He grasped the lid and to his delight, it turned easily. He kept turning until he felt it reach the end of the threads.

He paused for a moment. He could hardly breathe. "What is in here?" he whispered to himself. "What kind of key am I going to find? A document? What?"

He pulled the lid off and looked inside. He didn't see a document. There was some type of can inside. He turned the cylinder upside down and let the can slide into his hand. It looked like a simple metal spray can—like a can of hair spray, but smaller, and with no label. He looked back into the cylinder and saw another can. He turned the cylinder over again, and two more cans came out. He shook the cylinder but there was nothing left inside. Three cans. Three identical-looking spray cans.

"What's this all about?" he mumbled. "What am I supposed to do with three cans?"

He took one in his right hand, and sprayed a quick spray in the air. He sniffed and he thought he recognized the smell. It kind of smelled like bug spray. He grabbed another can and gave it a quick spray. Same thing.

"I don't understand … I just don't understand. What do these sprays have to do with time travel? How can they have anything to do with time equaling mass?"

He picked up the first can and sprayed it again, this time onto his arm. He smelled his arm, and it definitely reminded him of bug spray. He sprayed the second spray onto his arm, took a good whiff, and it had a very similar smell. He started feeling light-headed. He laughed.

"I need to be careful not to get myself high on this stuff."

He took a deep breath of fresh air to clear his head, but felt even more light-headed. He took a few more breaths and his head began to clear.

"Time equals mass. What is time equals mass really all about?"

He grabbed the third spray and sprayed just a bit on his arm. As he moved his nose toward his arm again, planning to take just a tiny whiff to see if it smelled like the others, something at the back of the store startled him. "A rabbit ... it's just a rabbit."

He looked down at his arm, and suddenly he was right next to the rabbit.

"What? How did you get over here so fast, little buddy?"

As the rabbit hopped away, and Walter lifted his head, his body jolted in shock. He was right next to the building. He glanced back and saw the huge tree where he had been, but he was nearly twenty feet away from it. The rabbit had not come to him; he had gone to it!

He dropped the spray can and stood erect. He kept looking back and forth between the back of the store and the tree. He had clearly changed location ... instantly.

"My God! I can't believe this!"

He grabbed the three small cans and put them in his pockets. Then he grabbed the cylinder, ran back to the tree, and carefully put the cylinder back in, replacing the bark cover. His mind was racing. The sprays had allowed him to change physical location. He could not believe it. He walked around to the front of the store in a daze. He entered and browsed a bit, still processing what had happened. The others were roaming around, gathering supplies. He was looking at some dehydrated meal packets when he noticed one of the employees standing near a map section about twenty feet away. There was no one around him, and he was standing with his back mostly toward Walter.

"I've got to try this again," he whispered to himself.

He pulled out the cans and did quick sprays of each of them on his arm, staring at the maps as he did so. He felt lightheaded, but nothing happened at first. As soon as he started thinking about the time equals mass concept, he was suddenly bumping into the map rack, knocking a couple maps to the floor. The employee snapped his head toward Walter.

"Where did you come from?"

"Oh, sorry to startle you. I was just looking at these maps here," said Walter as he quickly slid the cans into his pockets.

"Can I help you with something?"

"I was wondering if you could tell me where Wheeler Peak is," said Walter as he regained his composure.

"Certainly," said the boy, as he regained *his* composure. "You need to head on up to the Ski Valley, just a few miles from here. Just take Highway 150, also known as the Taos Ski Valley Road. You'll see signs all over. It will take you right to the Valley. Once you get there, you can ask someone for directions to Wheeler."

"Oh that's great to know. Is it a nice hike up Wheeler?"

"Nice Hike? You are not seriously thinking of climbing the beast, are you? It's beautiful, but it sure is tall, and the air is really thin up there. Better be careful. Don't push too hard … take it nice and slow."

"Sure, sure. Thanks for the tip."

"Not a problem."

Walter found the others, they paid for the supplies they needed, and headed up to the Ski Valley, with Patrick at the wheel this time. Walter sat in the back row, resting, when he noticed Alton staring at him. He looked perplexed.

"Walter, what happened back there?"

"What do you mean, Alton?"

"You know, my friend. At least, I think you know. If you don't, I may be losing my mind."

Walter noticed the others looking at him.

"What are you talking about, Alton?"

"Walter, I have never known you to hide things from me before, but something happened. I know it. I know I was not seeing things. I saw you move. I saw you change locations in the store ... instantly. You were there by the food. I was just coming over to talk with you, and you vanished. Then you were by the maps. You can't deny it! You instantly changed locations and nearly knocked over the whole map display when you did. What happened? How did you do that? Is there something from the scroll you gleaned that enabled you to do that? Something you read on the rocks?"

"Alton, I ... I am sorry. You know my deep respect for you. You know our friendship. I don't like to hide things from you. But I found something on the rocks at the wood island. Something I was not sure about. Something I needed to check out first."

"What? What was it? Tell me. It's vital we all know. What you have done is ... well ... I still can't believe it."

"It is complicated, Alton."

"We have plenty of time—please, my friend, tell me."

All the way to the Ski Valley, Alton quizzed Walter about how he had managed to change locations instantly. Walter kept telling him the key was truly believing and focusing on the fact that time equals mass. Then focusing on a different location.

Alton kept trying to change his location within the van, but nothing happened. He would squeeze his eyes tight in concentration, then stare a hole into the seat next to him. He watched the others trying as well. Walter felt bad as he watched them struggling.

171

"You'd better show us how you did it, laddie," said Angus. "If you don't, I'll personally send you to another location."

"I just can't now, Angus. I really need to rest."

"Awww, you poor little laddie."

"It's all right, Angus," said Alton. "Let him rest. He will tell us more soon enough."

Walter felt bad that he couldn't tell the others yet, especially Alton. He knew Alton was dying to know how he had changed location. But he was so afraid if he told him, any hope he would have of trying to use this new ability to find Ingrid would be dashed. At the least, my plan to find Ingrid would be slowed, he thought. I'll try to hold out longer. I just hope Alton will be okay with that.

\* \* \*

There was a storm raging in Alton's mind, not only as he thought about what Walter had done, but also as he dealt with the fear welling up in him about Sivvius. He was deeply afraid of the power Sivvius was attaining. He felt lingering effects from the second knowledge-destruction wave Sivvius had sent. It was short, but it still had impact. Alton knew he had been robbed of even more knowledge. He still couldn't recall the details about clotrons due to the first attack, and now he couldn't recall the results of one of his earlier studies of magnetic-field theory. He was afraid to think too deeply about other studies, afraid that more knowledge had been lost.

He felt awful as he heard the others discussing the formulas they had forgotten, the proofs they couldn't recall, and inventions that had once been simple to understand that were now a deep mystery. Even the cross-talking of the Letter brothers seemed negatively impacted—not quite as sharp and decisive. And no matter what they tried, none of them could seem to restore what they had lost from either the first or the second attack.

He knew he needed to finalize a dance that would restore lost knowledge. I must finalize this when we get to Taos Ski Valley, he thought. I must finalize it, and we must try it before we start our ascent up Wheeler—before Sivvius attacks again. But right now, I must know how Walter did what he did. We need this knowledge to help us against Sivvius. Why do I sense that Walter is hiding something from me? Why is he hiding something from me again?

*   *   *

Walter jumped when Alton yelled at him.

"Walter, you MUST tell me exactly what happened during the visit to the store. How could you do what you did so easily? Something must have triggered it! How could just thinking of time equals mass cause you to be able to change locations? It makes no sense. I've tried everything, yet nothing works. Tell me all you know! If you are hiding something, I can't imagine why, unless it's something I've done to offend you. Please my friend, tell me how you did what you did!"

After hearing Alton's latest plea, and seeing the look of despair on his face, Walter could hold out no longer. He felt deep guilt for holding back so long. "Okay, Alton, I will tell you. There is something I have discovered."

"What? What? Tell me. Please tell me now!"

"When we were at the wood island, and I was deciphering the etching on the rocks, there was more there than I mentioned to all of us. It was something that intrigued me—a reference to a camping store, a huge white ash, a trunk, a canister, and a tt key."

"A tt key?" asked Alton.

"Yes, a key. But not a key in the literal sense. I mean not like a key to a chest or to a house, or anything like that. It turned out to be something I would never have imagined."

"What, Walter? What was it?"

Walter relayed the whole story, how he found the cans, how he used them, everything. It was so hard to let go of his secret, Ingrid-finding knowledge.

Alton sat quiet, mesmerized. "So these sprays are the key, then?"

"Yes, Alton. I *think* the sprays are the key. The first time I used them, I changed location purely by accident, but the second time, I consciously made the jump. I sprayed them on my arm, looked where I wanted to go, thought of time equaling mass, and then I was there. It was that simple. I'm quite certain now that tt key means time-travel key—that the sprays are the key to time travel. Even though I only changed location, and did not appear to travel in time, with practice perhaps we can find a way to use the sprays to travel in time!"

"Fascinating. Simply fascinating. But why did you hide this from me, Walter?"

"It was so hard for me not to tell you, Alton. But … oh … its … well … it's Ingrid. I … I could not help but think about maybe being able to use what I discovered to find Ingrid."

"Awww, you got to be kidding me, laddie!" laughed Angus. "Find Ingrid? We're tryin' to save the world and you're thinkin' about Ingrid?"

Walter remained silent.

"Please, Angus, leave him alone. You know of his love for Ingrid."

"Aye. But still? After all these years? Can't you let go, man?"

"You know I can't, Angus."

"Walter, thank you for telling me how you did what you did," said Alton. "You did the right thing. We'll be sure to help you find Ingrid when the time is right. But right now we must focus on our mission. We must focus on stopping Sivvius."

Alton was silent. Walter watched him staring off into space. He could tell Alton was pondering deeply. He stayed this way for quite a while. The others were all talking feverishly about what Walter had said. They were analyzing and debating, every few moments asking Walter a question. But Alton just sat there, staring.

Finally, he spoke. "I'm completely excited by what you have told me, and am overflowing with hope right now. Yet as the leader of our Council, I sense we must be extremely cautious. What you have discovered has the potential to cause as much harm as it does good. I do not even remotely understand the logic and the physics behind what we've discovered yet, but I do know the incredible potential of what we have. We must follow the hint we've found and go to the peak. There must be more information there. I'm so tempted to cover myself with the sprays of three right now, but my experience and my wisdom tell me to wait. Do you have the sprays with you?"

"Yes."

"Please give them to me. I'll keep them with me and ensure they are not used again until we know the time is right. We must get to the peak first. Do not question me in this. You must trust me. If ever you needed to honor my leadership, now is the time."

In his mind, Walter struggled. He didn't want to wait. He knew the sprays were the key to finding Ingrid and winning her love. The thought of letting go of them was tearing him apart. I just don't know if I can do it, he thought. But I must. I must honor my friend. Ingrid is everything to me, but Alton is wise. He is right about the risks. I must wait. I must trust Alton. He reached into his pockets and pulled out the sprays. He stretched out his trembling hands to Alton, looking deep into his eyes. He saw the wisdom, and knew he could trust him: he placed the sprays in Alton's hands.

"Thank you, my friend. As it was in the beginning ..."

"So shall it be in the middle," Walter sighed.

"Yes ... so shall it be in the middle."

Walter didn't know what this saying meant, but he knew Alton held it as sacred, and as a sign of unbreakable loyalty.

Walter watched Alton looking at the others, waiting. They bowed their heads low and said together, "So shall it be in the middle."

"Excellent! We must get to the peak of Wheeler," said Alton. "Patrick, please step on it!"

# Chapter 18
# Wednesday, 7:30 p.m.

They reached Taos Ski Valley just as the sun was setting. The sky was filled with beautiful wispy clouds in shades of orange and red. Alton rolled down his window, breathed in the fresh, crisp air, and closed his eyes as the scent of mountain pines filled the van. It was at least thirty degrees cooler here than it was in Albuquerque, and he loved it.

As they entered the main parking lot, Alton asked Patrick to park near a wood bridge that spanned a gently bubbling stream. The stream ran beside a beautiful, quaint hotel that reminded Alton of a Swiss chalet. As they got out of the van, he motioned for them to gather in a circle.

"We shall begin our ascent of Wheeler Peak early tomorrow morning. It's vital we get a good night's sleep, and this hotel looks perfect for that. Let's check in, have a nice dinner, and settle in for the night."

*   *   *

They arose early the next morning, nibbled on granola and fruit, got their packs ready, and gathered in the parking lot.

"Before we begin our ascent up Wheeler Peak, I feel it's vital that we practice our dance of defense. Sivvius's last knowledge-destruction attack was very brief but also very effective. I know he is working on this weapon, maturing it, and without a strong defense, we could be in danger of massive knowledge loss when he attacks again. Let's practice."

They worked on their leg positioning, their hand positions, their balance, their stomps. Alton knew the dance was symbolic of stomping upon the serpent's head, and he knew that somehow God honored it, responding to it to usher in His power against the knowledge-destruction wave. When he felt like they had practiced the dance of defense long enough, he motioned for them to sit together.

"Excellent session, my friends. We should be better prepared when we face Sivvius again. This dance doesn't restore our lost knowledge, however. It can only protect against further damage. We need another dance to help us restore the knowledge we've been robbed of. I've been praying about this, and I believe what we need is something called the dance of balance. I sense that this dance will restore our lost knowledge."

"This isn't goin' to be some type of wimpy dance, is it Alton?" asked Angus. "I hate the wimpy ones. The ballet dances we do sometimes are so embarrassin'. I kind of like the dance of defense. At least with that dance we get to stomp. It's a wee bit more like a good fight."

"Please bear with me, Angus. It might seem a little soft for you, but it must be done."

"If it must, then okay," said Angus. "Doesn't mean I'm goin' to like it. Especially if it's wimpy."

"Okay," said Alton. "Gather in a straight line, one behind another, all facing in the same direction."

"Any particular order?" asked Walter as they began forming a line.

"No," said Alton. "This should work for now."

"How close together should we be?" asked Michael.

"Keep a good distance apart," said Alton. "Maybe five feet or so between each of you."

They completed forming the line, leaving a few feet between each of them.

"Now, what we are going to do is bend at the waist, so our upper bodies are parallel to the ground. Then we shall extend our arms out to our sides as if we are flying. After that, we'll each take our right arms and extend them forward, so they are parallel to the ground, while extending our left legs backwards. Each of us shall grab the left foot of the person in front of him. The person at the front needs to extend both hands forward, joining them in front, like the mast of a ship. Once we are set in this position, we'll all need to lift the balls of our right feet up, so we are each balanced only on our right heels. I believe you will see maintaining your balance is an extreme challenge; only with the help of each other will we be able to succeed. This will require physical and mental strength not only as you strive to maintain balance but also as you endure the inevitable burning in your right calves and shins.

"As we stay in this balanced position, each of us needs to focus on restoration of the knowledge we've lost; this is the most challenging part. The focus required for this dance to be successful must be much more intense than ever before. You will need to sense your brain rebalancing, and restoring its electrical connections. The perfect balance of your bodies, combined with your focused brain-rebalancing thoughts, will eventually restore balance to your mind.

"You see, during my prayers as I developed this formulation, I sensed more and more in my spirit that the knowledge we've lost is not truly gone. It's simply shut off from access. When Sivvius attacked us, it felt like fingers were massaging our brains. What was happening, as best I can sense, is that certain memory and knowledge centers were being sealed shut by the evil wave Sivvius sent upon us. It was like little fingers of electricity short-circuited specific electrical pathways in our brains, causing thought-flow imbalance. I believe with our new dance, the pathways can be restored, and our brains will be properly balanced again."

"C'mon on, Alton," said Angus. "This is just too far out there for me. This is another one of those ridiculous dances. If one of my fitness students were to see me doin' this, my reputation would be shot."

"Relax, Angus. I believe you will feel better once you see the results of the dance. Please, my friend, give it a chance."

Angus rolled his eyes but held his tongue.

"Go ahead and start the formation," said Alton. "I'll watch you all to ensure you're doing this properly."

Alton couldn't help but chuckle as he watched the antics. Some were too close together, some too far apart. There were feet brushing up against noses, hands flailing, trying to find feet. Some of them fell off balance and toppled to the ground as they attempted to rise up onto their right heels.

"Alton, what are you tryin' to do? I hear you laughin' at us! Are you messin' with us?"

"Sorry, Angus. It's hard not to laugh. If you could see what I'm seeing, you would laugh, too. I do not laugh *at* you my friend, but *with* you. Here, let me join you now."

Alton joined in and had some embarrassing moments of his own. He instructed them, encouraging them to determine proper distances, maintain the balance in all positions, and keep each phase of the dance to the correct length of time. He taught them how to focus on the mind becoming rebalanced as they translated the physical balance into mental balance. He encouraged them to believe the electrical pathways were being restored, and lost knowledge was going to be regained. Most importantly, he encouraged them to pray and ask God to send His restoring power into their minds. Before too long, many of the kinks had been worked out and the flow of the dance was more refined and fluid. Alton prayed intensely as they danced, and he felt a deep peace flow through his mind.

"Okay, that is enough practice for today. I already sense some healing in my mind. Toward the end of our session, details about clotrons started entering my thoughts again—details that had been completely blocked before. Excellent work. And thank you Angus, for your patience. I know it was hard for you to engage in such a delicate dance."

He saw the scowl on Angus's face, but also noticed the quick, reluctant head bob—a sign of satisfaction that at least he felt like Alton acknowledged the dance was beneath his superior level of physical ability.

"Did the rest of you sense some restoration?"

"You know, Alton," said Michael, "there was a recipe for lemon-basted lamb shanks I had lost when Sivvius attacked us the second time. It was one of my favorite recipes. At the end of our dance today, it came to the front of my mind!"

"Anyone else?" asked Alton.

Alton listened with joy as the Letter brothers entered into a lively and dynamic cross-talking session, displaying that their sharp analytical ability was back with a vengeance, surely fueled by restored knowledge. The others chattered excitedly as they disclosed restored knowledge about previous inventions and scientific discoveries they had feared were gone forever. Even Angus, albeit reluctantly, finally admitted the dance seemed to do some good, bringing some muscle-blasting techniques back to the forefront of his mind.

"And now it is time for us to begin our ascent up Wheeler Peak! Is everyone ready?"

The Letter brothers walked over to Alton and stood looking at him. They stood there for about thirty seconds, saying nothing. At first, it seemed perhaps they were struggling with more knowledge destruction, but then Alton realized they were struggling with deciding who would speak first. He saw Letter A's lips form a word, about to speak, but then Letter A would look at Letter B and see him doing the same and he would stop. Then Letter B would look at A and notice that Letter A was about to speak, so Letter B would stop. Alton watched this go on for quite some time. Letter A looking to Letter B. Letter B looking to Letter A. Looking, pursing lips, about to speak, deciding not to speak, and then looking again.

On and on it went. Alton considered helping them, but it was such a humorous display and he was enjoying the show. As Alton continued watching, the show got even more entertaining. Letter A would purse his lips, open his eyes wide, lean his head forward and stare at Letter B. Letter B would be doing much the same, except he developed a method of lifting his right hand up near his cheek with the fingers pointing forward, and then moving his hand forward as if he was about to push the words out of his mouth. Yet neither could seem to be the first to speak. Finally, Angus could take no more.

"All right already laddies, one of you belt out somethin'! This is a waste of time! The peak cries out to us!"

The Letter brothers looked to Angus, the pursing and the hand gyrations continuing. But no words came forth. Alton knew he had to intervene.

"Okay Letters. Let me help you. Why don't you go first, Letter A?"

The Letter brothers looked at each other again. The lips were pursing, the hand gyrations were getting wilder. Then they also started a strange head-bobbing activity. The look on Letter A's face was one of turmoil. Alton could tell he was trying hard to get the words out.

"Okay, Letter A, let the words out. You can do it. Let them come," said Alton.

Letter A's lips twisted into one final, massive purse, then his mouth opened wide, and he yelled out, "I'm scared!"

"I'm scared!" said Letter B right after him.

"Our knowledge is coming back, but what Sivvius did—"

"What Sivvius did—"

"To our minds—"

"Was—"

"Is—"

"Very scary—"

"I understand your fear, my dear Letter brothers. And I share it. As I'm sure we all do. But know that God is restoring our knowledge. Know He has shown us the restoration dance. We must trust in Him to protect us, and we must use the tools He has revealed to us. And just keep pondering on the fact that God's perfect love drives out all fear. Let us all sit for a moment and pray and ask for more of God's protection."

After they prayed for each other, the Letter brothers looked much more peaceful, and so they began the trek up the mountain. After they had been hiking for a while, the grade got steeper, and soon they were gasping. Alton called for them to take a break by a group of trees. They sprawled on the ground below the trees and meditated according to Alton's direction.

When Alton sensed they were ready, he called out for them to resume the climb. As they did, Alton's thoughts drifted back to Sivvius. He was getting so strong, so powerful, and his evil army was growing beyond all expectation. Now here they were, the first scroll read, the sprays in their possession, and yet he felt their progress was too slow. He could pull out the sprays right now, he thought. Pull them out, throw caution to the wind, spray them all over himself, think of time equaling mass, and try to go back to the past so he could stop Sivvius in an earlier time.

But even if he could use the sprays to travel to the past, the risks would be far too great. There were so many implications. So many variables. So many things to consider. He could make things even worse. No, I must not use the sprays yet, he thought. We'll need to approach use of the sprays very carefully. I must speak with the others more about this. We must consider all the implications and do controlled experimentation.

# Chapter 19
# Thursday, 12:00 p.m.

They continued their trek for the next couple of hours. With the air thinning and the pace slowing to a crawl at the higher elevation, Alton decided they needed to take another break. As they sat down to rest, Alton walked off to a secluded bluff to think. He prayed, seeking the Lord's strength and wisdom.

"You are right to think of me, Alton."

A wave of fear rushed through Alton. He peered over the edge and saw Sivvius sitting on a rock outcropping. He waited for the pain, or the wave of knowledge destruction. When he felt nothing, he got ready to run to the others. They must jump into the dance of defense.

"It was very wrong for you to mislead me about the island, Alton. I should wail against you right now, but I have not come to bring you pain this time. I have come to answer your longings."

"You can't answer my longings, Sivvius."

"Of course I can, Alton. My power and knowledge have reached new levels even I can't comprehend. Come with me, my friend. Why do you allow yourself to continue in this ridiculous quest when I have all the answers for you right now? Why do you keep on with your brutal trek up this mountain? You will find nothing at the top. You are wasting your time. I can show you all you seek right now. Don't you know my power is now greater than God's power?"

Alton felt a strong sense of the friends from beyond.

"Sivvius, you are so deceived. Your power is nothing compared to God's power. Putting yourself above Him will just ensure that your eternity in Hell is all the more miserable."

"Do not be foolish, Alton! Come with me. We can do mighty things together."

"NO Sivvius! I will NOT come with you. Let go, Sivvius. Let go of your friends from beyond. It's not too late. Do not be deceived into thinking you have more power than God does! That is not possible! He could crush you in a moment if He wanted to. But He will not. I tell you yet again, He gives us all free will. And He is loving. He is waiting for you to come to Him. He holds the door open. He still waits for you to choose Him."

"NOOOOO!" screamed Sivvius, with the sound and power of a thousand voices. Alton felt the ground beneath him tremble, and he saw chunks of rock break off from the cliff below him and roll down the steep mountainside.

"Stop with this foolish talk, Alton. I can't stand your childish banter. Do not stand against me any more. Remember my power. Recall how it has grown exponentially recently. Do not force me to use it against you again. The next time I use it may bring the end of your friends. Come to me, and I will allow them to live."

"Sivvius, you know I will never join you … ever."

He heard the others running toward him, yelling out to him. As they gathered around him, he peered over the edge. Sivvius was gone.

"What happened?" yelled out Walter, panting. "We heard a yell and felt the ground tremble. It sounded like Sivvius."

"It's okay," said Alton, his voice shaky. "He is gone now."

Alton gathered his composure. "We must press on. Sivvius has left for now, but he will be back soon. We must find the next scroll, and we must find the way to use the sprays to their full extent. We must move quickly. There is very little time."

Alton gathered them together and asked Walter to pray for them. Then he led the way, heading back up the mountain. He could hear the others behind him chattering away. They were worried, and they wanted to know more. But he couldn't speak more about Sivvius. He was afraid of what would be coming next, and he didn't want the others to sense his deep fear. He prayed for God's help as they hiked.

*     *     *

Sivvius reached the rendezvous point and saw three of his Sector Captains waiting at attention a few yards away. He shook the feelings of frustration and insanity from his mind. He knew he couldn't let the Captains see the internal struggle on his face. Their crisp salutes greeted him as he drew near.

"Reports," said Sivvius.

"60,000 recruits this past week, General Sivvius."

"Excellent work, Captain Stavius. What about you, Captain Tellitris?"

"I just missed my goal of 50,000, General Sivvius—but I exceeded my upper-class training rate by twenty percent!"

"Good work. This is what we look for. You missed your mark, but you made extra effort to compensate. Be sure to make up for what you missed in quantity this past week."

"Yes, General."

"And you, Captain Gratus."

"It's been a rough week. I missed my quota by nearly 30,000 souls. But I will do better next week."

"Did you exceed your quota in other areas?"

"I'm afraid not. It has just been so difficult. The people can be so hard to reach sometimes."

Sivvius walked up close to Gratus and slapped him with all his might. As Gratus stumbled backward, Sivvius walked up to him again and slapped him even harder, knocking him to the ground.

"Do not disappoint me again. The end of our war draws nigh. There is no time for failure. Stavius! Tellitris!"

"Yes, General."

"Take a few minutes to motivate Gratus. And make sure he never forgets to call me General again."

"Yes, General."

Sivvius turned on his heel and stormed off.

\* \* \*

After another hour or so of hiking, as Alton was still struggling in his mind, he overheard Walter and Angus get into one of their crazy discussions. He felt better as he listened. Another chance for them to bring him joy, he thought. It was such a nice escape from the weight upon his shoulders.

"I wish I was a couch," said Walter.

"Why do you say that laddie?" panted Angus.

"Because all I'd have to do is sit there. I wouldn't have to be engaging in all kinds of motion. I wouldn't have to think about what to do next, or where to go. I could just be there … doing nothing. Maybe occasionally I'd have to allow whoever was sitting on me to extend me into the reclining position. If I were a foldout bed, I'd have to let them fold me out sometimes. But that's about it. I'd be so relaxed."

"That is yet again one of the most ridiculous things I've ever heard, laddie. Besides, being a couch is probably not all it's cracked up to be. Just think about the drawbacks."

"Like what?"

"What if your owner was a stinky man who hardly ever showered? Layin' all over you, stinkin' you up."

"That's an awful thought."

"Sure is, and it could happen."

Angus paused for a few moments, letting his heart rate slow, gaining strength for the fun. He motioned for Walter to stand by him.

"And what if your owner was a spiller? What if he spilled all kinds of things on you all the time and then never cleaned you up? Just imagine milk spillin' on one of your cushions, and then the owner givin' it a weak clean-up by just dabbin' it with a paper towel. All that milk that sunk deep into you, permeated through your couch cells, stuck in there forever, gettin' rancid ... stinkin'. And what if that owner was the stinky man? Now you'd have the stench from the man, the stench from the milk, and the stench of God only knows what else. How can you get excited about that? You would be wishin' at that point that you *could* move. And you'd be stuck there, stinkin'."

"You do have a point," sighed Walter. "Perhaps I should just try harder to make the best of my grueling life on this mountain, exhausted from lack of oxygen and food."

"That's better, laddie! Quit your whinin' and take it like a man."

"You're right, Angus. Let's press on."

Alton felt better, but the oxygen levels were so low the best he could do was to take three steps at a time before he would have to stop to catch his breath. He could see the others struggling as well. But they pressed on and eventually reached the summit.

"Here we are!" exclaimed Alton with a huge smile. Reaching the summit brought a new sense of anticipation into his mind. "We made it to the peak! Now we must find why we're here. Walter, our reader of the scroll, what do we do now?"

"That I don't know."

"You don't know, laddie?" asked Angus. "You mean to tell me the hint said nothin' of what we must do once we reached the peak?"

"You heard me decipher it. Did you hear any details of what we should do up here?"

"No, but you have a history now of neglectin' to tell us certain things, so how am I to know there's not more you've hidden from us?"

"I assure you, Angus, there is nothing more about the peak. You know as much as I when it comes to what we do now."

"If that's the case," said Alton, "then perhaps we should just walk around until we find something that looks unusual."

Alton looked all around the peak. Every so often, he would find a pile of rocks or some sign that others had been there, but he found nothing out of the ordinary. After nearly two hours of searching, and none of them finding anything, he started to feel discouraged again.

"Wait a minute," said Michael. "As both Travel Director and Apprentice Dietician, I have just experienced a combination thought that may lead us to that which we seek."

"Tell us!" said Alton.

"We made it to the top but have found nothing. But perhaps all we needed to do was *make it* to the top, and what we seek is on the way back down."

"That makes no sense, you pork shank!" shouted Angus. "Don't you think we would've seen it on the way up?"

"Not necessarily. Think about it. Often times in my travel directing, arrival at a destination is not what brings the greatest discovery or excitement. What happens is that during a trip, something else more interesting is discovered that has nothing to do with the planned itinerary."

"That's probably because you're always gettin' us lost so we end up in a better place than what you'd planned anyway," snickered Angus.

"Very funny, crazy man. But seriously, the perspective going down will be different from when we went up. We were all so exhausted and oxygen-deprived on the way up that all we could think of was our next step. We were not looking for anything on the way up. I say that we must head back down. I believe we'll find what we seek on the way."

"Oh c'mon laddie. You've no idea—"

"Hold on Angus," said Alton. "Michael may be on to something. We've found nothing up here after quite an extensive search. We can at least start down and see if we come across something, as Michael suggests."

"But if we don't, that means we've got to hike all the way back up again," grumbled Angus.

"That is a chance we must take. We must try something different. We shall follow Michael's suggestion and head down. Look carefully for anything unusual on the way."

\* \* \*

Michael led them slowly downward. Alton watched him snap his head back and forth, trying to spot something. Suddenly Angus ran off the trail, stopped, and stood there, gazing into the distance.

"Hey, laddie," he yelled to Michael. "Why's there a tree up here? I thought we were still well above tree line."

"Where do you see that, Angus?"

"About twenty yards from where I am. It looks like there's a tree partially obscured by a boulder over there."

Michael trudged over to where Angus was and gazed intently toward where he was pointing.

"See?"

"Ahhh … yes, I see what you're talking about. There should be no trees up this high. Let's go look."

Michael ran toward the tree, causing rocks and pebbles to start rolling down the mountain, all the while his feet slipping and sliding. Fortunately, he made it to the tree without incident, much to Alton's relief.

"Oh my," Alton barely heard him say.

"What Michael? What is it you see?" questioned Alton.

"The tree is not real. It's an artificial tree! And the trunk appears to be hollow. I can press the outside edges of the main trunk inward."

"Let me see," shouted Alton as he rushed over toward the tree. As soon as he got there, he touched the tree and thumped the trunk.

"It appears to be hollow. Let's see if there's something inside."

Alton felt all around the trunk to see if there were any holes or openings. One of his fingers found a small hole, and when he inserted his finger, he felt something like a metal tube.

"I feel a tube inside!" yelled Alton. "Help me get it out!"

Alton's mind was racing. Hope surged in him again. The epic battle was about to shift back to the side of good again. They were all there now, pawing at the tree, trying to pull it from the ground. But it wouldn't budge.

"There must be a way to get at the tube," said Alton.

"Wait, let me try," said Walter. "After all, I was the one destined to read the first scroll. Surely the second is meant for me to read as well."

\*   \*   \*

Just as Walter touched the tree, the front of the trunk opened and the tube shone forth in all its mysterious brilliance. He grabbed it, and as he gazed at it, he felt a tingling in his hands, and heard the humming as he had with the box for the first scroll. He was not afraid this time. Suddenly he heard a popping sound as one end of the tube sprung open. He reached in and felt a rush of joy and anticipation as his fingers contacted the parchment within.

"It's another scroll!" he yelled.

"Take it, Walter! Read it!"

Walter gently took out the scroll, and saw the same type of ribbon and seal upon it as they had seen on the first scroll. Remembering how the first seal had been released, he placed his thumb upon it and waited. He heard the sound again like a distant ocean wave crashing upon the shoreline as the seal released its hold. He removed the red ribbon and slowly rolled open the scroll. He recognized the writing as the same style that was on the other scroll they had found: the strange symbols, the code. He engaged in the deciphering process and after a few moments, his mouth gaped open, and his eyes misted. He could not believe what he saw.

# Chapter 20
## Thursday, 4:30 p.m.

"What is it Walter? Please tell us," said Alton.

Walter could not speak. Tears streamed down his cheeks as he pondered what he saw in the scroll. The scroll mentioned a special name, his name, a pet name his parents had given him when he was a boy: Walty the warrior. The name he had gone by for so many years yet chose to forget when his mother died in the car crash. Never again had he allowed himself to think of this name, and yet here it was. The past flooded his mind. Memories of his parents, their days together in the parks, the trips to the country, climbing trees together in the forest, exploring caves.

Memory after memory of excitement and discovery came back. They had birthed in him the intense desire to learn, to study, and to search. That desire never faded, and led him to this very moment. He was confused though—only his father and mother had known his secret name. Who else could possibly have known? They had sworn to each other never to speak his secret name to others. It was a sign of the love between them, between the three musketeers, as they called themselves. He recalled how after his mother had died, his father had fallen into a deep depression and spent most of the time in his study, constantly reading. He recalled how he would ask him into his study sometimes, and show him some fascinating books, many of them about other cultures and science, and even one about code deciphering. He was always amazed at his father's incredible intelligence.

Could it be that my father was involved in some way in the development of the scrolls? Could it even be that he was the author? To write something that could change the fabric of time? Could my father really have done that? Yet if not my father, then who? And why? And why to me? Yes, it had to be my father. If anyone could have done it, he could have. And there is no way anyone else could know my secret name. I can hardly believe it! My father must be the author of the scrolls!

Walter jumped when Alton touched him on the arm.

"Well, my friend, let us hear the words of the scroll."

"Sorry, Alton … I was lost in my thoughts. I have discovered something beyond my wildest imagination."

"What is it, Walter?"

"I … well … I believe … I believe my father is the author of the scroll!"

"Your father?"

"Yes, Alton. My father. The scroll mentions my secret name—a name only he and my mother knew. We swore to each other my secret name would never be revealed to anyone other than the three of us."

"What is this about secret names, laddie? Just read the scroll already, will you?"

"But Angus, can you grasp the significance of this?" said Patrick. "The author of the scrolls could be Walter's father? This is just … this is just—"

"Amazing," said Michael. "This is just amazing."

"Amazing," said A.

"Amazing," said B.

"Just amazing," said A.

"Just amazing," said B.

"More than amazing," said A.

"More," said B.

"Much more," said A.

"Yes, Letter A and B," said Alton. "You're right. Much more than amazing. Especially if we really think about this.

After all, even Einstein, who explained time as no one else ever had, couldn't literally alter time. And in all the years since the scrolls were written, not even one of the world's greatest scientists has even come close to conceiving anything like the incredibly powerful and elegant formula discussed in the first scroll.

"Walter, let us assume for now the author truly is your father. Your father must have met with Einstein in the hopes of getting Einstein's review and confirmation of your father's elegant formula. Einstein must have considered this formula to be of such profound significance, beyond even his own work, that he chose to collaborate with him, by handwriting an inherently unique book about the formula—not even specifying the formula—but explaining that it could be used for time travel. He must have considered your father to be an even greater genius, with perhaps the greatest scientific break-through of all time. He therefore wrote the book to honor and pay tribute to him, and through all the math, physics, and other sciences involved, found your father's proof so absolute that he had no need or reason to prove it himself in writing. His book is therefore a tribute to your father, a confirmation of your father's discoveries, and a summary of key facts from your father—facts that would be needed to enable discovery of the scrolls.

"And to think how your father conceived of a complicated quest that began with me finding Einstein's only copy, a handwritten book, and then, inspired by Einstein's words, I found you. And now, here we are, still working through the mind-boggling, admirable intricacy of the incredible plan of your father."

"Do you know what else is utterly amazing, Alton? Einstein died in 1955. The only way my father could have met

Einstein and collaborated with him was by going back in time!"

Alton tilted his head back and stared into the sky. After a few seconds of pondering, he snapped his gaze toward Walter. "You're right! There's no other way. Your father must have convinced Einstein of the reality of time travel into the past—and surely that blew Einstein's mind and radically altered some of his theories. It must have been close to Einstein's death when your father met him, or Einstein would have surely re-written some of his other texts to take these revolutionary discoveries into account. Einstein must have gone to his grave very humbled."

"So true, Alton. Something else just hit me. I wonder if part of why my father met with Einstein was because my father knew of my radical passion for all of Einstein's works. Surely my father knew if I was shown the obscure Einstein text, I would devour it and ultimately end up going on this epic quest!"

"That makes sense, Walter. It may be your father wanted to ensure you would carry on with the battle against evil after he died. Your father must have known of Sivvius's plans long before we did. This is all so incredible. My mind is on fire!"

"As is mine, Alton! I'm amazed beyond more words."

"Thank God, laddie," spouted Angus. "If you're finally out of your own words, let's hear what the scroll has to say!"

"But Angus, aren't you the least bit amazed at this revelation?" asked Walter.

"Yes, laddie. I admit it's amazing. Now, can we hear the words of the scroll?"

"Okay. I shall read now," said Walter as he tried to regain his composure. "Let's see—"

Walter opened the scroll slowly, his anticipation high, as he read his father's words out loud.

"You have found that which you have sought, Walty the warrior. Well done. More deep truths will be your gift. Now listen to what I have to say. You have made it this far because you were meant to be here. You and your friends have had to spend much time getting to this point because it was necessary for you to be ready for such knowledge and use of the formula. You and your friends have avoided the control of Sivvius because your passion drives you to success, and especially because you stand with God. Very good. Now we must move quickly in the teaching, since time is short.

"I gave you the insight into my time equals mass formula. Since then, if you discovered one of the mysteries of the three sprays, you are on your way to understanding the true power of the implementation of my formula. If you have not yet discovered the three sprays, you must go back to the camping store and complete this task. I am confident you have made the discovery, however, so I press on.

"I am also confident that you exercised caution in using the sprays to this point, especially once you realized the potential power of the time equals mass equation. I made it possible for you to have the chance to implement my formula only because I know you are wise, based on the years of searching and studying you have done. Now that you are here, and you have survived, it is time to go to the next level of understanding.

"Read this part carefully and apply all that I say with precision and seriousness of thought. You will remember the proofs I gave of my time equals mass equation. Simple on the surface, yet complex in the results. What you must now realize is that you hold in your hands the ability to alter time. If you dabbled with the sprays, you have seen how they can cause alteration in space-time. You will most likely have experienced location jumping at some level. This alone is not enough, however. Without the proper use of the sprays, there is risk you could cause a warping or distortion of the space-time continuum."

"Wait a minute, laddie! What is this about a warpin'?"

"I'm not sure, Angus. Perhaps the rest of the scroll will give us more insight."

"All I've got to say, you pork shank, is I hope you haven't already caused some warpin'."

Walter ignored Angus's comment and got back to the reading of the scroll.

"So, what is the proper usage? First of all, proper application of the time equals mass equation is vital. This part is not difficult, but it must be done. It is as simple as thinking firmly that time equals mass. Second, it is imperative you have a focused mental picture of the destination in mind. By destination, I mean not only physical location, but also time location. It is possible not only to change physical location, but also to change time location—forward or backward. As you think it, so shall it be: so think VERY carefully.

"It is also vital to understand that as you use the sprays, the sequence of usage, the duration of each spray, and the time delays between each spray all play a huge role in the end result. This is a bit more tricky since there will be seven of you. In my experiments and in my travels, it was only me. I spent much time working out the durations and sequencing, and even where on my body I sprayed the sprays. But this was done with only one person in mind. You will need to experiment with durations and sequencing. I can tell you a fairly safe start will be to use them on just one of you, in sequence A, then B, and then C—you can see the engraved markings on the bottoms of the cans—and be sure to make your spray durations short. Just a quick press on the nozzles will be adequate. Regarding delays between using A, B, and C, a second or two between each will be fine to start with.

"If you keep this part of the experiment controlled, you will be able to work more effectively on your mental-focus skills. A stray thought of location or time can get you into serious trouble. As you master the basics with one person, you can eventually build up to the point where you can use them on your full group of seven. Again, duration and sequence testing will be vital. Here is where you will need to experiment with range factors as well—how close must a person be to the source of the spray activity to be pulled through space with the sprayer. As you become more advanced, you will learn how the sprayer can stay in his current time location, yet send another to a different location. I have done this with mice, and am quite confident it can be done with humans as well."

"Now hold on a minute, laddie. He's quite confident? So he hasn't done that last part on a human? Blast! All I've got to say is I won't be the one this theory is tested on."

"Be patient, Angus. Please hear everything first. We will use all we learn from the scroll and do our experiments in a very controlled manner. Now let me get back to the reading."

Walter sighed, scanned the scroll to find his place again, and resumed reading.

"Let me also briefly explain the differences between travel forward in time and travel backward. This is unbelievably complicated, but I will sum it up at a very high level. Regarding travel into the future, the sprays allow you to travel into other people's futures. Your time reference is changed so as you spray to the future, your aging is essentially stopped, but those around you continue to age and to live out time. You are familiar with Einstein, of course, and his theory of relativity is the key. In essence, time passes more slowly for objects at high velocity *relative* to objects at rest. The sprays allow travel through space-time at such a velocity that time essentially stops for the traveler, while time on the earth continues to pass at its normal rate. Therefore, the sprayer is able to travel into the future of the rest of the world. The sprayer is still the sprayer—there will not be two of a person at different ages in the future. Fortunately, if need be, the sprayer can spray back to the original time as well, but this is a bit more risky and takes much precision of thought.

"Travel into the past is a bit more complicated, and carries far more risk. Travel into the past is *not* relative to the point of origin. In other words, travel into the past will bring one truly into the past—one's younger self will be there ... somewhere. As you can imagine, you should approach this with great care. Fortunately, when jumping back from the past to the point of origin, the sprays prevent the relativity issue associated with future-jumping. In other words, you could jump back thirty years, and when you jump forward thirty years to the original point of origin, you and your surroundings will be as they were when you left—except for the fact that you will recall what you experienced in the past.

"I must also warn you that there is significant risk in using the basic store-variety sprays without care. Although they work when combined properly, they are unstable. Amazing, isn't it? That bug spray is the key to time travel? Who would have thought? But the implications of misuse are mind-boggling. Fortunately, the chances of a layman ever using three bug sprays at once, with each being of the exact variety and chemical makeup that is required, are near zero percent, or rather, hopefully, *at* zero percent. The sprays you found in Taos had been secretly placed there by me. They are of the enhanced variety. You see now my trust in you. You had the power to mess up the entire universe with a few sprays of insect repellant!"

"Laddie! Blast, blast, blast! Mess up the entire universe? I sure hope you haven't done that!"

"I'm sure everything is fine, Angus. My usage was very minor. Now please! Let me finish reading the scroll."

"Yes, Angus," said Alton. "Please let Walter finish. We must hear all that is in the scroll and then work together to do the controlled experimentation."

Angus was about to say more, but Walter jumped right back into the reading.

"So what are the enhanced sprays? They are more than just insect repellant. They are modified insect repellants; basic insect repellants combined with chemicals I gathered from alternate times as I implemented my time equals mass formula. You see, although time alteration is possible with the right combination of basic bug sprays, and even through some other means I have discovered, the chemicals I gathered from various time locations enhance and simplify the application of my formula. In the past, before I developed the enhanced sprays, altering time through application of my formula was much more difficult and risky.

"You might wonder how I ever stumbled upon the idea of using bug sprays in the first place. Well, it was through painstaking and disciplined experimentation. I had tried many different chemicals and liquids and eventually determined there were some chemicals that caused a slight variation in space-time. As I studied this, I realized some of the chemicals were contained in every-day bug spray. That is when I moved into an in-depth study of bug sprays. I needed to confirm if simple bug sprays could in fact enable the time equals mass equation to be implemented. Eventually, I did confirm my hypothesis one day when I was working with a combination of three slightly modified sprays. I was experimenting with sending a test mouse, and after spraying the sprays on my arm and thinking of sending the mouse, it disappeared from its cage!

"I searched everywhere for the mouse. Had the usage of the sprays killed it? Or had it moved in time somehow, as I had hoped? I looked around the lab and found it in the humidity test chamber where it had been the previous day. I was certain it was the same mouse since it had the identical numeric marking upon its left hind leg as the mouse that had disappeared. Somehow, the sprays had caused the mouse to travel in time to the prior day, and I had traveled in time with it! I noticed the breakfast from the previous day sitting there, uneaten! Fortunately, I was able to do some quick analysis, focus very carefully, and spray forward to the original day and time. This enabled me to avoid contact with my one-day-younger self—I was not quite ready to handle this type of situation without full preparation.

"Over the next few months, I engaged in numerous experiments, and learned various ways to alter time through the equation and the sprays. Ultimately, I was successful in spraying myself through space and time in a very precise manner. I did find, however, that some negative consequences could occur ... strange things. I would sometimes notice that after time travel, my lab would be different in some ways when I returned to the original time from which I left. I would notice a counter shaped in a strange manner, a light fixture no longer there, a door gone. This is when I realized the combination of the sprays I discovered, although effective, was somewhat unstable.

"As I began to narrow down to what could be causing the instability, I realized I needed other chemicals to help with the stabilization. Yet I could find nothing on the earth in the present time that would help. That is when I decided to take a huge risk and do some long-range location jumping and time traveling to the future, to search for stabilizing chemicals. Over the period of many months of searching and testing, I found chemicals that enhanced the sprays to the point where I could use them in a completely safe way.

"Believe me, the sprays work and time truly does equal mass. However, do not use them for major jumps until the time is right. You will know when the time is right. If you use them when the time is wrong, you could mess things up for all of humankind and for all of mass. Until the time is right, practice in very controlled experiments, and prepare for the time when they will be needed for your critical destiny.

"Lastly, fear not that you will run out of spray. The way I have designed the spray chemicals, combined with the ultra-low spray volume nozzles, will allow for thousands of sprays from each can. Nevertheless, at some point, it would be wise for you to do a chemical analysis of each spray. You have adequate skills to do a complete composition analysis, and you will see that you can create the sprays on your own, using chemicals within your current time location. Even the stabilizing chemicals I found in the future can be recreated with combinations of various chemicals in your time.

"Now, go to a place with two between two and you will find what you need next. Be ever watchful. And as you go, always walk with God."

Walter stopped reading. He paused for a long time, deep in thought.

"Everything makes so much more sense now, Alton. Now I know why my father taught me so much about language, code deciphering, and science when I was a child. He must have known that someday I would need to decipher his writings. You know, my dad would often work in his lab for hours on end. I remember many times around the dinner table, he would speak of things he was working on. Some of the things were so unbelievable to me at the time, I thought maybe he was just joking. But now I know he was not joking or dreaming. Now, for the first time ever, we've been given the honor of seeing the incredible results of all his work!"

Walter rejoiced within himself. The author of the scrolls was his own father! He could not believe it. He knew they would find the rest of his writings and learn how to stop Sivvius. And most importantly, the writings would show him how to find Ingrid. Yet something bothered him.

"Alton, why do you think my father didn't just tell me earlier, when I was a boy? Why make me spend so much time struggling? Why let me have to battle Sivvius for so long? Why not protect me? Warn me? Why let me go on, unknowingly preparing to save the world? He knew of the future! Why not warn me!"

Alton closed his eyes and paused for a few moments. When he opened them, he looked deeply into Walter's eyes and spoke in a soft voice. "My dear, dear friend Walter. I am absolutely certain your father loved you, and had only the best in mind for you. I'm sure he realized if you knew in advance what was coming, you would make different choices, causing the future to change for the worse. Your father was an extremely intelligent scientist, and surely he knew what the future would be if he *had* told you. Surely the future he would have envisioned would have been terrible for you and for the world. I'm certain he hated to know you would struggle, but I'm also certain he knew the alternative would have been far worse for you. And remember his words on this scroll: we needed to spend time getting to this point because it was necessary for us to be ready for such knowledge and use of the formula."

Walter was silent for a few moments. He felt a deep peace from what Alton had said. He felt a joy building up within himself.

"Yes, Alton, yes! You are absolutely right! He did know best. Oh God! Can you believe it? The author of the scrolls is my father!"

"Yes, Walter. This is incredible. You truly have been given great honor."

Alton reached over, grasped Walter's shoulder and squeezed gently.

"Congratulations, my friend. You are the son of the greatest scientist of all time. If not for your father, Sivvius would already have won the world."

\* \* \*

They discussed the hint at the end of the second scroll as they continued their descent of the mountain. After just a few minutes, Alton's heart froze when he heard a light cackling and saw Sivvius emerge from behind a large boulder a few feet to the left of the trail. The cackling grew in intensity.

"Council members—quickly. Prepare for the dance of defense."

"Don't waste your time, Alton. Although I could unleash the knowledge destruction again, I know you and your ridiculous sidekicks would defend against it. And I know of your silly dance of balance to restore what I destroy. It's all just so boring. I destroy, you block. I destroy, you restore. It just goes on and on. But you underestimate me, Alton. Don't you know I have something else now? Don't you realize you will never be able to keep up with me?"

"Sivvius, you are nothing compared to Go—"

"SILENCE!" shouted Sivvius, sending a quick pain wave that knocked them to the ground. "Shut up and listen."

"But Sivvius," said Alton, his voice wavering as he tried to stand up.

"SILENCE!" shouted Sivvius again, sending another pain wave, knocking Alton back to the ground.

"What I have for you now, thanks to my friends from beyond, who I might add, are far more powerful than you or your God, is something you will fear beyond all fears. I warned you before, Alton. To continue to stand against me would be your end."

Alton rolled onto his side and looked at Sivvius. He saw him standing tall with a crazed look in his eyes, a warped smile on his face. Alton sensed the presence of the friends from beyond at a level greater than ever before.

"Grrrraaaaaah!" bellowed Sivvius. "I am on the top of the world, and my army is massive, my friends from beyond, mighty. I stand on the precipice of victory. And you can't stop me! I have a new weapon for you to enjoy, foolish Alton. I can't have you finding more scrolls, and I'm weary of having to track you. I need to devote all my time to building my army. My friends have given me a new power. Oh, I love just thinking about it, and reveling in your fear as you wonder what it is. It's almost too much fun to look at your face. I can imagine the dread you must be feeling now. You must be scared like a little baby, wondering what great wrath I'm going to unleash upon you. I'd stay here all day and watch you suffer with agonizing anticipation, but I've really got to get going. Got a world to conquer, you know.

"Alton, what I have for you today, is an ingenious idea. It is so perfect. What I have for you is something called STOP MOTION! I know how you thrive on motion! Just about everything you've done of any significance is motion-based. So today, you lose this ability. Today, you lose the ability to move. Today you become vegetables. Vegetables in my garden! Ahhh, yes! I love that thought. The earth is now my garden, and I turn you into my vegetables. I'll feed you once in a while, just to keep you alive so I can stop by now and then and enjoy your helplessness."

Alton watched Sivvius raise his hands into the air, starting the wild gyrations again—the gyrations that always ushered in some terrible attack. Alton felt utterly helpless, so discouraged and fearful, he couldn't even find the strength to pray. Sivvius swung his hands downward, and as he did, Alton felt a hot sensation rush through his body. Not painful, it was more like the feeling he had experienced when he walked into a steaming-hot sauna. The sensation rushed throughout his body, up and down his limbs, around his chest, up into his head. He felt increasing heat. Just as the level of heat was getting painful, he felt it diminishing, seeping out of his body. As it seeped out, what it left behind was numbness. He tried to stand, but couldn't. He tried to lift his arms, but they were without feeling. He could move nothing. He was completely paralyzed, unable even to turn his head.

A few minutes later, he heard footsteps. Then he heard the cackle, full and heavy. A face appeared above his, filled with a huge, demented grin, looking down upon him.

"Ohhhh, Alton. You should have listened to me before, while you still had a chance. You could have joined me. Now ... well now ... it's just too late. You look so pathetic, Alton. All your struggles have been such a waste. Don't you see now I was right about your God? He is nothing compared to me."

Alton heard more footsteps as Sivvius walked around the area. He saw him walking toward Walter. At least my head froze in a position where I can see Walter, Alton thought. At least I can still move my eyes. He watched as Sivvius found the scroll lying on Walter's chest. He watched as he bent down to pick it up.

There was a loud crackling sound as Sivvius touched it, and Alton saw him jump back, holding his arm close to his chest, rubbing it furiously. Sivvius walked back to the scroll, approaching it tentatively. He stood for a few seconds, staring at it. He slowly reached down again, a shirt wrapped around his hand this time, but as soon as his shirt-covered hand touched the scroll, Alton saw Sivvius fall to the ground in pain. He sat there for a few moments, spewing angry words at the scroll. He eventually calmed down, stood up, and walked back over to Alton.

"No matter, Alton. I don't need it anyway. And you sure can't do anything with it!" The cackle started softly, then grew into a wild, crazed laughter.

"Well, got to go. It's hard to believe it was so easy to stop you today. I guess I'm just that powerful now."

Sivvius flashed his demented grin and shouted: "Enjoy my garden, you pathetic vegetables!"

Alton lay there, helpless. All he could do was silently pray. Oh God, how could this have happened? How could Sivvius have done this to us? Oh God, please help us. Please, Lord Jesus, bring a miracle. Help us to move again. Only you can do it! Alton waited, but felt nothing changing. He kept praying, kept hoping, but nothing changed. He felt agony within himself like never before. He could imagine nothing worse. To be without motion: the ultimate pain. He looked upon Walter, helpless and motionless as well. His heart ached for his friends. How could he have let this happen to them? Why had he not anticipated this ... prepared for it?

As Alton continued lamenting, he thought for a moment he saw Walter flinch. It couldn't be. Then again, he swore he saw him flinch. He saw his right hand move. Was he seeing things? He saw Walter's right arm lift up, then his left. He watched him roll onto his side and push himself onto his knees with his hands. He stood, grunting as he did. Alton couldn't believe what he was seeing. Alton tried to move again, but still had no feeling in his body. Walter walked over to Alton, very slowly, stumbling along the way and collapsing on the ground next to Alton.

"Alton, Sivvius truly dealt us a massive blow this time. Yet somehow, I was mostly spared. All I can think of that might have helped is I jumped right into the dance of defense on my own as soon as I heard Sivvius, and I was also singing praises to God right when Sivvius attacked. I've been working on a new praise song for a while and really focused on it today. I was paralyzed just as you were, but the effect wore off very quickly."

Alton looked deep into Walter's eyes. He was so relieved his friend was okay, yet he couldn't help but agonize about his own condition, and the condition of the others. The agony must have shown on his face.

"Alton, take heart. I believe none of you are permanently paralyzed. Perhaps if you praise God right now, even if you can only do it in your mind, it will eliminate the paralysis."

Alton felt hope building within him, and he praised God as he looked at his friend. He was singing a song of praise to God in his mind when he heard a sound from his throat. It was a grunting sound. He consciously tried to make a noise, and another grunt seeped out. Then a squeaky something rolled across his tongue. He kept pushing, and soon he could hum his song of praise.

"Praise God, Alton!" shouted Walter. "You are reviving!"

Alton continued humming, and was eventually able to start singing. He praised God in song like never before. He felt his right arm twitch, then his left. He felt life seeping back into his legs. He could move his neck, and turn his head. He eventually managed to rise to his knees, as he fought through the pain and stiffness. He continued singing praises, and with Walter's help, he was finally able to stand.

"Praise God, Walter! He has restored us! Praising God, even in the worst of circumstances, has brought healing to my body!"

Alton raised his hands to God in praise, his arms trembling as they were still regaining strength. "Father God, Lord Jesus, Holy Spirit: you are a mighty God! Three and yet one. One and yet three. I praise you with all my heart."

Alton sobbed as he prayed. It felt to him as if he had been given a new life. He had felt more anguish than ever before in his life at the thought of lifelong paralysis, but now he was released from bondage. He stood there for some time, just praising God. Then he remembered the others.

As he turned to them, he saw them lying helpless on the ground. His heart ached. He felt deep compassion for them, but he felt even more than that. He thought of all the souls Sivvius had brought to evil—souls held in eternal bondage in Satan's kingdom. Not physical, but spiritual bondage. He knew how his physical bondage had been indescribably awful, and his heart went out to those on the earth struggling with paralysis, but it went out even more to those in spiritual bondage. Their bondage would be for eternity. He knew time was short, and he knew they must step up the pace and do everything possible to stop Sivvius from leading more souls to eternal damnation.

As Alton and Walter walked toward the others to help them revive, Alton realized once more the power of praising God even in times of great trouble. He would remember this when the final battle drew nigh. He had more confidence than ever that they would be victorious in the final battle, and that Sivvius would be drawn to repentance.

# Chapter 21
# Thursday, 6:30 p.m.

All of them eventually rose and began walking around. Their walking was more like dragging of feet, and there were many grunts and groans. The stop-motion attack had taken a severe toll. But they were all alive and in motion.

Before they revived, Alton had encouraged them to praise God with all that was within them as they were lying on the ground, even in the face of their agony. Some had taken quite awhile to revive, but Alton had just kept singing praises as he sat next to them, encouraging them to join him with their hearts and minds.

Now that they were healed, Alton's heart was rejoicing. He felt a strong sense of God all around them.

"God has done a miracle today! Praise to God Almighty who has freed us from physical bondage. We must cry out to God in praiseful song whenever Sivvius attacks us. Let this be a lesson to all: we must thank and praise God in everything.

"Let us also work more on our dance of defense. We must enhance it to be more effective against attacks such as the stop motion. Each of us must have full confidence to be able to do it quickly and independently if needed. Let us also work some more on our dance of balance. Perhaps we can refine it to be effective in bringing healing in other areas. Not just in knowledge-loss healing, but in whatever Sivvius might have for us next. And he *will* have more for us. He will be furious when he finds out we've been revived from his stop-motion attack.

"His power is exponentially increasing, as is his rate of soul conversion. We must ratchet up all we are doing. We must find the next scroll very quickly and learn how to stop Sivvius before it's too late. But let us practice the dances before we move on, and then I'd like to try something else."

They practiced the dance of defense for a while, working especially on ways for it to be effective when they were separated, and on ways for it to be effective in defending against new and different attacks. They spent much time discussing the importance of prayer and praise during the dance. Alton knew the power was mostly in the praise. They also spent time on the dance of balance, discovering new ways to use it to heal future damage, even from new attacks.

As they were finishing their practice, Alton gathered them into a circle.

"We are nearly ready to continue down the mountain. But first, we must do some minor experimentation with the sprays. I ask that the rest of you not sit too close, since I'm uncertain about the range of what we are going to attempt."

Alton walked about fifteen feet away from the others, still within earshot but far away enough to reduce risk.

"Walter, your father mentioned about properly applying the time equals mass equation when using the sprays, ensuring a strong mental focus of imagining time equaling mass. He also mentioned having a focused mental picture of the destination in mind—both physical location and time location. I recall, Walter, when you told us of your experience in the camping store, you did in fact apply these principles at some level.

"Yes, that is mostly true," said Walter. "But I was not specifically focused on time location—perhaps since I was so focused on a physical location I could see in present time, time travel was prevented."

"Very likely," said Alton. "However, as we start with location-jump experimentation, we'll need to ensure we focus very intensely on present time. I don't want to leave anything to chance and inadvertently travel in time. And I feel it is too soon to consciously attempt any time jumping. Let's first perfect location jumping.

"Regarding sequence of spraying, and duration of sprays, all we have to go by is the suggested starting point of the A-B-C sequence, with a quick spray of each, and no more than a second or two between each spray. We will learn much more about this. And through careful experimentation, we should be able to learn how to modify the process to work for groups. For now, we'll try this only on me, and attempt a very short location jump."

"Wait, Alton," said Angus. "As our leader, I don't think you should be the one to take the risk on this first attempt."

"I appreciate your concern, Angus, and also your offer to be first, but I must be the one. I've brought you to this point, and I can't allow anyone other than me to take this risk."

"Actually," said Angus, "I didn't mean for me to be the one to try it. I was goin' to offer up Michael."

"What?" said Michael. "Thanks a lot, Angus."

"It's my pleasure, laddie. After all, you are our Travel Director. You really should be the one."

"No, no," said Alton. "Do not worry, Michael. I would not ask this of you. I shall be the one."

Alton breathed in deeply, and then exhaled slowly, releasing as much tension as he could.

"I shall focus on the large boulder about ten feet away from me. I'm going to picture myself moving to that location in current time. I'll also be focusing on time equaling mass. I'll do short, quick sprays, in the A-B-C order."

Alton concentrated deeply, doing his best to clear his mind. Then he prayed for help and focused his thoughts on the location near the boulder in present time, and time equaling mass. He took the first can and sprayed the back of his left hand, feeling nothing. He quickly sprayed from the second can

THE SECRETS OF TIME TRAVEL: PART II — A Taste of Time

and felt slightly light-headed. He did his best to focus as he sprayed from the third can.

The odd feeling in his head grew rapidly, and he started feeling lighter in his body as well. He was focusing on the rock, staring at it, when suddenly he couldn't see it. He looked down at his hands and saw the third spray bottle in his right hand. He couldn't see the boulder, nor the others. "Oh my God, where am I?" Alton exclaimed.

"Alton, is that you?"

"Walter, where are you?"

"I'm up here, Alton!"

Alton turned around, looked up, and saw Walter standing with the others.

"Wow!" yelled Alton. "They worked! The sprays actually worked! I ended up over here below the rest of you, but at least the sprays really enabled me to change location!"

"How do you feel, Alton?"

"I feel great!"

Alton saw Angus staring down at him.

"Well, I'll be dog-shanked! I can't believe it!"

They all loped down the hill to Alton, hugging and rejoicing when they reached him.

"The sprays really work," said Alton. "They worked with Walter, and now they have worked here in a more controlled experiment. But we'll need much more experimentation. I'm sure a combination of my lack of focus combined with many other factors such as duration and sequence of sprays, and even where I sprayed the sprays on my hand all played a critical role in effectiveness and accuracy. We'll need to work on these things with much care and seriousness of thought. Let me try another jump with a slightly different spray duration, and see what that does."

Alton tried various durations, and then sequences, working to refine the accuracy of the sprays. Sometimes he was able to get within a foot or two of the desired destination, but sometimes he was quite a few feet off. Eventually, Walter coaxed Alton into trying to send him to the boulder. After a few failed attempts, Alton was eventually able to transport the two of them together, but they ended up far away from the boulder. After more practice, he was able to transport just Walter, but again, far away from the boulder. Alton was amazed at what they were able to do, but he knew it would take much more practice to get all the variables right. It would be far too risky at this point to attempt any long-distance jumps or time jumps.

It was getting dark, and they decided to set up camp for the night. They found a flat area a little farther down the mountain, had a light dinner, and sat around the fire talking. They were exhausted by what they had endured from Sivvius, but quite excited about the sprays. It was nearly midnight when they reclined in their tents. As Alton bundled up in his sleeping bag, he pondered what they had done with the sprays. He could not stop thinking about it. He was especially excited that he was able to transport Walter. "Oh God," he whispered, "I had hoped this would be possible … to transport another." Alton continued to pray quietly, asking God about a very specific and radical idea percolating in his mind. He drifted off to sleep as he prayed.

# PART III:

## *The End of Good or Evil*

# Chapter 22
## Friday, 11:00 a.m.

Walter snapped awake. Thoughts of eventually using the sprays to find Ingrid raced through his mind. He looked at his watch and was shocked that it was already 11:00 a.m. He climbed out of his tent, and noticing he was the first one awake, got the fire going and filled the coffee kettle with some of the water they had hauled up. He roused the others, and after finishing off the coffee and some granola bars, they packed up camp.

"We need to get going," said Alton. "I can't believe we slept so late, but I guess we needed it. We must determine where the next clue is leading us. Perhaps we should engage in a motion activity to help stimulate our thoughts."

"I agree," said Walter.

"How 'bout the ball of death?" asked Angus. "Are you ready for some serious thinkin'?"

Walter grimaced when he heard Angus mention the dreaded ball of death. They had used it only one other time, and although highly effective, it was by far the most dangerous motion activity known to the Council.

"I don't know about that," sighed Alton. "The risk is just too high. Let us rather engage in the skip of life. As we skip, think of the clue of a place with two between two."

Walter sighed with relief at Alton's suggestion of using the skip of life. It was a great thought-enhancing motion, and far safer than the ball of death. He glanced at Angus, who had become silent, and noticed the look of disgust on his face. He chuckled, since he knew Angus hated the skip of life. The thought of skipping down the mountain in perfect unison was not Angus's idea of manly motion. He could see that Angus was dying to complain, but was managing to hold his tongue, probably out of respect for Alton.

As the skipping began, Walter knew Angus was in agony. He had to work hard at not watching him; he knew the look of frustration and embarrassment on Angus's face would cause him to laugh, and then his concentration would be broken. Walter kept looking into the distance as he skipped, focusing on the clue. He started to feel the energy in his mind intensify; he felt an answer already forming in his mind. Eventually they came to a level area and Walter stopped dead in his tracks.

Alton stopped behind him, nearly running into him. "What is it, Walter? Why did you stop?"

"I know."

"What is it you know, laddie boy? That you're enjoyin' the skippin' and you want to do it for the rest of your life?" laughed Angus.

"Please listen, Angus," said Walter. "I know the answer to the clue!"

"Really?" asked Alton as the others gathered around him.

"Yes, Alton. I truly know. Gaze into the distance. What do you see?"

"I see mountains. I see trees. I see plants. And I see your wimpy face!" laughed Angus.

"Okay, Angus. I've about had it with you. I'm going without you."

Walter located his destination and sped down the mountain.

"Where're you goin' laddie?"

"Wait up, Walter. I'll go with you," yelled Michael as he ran toward Walter.

"Oh that's just what we need," barked Angus. "Spaz-man Walter, coupled with a Travel Director who couldn't find his own foot in his shoe. We'd better follow."

They all ran after Walter and Michael, and soon arrived at the edge of a beautiful, crystal-clear mountain lake.

"This is it!"

"This is what?" Angus asked Walter. "This is the point where you finally admit you're an idiot?"

Walter ignored him. "This is the answer to the clue. Did the skip of life not show you what it showed me? Think! A place with two between two? Anything?"

"No, not really," said Alton with a puzzled look.

"Think! Two between two. Think of a scientific designation!"

"Let's see ... two between two. Maybe 222? But what would that designate?" asked Alton.

"That's actually two between twos, not two between two— but a good guess, nevertheless. Any other ideas?"

"Hmmm. We know there must be a two in the middle of some designation. Or could it be signifying us? Maybe two of us between two others? Maybe a certain order of alignment of how we stand to enhance spray usage?"

"Great thoughts, Alton. But still not quite it. Look!" said Walter as he pointed to the water.

"The water? How does the water fit into this? It—oh wait! Yes! Of course! It's not all numbers. It's the two between two of something else ... in this case letters!"

"Precisely, Alton. The answer to the clue is H2O. Two between two, or the number 2 between two letters—two between H and O. H2O! Water!"

"Excellent analysis, Walter. A place with two between two is water. And here we stand by a mountain lake. We should enter the water and see what we find. But who? Who should go?

"I should be the one," said Walter. " I have a strong desire to follow the clue. The answer came to me in the skip, so I feel that I should be the one."

Walter could tell Angus was about to object, when Alton spoke up and saved Walter from another verbal wrestling match.

"I agree, Walter. You have interpreted the clue and now you should be the one who has the honor of the next step. But before you enter the lake, let us take a few moments to pray for your safety."

\*  \*  \*

Sivvius stayed hidden behind a tree near the lake where the Council members were gathered. He couldn't believe they had recovered from the paralysis. He wondered how they had done it. How could they possibly have broken free so quickly? How could they have broken free at all? I thought my friends from beyond had given me the ultimate weapon. I thought Alton and his idiotic sidekicks would be my vegetables forever. "Oh my friends," he whispered, "how could they have broken free of the stop motion? What have I done wrong? Please help me to do better next time."

His body tensed as he felt anger and frustration pulse through his mind, fueling his insanity. He did his best to clear his mind and think of something positive. "At least I have the two," he whispered. "If Alton only knew how I've reached two of his group already. He still seems to have no idea. I need to keep it that way. I will play my trump card when the time is right."

\*  \*  \*

After a time of great prayer, Walter was ready for his journey into the lake. He stood up and looked at Alton.

"Are you ready, Walter?"

"Yes, Alton. I feel that I'm ready and the time is right."

"Then venture into the lake. May you have both success and safety."

Walter walked to the edge of the lake and waded in. The water was icy cold, but also invigorating. His legs burned from the cold, but his heart was hot with anticipation of what he would find.

He looked very closely for anything unusual as he waded through the shallow water, and eventually noticed a large rock just below the surface. It looked quite unique—circular in form and about the size of a volleyball. He bent down and rubbed his fingers along the surface. His heart raced when he felt some type of etching. He lifted the rock out of the water and was able to hold it while he inspected the etching. It was the same type of code that had been on the scrolls! He paused for a moment to still his racing heart.

When he regained his composure, he deciphered the code, and was puzzled. The first part made some sense. It simply said North Texas—land of plainness and O. It surely meant they needed to do something in North Texas, although he wasn't sure about the plainness and O part. But the second part was more confusing—it said to think of a direction and think of that which you might need when food comes to mind. He read it a few times to commit it to memory, then placed the rock back in the lake. He looked back at the others and saw them waiting for him at the water's edge. He thrashed over to them with wild abandon.

"What happened, Walter?" asked Alton. "Did you find any clues?"

"I can't believe it, Alton! I found a very unique rock in the lake and it had the same code we found in the scrolls!"

"What did it say?"

"Well, the words are clear, but I'm not sure of the meaning. It translated as: North Texas—land of a plainness and land of an O, and also said to think of a direction and think of that which you might need when food comes to mind."

"That is all there was?"

"Yes, Alton."

"Hmmm. Interesting. I get the North Texas part, but the rest … hmmm. We'll need to ponder this."

"Yes, I agree, Alton. Can we rest a bit first? I'm exhausted."

"By all means. We'll talk more when you're ready."

Walter walked over to a secluded tree and sat down, resting against the trunk. It felt good to relax and let his mind shut down. He had hardly slept the night before. Just as he was starting to doze, he heard a yell from down the main trail.

"Hey! Have you guys been up Wheeler Peak?"

The man got up closer and extended his hand to Walter. "Name's Ralph … Ralph Palmer. I'm the local forest ranger. You guys doing okay up here? You been up to the peak?"

"Yes, sir. We're doing just fine."

"Looks to me like you have had a rough time of it. Climbed up and down too fast did you?"

"Oh, I've just been pretty stressed lately."

Walter was being very cautious. Something about the man just didn't seem right.

"I see. Looks like you've been in the water. Maybe fishing? Do you have a permit?"

"No sir, I have not been fishing. I was just trying to get refreshed with a little swim."

"Mmm hmm. So you say. You didn't happen to find anything in that old lake did you?"

"What do you mean?"

"Anything interesting? I mean, other than the fish you probably caught without a permit."

"But I wasn't fishing! I don't even have a pole with me."

"You'd better be careful with that attitude of yours, or I'll have you hauled in for trespassing."

"Trespassing? What are you talking about? This is not private land. Who are you?" Walter stood and faced him.

The man got a strange look on his face and his eyes starting twitching out of control. As the twitching subsided, he looked deep into Walter's eyes.

"Can you see out of that left eye all right?" asked the man.

"Why do you ask?"

"I noticed a little bit of swelling in that eye, and as an ophthalmologist, I have a natural concern for eye health. You should schedule an appointment with me."

"But I thought you said you were a forest ranger!"

"Forest ranger? Where did you get that idea? I'm not a forest ranger, at least last time I checked! Now, let me see that eye again."

Out of the corner of that eye, Walter was peeking over to where Alton stood. He noticed that Alton was motioning for him to stay calm. He appeared to be mouthing some words to him, but he couldn't quite make them out.

"Look straight ahead, please!" said the ophthalmologist impatiently. "I need to look deep into your pupil to determine just what type of problem you may have."

Walter looked straight again, but was agonizing over not being able to see what Alton was trying to tell him. He darted his eyes back toward Alton, just enough to see he was mouthing something like "un ear."

"Back to me, you impossible patient. Back to me with your eyes!"

Walter glanced back to the man for a few seconds but then back to Alton for another glimpse. He squinted and looked very closely ... Alton was saying, "Un eer ... run ... eer ... run here!"

"Uh ... doctor ... I think you may be right. I may have a problem with my eye, and I'd love for you to treat it now, but we have a critical meeting in a nearby town. Is there any way I could set up an appointment with you?"

"Well, I hate to let this wait, but if you must go, you must go. Let me give you one of my cards. You can call my office and make an appointment with my secretary. Oh, wait. Here she comes now. You can set it up directly with her. Shirley? This gentleman here would like to set up an appointment to see me soon."

"I don't see her, doctor. Is she coming up the trail?"

"What is that you say, young man? Is who coming up the trail? Now what about that appointment? Can you make it ... say ... next week on Wednesday?"

The doctor's voice had changed to that of an elderly woman's, and even his facial expressions changed. If one were not to look too closely, it might be believable that this was in fact an elderly woman.

"So ... next Wednesday?"

"Where is the doctor?"

"Oh, he had to go. There was another patient needing help. So ... Wednesday then?"

"Yes, yes. Wednesday is fine."

"Morning or afternoon?"

"Oh I don't know, I guess morning would be fine."

"Good. Say 9:00?"

"Yes. 9:00 will work. Now we must be going."

"Very well, but, before you go, let me get some ..."

Her voice trailed off and her expression tensed as she shifted her gaze over Walter's shoulder. Walter felt fear chills race down his spine. He snapped his head around as he felt a cold hand rest upon his shoulder.

"Do not fear me, my young friend, Walter," Sivvius whispered into his ear.

Walter glanced over at Alton and saw him getting the others ready for the dance of defense.

"I can help you," Sivvius continued. "I can help you find your beloved Ingrid. And I can make sure she will love you; I can help you to become all she would ever want. It's a tragedy she was pulled away from you by destiny. It's just not right. She was the one meant for you, and you for her. Let me help you. Tell me what you found in the lake and we can decipher the mystery together. Then I can lead you to Ingrid. You will never find her on your own. Do you not realize this?"

Walter's mind was racing. How could Sivvius help him find Ingrid? Can he really help me find her? Can it be true? But how can I even be thinking this? I can't trust him. I can't betray my friends. I must stand firm. Surely I'll be able to find her with the help of the scroll. He glanced over at Alton; it helped him to see his leader and friend looking at him with reassurance as they were beginning the dance of defense.

"You are wrong, Sivvius. I can find Ingrid on my own. The scroll will help me. Alton will help me. God will help me."

"God can't help you! If He cared about you, why didn't He give you Ingrid when you were a boy? I can give her to you right now."

Walter felt a burst of pain. He had asked himself the question before—how could God have allowed him to lose Ingrid? But no, he thought. This is not God's fault. I must not question God. I'm the one who didn't get her number, and I'm the one who didn't kiss her sweet lips. Yet all things work together for good, this I know to be true. My day with Ingrid is coming.

"No, Sivvius. It's not God's fault I didn't get Ingrid. And I certainly don't need your evil in my life; even if you help me find Ingrid, there will be something not quite right. I just know it. And you just paralyzed us yesterday! How could you ever expect me to trust you? Now please, leave me alone."

"Oh foolish Walter! You do not know what you are saying. You have no idea what I could do for you, what power I could offer you. Your ignorance is hurting us both. Don't hide from me that which is rightfully mine. I know you saw something in the lake. Tell me what it was. Submit to me now, and find great wonders, or continue against me and suffer."

Walter stood in paralyzed fear. He was face-to-face with Sivvius, and felt utterly helpless.

"Well, Walter? I'm waiting. Tell me what I seek before I paralyze you again."

Walter noticed out of the corner of his eye that Alton was reaching for something in his pocket. Walter knew what it was.

"I will tell you what you wish to know, but you must first let my friends go," said Walter.

"This can't be done! I have so much to offer all of you, Walter. All you need do is bend your knee to me and follow my ways. I will bring great things to you. I desire to help you, Walter."

"You do not really desire to help me. All you want is to control me," said Walter.

"But my control is good. I can bring you such incredible things. Just remember, if you stand against me, you will live out the rest of your life in agony. And you will never have Ingrid. I'll make sure of that."

Walter continued pleading with Sivvius, trying to stall, trying to allow Alton time to prepare. Then he saw the cylinders. The three cylinders. The sprays. Alton was spraying the first upon his arm.

"Okay, okay!" said Walter. "I will tell you what I saw, but you must promise me that you won't harm us."

"Promises I do not make. And advice I do not take. Do not anger me. Just tell me what I wish to know. If I'm pleased, I may be merciful."

"If this is as it must be, then I will tell you. When I waded into the water, I spotted a strange box just below the surface …"

Alton was spraying the second spray upon his arm, motioning for Walter to run over to them.

"… I noticed some writing on the box … something about a northern city. Something that looked like Duffallo … or perhaps it was Chuffallo … I couldn't quite make it out …"

Alton was about to spray the third spray upon his arm.

"… and as I looked, I saw what I thought might be—"

"You are lying," bellowed Sivvius. "You dare to lie to me?"

"No! No! I'm telling you what I saw!"

"No, you are not. I know you're lying. Now that you have not only lied, but also lied about lying, your suffering will be far greater than the suffering of all the others put together. Prepare to begin your pain—wait, what was that?"

Walter felt a tremor beneath his feet, a tremor that was intensifying. He broke into a run toward the others. As he was running, he saw Alton spraying the third spray upon his arm. He dove at Alton's feet, wrapping his arms around his ankles. He noticed that his arms were getting lighter in color, starting to take on a slight transparency. He felt light-headed.

"What's happening?" asked Sivvius, his voice rising in volume and intensity.

Walter saw his arms getting more transparent, then his legs. He could see it happening to the others too.

"STOP! STOP NOW OR DIE!" screamed Sivvius.

*     *     *

Sivvius watched them disappear from his view, unable to stop them. He let out a roar that caused the trees to tremble. He couldn't believe they had escaped. He collapsed on the ground in agony. He felt a strange lightness in his head, then in his body. Suddenly he was somewhere else. He didn't know where. He sat in a field, and saw cattle in the distance.

"Where am I?" he bellowed into the sky. "How can I keep failing to stop them? What have they done now? What is this power they have, to be able to disappear from my sight? And where have they sent me? Oh, my friends, forgive me. Help me. Help me to find out where I am, and help me to get back to them—to stop them. I must stop them. I must turn them. I must find a way. They are a huge threat now. The scale has tipped the other way again."

He sat on the ground, filled with frustration and anger and hatred. He thought about what to do next. All he knew to do was to look around and get his bearings, to figure out where he was. Then he could focus on finding them. He sat for a while longer, thinking. At least there are two of them already taking my bait. But I must reach the others: I *will* reach the others. But I must find them first.

# Chapter 23
# Saturday, 10:45 a.m.

"Where are we? What just happened?" asked Walter. "I thought we were about to be killed. Did Sivvius kill us? Are we dead?"

Alton looked around with a keen eye. They were not where they had been, that was for sure. This place was flatter with hardly any trees and the wind was much stronger than what it had been just a few moments before. There was no lake, either. Everything was different, but it felt like it was different in the right way.

"Yes, what happened?" asked Michael. "Where are we? I felt the earth tremble, then I heard Sivvius scream, then I felt a strange feeling in my body and mind, and now here we are!"

"I used the sprays for a long-range jump. It had to be done."

"What about the risks, Alton?"

"I hope against all hope there were no negative consequences, Walter. I believe I had no choice but to use the sprays. Sivvius was upon us and he had the upper hand. I just hope our previous short-range practice with the sprays was adequate to make this long-range jump safe. I applied what we had practiced earlier as best I could. I think the motion activity we did prior to the jump helped as well. I think it's critical that we engage in motion before all long-range jumps.

"But believe me, I was petrified of misusing the sprays. We had not perfected the accuracy of our local launches, and to attempt a long-distance jump was very risky. But I was afraid a local jump wouldn't be effective. I was afraid Sivvius would still be close enough to get to us, and possibly even steal the sprays. I knew we had to risk a huge jump.

"We'll see what happens from here, and if we caused any problems. If we messed things up, we'll do what we can to repair the issues. Right now, all I know is we are free of Sivvius, we are safe, and we are together. Is everyone okay?"

They all nodded their heads in agreement.

"Good, then let me tell you where we are."

"You know?" asked Walter.

"I think so. I think the sprays have allowed us to travel to the location the rock gave us clues about. As I sprayed, I thought of North Texas and time equaling mass. And, I guessed at this next part, but I think I'm right. The clue talked about the land of plainness and O. At first I thought the clue was referencing plainness as in the sense of a city that was very plain or simple or flat, but that could be almost anywhere. Then as I played with the words, it hit me. There is a city called Plano. I had heard of it before. Plainness and O—it made sense to translate the clue words into Plano.

"I hope I was right, and I hope that if I was, we are actually *in* Plano. I must say this at least feels like North Texas would this time of year: hot. So even if we're not in Plano, hopefully we're close."

"This is amazing!" said Walter. "We might have really done a long-range jump!"

"Wow, Alton! That is excellent!" said Patrick. "I must apologize in advance though because all this travel has made me intensely hungry."

"You know, now that you mention it, I too am filled with a hunger. We must consume massive amounts of food. I'm thinking of a large buffet of pizza or perhaps a feast of hamburgers."

"Ahhhh, both tempting, Michael, my young apprentice," said Patrick. "I can remember one time in my youth, when I engaged in one of the most thrilling mass consumptions of my lifetime."

Alton looked over at Patrick and Michael. He knew they were about to delve into one of their zany food conversations. The brothers in food are at it again, thought Alton. He knew he would enjoy their conversation, but he also knew they must move quickly to solve the latest clue.

"My fooderific friends, I'd love to hear your discussion of prior food consumption, but time is short. I recommend we find a restaurant in that strip mall over there, and fuel our bodies so hunger won't block our minds. I know you two love chicken wings. Why don't we see if we can find some?"

"That sounds most excellent," said Michael as a huge smile spread across his face.

"Sounds great to me as well," said Patrick.

\* \* \*

They found a wing restaurant in the strip mall, and Patrick lunged toward the door and attempted to yank it open, nearly dislocating his shoulder in the process.

"It's locked!" shouted Patrick. "How can it be locked?"

"Perhaps the place is not yet open for business," said Alton.

"But it's after 2:00. How could they not be open yet?"

"What I mean is perhaps this is an entirely new business that is still under final construction."

"No, no, no. That can't be. Look inside. Everything is there: the chairs, the tables, the paper towels on the tables, the cash register, TV's. I even see someone at the counter now."

Patrick hammered on the glass. "Hey you!" he yelled. "Why is the door locked?"

The person at the counter mouthed something, but Patrick couldn't make it out.

"What?"

The person inside pointed to his watch and yelled something.

"What is he saying?" asked Alton.

"Hard to make it out, but he keeps pointing at his watch and yelling. Sounds like something about fifteen minutes, or eleven, or something like that."

Patrick hammered on the glass again. The man finally rushed up to the door with a frustrated look on his face. "We don't open until 11:00," he yelled through the glass. "Please be patient!" Then he ran back to the counter, resuming his work at the register.

"What did he say?" asked Alton.

"He said they don't open until 11:00."

"11:00? But it's already after 2:00! Isn't that right?" The others looked at their watches and they all confirmed it was after 2:00.

"What's going on?" asked Patrick as he tilted his palms upward. "Is this guy batty or something?"

"I'm not sure," said Alton. "Let's check some of the other stores in this strip mall. Let's see what time the clocks show in those, and ask some people the time as well. Maybe something happened to our watches in the location jump."

They dispersed to check out other stores and ask various people the time. Within a few minutes, they met back by the wing restaurant, and all confirmed it was nearly 11:00. Alton looked at his watch again. He walked away from the others, reflecting back to where they had come from. He knew it had been 2:00 there. He checked his watch just before they had left. He had been checking his watch throughout the day as they descended the mountain, and as they waited for Walter to come out of the lake. He spun back toward the others and ran to the wing restaurant. He veered off at the last moment and finished his sprint near a newspaper dispenser. After staring into the dispenser for a few seconds, he turned back toward the others. He walked to them slowly, glancing at his watch every few steps. When he got to them, he stood silent for a few moments, continually checking his watch. The words finally came.

"Well ... we have not only left New Mexico and traveled to Texas, but we also managed to travel forward in time. Even though it's an earlier time of the day than when we left—that is 11:00 as opposed to 2:00—it's also a different day. We have traveled into tomorrow!"

There was silence. Alton saw the looks on the faces of the others—a mix of wonderment, joy, and fear. He walked off by himself, all kinds of thoughts running through his mind. They had done it. What had happened to Walter at the store in Taos and what they had practiced on the mountain was amazing enough. They had done much location jumping. But this time, they not only did a long-distance location jump, but a time jump as well. It had really happened. The sprays enabled them to travel forward in time. Perhaps we really can stop Sivvius with what we are learning from the scrolls, he thought. Alton glanced over at Walter who appeared to be in deep thought as well.

\* \* \*

I can't believe what just happened, thought Walter. We really traveled in time! Thoughts of Ingrid raced through his mind. Surely, the ability to travel in time could help me find Ingrid and possibly even change what happened in the past. But could I really do it? Could I travel back to my childhood and change that day when I first met Ingrid? Could the sprays really make it possible? I just don't know for sure. We must find out more.

\* \* \*

"We really have traveled forward in time, at least in a relative sense," said Alton. "I'm not sure how. I did not think of a future time when I used the sprays. It could be I had a thought of what we would do the next day, but if I did, it would have been very fleeting. These sprays are very powerful. I hope I haven't caused some huge rift in the continuum. It's so vital to have perfect mental focus when we use the sprays. One thing I must say, is that this gives me great hope. If it was so easy to jump a day ahead, imagine the possibilities! We might be able to jump weeks, or months, or years ... or even decades through time. Can you imagine—"

"Okay, now we're open," said the man with a look of disgust on his face as he opened the front door.

Alton just stood where he was, motionless. He saw that the others were also unable to move. He knew they were all still trying to process the fact that they had just traveled into the future. He knew they had all kinds of thoughts racing through their minds.

"Well?" asked the man. "Are you coming in or not? After all that banging on the glass I sure thought you were anxious to eat!"

"Yes," Alton finally managed to say. "We are coming in."

"My friends, let us consume wings. What has just happened to us is beyond comprehension. The sprays really do work, but we must engage in food consumption to stimulate our minds. We have much to process. We must determine where we need to go next. Let us enter in."

Patrick led the charge to the nearest table, placed the order for the group and before too long wings started arriving. Alton was so relieved; the recent events had stirred his appetite. They were silent as they ate voraciously. Every half hour or so Alton would hear a muffled cry from one of the others as they asked for more wings. Alton decided they would spend the day there. It was a great place not only for wing consumption, but also for pondering and discussion. Anyway, they couldn't move on until they solved the latest clue.

Every so often, they would lie on the floor to stretch out and ponder. Alton knew this had to look ridiculous to some of the other customers filtering in and out through the day, but he didn't care. He knew they must do whatever they had to, so they could determine where they should go. They had to stay ahead of Sivvius.

Alton had a number of thoughts about Sivvius. Oh God, he prayed silently, *is it possible Sivvius somehow came with us to this time? I didn't see him anywhere when we arrived, and I looked all around. If he did somehow come with us, will he know we traveled into the future—at least in the sense that the scroll described travel into the future? If he knows of this ability, he may be forced to do whatever he must to stop us now, even to the point of killing us. I don't think the small good left in him will hold him back, because we now possess this mighty ability. The stakes are too high. Oh, God, please help us.* Suddenly, the manager spoke.

"Gentlemen, I appreciate your business, but unfortunately the restaurant is closing."

"Have we really been here that long?" asked Alton.

"I'm afraid so, sir."

"But we have not yet determined what it is we are to do next."

"What do you mean?"

"You would not understand."

"Why do you say that?"

"You would not understand the clues we've been given to help us find what we seek in this great quest of ours."

"A great quest, you say?"

"That is correct, young man. A very great quest indeed. But we've not the time to give you all the details. We must find that which we seek."

"Well, what are you seeking?"

"Again, you would not understand."

"Try me. I may be just the manager of this wing store to you, but in my heart of hearts I'm a great sleuth who loves to solve a mystery."

"All right. I guess it couldn't hurt for you to try," sighed Alton. "The clue we found stated that we needed to think of a direction and also think of that which one might need when food comes to mind."

"That is all you have?"

"I'm afraid so."

"Let me see ... let me think ... hmmmm ... direction and something needed with food. And this is supposed to be some sort of place?"

"Yes, we do believe it's supposed to be a place here in Texas where we are to find our next clue."

"Okay, a direction. I guess a direction could be up or down or sideways or forwards or backwards. Something needed with food could mean just about anything. It could be salt, it could be milk, it could be a napkin ... the possibilities are endless. I need more information."

"Yet I'm afraid that is all we have," sighed Alton. "Have you tried engaging in motion to stimulate your thoughts?"

"What?"

"Motion is the key to knowledge, you know. That is why we are here. You think we are consuming massive quantities of wings only because we like them? No, I tell you. We are engaging in this eating motion to stimulate our minds."

"That sounds a little weird."

"Maybe to you, but that's only because you don't understand. Now please, either engage in motion to stimulate your thoughts or stop wasting our time."

"But as I've said, we are closing."

"May we stay here and brainstorm through the night? The wonderful odors in this establishment are very inspiring. We'll pay you well for the privilege, and you can stay with us and think with us if you like. I think you will find our discussion fascinating."

"I'm just not sure about that. I mean, this is intriguing and all, but you guys sure seem a bit out there. But, oh, I don't know. I guess … you know, why not? I'll probably get in some type of trouble for this, but I must admit you have me curious. I'm not sure who you guys are or what your great quest is all about, or even if you guys are sane. But this is the most interesting conversation I've had in a long time."

Alton smiled as the manager pulled up a chair. They talked through the night, taking catnaps as needed. The brainstorming was intense. Notebook pages were strewn all over the table and floor, some with wing-sauce stains, some partially crumpled, some torn. As the morning sun peeked through the front door, they continued brainstorming, unfazed by how much time had passed. With not much morning left, Walter said something that struck Alton.

"Maybe the direction has to do with compass points. North, south, east, or west? And maybe the food thing has to do with what we use to eat the food?"

All were silent. Alton sensed that Walter was on to something.

"Yes!" shouted Walter. "A direction and something we eat the food with. This feels right! Something we eat with ... let us see ... our mouths? Our tongues? How about a fork?"

"Wait! What did you just say?" asked the manager with both a smile and wing sauce on his face. "Did you say fork?"

"Yes, a fork." said Walter. "Does this mean something to you?"

"I think so. I think it might. You said north, south, east, or west, and you said fork. Right away when you said fork, I thought of Southfork Ranch in Parker, Texas!"

"Southfork Ranch?" questioned Michael. "What is that?"

"You have not heard of Southfork Ranch? The place where they filmed the old television series Dallas?"

"This doesn't ring a bell," said Michael. "Is this place near us?"

"You are not far. Parker is near Wylie, and both are but a few miles east of Plano. All you need to do is head east on Parker Road and it will lead you to Southfork."

"Hmmmm. Southfork," said Alton. "It feels right ... a direction ... something about food. I guess it couldn't hurt to try it out. I'm not sure why the other part of the clue led us to Plano and not Parker, but perhaps it's just more of the complexity required for our search—the complexity that ensures not just anyone could find what we seek. We will go to this Southfork Ranch. Young man, is there a car-rental facility near here?"

"Actually, right down the street," he said as he pointed. "You can walk there fairly easily."

"Excellent! Thank you so much for your help. You have proven to be highly competent. If we were not already seven, I'd consider inviting you along."

"Oh, that's okay. Just glad to have been able to help. Besides, I have my restaurant to take care of. Speaking of that, I need to get ready for tomorrow—I mean ready for today. Good luck in your quest."

"Thank you. We wish you the best of luck with your restaurant. By the way, what do we owe you?"

"This one's on me. I feel like I was hanging out with family these past hours, and I just don't feel right billing family. Here, take my business card and call me some day to let me know how your quest turns out."

"I really appreciate your kind offer," said Alton, "but I can't let you do that. We ate a lot of wings. And you helped us solve a very difficult clue. You run a nice business here, and deserve a fair wage for a job well done."

Alton pressed five one hundred dollar bills into the manager's palm as they shook hands.

# Chapter 24
## Sunday, 11:00 a.m.

They rented a minivan, and it took only fifteen minutes to get to Southfork. It was a beautiful, sprawling ranch house, with lovely grounds and Texas longhorns grazing nearby. Alton directed them to head on in since it appeared to be open to the public. Once inside, Angus stepped up to the desk where a woman was collecting the tour fee.

"Well, hello there," said Angus with a confident, sly little smile.

"Hello, sir. May I help you?"

"Oh, that you may, beautiful lady. I could not help but notice that you're the most gorgeous lass I've seen in these here parts for a long, long time."

Alton recalled that Angus had a fascination with Texas history. He learned not only the history, but also developed a love for the classic drawl and unique Texas sayings. The problem was that he tended to get his approach with the words and sayings a bit messed up. He also seemed to have trouble segregating his Texas and Scottish words. Alton prepared to be amused.

"Why sir … you surely flatter me," she said, blushing a bit.

"So, tell me, young chicken girl, did you happen to see that ole' high-length steer out front?"

"Oh, you mean the longhorn?"

"Aye! The longhorn. Ain't he a purdy sight to lay one eye on?"

"Oh he sure is pretty."

"You know girly girl, I once took down one of them big horns just as quick as an armadillo takes down a jackrabbit!"

"Is that a quick thing?" she asked. "I mean, can an armadillo take down a jackrabbit real quick? I'd never heard of that."

"Aye, lass. You'd see that rabbit go down like the underside of a Texas turtle slidin' down a hill of ice! Better yet, it's like a large flock of horses sittin' down on the range! Aye, sugar lass. It's really a hot-diggity kind of thing for all y'all."

"Sir, I am not quite sure what you just said, but it's cute. You are such a cute fella. I'll tell you what ... why don't you take my phone number here, and give me a call someday? Maybe we can do some two-steppin'."

"Why thank you. You're a darlin' little possum if I ever saw one. Sure, we can do some two-steppin' someday, or even some three or four-steppin'!"

"You're just so cute," she said.

"Thanks again, pretty steer girl. You're a sweet bowl of fried okra if I ever saw one!"

"Thanks, you old bull dog," she said with a glimmer in her eyes.

Alton was still chuckling at Angus's antics as they started the tour. They walked through the Southfork home, and saw some incredible things. Alton loved the massive staircase, the gorgeous furniture, and a bathroom off the upstairs bedroom that was heavenly. Yet they struggled to find any clues. Alton was checking out the main bedroom when he heard Walter yell from the bathroom.

"What is it Walter?"

"Come on over to the tub. I think I've found something!"

Alton recalled how Walter had a fascination with bathtubs. When he got into the bathroom, he noticed that Walter was checking out the tub in detail. He had even crawled in and sprawled out, looking at something on the side of the faucet.

"Is he in a tub again?" asked Angus with more than a little frustration. "Seems like all he does is take baths. Even when we're in the wilderness, he drives me crazy, constantly diggin' huge holes and fillin' 'em with water. He spends more time makin' his fancy forest baths than he does anything else."

"Be nice, Angus," cautioned Alton. "You must admit he comes up with some incredible ideas after he's been in the tub for a few minutes."

"Minutes? What do you mean minutes? How 'bout hours?"

"Yes, you are right, sometimes hours. But it seems to work. Let's see what he's found."

"Oh all right," sighed Angus.

Alton leaned over the tub.

"It's on the side of this faucet, Alton. Look! I found an etching that is in the same coded structure as the scrolls!"

"What does it say?" asked Alton.

"It says that we will find what we seek just north of J.R. yet south of the liquid redness."

"What does that mean?" asked Michael. "Here we go again with these cryptic directions. And you guys wonder why I have trouble finding things. Sure would be nice to have some good directions for once."

"Actually," chimed in Angus, "I think I might know what at least part of it means, at least the J.R. part. I remember that one of the characters on the old television show Dallas, which had some filmin' done here, was a J.R. Ewing. North of J.R. must mean north of Southfork since this was the home of J.R. in the show."

"Excellent, Angus!" said Alton. "It makes sense. But what about the liquid redness part?"

"I believe I know what that is also. There's a huge river near the Texas and Oklahoma border called the Red River. Red River sure sounds to me like liquid redness!"

"Great work Angus. Now how does it all tie together? North of here, but south of the Red River. How far is the Red River?"

"Unfortunately Alton, it's pretty far, so there's a lot between here and there, but at least we know more than we did before."

"True, Angus. Was there anything else, Walter?"

"Yes, but it's hard to understand. Translation of the rest of the code results in the following: M&Y south of where the hill follows the foot and baskets are strong."

"Where baskets are strong? What in the name of all things Scottish does that mean, laddie?"

"You know as much as I, Angus. I'm lost on this one."

"Very interesting," said Alton. "This is extremely vague and challenging. We'll need to ponder this. What do you think Michael? You are our Travel Director. What should we do next?"

"I recommend we start by heading to the Red River. We can ponder more as we go."

"Sounds like as good a recommendation as any. Let's hop in the van and head to the Red River!"

\* \* \*

As they left Southfork, Walter looked back at the huge balcony. He imagined standing there with Ingrid, holding hands. He would be telling her how he found so many clues that led him to her. He would tell her how he discovered how to use the sprays, how he deciphered the clue that led them to the underwater cave, how he found the etching on the tub faucet, and most important of all: how he never gave up in his search for her. She will be so proud of me, he thought.

\* \* \*

After a few miles of driving, Michael turned the van around and went back the other way.

"What's goin' on Michael?" asked Angus.

"Oh, nothing. Just getting us warmed up a bit before we head north."

"I see. Just a warm-up, eh? What just happened had nothin' to do with the fact that we just passed a sign that said we were headed south?"

"Oh I knew we were headed south, Angus. How can you go north in an effective way if you don't go south first?"

Alton laughed to himself. He watched the signs as they headed north. This is so exhilarating, he thought. He had no idea what they would find. Yet he knew they would find something. Every clue so far had led them to another great revelation. He felt full of life as he watched God's glorious creation pass before his eyes. As they drove through the cities of Allen, McKinney, Anna, and Sherman, he saw the trees, the grass, the clouds, the expanses of unspoiled land as they got farther north. Oh, how I love this earth, he thought. How I love the beauty God has made. We must not let Sivvius destroy any more of it.

"Alton!" yelled Michael.

Alton snapped out of his contemplative mode.

"Alton, I see the Red River ahead!"

Alton looked ahead, and saw the river. He motioned for Michael to pull over. They got out of the van and looked at the river.

"My friends," said Alton, "Michael has led us to the Red River. A great accomplishment, indeed! This incredible sight awes me, yet I'm troubled, because we've found no clues on our ride northward. Here we are at the Red River, and I sense nothing revelatory. Does anyone else sense anything?"

He looked to the others and saw no indications of revelation.

"I believe it's time for us to seek deeper knowledge. We need some motion. I believe it's time for the circle walk."

Alton reserved the circle walk for times of exhaustion when they had little energy left for significant motion. They were weary after the all-night chicken-wing feast. The circle walk was one of the simpler mind-enhancing processes, yet he was always amazed how it worked so well. He directed the others to gather into a circle and begin the walk. As they walked, each facing another's back, Alton pondered their dilemma and prayed. They had found the Red River, yet now were stumped. He hoped the walk would bring some insight. The walk went on in silence for quite some time. Alton was not sensing any ideas, and apparently neither were the others. He was about to suggest another approach when Patrick broke the silence.

"McKinney!" exhaled Patrick loudly. "We must go to McKinney!"

"How do you know this?" asked Alton.

"The circle has inspired me and brought wisdom. Remember the clue from the tub?"

"What clue, laddie? You mean the part about baskets?"

"No, no. The M&Y. It must surely stand for McKinney!"

"But what about Melissa?" barked Angus. "We passed a town called Melissa on the way north as well. It doesn't have a Y but maybe the Y means somethin' else."

"No, no, no, Angus! It can't be Melissa. I just know it! It must be McKinney, especially since it has a Y in it. And it's south of the Red River."

Alton noticed a strong look of skepticism on Angus's face.

"Everything okay, Angus?" asked Alton.

"Aye, Alton. I think so. Just somethin' that doesn't feel quite right. Could be I'm just tired."

"Well, try not to worry, Angus," said Alton. "What Patrick says makes sense. And we must try something. Let us head to McKinney!"

Patrick grabbed the keys from Michael, hurried everyone into the van, and headed south. He drove well above the speed limit, and they reached McKinney in record time. To Alton, Patrick seemed overly intense, but he continued to trust that Patrick knew what he was doing.

# Chapter 25
## Sunday, 2:00 p.m.

"I know right where we need to go!" said Patrick excitedly. "I know we will find what we seek right here on Louisiana Street."

"How do you know this, my leader in food?" asked Michael. "As my master in all things of food, you have never given advice in the area of travel."

"Ahhhh, you shall see. Soon you shall see the wisdom of my ways. In fact, look ahead, my food apprentice. Look ahead on your right!"

Alton noticed Michael's eyes open wide, but couldn't figure out why. He saw nothing unusual or exciting. What he did see was a look of something unpleasant forming on Angus's face.

"Do you see it now?" asked Patrick.

"Oh yes great master of food," Michael responded. "You are so sneaky in such a delightful way!"

Alton looked everywhere, but still couldn't see anything remarkable. Patrick took a hard right turn and entered a parking lot. He parked the van, jumped out, and boldly walked up to the front door. He turned around, beaming. Alton realized what Patrick's scheme was, and he thought to himself how effective he had been in getting them all here. He chuckled to himself. He knew he had been duped. He noticed Angus was not taking it so well, and could see the agitation building on his face. Just as it looked like Angus was going to unleash a vicious tirade filled with all kinds of terrible words, Patrick cut him off at the pass.

"Angus, our leader in all things physical. Alton, our honorable leader of leaders, and all of you, my esteemed colleagues. Please do not be angry with me. This stop is essential, I believe, to the success of our mission. Yes, here we are at a Dairy Queen. But this stop is about much more than food! It's that which will prepare us for what is next. We must be at rest, and have no hunger distractions as we delve into our next adventure."

"I knew it!" shouted Angus. "You led us through all this just so you could have your blasted ice cream with hot fudge."

"But Angus, it's about more than the hot fudge! We must prepare for the search ahead."

"There are many things I'd like to say, most of which you wouldn't enjoy. But I'll hold my tongue for now, and hope your piggery somehow inspires you to do somethin' productive. But if your lust for the hot fudge has led us astray—"

"I think Patrick might be leading us on the right path, Angus," said Walter. "I can't fully explain it yet, but the more I think about the clues on the tub faucet, the more I think McKinney is the right place."

"Could be," said Angus. "I hope you're right. Patrick, you'd better hope what Walter just said is right!"

"Of course he's right, Angus," said Patrick with a huge smile. "So let's go in. Let the piggery begin!"

Patrick led the charge into the DQ. Michael rushed in right behind, nearly trampling Alton. Alton was looking forward to hearing them place their orders—he knew this was going to be really good.

"Can I help you?" asked the young girl at the counter.

"Yes," said Patrick, "I'd like three hot-fudge sundaes with extra hot fudge, two strawberry sundaes, and a caramel sundae. Please drizzle the toppings generously and evenly over the ice cream, and be sure to add five cherries to each of the sundaes. I'd like the cherries embedded within the ice cream itself rather than placed upon the outer surface. A layering technique should prove effective. Please also ensure each column of ice cream extends precisely four inches above the top edge of each dish, and do not allow there to be any columnar lean."

"Sounds a bit tricky, sir, but I'll do my best. And what about you, sir?" she asked Michael.

"I believe I'll go with the banana split, but with slight modifications to the design. I'd like the tips of the bananas sliced off and placed at either end of the dish so there will be banana content on all four sides of the dish. I'd also like the three toppings to be hot fudge, strawberry, and pineapple, but with the toppings only along the outer edges of the bananas. And please ensure the pineapple is only placed at the ends of the dish, not on the sides. Please also ensure you do not allow the pineapple to touch the other toppings. I prefer to let the toppings gently mix over time as the ice cream transforms into a less-solid state. Next, please hide three cherries somewhere within the ice cream ... let your creative side have some fun with this. Could be you put them in separate locations, or perhaps two together and one apart, or possibly even three together. This adds so nicely to the mystery of the consumption! Once you—"

"Hey, come on laddie! Are you gonna take all day? It's bad enough Patrick dragged us here, but now I have to listen to your endless request?"

Michael sped up his request, Angus glaring at him the whole time. When their orders were ready, Michael and Patrick settled in at the nearest table and began feasting. Alton walked over to join them, but the wild flailing of their elbows posed so much danger as they aggressively consumed their concoctions, Alton was forced to sit at a different table.

After they finished the last spoonfuls, Angus prodded Patrick, asking if the ice cream had inspired him enough to know what they were supposed to do next.

"Of course I know, Angus. But I must first visit the men's room. I'll join you outside soon."

As they were leaving the DQ, Patrick pulled Michael aside. "Michael, do you have any idea what we need to do next?" They had not noticed that Alton was still inside, studying the ice cream flavors. He listened to the two intently.

"I'm sorry master. I have no idea."

"Oh dear, what are we going to do? Angus is going to kill me."

"Can you not think of anything else other than that we are supposed to be in McKinney? Nothing about a hill or a foot or baskets?"

"My wise apprentice, let me give you a tip about true mastery of things: Sometimes, the food is what it's all about."

"You mean—"

"Yes. My goal was the ice cream. But you know, I really did get a sense about the M&Y clue. The McKinney part makes sense. And even Walter agreed about McKinney. But what to do next? I'm at a loss. Can you take over and make up something about how to get someplace, like you normally do, and get me out of this mess?"

Alton couldn't help but chuckle.

"What do you mean make up something like I normally do? I am the Travel Director!"

"Then please do some directing, my friend."

"Very well … let me see … oh I know. I know what we need to do! Why don't you say we need to go to the library? Surely McKinney has a library. We can go there to check out some books and find some inspiration about where we need to go next. Perhaps we can do some wallowing in the books and get some type of insight about a hill, a foot, and strong baskets."

"Well ... I guess it's possible this could pacify Angus. He does love libraries. Any idea where the library is?"

"Hang on a second, I'll be right back," said Michael.

Alton hid behind a display as he watched Michael go back to the counter and wiggle his way to the front of the line.

"Excuse me young lady, can you tell me where the library is in this town?"

"Sure! Just head on down the street we're on," she pointed, "and you'll get to the square. It's on one of the streets just north of the square—I think it's Hunt Street. Ask around if you can't find it. There are always plenty of people walking around."

"Why, thank you young lady. You have been most helpful and courteous. Thank you again for making such wonderful creations for us. We shall remember you whenever we partake of ice cream."

"My pleasure, sir."

Michael walked over to Patrick and advised him that he knew the way to the library. As they headed outside to make their announcement that the library was the next place they must go to, Alton remained behind to wait a bit before joining the group. He was still laughing when he eventually left the building, but his laughter stopped cold when he got outside.

\* \* \*

"We meet again, Alton."

Alton froze. The appearance of Sivvius had caught him completely by surprise. He felt a disturbing, sickening, evil presence permeating the air around him. He glanced around for the others but they were not in sight—probably gathered around the side of the building.

"Did you really think you could lose me so easily, Alton? Did you not realize I could easily repeat your jump to Texas? Do you still not comprehend my power?"

Alton stood still, dumbfounded. Could Sivvius have also jumped in time? Could his friends from beyond have shown him how? Surely not. He had to be bluffing. He must have somehow come along with us when we jumped, he thought. It could be since we were in such a stressful situation, I failed to focus clearly enough on only the seven of us jumping. I wonder if he knows we traveled a day ahead. Alton played along.

"Of course I know your power, Sivvius. You have shown me many times. You nearly paralyzed me for life not too long ago."

"Yes, that was incredible, wasn't it? But I'm not going to waste time talking with you today, or telling you about the hundreds of thousands of souls being added to my mighty army. I'm going to use my power again to stop you once and for all. This time you won't recover."

Alton immediately entered into the dance of defense, and yelled at the top of his lungs: "Praise God!" It was the signal they had agreed to use if any one of them needed help. He started singing praises to God.

Sivvius cackled, and began waving his arms in the air above his head. Alton sensed the evil presence growing, thick in the air. Alton sang louder, with more conviction, noticing the look of pain on Sivvius's face. Alton heard the sound of running feet, and soon all members of the Council entered into the dance of defense. They sang together, praising God. Sivvius intensified his gestures, but at the same time, the grimace on his face grew contorted and warped. It was clear he was straining with everything he had to stay focused. He brought his hands down in force, sending the wave. Alton knew it had to be the stop-motion wave. He felt heat, but it was mild. He did not sense any paralysis. He did not sense any loss of knowledge either.

Sivvius raised his hands again and swirled them with more intensity. Alton sang louder. As Sivvius thrust down his hands again, the Council members sang praises and stomped, battling Sivvius with full unity and conviction. Alton felt another mild wave of heat, but nothing drastic. Sivvius thrust his hands down again, and again, and again. But Alton felt no paralysis, no loss of knowledge. Only a mild heat, and a mild tingling sensation. Sivvius was trying knowledge destruction and stop motion, but both were blocked by the dance and the praise.

Sivvius stopped his gestures and stared into Alton's eyes. Alton could see the rage there, amid a deranged look on his face. It was a look so twisted and warped that it was hard not to break his eyes away. Sivvius pushed past Alton, and hurried toward the side of the building. Alton heard a car door slam shut, then a roaring engine and screeching tires as Sivvius swerved the car out of the parking lot and onto the street, nearly slamming into a pickup truck passing by the entrance. As he sped away, he yelled at the top of his lungs, "Enjoy this day, Alton! It could be your last! What we bring next you will never endure!"

Alton watched the car speed off into the distance. When it was out of sight, he gathered the seven into a circle. "Oh God," he prayed, "thank You for Your help today. You are truly a mighty God. You have protected us from evil. I sensed the evil thick in the air today, but You are far more powerful than any evil force. We continue to praise You and thank You for Your mighty power and Your deep love. Thank You for honoring the dance, and showing us how to enhance it, and thank You for inclining Your ear to our praise of Your mighty name!"

"My friends, God has protected us mightily! Sivvius could not hurt us today! No paralysis! No knowledge destruction! Nothing! Praise be to God!"

"Amen!" they all shouted with joy.

"But I know Sivvius won't wait long to try again. I don't know if he realizes yet that we've traveled into the future, but at a minimum, he clearly sees God's power at work in us. The scales are tipped heavily in our favor now. He will be desperate. He already knows of our new ability to change location, but if he realizes we also have the ability to travel in time, he will surely find a way to kill us. He will be so desperate that the small speck of good within him will no longer stop him. I fear we may be just days away, maybe only hours away, from a final confrontation. We must spend much time in prayer, and we must find the answer to the last clues as soon as possible."

"I agree," said Patrick. "Alton, as I recently told the others, I believe we need to go to the library next. I think—"

"I'm still not sure about that, laddie," barked Angus. "Alton, how can you trust Patrick? We all know he brought us here just for the ice cream. I wonder what he has in store for us now. When we get to the library, will it be for more food? For all we know, they're probably havin' some type of food festival there today."

"But Angus," said Patrick, "it's not for food that we go there. The ice cream has already brought the inspiration!"

"Laddie, it's hard for me to believe anything you say when food is involved."

"But believe me, Angus, the library is a good move. Surely that's where we will find inspiration as we wallow in the books."

"Well?" said Angus. He looked to Alton.

Alton nodded his head gently. "We need to try something, and wallowing in piles of books has proved to be of benefit in the past. To read a book while surrounded by books, consumes us with words, and immerses us in knowledge."

"Well, all right. I'll follow you Patrick," said Angus. "But all I've got to say is you'd better be right about this, or I'll put you through a physical-trainin' regimen that will have you cryin' for your mama."

# Chapter 26
## Sunday, 3:30 p.m.

A few minutes later, Patrick pulled into the McKinney library parking lot. Walter bubbled with anticipation as they entered. I just hope we'll find something useful here, and I hope we find it soon, he thought. I can hardly wait to find the next scroll and decipher more code. Walter thought about the last scroll. It was still so hard to believe they had discovered the keys to time travel. So many had tried for so long, and most of the attempts were so futile and filled with complexity and complication. His father had made it so simple.

He brought his thoughts back to the library, and gazed with wonder at the vast collection of books.

"Look at all these books!" he blurted out. "Isn't this wonderful? I'm so happy to see this library keeps so many actual books. Everything's so virtual nowadays. This is so refreshing!"

"Please be quiet, sir!" scolded the librarian. "We do have people trying to concentrate, you know."

"I'm sorry, but this place is so amazing. And I believe it will help us."

"Well, that is great, but as you are helped, please be helped in a quiet way."

Walter leaned over to Patrick, and whispered in his ear, "Where should we wallow?"

"It's probably best if we go to one of the back sections away from people, so we can wallow freely," said Patrick. "Follow me."

Patrick led the others to an area far away from the front desk, and found an aisle with no people. The group migrated toward the end of the aisle and Patrick started gently removing books from the shelves and placing them on the ground. The others did the same until the floor was covered in books.

"Okay," said Alton. "It's time to wallow. Now remember, as we—"

"Sir! What are you doing?" The librarian stood at the end of the aisle, scowling at Alton.

"I'm so sorry, miss, if we've caused an issue here, but we need to engage in a wallowing session."

"Well, I'll say you've caused an issue! Look at this mess! What is wrong with you men? Have you no concern for order and proper conduct?"

"Again, miss, we meant no harm—"

"Let me handle this," said Angus.

Angus sauntered over to the woman, put his arm around her shoulder and gently led her away from the aisle. Walter could not hear what was said, but the sweetest laugh eventually drifted down the aisle. He saw the librarian appear at the end of the aisle again, holding a hand over her mouth to mute the laughter. "You boys can wallow for a bit if you like. Mr. Angus here is such a gentleman, and has helped me to understand what's going on. Please, Mr. Angus, tell me more."

Walter remembered how Angus had shown himself to be a bit of a ladies' man at Southfork, and had apparently used his sweet-talking again. After they finished their wallowing and were on their way out of the library, Walter noticed the librarian flashing Angus a smile. One day Ingrid will flash me a smile like that, he thought.

Once outside the library, Alton gathered them together. "Has the wallowing brought insight to anyone?"

"Wallowing," said A.

"Wallowing," said B.

"Books all around," said A.

"Books," said B.

"A foot," said A.

"A foot," said B.

"A hill," said A.

"A hill after a foot," said B.

"A hill after a foot is foothill!" shouted A.

"Foothill!" shouted B.

"South of a foothill," said A.

"Where baskets are strong," said B.

"South of a foothill," said A.

"South of foothill," said B.

"Foothill could be a street," said A.

"Foothill must be a street," said B.

"South of Foothill must be baskets," said A.

"Baskets south of Foothill," said B.

"Baskets south of Foothill," said A.

"Find Foothill," said B.

"Find Foothill," said A.

"I think you may have it!" said Alton. "I think you're onto something. I believe the wallowing has brought insight. The clue may truly be referring to a street in McKinney called Foothill. We need to find this Foothill and then look south of it for baskets."

Walter pulled out his cell phone and did a Google search for Foothill Road in McKinney. His heart raced when it pulled up a location. "Here it is!" he yelled as he pointed to his phone. "Look! Foothill Road. Let me get some directions from here to there." He tapped the location and played around with the map. "It's really close—just on the other side of highway 75 and a bit south."

"Let's go!" said Patrick. "What did I tell you Angus? You see the power of the hot fudge? It led us to the library and now to Foothill Road."

Angus just shook his head, almost spoke, then shook his head again.

They piled into the van, with Patrick at the wheel and Walter serving as navigator, and quickly arrived at Foothill Road, just off Park View Ave in McKinney. They sat in the van for a few minutes looking around.

"Well now what, you bunch of wilddoggers?" asked Angus.

"I believe the oilman term for that would be wildcatters," said Patrick.

"Are you questioning my vast knowledge of Texas oilman culture, you pork shank? Better keep that yap shut or I'll wilddog you right into the next county."

"I say we simply park the van here and walk south of Foothill," said Alton. "These baskets we're looking for could be anywhere, perhaps even a decoration in someone's yard, and I would hate to drive right by them. Keep your eyes peeled for anything looking like a basket."

The others nodded their heads and followed Alton as he left the van and walked west on Foothill. When they reached the end of Foothill, they headed south on Inland Lane and eventually reached North Brook Drive. As Walter looked west on North Brook, he noticed an area on the left that looked like it could be a park.

"It looks to me like there may be a park on the left side of this street just west of here," said Walter. "I find it interesting there would be such a major feature south of Foothill Road. It could be of some significance. Let's check it out."

After walking around the park for a few minutes, they noticed a paved bike trail and decided to follow it. After about a half mile of walking, Angus grew impatient.

"This seems to be wasted time," said Angus. "How are we supposed to find baskets on this trail? Shouldn't we head back to the houses? And you're walkin' so slow, Walter. Are you daydreamin' about your lost lass again? I think it's time we—"

"Wait!" shouted Walter. "What's that ahead on the right?" Walter ran ahead of the others into a small clearing on the right of the trail. He stopped his breath short as he confirmed his first impression. He saw what looked like a basket. A metal basket. A *strong* basket. It was one of the baskets on a Frisbee-golf course.

"Alton!" he screamed. "Alton! A basket! I found a basket! A metal basket. On this Frisbee-golf course. I think the clue was about these metal baskets. They are south of Foothill and they are strong. Very strong."

When they all reached the basket Walter had found, they began examining it, fumbling over each other. They checked the basket chains designed to cause a Frisbee to drop into the bottom area, they checked the pole mounting the basket into the ground, and ultimately checked every square inch of the structure.

"Well I can't believe I'm gonna say this," said Angus, "but I think Walter came through this time. I don't see any clues on this basket, but where there be a basket, there'll be more baskets. Let's move on and find some others."

A short distance farther along the trail, they crossed a bridge over a creek, and on the other side of the creek, Walter saw more baskets to the left. He ran over to one of them and started inspecting it. The others spread out to check the other baskets in the area.

"Make sure you check the poles very closely," Walter yelled to the others. "If there's going to be any type of clue on one of these baskets, it sure seems like it would be etched into the pole. That's the only part of the structure that appears to have enough surface area to contain a message."

After a few minutes of close inspection with no results, Walter looked around to find another basket. The baskets in the immediate area were still being inspected by the others, so he walked back toward the path after the bridge and noticed more baskets on the other side of the path. He arrived at one in a secluded area by the meandering creek and began his inspection. He traced his fingers along the pole's surface, working from top to bottom. He felt a surge of hope as his fingers passed over a rough area near the base of the pole. He knelt by the basket, detached a magnifying glass clipped to his pants, and looked closely at the base of the pole. He jerked when he heard Angus. Walter had been so focused, he hadn't even heard Angus approaching.

"Did you find somethin', laddie?"

"There's etching, Angus. And it may be the same type of code we've seen in the scrolls. Let me see—"

"Hey, Alton!" shouted Angus. "Get the others over here. Looks like Walter might've found somethin'."

After a few minutes of focused inspection and with all the others now gathered around the basket, Walter lifted his head and beamed a smile toward Angus. He looked back to the base of the pole and stared through the magnifier.

"The markings are very tiny," said Walter. "And I can barely make them out with this magnifier ... but it's definitely the same code as was on the scrolls ... and yes ... it says ... it translates as ... brother and sister together ... near the land ... that let you ... that let you in ... a view to the left ... and a ... and a ... hum. That's it ... brother and sister together near the land that let you in. And then the comment about a view to the left and a hum."

"That's it? What do we do with that, laddie? What is this talk of a brother and a sister? We haven't met any brother and sister. And what land? This is much too vague. What in all things Scottish do we do with this?"

"Hmmm," said Alton. "Definitely vague, but interesting. Especially the hum part. Letters … any ideas?"

"Brother," said A.

"And sister," said B.

"Brother and sister," said A.

"Hmmm," said B.

"Hmmm," said A.

"Not sure," said B.

"The land," said A.

"The land that let us in," said B.

"It let us in," said A.

"What land?" said B.

"The land that let us in," said A.

"Let us in to what?" said B.

"In to the land," said A.

"It let us in," said B.

"Let in," said A.

"In … let," said B.

"In … let," said A.

"Inlet!" shouted B.

"Inlet!" shouted A.

"You have done it again, Letters," said Alton. "The land that let us in is Inlet. It makes perfect sense. We must go back to Inlet! I'm not sure about the other parts of the clue yet, but it seems that we may find the rest in the very place we were before."

"Alton," said Michael, "I wonder if we should use the sprays again to save time. Should we consider spraying to Inlet?"

"The sprays you say? I know we need to save time, but the sprays? I'm not sure we dare try them again before we receive more direction from the next scroll. Although it seems we've used them successfully so far, we can't be sure if we've done so without negative repercussions. To use the sprays again, so soon, appears to me to be a great risk. I don't feel the time is right."

"But Alton," said Michael, "how can we afford to wait? Knowledge calls us. Sivvius seeks us. We must move fast!"

"Yes!" agreed Walter. "We need to move quickly, Alton. Are you sure we can afford to lose so much time arranging flights and such?"

"You put me in a precarious position. I'm afraid to release the sprays again so soon. We have not fully investigated the repercussions yet. Our last jump to Texas moved us ahead in time, and I had not intentionally done that. I had planned for only a location jump. A fleeting thought of the next day could have caused it. Or maybe my durations were off since there were seven of us in the jump instead of just one. We need to do more experimentation before we risk another long-range jump.

"I think it would be wiser to fly. We can spend the evening in a hotel here in McKinney and head to the airport in the morning. That way we can take tonight to do more testing. Even though I don't want to use the sprays for a jump to Inlet, we need to get ready for what is coming … for who is coming … for the final battle that is imminent. I have an idea of how to stop Sivvius for good, but I'm not ready yet."

\* \* \*

They got back to the van, left Foothill Road and soon found a nice hotel in McKinney, not far from where they were. They gassed up the van and then went back to the hotel to check in. After settling in, they met back at the van and drove to another local park that the front desk attendant had mentioned was very quiet and would be relatively empty so late in the day.

They spent time perfecting short-range jumps of one person and then two people, eventually working up to where the entire Council could jump together. Many of the jumps, especially with six or seven, were highly unpredictable, with the Council members arriving at the desired destination spread quite far apart. They had to try many variations of durations and sequences to get it more precise when moving the full Council. Alton thanked God they had somehow managed to stay relatively close together when they had done the spontaneous jump to Texas.

Alton then practiced sending one at a time on a jump, while he stayed fixed in place. He spent a long time on this, getting confidence to try the next, much more risky jump.

"I'm going to try a short time jump for the first time. I'll do it with just me to start with, but before we retire to our hotel tonight, I'd like to attempt to send someone else to the past for a few brief moments. Then I'll join them in that time and bring them back to our time.

"I'm going to think of a very recent time, about two hours before we got to the hotel in McKinney. I don't want to take any risk of being seen by anyone when I appear, so I noticed that little gas station we stopped at near the hotel had a secluded area off to the side with no parking—just a Dumpster and some old wood pallets. It appeared to be an area where people wouldn't hang out or even walk by, unless they were attending to garbage or stashing pallets. I can also pop in to the convenience store at the station when I get there to do a quick day and time check—there are newspapers and a clock in there. I'll be there before we got there earlier today, so there's no risk I'll see myself or any of you in the past—just too many ramifications to that at this point. As soon as I verify the day and time there, I'll jump back to this time. I may be seen when I enter the store, but at least I won't be appearing out of nowhere."

Alton saw the others fidgeting and noticed the concern on their faces.

"Don't worry. I shall be careful. Pray for me. And please, stand a good thirty feet from me."

Alton was very tense, and wanted to get this first attempt done before fear overtook him. He had thought the process through many times and was as ready as he'd ever be. He focused intensely on the location by the Dumpster, and on the exact time he wanted to arrive to. He thought of time equaling mass as well. His thoughts were in a steady cycle: location, time, time equals mass … location, time, time equals mass. On and on it went. He then pulled out the sprays and sprayed the first, then the second, then with his heart racing, the third. He felt the lightness, and then he was standing by the side of the gas station.

"Oh my God! I think it worked!"

He touched his arms and legs, felt his head—he was all there. He felt no pain, no ill effects. He felt perfectly fine. He darted into the convenience store and quickly checked the date on the newspaper and the time on the clock. He felt joyful as he verified it was the right day, and within about five minutes of his desired arrival time of two hours earlier. He stood there for a few seconds, taking in the surroundings, making sure everything looked and felt okay.

When he was convinced all was well, he darted back outside to the side of the building, went through his thought process, focusing on the exact time and place he had just left from, and then sprayed the sprays. After he sprayed the third, the lightness came, and he was standing around the others again. He breathed a huge sigh of relief as they gathered around him, and his wristwatch confirmed he had been gone only for a few minutes.

"Alton, you're back!" yelled Walter. "How do you feel?"

"I feel great. What did it look like when I left?"

"Just the same as when we did our other location-only jumps," said Walter. "You faded and then disappeared. What was it like there? Did it work? Did you really go back in time?"

"Yes, I went back in time. Within five minutes of the target time."

The others went wild, jumping around, yelling, slapping each other's backs and shaking hands.

"It's still hard to believe it really worked," said Alton. "But it did. It really did."

They continued jabbering for nearly fifteen minutes, discussing the implications and the possibilities. They could have gone on for hours, but Alton was anxious to try the next experiment. He did the next jump with Walter at his side, then with Angus. Both jumps were successful, there and back.

When it was time to send someone else alone, Alton was very nervous, especially since it was his dearest friend Walter who insisted on being the first. Fortunately, the jump with Walter worked fine as well. Alton sent him alone, went to meet him thirty seconds afterwards, and they returned together. No major issues or problems. Some minor inaccuracies occurred as they practiced more—a little too close to the Dumpster once, off by a few minutes of target time most times, but nothing substantial. With practice, they would get much better. They had done it. They had really done it. Alton could not believe it was true.

They piled into the van and drove back to the hotel, unable to stop talking about one of the most incredible nights of their lives.

# Chapter 27

# 30 Years Earlier

"That's a good boy, Eddie. You are such an angel."

"Thank you, mama! I love to read."

"And such a good reader you are. Do you realize you read all the way through the book of Matthew without one mistake?"

"Really, mama?"

"Yes, my sweet little Eddie. All the way through with no mistakes! Now tell me, what do you remember most about what Jesus said in the book of Matthew?"

"I like the part best where Jesus talks about loving each other. It's so beautiful, mama! Jesus has such love and He always gives it. It is super-neat how Jesus wants us to love each other the way He loves us. I want to love like that, mama."

Eddie's mother paused for a few moments. She had a hard time holding back tears. She could not believe what her sweet little son had just said. He had grasped what most never find. He had grasped what she was finally starting to see that her husband had only pretended to find. What she thought was her husband's love was nothing more than his selfish desire for all his needs to be met. And now that she was older and not quite as slim and gorgeous, her husband showed her less affection each day. She saw less and less of him in the evenings. Late nights had become the norm. She knew there were other women. She could smell the evidence as he snored away the nights in their bed.

She wanted to confront him, but each time she would try to bring it up, she would regret it. Her arms still hurt from the previous night when he squeezed them until she screamed. And she could not even touch her stomach; he had hit her so hard she had lost consciousness. She was afraid of him like never before. And just as afraid to tell anyone about it for fear that he would follow through on his threat to hurt Eddie if she did so. She had become an expert at hiding her wounds; clothes took care of that, since he was careful about never hitting her face and exposing his brutality to the world.

She looked lovingly upon her sweet, gentle son, and she feared for his safety. She hoped and prayed with all her heart that her son's desire to love as Jesus loved would not be destroyed by her husband.

\* \* \*

Eddie sat in the woods near his house, brooding. He could not believe it had been almost half a year since his father had beaten his mother so badly that it damaged her brain. His father had mastered the technique of punching her on the back of her head so the bruises would be hidden by her hair, but the hair could not hide the effects on her brain. She lived in that strange place now, wandering around … mumbling. So many times he had gone to see her but she did not know who he was any more. She didn't know who anyone was any more. She wasn't really even his mama any more. His mama was gone and the uncle that had moved in to take care of him was just as mean-spirited as his father was. He hated what his father had done. He hated what he had done to him. It didn't ease his pain in the least when his father was sent to prison. That did nothing to make his mother well. It was too late for her. He hated God for letting his father hurt them so. He grew to hate God more and more each day. He grew to hate even those who followed God in any way. He gripped the sickle tighter in his hand.

\*    \*    \*

Young Alton sat in the woods behind his house, watching the leaves of his favorite tree blow in the wind. The massive leaves of the mighty red oak made such a peaceful noise as the wind caused them to flutter. Sometimes when he closed his eyes, the sound of the leaves was like the sound of the ocean. He would imagine himself sitting by the water, feeling it lapping against his legs as he breathed in the sweet salty air. He could almost taste it. And sometimes he could swear he heard God speaking to him through the leaves. He could swear he heard God answering his prayers through the leaves.

He heard a woodpecker bang wildly against a branch above him. He thought it was so neat how the bird would show up every time he sat by the tree. It was a tapping that had been magical to Alton, a special kind of bird-music, a master musician at work, a bird that lived as the drummer in God's magnificent bird-band.

Alton was mesmerized as he breathed in the wonderful aroma of jasmine and the sweet, fresh scent of blackberry bushes. He felt such peace as the gentle breeze blew across his face and ruffled his hair. All of it was incredible to him: all a sign of God's love. It reminded him that God cared for him, that He had made the earth for people to enjoy.

His mind drifted to thoughts of his best buddy, Eddie. "Oh God," he prayed, "I am so sad for Eddie. And I miss our times together so much! We had so much fun, and we discovered so many things together. God, I hate seeing what's happened to him. He's so mean and so evil. He never used to make fun of the other kids in school. And the names he calls them … I can't even believe it … and the way he beats them up … it's awful. He won't even listen to me when I ask him how I can help. He just looks at me in that strange way. Oh God, I miss my bud so much! Please, God, help him. He has no love left in his life. With his mama locked away in the home, Eddie has nobody. He won't ask me for help, and I know he hates You. Please, God, help bring out the good in Eddie again … I know it's still there."

Alton was startled when he heard footsteps behind him. He whipped his head around and saw Eddie walking toward the tree.

"Eddie! How you doin', bud?"

"Shut up, freak of nature. What are you doing by that stupid tree? What are you looking at anyway? It's a tree, all right? How many times can you look at it? I suppose you're praying again, too. I just don't know why you waste your time. God doesn't care."

Alton sat frozen. He saw the sickle in Eddie's right hand. Eddie was waving it back and forth, right next to the blackberry bushes on the trail. The look on Eddie's face was contorted and filled with hate. The hate scared Alton so much that he dry-heaved, choking on the fear that filled him. He felt chills of terror race up and down his spine.

He had never sensed such hate from Eddie. It was as if something had snapped in him. He watched him move closer to the blackberry bushes at the edge of the trail. He stood there, slowly waving the sickle back and forth, just at the edge of the bushes. He kept staring at Alton, the scowl on his face growing more grotesque by the moment. He began waving the sickle more quickly, and inched closer to the bushes. The sickle started to clip the edges, leaves started to fly off, and branch tips started to snap.

"No Eddie!" screamed Alton. "What are you doing?"

Eddie laughed, a sick, demented sound, and swung the sickle wildly, thrashing the bushes, scattering blackberries and leaves and branches all over the trail. The slashing intensified as Eddie started barking out strange words Alton had never heard before.

"Stop, Eddie! Please stop!"

"Shut up freak-boy—nature wimp. Shut up before I slash you with this sickle. See how easily I destroy what God made? Just like He let my father destroy my mother."

Eddie's slashing got wilder, ripping life from the bushes. Then he moved to some flowers, scattering the petals into the wind. Alton sat in bewildered agony. He felt terrified and completely helpless.

Eddie suddenly stopped his slashing. Alton stared as Eddie stood there panting, leaning on the sickle. Then he walked toward Alton, a scary cackle seeping out from his throat. He waved the sickle back and forth as he approached. All Alton could do was sit there paralyzed with fear, helplessly waiting for Eddie to slash him. But Eddie walked right by Alton and up to the base of the mighty oak. He swung the edge of the sickle down hard into the truck, gouging out a chunk of bark.

"No Eddie! Not the tree! Please stop!"

Eddie glanced back at Alton with a deranged, possessed look on his face. His cackling laugh continued as he turned back to the tree, swinging the sickle into the bark again and again. Huge chunks fell to the ground. He began jumping up and swinging at the lowest branches, ripping leaves from limbs, tearing off branch tips. He kept slashing as sweat poured down the back of his neck and dripped off his arms. All Alton could do was sit there in agony, watching his beloved tree being ravaged. He was too afraid to try to stop Eddie.

Finally, Eddie slouched to the ground, his back resting against the scarred trunk, his chest heaving. He stared deep into Alton's eyes.

"What do you think of this stupid tree now, freak boy? It looks like crap. Did your so-called God do anything to stop me? Did your God protect the tree? No! I tell you again, you moron ... He doesn't care. Don't waste your time trying to talk to Him."

"Eddie, what's happened to you? We used to have so much fun. You used to like these woods. We used to explore them together. And you never used to hate God. Let me help you. Can I pray for you?"

"What! You've got to be kidding me! Pray for me? You are so stupid, Alton. Your prayer will do nothing. I'm so sick of seeing you sit by this tree every day, praying to a God who is way too busy to listen to us. That is, if He even really exists. I begin to wonder about that."

Eddie grabbed the backpack he had thrown by the base of the tree. He attacked the zipper, opened the pack and reached in. Eddie's cackling laugh started in again as he pulled something out. Alton heard a sloshing sound, like water in a canteen. As soon as Alton saw the top of the container, he knew what it was. He caught a subtle whiff of what was inside.

"Oh God, Eddie. Please ... no ... please ... stop."

Eddie said nothing. He just stared at Alton as he pulled the container out of the pack. He unscrewed the cap slowly, appearing to savor the moment. When the cap fully released its hold, Eddie let it fall to the ground. The odor was unbearable to Alton. He never minded the smell of gasoline before—even kind of liked it when his dad would fill the car. But today the odor was awful, evil. He knew he would never like the smell again. He watched helplessly, paralyzed by disbelief and fear, as Eddie poured the gasoline all over the base of the tree. His cackling grew into a wild frenzy as he swung the container frantically back and forth, splashing gasoline as high onto the tree as he could.

Alton pushed himself up off the ground. He knew he had to try to stop Eddie. But just when he got to his feet, Eddie ran over, punched him in the gut, and kicked his head hard when he doubled over. Alton fell to the ground, whimpering in pain, barely able to breathe. He had all he could do just to watch Eddie as he ran back to the tree, striking a match and throwing it at the trunk. Flames leapt up the tree. There had not been rain for days, so the bone-dry tree flared up quickly. It was like a nightmare. Alton watched helplessly as the flames consumed the tree, burning away the bark and the leaves. He felt the heat from the inferno against his face. He heard Eddie laughing, saw him staring at him, enjoying watching the tears stream down Alton's face. The sound of the leaves and the branches cracking and popping as they were consumed, coupled with the fanatical laughter of Eddie, forced Alton to clamp his hands over his ears. He closed his eyes and turned his head away. He could not believe what was happening. He prayed with all his might for God to save the tree.

Eddie kicked Alton's left leg.

"Pray all you want, moron. It won't matter. Just enjoy the campfire!"

Eddie walked off with a bounce in his step, cackling as he went. When Alton could not hear him any more, he screamed out in pain and sat there helpless, sobbing, as the tree continued to burn. He prayed for God to save it. He prayed and prayed, refusing to leave his beloved tree. He prayed until he could not keep his eyes open, and drifted off into sleep.

He slept for hours, curled up in a fetal position, until he was jarred awake by a cracking sound. When he opened his eyes, he didn't know where he was. He thought maybe he just had a terrible nightmare, until he smelled the charred tree. It smelled the same as his neighbor's house did after it had burned to the ground just a month before. It was an awful smell, an odor he could taste. It had been like someone forcing him to eat burned, black-as-coal, bone-dry toast that clung to the inside of his mouth and got stuck in the back of his throat.

His stomach heaved as he walked up to the tree and looked at it more closely. At least it was still there, but the leaves were all gone and the intricate bark he would study every day had lost its features. The trunk looked like a burnt-out log in a fireplace. His stomach knotted in agony and he could barely hold back the vomit. He heard the cracking sound again, and realized it was the branches above, weakened by the inferno, cracking from within.

Even in the midst of this living nightmare, Alton still felt hope. At least God had not let the tree burn away into nothingness. At least the shell remained. He looked into the sky and prayed with all his might. He asked God to heal the tree and make its leaves grow back. Tears streamed from his face as he cried out to God. He cried until it felt as if there was no liquid left in his body. He focused so intensely during his prayer that his mind felt washed out, drained of its energy. It was as if someone had gotten inside his head and scrubbed away all his thoughts with sandpaper.

When he had no strength left for prayer, he stood and walked away. He could not believe what had happened. He could not believe what Eddie had done. Eddie has truly lost it, he thought.

As he trudged along, walking back toward his home, hope for his tree now virtually gone, he heard a cracking sound again, very loud this time. He glanced back, expecting to see a branch fall from the tree. But he saw no branch fall. He heard another loud crack, but again, no branch fell. He continued looking up into the tree, and he could swear he saw a glimmer of something green on one of the branches.

He ran back toward the tree and stared into the branches, squinting, focusing so hard it hurt. As he stared, he definitely saw something green. And it seemed like more green was appearing. He rubbed his eyes with his fingers and looked up again. More green! There was something green appearing on the branches! As he continued to stare, more green appeared ... taking shape ... many small bits of green seemingly growing larger. Then a branch right above his head magically sprouted an array of beautiful, wonderful, magnificent leaves. Bright green leaves, with huge veins forming along the surfaces! He could hear the tree rustling as the leaves grew everywhere. A beautiful, wonderful rustling. It was music to his ears. As he looked at the trunk, he saw fresh, new bark forming. It grew as he watched, flowing up from the base of the tree like hot wax flowing across a table.

He fell on the ground in disbelief, gawking at the tree as it completely regenerated into what it had been before the terrible burning. But it was even better than before. The leaves seemed larger and greener. They were so vibrant he could almost feel the life in them. Their veins looked like they were pulsing with life. The bark formation was so intricate that he longed to study the patterns, to see what new intricacies God had created. He knew God had answered his prayer, performed a miracle, and fixed the tree. He bowed his head in a prayer of thanksgiving.

\* \* \*

Eddie watched from a distance, utterly baffled. He kept rubbing his eyes and shaking his head, not believing what he was seeing. The tree, just as it was before he lit it up. No— better. Such a vibrant green, the branches full with leaves "How can this possibly be?" he whispered. "I burned the tree! I saw it! It was in flames. Now there's not even a black spot on it.". Then he noticed Alton kneeling by the trunk, hands raised high.

As he walked closer, he could hear Alton thanking God for answering his prayers and miraculously healing the tree. His face flushed with rage as he heard Alton's prayers. He refused to believe Alton's prayers had anything to do with it. It was not God who fixed the tree, he thought. It was a freak of nature. God doesn't care. There is some logical explanation. The flames must have gone out right after I left. I probably didn't put enough gas on that stupid tree. It's a good thing I brought more ... this time I'll make sure I do it right. And I'll wait this time. I'll light up this tree and I'll sit here and wait until it collapses in a heap of ashes.

"Hey, freak-boy!"

Alton snapped out of his prayer and jumped up.

"Eddie! Look what God has done! See His power? See His wisdom? Isn't it beautiful? Even more awesome than before! Look at the leaves. See how they look alive? And look at this bark ... it is so beautiful. Eddie, God really is awesome! Can you believe what He has done? See? He does listen ... He does care!"

Eddie stood there, completely disgusted. He hated Alton's joy. He hated the tree. He took off his backpack and pulled out the container. He said nothing. He just walked past Alton, up to the base of the tree and started splashing gasoline all over it again.

*   *   *

Alton did not understand. "Mighty God, doesn't Eddie see what You have done? How can he not believe this is a miracle from You?" Alton smelled the gas as Eddie splashed it on the tree. He heard Eddie's sickening, cackling, laugh again. Alton knew there was no way he was going to let him hurt the tree again, especially since God had personally healed it.

He ran up to him and pushed him to the ground, fueled by his passion to protect God's miracle-tree. Eddie jumped up and punched Alton in the face. They fought hard, kicking and punching, with flurries of blows everywhere. He eventually managed to throw Eddie against the tree, hearing the whack of Eddie's back as it slammed against the trunk. Eddie sloughed to the ground and stared up at Alton. The pain on Eddie's face softened Alton for a moment.

"I'm sorry Eddie," he gasped. "I don't want to hurt you, bud. Let's stop. Let's talk ... like we used to. Remember our talks?"

Eddie's gaze hardened and he cackled as he pulled something from his pocket. A book of matches. He struck one.

Alton felt helpless, paralyzed, begging Eddie with his eyes not to light up the tree again. But Eddie sat there, staring, laughing eerily, the match continuing to burn. Alton had to think quickly. He grabbed a rock and threw it toward Eddie's arm, hoping to knock the match away. When the rock hit Eddie's shoulder, his grip on the match let loose and the match fell right onto his pants. There was just enough of a flicker remaining to cause his gas-splattered pants to catch fire. The fire spread lightning fast.

Alton screamed and tried to help Eddie by throwing dirt on his pants, but the flames were too intense to stop. Eddie jumped up and his shirt and hair caught on fire. Alton yelled out for Eddie to roll in the dirt, but he ran around like a chicken being chased down for slaughter. The flames flaring off Eddie were so hot Alton could not even get near him. He continued throwing dirt on him and yelling for him to roll on the ground. Eddie tripped on a root, and fell into a roll right to the edge of a nearby ravine. Alton helplessly watched him tumble over the edge and down the steep hill. Alton ran to the edge of the ravine and saw Eddie rolling and flaming, his limbs flailing wildly. When he reached the bottom, he ended up at the edge of a stream, his body still in flames. Alton ran down, half sliding, bouncing off trees, tripping on roots, barely staying on his feet. As soon as he got to Eddie, he pushed him into the water. He heard the sizzle as water met fire. It was a battle between the two elements, and the water won.

But the damage had been done. Eddie's shirt had melted into his back. His legs were shaking uncontrollably. The backs of his arms looked like blackened catfish, hot off the grill. His hair was gone. Alton inched up to him.

"Eddie ... how can I help? Let me help."

Eddie rolled over and looked at him. It was more than Alton could bear. His face was a bubbled mess, with parts of it appearing featureless, like candle wax that had gelled after the flaming wick was snuffed out. He expected Eddie to cry out for help, and Alton was ready to do whatever he could to ease his pain. But Eddie just looked at him, his deep blue eyes still somehow shining brightly, and he laughed. It was a sick, haunting, cackling laugh that Alton would never forget.

"I swear I will get you back for this someday. I will destroy everything you love."

"But Eddie, it wasn't my fault. I tried to help you!"

Eddie's haunting laugh started to fade. Alton saw his eyes glassing over, the lids half shut. Just before he passed out, his half-open eyes stared into Alton's and he gasped out a few final words.

"You're wrong, Alton. It *was* your fault. I will never forget ... what you have done. And I will never ... ever ... forgive you. You will pay for ... what you have done."

# Chapter 28
# Monday, 6:00 a.m.

Alton arose early the next morning, excited about getting to the airport and heading to Inlet again. He was still full of wonder about what had happened the previous night. He rousted the others and relentlessly pushed everyone to get ready as quickly as possible. Michael insisted on driving to the airport and after they had been on the road for a while, Angus was getting noticeably impatient.

"Michael, are you sure you know where you're goin'?"

"Of course, Angus. I am the Travel Director."

"Like that means anything, laddie. Are we gettin' close to the Dallas Fort Worth Airport?"

"Absolutely. I believe we are, in fact, getting close."

"How close?"

"Oh, I'd say pretty close. You know, with so much travel-directing experience, I've just kind of developed a special sense about these kinds of things."

"So you mean to tell me you really don't know how close we are, I mean, as in miles, or some sort of concrete way of measurin' distance?"

"Oh, no. I never track by miles, it gets too confusing."

"How do you track, then?"

"I just kind of feel it out."

"Feel it out? Have you lost your small mind?"

"Yeah ... I just kind of feel it out. It feels like we're getting close by now. I mean, after all, we've been driving for a long time, so we must be getting close."

"Michael, you double shank wedge. You've got me stressin'. At least tell me which town is close to the airport so we can watch for it."

"Oh I don't track by towns either. That can be dangerous, you know. You could plan a whole trip around reaching a certain town and when you get to where it was supposed to be, maybe the name was changed and you didn't know it so you keep going, looking for the town, and end up driving all the way to some foreign country we are at war with and end up getting shot or thrown in jail. I can see it happening. Town names scare the heck out of me. I know I don't want to get shot … do you?"

"Michael, I just dunno' what to say."

"Pretty amazing insight, eh?"

Angus narrowed his eyes and clenched his fists. Alton figured he'd better jump into the conversation before Angus let loose.

"Michael, let me make sure I understand. You're saying you have no idea how many miles away from the airport we are, and you're also saying you have no idea which towns we are supposed to be passing through. Yet you feel like we're getting close?"

"Yes! See, Angus! Alton understands."

Angus lifted his eyes and glared at Michael.

"But, Michael," said Alton, "you do know we are at least heading in the right direction, correct?"

"Of course!"

"How do you know?"

"Well, if you must know, although I don't track by town, I do occasionally check out the state we are in, and we are still in Texas. Therefore we can't be that far from the Dallas/Fort Worth Airport."

"But, Michael, Texas is a huge state!"

"And?"

Angus jumped back in to the conversation.

"We could be a long ways away from the airport, laddie! We've been drivin' for nearly two hours now! In fact, wait— here comes a sign. Let's see ... it says Corsicana."

"Oh good. Corsicana. We should be getting close then. Dallas should be just south of Corsicana."

"Laddie, Dallas is not south of Corsicana! It's the other way 'round. Do you understand?"

"Oh yeah, but not really."

"What do you mean oh yeah but not really? What's that supposed to mean?"

"It means, oh yeah I realize what you're saying, but yet not really."

"Laddie, you don't have the slightest idea where Dallas is, do you?"

"I feel that I do."

"Did you look at the map or your cell phone? Does the map show that Dallas is south of Corsicana?"

"I hadn't thought about checking the map. I don't like them too much. They kind of confuse me. And you really can't trust the cell phone map apps."

"You mean to tell me you're our Travel Director but you don't use maps of any kind?"

"I guess you could say that."

"You guess I could say that? I did say that, laddie. So what do we do now?"

"We press on, of course. We take it one step at a time. Dallas will find us!"

"Dallas won't find us, hip shank. Give me that map."

"You'll be wasting your time."

"Laddie ... just give me the map!"

"Geez ... all right ... I'll get it."

Michael reached into the door pocket, grabbed the atlas, and handed it to Angus, who opened it, paged through it, and found the map of Texas. He was bouncing his leg up and down while he looked at it, and then he suddenly stopped, still as a stone. Alton could see his face flushing and eyes squinting.

"Michael, look with me," said Angus.

Michael peered over at the map.

"What do you see?" asked Angus as he pointed to Dallas.

"I see Dallas. See! I told you, we are almost in Dallas! I'm right on track."

"Do you see Corsicana?"

"Well, it's right there, isn't it? Just above Dallas?"

"Do you see it above Dallas?"

Michael looked a little more closely. Then he looked even more closely. Then he looked so closely that his nose nearly touched the paper, and the van swerved.

"Be careful, laddie," yelled Angus as he grabbed the wheel. "Are you tryin' to kill us all?"

"Uh, Angus, I don't see Corsicana. This atlas must be out of date."

"Out of date?"

"Yeah … out of date. This must be from back in the 1980's or so, before Texas was considered a state."

"Laddie, Texas was a state long before the 1980's! Besides, this atlas is only two years old. I see Corsicana."

"Oh you do? Oh good! I knew it had to be there! You must have found some small print, eh? Maybe Corsicana gets smaller print since it was not added until later. It's just north of Dallas, isn't it? I bet we're really close, aren't we?"

"Michael, follow my finger."

Michael glanced over at Angus's finger.

"Here's Dallas."

"Yes, I see."

"Now watch where my finger goes."

Michael watched as Angus's finger slowly traced itself downward. It kept going until it stopped just below Corsicana.

"Do you see where my finger is now?"

"Yes, Angus," said Michael, his face reddening.

"Now look at the word above my finger."

"It says Corsicana."

"Exactly, laddie. It says Corsicana. Now, where's Dallas again? Is Dallas above Corsicana? Let me answer for you— aye, it is. And does that mean we've already driven past Dallas? Let me answer for you again—aye. Here's Dallas, and here's Corsicana ... see? Here's Dallas, and here's Corsicana."

Angus kept sliding his finger back and forth between Dallas and Corsicana. He did this for about ten seconds, back and forth, back and forth. Then he gently placed the atlas on his lap, reclined his seat, slouched back, and let out a massive sigh.

"Turn this hunk of metal around, laddie."

Michael eventually got them to the airport, after ongoing and very close supervision from Angus. After they returned the van, they walked toward the airport shuttle area. A shuttle bus pulled up to them well before they reached the boarding area where all the other people were, and the driver asked them to board quickly since he had an emergency pickup at the terminal. They climbed aboard and the shuttle lurched ahead. Just as Alton was wondering why they appeared to be heading away from the airport, the shuttle pulled into a vacant lot. The driver parked at the far end of the lot, in a very secluded area.

"What's going on, driver?" asked Alton. "Is there a problem with the shuttle bus?"

There was a cackling laugh from the front of the shuttle as the driver pulled off his hat and removed the wig.

Alton felt chills of fear race through his body.

# Chapter 29
# Monday, 11:00 a.m.

Alton stared at Sivvius in disbelief. How had he not sensed him? It must have been because he was still so consumed with thinking about their successful time-jumping experiments. He had let his guard down again. It was so hard to stay on guard every moment.

"Surprised, Alton?" cackled Sivvius.

Alton remained silent.

"Well, now I have you where I want you. Our last encounter at the Dairy Queen was not a good day for me … not a good day at all. But this is a new day. And do you know I discovered something, Alton? I was so amazed at how you pulled me to Texas. Had no idea how you did it. I was thinking how awful that was, how you had such an incredible ability. But then I realized it was even worse than I thought. I found out there had never been anything wrong with my watch. I kept thinking both the time and the date were incorrect due to a bad battery, but then today I saw the newspaper. Today it finally hit me. Today I realized that today is really yesterday, at least as far as our chronological ages are concerned, relative to everyone else.

"So see, now I know, Alton. Now I know what ability you really have. It's far more than I ever imagined you would be able to do. It's just far too much for you to have. But you know why that doesn't bother me? Do you know why I'm not shaking in my shoes because of your new ability? It's because I have something as well. I have something from my friends that I plan to use against you right now. You give me no choice at this point. Any fear I have of using this new gift, or anything within me that blocks it, I've decided to suppress. I've decided to do what I have to do to stop you. I'll deal with the guilt and the consequences later. You have just simply pushed me too far. You and your moronic friends are getting too dangerous for me to let you ever get away from me again."

Alton was aligning sprays A and B in the large right pocket of his pants. He had made notches on the cans so he could tell the difference between A, B, and C. He also kept C in his left pocket to make the process even easier to follow. Fortunately, the night before, they had practiced the spraying of the seven of them together many times. They had also worked very carefully on how to do directed sprays, so only certain individuals could be jumped without the others going along. He had not tried it with an undesired target so close, but he had no choice.

His hands were trembling as he aligned the cans. He trembled not only because he feared Sivvius, but also because he feared such a long jump again. He hoped their practice sessions would keep this latest jump from becoming an unintended jump. He also hoped he could concentrate enough on the location and on time equaling mass, considering the circumstances.

"Don't do it," said Sivvius. "If you do it, you'll cause rifts in the space-time continuum. When you left me before by using the sprays, you have no idea what problems you set in motion. You can't begin to comprehend how you have already altered the mix of time, space, and matter that you see and feel around you. Use the sprays again and you will see what I speak of. Now, take your hand out of your pocket."

"Sivvius, you know not what you speak of."

"Oh, Alton, you truly are a fool," said Sivvius. "Letter A and B, take the sprays from Alton. Do not let him destroy time. Do not let him alter the delicate balance of the universe. Do not let him stop you from your quest. It's your destiny. You must know that. You know it's your destiny to fully submit to me. With me, you can have all things. Fight against me, and you will end up with nothing. Follow me. You will see that I am the better way. I can make you complete. I can fulfill all your dreams ... right now."

Alton looked at the Letter brothers and saw tormented looks on their faces. He wondered what Sivvius had said to them before. What had he shown them? How could they believe his lies about problems caused by usage of the sprays?

"Sivvius—"

"Silence!" he bellowed. "Letter A ... Letter B ... it's time to prove yourselves. Take the sprays from Alton."

The Letter brothers looked toward Alton.

"Good. Now get the sprays. Give them to me."

Alton broke out in song, praising God. The others joined him, except for the Letter brothers. Alton could tell they were in agony, torn between the Council and Sivvius. At least they seemed unable to fully betray the Council and grab the sprays.

"Oh, Alton," laughed Sivvius. "Such a fool you are. To the very end."

Sivvius raised his hands and started the wild circular motions.

Alton was getting spray A aligned in his pocket. But Sivvius was just about to release whatever it was he had this time.

"Alton, this time, you will die. I think I will miss the opportunities to hurt you again and again, but, still ... you must die. And Letters, you lost your chance. Now die with your moronic leader."

Sivvius's gyrations were at a peak and Alton could tell he was just about to thrust down upon them some unspeakable final blow. Alton thought he had spray A in his hand, but felt the notching on its underside again and realized it was B. He fumbled to find A.

"Goodbye, Alton!" shouted Sivvius.

Alton found A, lined up B next to it, yanked his hand out of his pocket, spritzed A on his arm, then B, grabbed C from his left pocket, and just as Sivvius's arms were coming down, he spritzed C. He focused with all he had in him on time equaling mass, Inlet, the current time, and only the seven of them jumping. The word "sister" slipped into his thoughts but he tried to focus mostly on the word Inlet. He heard Sivvius yelling something, but the voice was drifting away.

He felt lightness, but also heaviness … deep heaviness … death. He felt suspended between two realities, life in one and death in the other. He focused hard and cried out to God.

\*　\*　\*

Alton felt cool air as he collapsed. He was dizzy and fought to stay conscious. He looked around and saw the others on the ground as well.

"One, two, three, four, five, six—oh, thank you God, we all made it," said Alton as he gawked at the beauty around him. They were on a foot trail in the woods, surrounded by massive trees of all varieties, with the sun filtering through the rustling leaves. He couldn't help but sit there and take it all in for a few moments. He finally pushed himself up to check on the others. As he walked toward Walter, his eyes darted everywhere. He was petrified he would see Sivvius, but didn't see him, and sensed no evil presence.

"Are you all okay?" he asked as he helped Walter. There were grunts and groans as the others struggled to stand. Alton checked on all of them. Just as he finished verifying everyone was okay, and there was no evil presence around them, Angus approached him.

"I sure hope you got us to the right place, laddie. Looks like we're on a maintained hikin' trail—I wonder if we're near any trail markers to help us get some bearings?"

"Good question," said Alton. "These look like the same types of trees we saw when we were in Inlet before, but it's hard to know for sure if we're really in Inlet or not. I think I hear some highway traffic nearby. We must be near a main road. Let's follow the sound and see if we're near a trailhead."

They soon arrived at a trailhead with a small parking area right off a main two-lane highway. Alton found a trail marker and his heart leapt when he read it. He motioned for the others to gather around.

"My friends, look at this. It shows mileages to different lakes here. Notice that one is called Sis Lake. I don't see one called brother or bro, but there is clearly a Sis."

"I see," said Walter. "And there is a Bubb Lake. I guess I could see where Bubb could be a very loose, informal meaning for brother. Especially since there is a Sis Lake. Perhaps too strong of a correlation to be meaningless. And it shows Bubb Lake as five tenths of a mile from here, and Sis Lake as nine tenths of a mile from here. Pretty much together."

"What about the Vista Trail?" asked Alton. "It shows to be just two tenths of a mile from here. Why does this Vista sound familiar to me?"

"Wait a minute," said Walter. "The clue talked about brother and sister together, but also about a view, or something like that. This Vista Trail ... could that be what the view comment was about?"

"Now hold your horses, laddies. You're on a wild spin of thought. We don't even know if we're in Inlet. And how did we end up on a trail?"

"When I was getting ready for our time jump," said Alton, "I was thinking mainly of Inlet, but the word 'sister' from the clue snuck into my thoughts. I remember trying to clear the word from my mind to make sure we got to Inlet, but the short form Sis kept rumbling in my mind. And here we are at a trailhead with a sign that shows Sis Lake. Perhaps since I was thinking of Inlet and Sis in the last moments before the jump, the sprays picked one. Even if Sis Lake is not officially in Inlet, it could be close enough for the jump to end here. Hard to know for sure, but it seems plausible."

"I agree," said Walter. "And back to the Vista Trail ... it's only two tenths of a mile from here. It's near Bubb and Sis lakes that are essentially together, and the name Vista is like a view. I remember the last clue about brother and sister together near the land that let us in, and then the comments about a view to the left and a hum. And wait! The clue said brother and sister together *near* the land that let us in. We don't even have to be exactly within Inlet ... just near it. Let's go check out this Vista Trail, and at least see if it's on the left side of the main trail."

"Yes, Walter," said Alton. "I agree. Let's go check out this Vista Trail."

Angus let out a sigh but forged up the trail, leading the way at break-neck pace. "Let's get this done with, laddies. We still have no idea if we're even near Inlet, but whatever we do, we need to do it quickly. No tellin' when that scum of the earth will track us down again."

Within a few minutes, they arrived at a spur trail to the left with a marker identifying it as the Vista Trail. Walter let out a yelp.

"I knew it!" said Walter. "Look! The Vista Trail goes off to the left of the main trail ... a view to the left ... just like the clue said. Let's go!"

"Alton?" said Patrick.

"What is it, Patrick?"

"Are we really okay? Are you sure the jump worked right? Are you sure we didn't cause some type of imbalance?"

"It's hard to know for certain, but it does appear our jump was successful. I can't believe we made it with all that was going on around us in the shuttle. I just hope we didn't cause some major negative space-time consequence by jumping so carelessly, and I hope we are in same time ... not future or past. I hope our practice from last night was good enough."

"But Alton, what was it that Sivvius was trying to do to us? I felt ... I felt like I was dying," said Patrick.

"Me too," said Michael. "It was like nothing I had ever felt before."

The others expressed what they had felt, and fear of a future attack became the main topic of conversation.

"We must not live in fear," said Alton. "Sivvius will attack us again, but we must not fear it. God is with us, and God will help us. Yet we must do our part. We must be ready. We must focus and plan on how to fight such an attack. I believe Sivvius would have killed us if we had not jumped. I heard him yelling something before we jumped, and it sounded like he said essence death."

"Essence death?" asked Patrick with a look of horror on his face.

"Yes, Patrick ... essence death. I believe he has been given his most powerful weapon yet: the ability to completely destroy the life essence of someone. I did not think it possible due to the small good I sensed was still in him, even now. But it seems he was able to suppress it. He must be so desperate. He must know he is on the verge of potentially losing the epic battle."

"Where is he, Alton?" asked Patrick.

"I hope he's still back in Dallas, but we can't count on that. We were under great stress when we did the last jump so I may not have focused clearly enough on only the seven of us jumping. We must be on full alert at all times. We can't afford to be caught by surprise again. We were very fortunate this time. But next time will be our last if we're not ready. Let's spend a few minutes practicing our dance of defense before we check out this Vista Trail. We need to enhance it to be able to stand against the essence death he has in store for us. We must also pray. Our faith must be at its fullest, and our hearts must be steadfast in God."

They practiced the dance of defense, and strategized about how to stand against Sivvius when he would inevitably attack again. Alton sensed very strongly that it would not be long before they faced him once more. As they practiced, Alton noticed the others continuing to glare at the Letter brothers. They had not said a word after the location jump. Angus threatened physical violence but Alton told him to refrain.

Alton noticed the Letter brothers looking at him in agony numerous times. He knew they felt awful. He just hoped they felt awful enough to stand against Sivvius the next time. He walked over to them and put his hands on their shoulders as he spoke to the group.

"Let us begin our ascent up this trail," said Alton. "Let us not fear the unknown. Let us climb as we've never climbed before! Let us find that which we seek before Sivvius finds us again. Whatever he has done, we must find a way to undo it. For he can't be the author of anything good. This I know to be fact. Let us ascend as one. We need each other. Together we can save the world. Apart, all of us will suffer. Be sharp, and listen for the hum the clue mentioned. I hope beyond all hope we will hear the hum."

Angus led them up the trail at a feverish pace initially, but the pace slowed as they ascended the extremely steep slope. After less than ten minutes of climbing, Walter stopped by a group of trees, asking the others to be quiet.

"Aw, c'mon laddie! We're just gettin' under way!"

"Wait … I think I hear something."

\* \* \*

Walter strained to listen. He definitely heard a sound—a very subtle humming. He stepped off the trail and began analyzing some of the trees. The humming seemed to be loudest near one particular tree. As he drew close to the trunk, the humming intensified. He moved away and the humming softened.

"Do you hear it?" he yelled.

"I hear it, Walter!" said Alton. "There is definitely humming. And it got appreciably louder when you drew near to that huge tree."

Walter walked closer to the trunk again, and as the humming intensified, he looked all around the base, hoping to find some secret compartment. He froze.

"What is it, Walter?" asked Alton. "What do you see?"

"There is some sort of marking on this tree. I think it's the same type of coded writing I saw in the scrolls!"

"Really, Walter?" asked Alton. "Read it, Walter, read it!"

"Let me see. It's somewhat hard to read. Let me see. It says … the third … the third … ahh yes … it says the third of three awaits. Then it says … it says … it says that the tips tell the tale. And it says, hum to the tips."

Walter froze again.

"What is it, Walter?" asked Alton.

"I think I see a signature at the end of the inscription on the tree."

"A signature?" asked Alton.

"Yes, Alton, a signature. Let me see if I can decipher it."

Walter leaned closer and studied the signature. His heart was racing. It looked familiar, but still in code. He deciphered the code in his mind. He could not believe it. A tear rolled down his cheek.

"What is it, Walter?" asked Alton. "What is the signature? What moves you so?"

"The name ... the name is ... Jonathan Briggs," said Walter. "It's a confirmation of what I've known in my heart and confessed to all of you when I read the second scroll. Jonathan, my father, is confirmed in writing this day ... as the author of the scrolls!"

"Is the writing he left on this tree the same as that of the scrolls we've seen?"

"Yes, Alton. It's exactly the same."

"Then you are right. It is officially confirmed, as expected. The author of the writing upon the tree and the author of the scrolls is most definitely your father, the greatest scientist of all time!"

Walter's heart leapt as the others cheered and yelled out congratulations. The cheering was cut short with the bark of Angus.

"Okay, laddie—great. Now, what about the clue that was written on the tree?"

"Yes," said Alton. "Let us think quickly. It says that the third of three awaits—clearly a reference to the last scroll. But what of the tips comment? And what could hum to the tips mean? Any ideas?"

As he pondered, Walter felt the ground shift beneath him. A boulder field appeared a few feet away from them. He felt the ground pushing up on his feet. He saw Alton struggling to stand still. Hail fell and then stopped. Lightning shot through the sky and then the sky cleared. Something terrible was happening to the earth.

"Think!" said Alton. "We must find the next scroll now! We must find out how to stop what is happening to the earth. I fear that Sivvius's final attack has begun! Think! What do the words on the tree mean?"

"Alton! We think we have it!" said the Letter brothers.

The others became silent. Even in the midst of the chaos, they held their tongues. Walter watched Alton look deeply into the eyes of the Letter brothers, first A, then B, then back to A. Surely he must be deciding if they could be trusted.

"Please, Alton, let us speak," said A. "Let us help. Let us at least *try* to atone."

"Atone," said B.

Alton looked even deeper into their eyes.

"Tell us, Letter A and B … what is it you have realized?"

"The tips," said A.

"Look to the tips," said B.

"Tips at the top," said A.

"Top tips," said B.

"Tips of the branches," said A.

"Look to them," said B.

"See nothing," said A.

"See nothing but the tips," said B.

"Hum to the tips," said A.

"We hum to the tips?" said B

"Not us, but the tree," said A.

"The tree hums," said B.

"Hum the tree, look to the tips," said A.

"Close to the tree, hum the tree," said B.

"Make the tree hum, then look to the tips," said A.

"Make it hum and look to the tips," said B.

"That's it!" said A. "Walter, you must stand as close to the tree as you can and make it hum as loud as you can. While you do that, we need to be looking to the tips of the branches."

"Letter brothers ... know now you have been with us for a reason!" said Alton. "It was your destiny to be the ones to decipher the clues upon this tree. Know that Sivvius is not the way to good things. He can only lead others into a life of pain. Now, Walter, stand close to the tree and make it hum as loudly as you can. The rest of us will gaze up into the branches and look for a sign."

# Chapter 30
# Monday, 12:00 p.m.

As Walter stood by the tree, Alton felt a steady rumble beneath his feet, as if the earth were percolating, preparing for something awful. He felt the wind pick up, and saw surreal flashes in the sky: black lightning.

"Sivvius's attack upon the earth is building! Look with great intensity into the branches of the tree. Walter, get closer to the tree—grasp it with your hands."

Alton heard the humming of the tree intensifying.

"Look! Look into the branches! Oh God, please help us!"

As Alton looked into the branches, he noticed something strange about one of them. He strained his eyes and could clearly see that it appeared to be glowing, even pulsating, with some type of energy.

"Look into the tree! Do you see the branch with the strange light? It looks like—"

"Alton!" screamed Walter. "I see it too! There is a branch that appears to be glowing."

"Quickly Walter," said Alton. "Climb the tree—see if it holds the scroll that awaits. Find a way to get it and bring it down here immediately!"

Without a word, Walter scurried up the tree. Alton watched as he reached the glowing branch, almost falling as he reached toward where the glow was the brightest.

"It looks like there is a cylinder attached to the branch!" yelled Walter. "Let me see if I can get to it!"

"Be careful, Walter!" yelled Alton as he watched him dangle precariously, straining toward the branch.

"Yes! I can feel it! It's smooth and hard, except, yes, I feel some type of latches. Let's see ... yes! I can slide them open! Yes! Yes! I feel parchment within! It's a scroll!"

"Quickly, Walter, bring it down!" yelled Alton.

Walter closed the latches, scurried back down the tree, dropped to the ground and sat panting. He opened the latches again and removed the scroll. "I can't believe we have the third scroll!"

The black lightning and wind were intensifying as Angus bellowed, "Come on, laddie! Read it!"

"Yes," said Alton. "Do not delay!"

Walter pressed his thumb on the seal, heard the familiar release, and removed the ribbon. He rolled open the scroll, the parchment shaking in his hands.

"It's the same code as the others! It says:

"You have found this scroll because it was your destiny, my great son Walty the warrior. You have done well. You have fought the good fight against Sivvius. You have endured much pain and agony. Unfortunately, the world will most likely be on the verge of being completely controlled by Sivvius as you read this, with evil rampant throughout the earth, and devastation across the land. I know that the evil you are facing is spiritual. It is demonic. I never saw demons in my time travels, but from what I did see—all the devastation and agony on the earth—I knew no human could have caused it. I knew there was far more at work than just Sivvius and his evil army. Behind his army is truly a vast network of demons, working throughout the earth.

"I hate that you had to go through so much, my son, but it had to be this way. I studied and analyzed all the possible scenarios. If I killed Sivvius when he was young, his death would have led to horrible consequences for you. If I had given you any of the information in the scrolls before the time was right, the consequences would also have been horrible. You see, my son, I trained you for the days of the scrolls. I also knew it would take more than just you. It would take all of you, deep men of science and of God, working as one, preparing for what was to come. And even when the time came, the scroll information could not be revealed too soon, and not all at once, for many reasons—reasons that would take far too long to explain in this scroll. Just trust me that everything had to happen the way it did.

"Regarding Alton, without him, none of this would have been possible. I learned of Alton in my time travels. I learned that he knew Sivvius as a boy, and that he saw Sivvius change from a good, pure boy into a raging maniac—yet he would never give up trying to encourage him to come back to God. I also learned that Alton was a great scientist with a deep love for Einstein's work, that he was a man worthy of trust, and a man of very strong faith in God. It was these traits that enabled me to trust him with the secret Einstein text that would eventually lead you to the first scroll.

"Much to my delight, Einstein asked to write the text himself as a tribute to me, and as a validation of my formula— a formula for which he praised me many times. I thank God I was able to travel back in time to meet Einstein. He was a friend who I could tell my greatest discoveries to in complete confidence.

"I hope you and your friends are all strong in your faith in God Almighty. I hope what I taught you as a boy stayed with you, and I hope Alton has been a strong mentor to you in the ways of God. You will need every ounce of your faith in God during the final battle against Sivvius. You will need to overflow with praise to God, and you will need to completely trust in Him—you must not let fear consume you. Cry out to God with praise and prayer and He will place a mighty hedge of protection around you. And you must do this together in unity.

"With the demonic forces at his side, Sivvius has surely won many souls for evil, and his power will be vast and deep. Only the power of God can enable you to win the final battle. Trust God. Praise Him. Rejoice. Stand as one against Sivvius.

"And remember that time equals mass is a proven formula, and holds great promise. The location jumping aspect of the formula is powerful, but the time-jumping aspect is even more so, and must be used for a very special good when Sivvius is at his weakest. The only way for Sivvius to repent will be by seeing himself in another way. Consult with Alton on this. I believe he will know what to do."

Walter paused.

"Is there any more, Walter?" asked Alton.

"Well—"

Black lightning fingers raced across the sky as small marbles of electricity dropped to the ground. One landed near Walter, fizzing with its electric voice, dancing on the ground, leaving burn marks and puffs of smoke. The wind howled, and the ground rumbled louder.

"Time is short!" yelled Alton. "Sivvius's desolation wave is growing rapidly. We need to do motion now. I sense that Sivvius will be coming in for the kill at any moment. He tried to kill us in the shuttle bus with his terrible power of essence death, and there is no reason to believe he won't use it again when he finds us. I doubt he will waste any time with knowledge destruction or stop motion—he will surely channel all his strength into one final blow against us. So we need to practice the dance of defense one more time, with a laser-sharp focus on defense against the essence death. And as we dance, let us ponder on the deep truths from the third scroll. But first, let's get back to the main trail where it's more level and we have more room to practice."

They rushed back down to the main trail and entered into the dance of defense, honing leg and palm positioning, practicing their stomping, praising God together in song. The sound of the seven men raising their voices to God in unity brought chills through Alton's body. He knew the praise was the most powerful aspect of the dance, and he sensed levels of peace and confidence beyond any he had ever experienced.

He was jolted from his peace as he felt the earth crescendo and shift beneath his feet. Massive chunks of hail fell, chipping away at the trees. The wind was whipping around them, making it difficult to remain upright. Hot gas and fire shot from the ground, engulfing nearby trees in flames. The black lightning grew in intensity as it did its menacing dance of destruction—striking tree after tree, causing even more fires.

"Here it comes! Sivvius, with the help of his Captains, is unleashing an all-out, final assault on the planet: a final devastation. Everything is being altered around us. I just pray that what Sivvius is doing is not causing permanent damage. I hope that once we stop him, the earth will settle, and it will heal."

He could see the others were filled with fear. "Oh God, help us! The devastation is upon us! The end draweth nigh!"

"Alton, I'm not sure we're going to make it," said Michael. "Look at what's happening all around us. What should we do? The trees, the earth ... shifting ... changing ... burning. I've never felt such fear!"

"Michael and all of you, listen to me. I'm just as afraid as you are. But we must stay focused. I refuse to believe we came this far only to have it all end here. Trust in God. We've made it to this point for a reason."

Clouds swirled, torrents of rain battered the land. Then the rain stopped. Then it fell again. Electric balls were dancing everywhere. One bounced off Alton's sleeve, leaving a black burn mark. The ground was covered with patches of black smoke from the spouts of flame that were sporadically erupting. Alton was sure he felt the ground softening beneath his feet. He had been so worried about the flames and the lightning, but had not conceived of his body sinking into the ground. The world seemed to be spiraling out of control. Alton feared they might not make it. He prayed as he had never prayed before.

"Alton! What do we do?" screamed Walter. "We are going to die!"

"No Walter! Don't say it. Don't give up. Keep singing praises to God. He will protect us!"

"Alton, I'm sinking into the ground!" cried out Michael.

Black, menacing clouds began filling the sky around them. They moved in closer. Alton felt the air pressure around him increasing. He watched helplessly as the clouds continued moving toward them, from above and on all sides. The clouds were so black he soon couldn't see anything. It was completely dark.

"Alton," cried out Patrick, "fear consumes me!"

The others were crying out in fear as well, as they were completely isolated in deep blackness.

"Keep the faith. Keep praising God!"

Suddenly the wind died down, the terrible sounds of devastation around them softened, and light began to appear gradually, as if someone was turning up the dimmer switch on a lamp. Alton breathed a guarded sigh of relief as things settled.

# Chapter 31
# Monday, 12:45 p.m.

"Foolish ones," boomed a voice from the distance. It was a deep, strong voice that penetrated to the marrow of Alton's bones. Alton looked down the main trail and saw Sivvius walking toward them. He felt the eyes of evil boring into his very soul. He felt a chill and emptiness filling him. He felt paralyzing fear race through his body.

"Did you think I would not find you again? You escaped me in the van, but this time there is no escape. Now you shall die! Even you, Letter A and B. I gave you your chance in the van, and you betrayed me. And Walter, you shall never have Ingrid now—you will be far too dead!"

"Focus on the dance of defense and keep praising God!" screamed Alton.

The chaos around them resumed, this time more furious than before. The wind, the lightning, the hail, the electric balls, the splitting ground. Hail was hammering Alton, pelting his body, some chunks so big they left welts on him. Alton felt the ground beneath him becoming more unstable, and his feet began to feel the heat from a boiling mass below the surface.

"Praise God! And dance as you've never danced before! Use the precise techniques we've practiced!"

"Your dance is futile, you imbeciles!" shouted Sivvius as he waved his arms. "Don't you know your end is coming right now? You will be dead and gone, and with my final devastation completed, the millions of souls that are on the verge of turning from God to evil, will finally turn. They will become soldiers in my mighty army! Now, DIE!" He thrust his arms toward them.

Alton felt the darkness rush into his mind. His thoughts were a jumble of praise and fear and darkness. It felt like tentacles of death were wrapping around his brain, squeezing, squishing, like an evil hand draining a sponge of its water. He looked to the others and saw total fear on their faces. He looked at Sivvius and saw power and confidence on his face. He saw the devastation around them intensifying: trees burning, the ground churning, lightning striking everywhere.

"You can't escape my essence death this time!" shouted Sivvius. "This very moment you are dying. In a matter of seconds, you will be dead. And I'll finally be free of you. There will be nothing to stop me from my final victory. Thank you for this death power, my mighty friends from beyond! I am enraptured with your evil might!"

Alton felt the tentacles of death tightening. He felt the life being squeezed out of him. "Don't give up! Don't let the essence death of Sivvius destroy you. Focus on praise! Let us sing together as we've never sung before! There is power in the praise!"

They intensified their praise to God, their voices rising toward heaven in a sweet chorus. The power and unity of the seven voices brought joy to Alton's heart. He felt the pressure on his brain subsiding. He felt the tentacles easing their grip.

"Alton!" shouted Walter. "I feel strength coming back! I feel this essence death seeping away!"

"Me too!" shouted Letter A.

"And me!" shouted Letter B.

"Aye," barked Angus. "You scum dog, Sivvius! Your essence death is nothin'!"

"Keep praising!" shouted Alton. "God is pouring out His massive protection. He is honoring our praise and our trust in Him!"

The voices of the seven rang out with power as Alton felt the essence death continue to seep away. He saw the contorted, agonized look on Sivvius's face.

* * *

Sivvius could not believe what was happening. "This can't be possible," he screamed into the air. "They can't be defending this. They should be dead." He looked into the sky and yelled with all his might: "My friends! Help me! Bring power to me greater than any ever before! Help me to release a wave of essence death that cannot be stopped!"

Sivvius waved his arms in the air as he reached out to his friends with his mind. He felt power filling his body. He felt it welling up, sizzling through his brain, pulsating in his heart. He felt madness raging through his mind. He shot his arms toward the Council members, releasing the essence death. He watched with joy as Michael and Patrick fell to their knees. He rejoiced as he saw the look of pain on Alton's face. He cackled as he watched fear consume the faces of the Letter brothers.

* * *

Once more, Alton felt the tentacles crushing his brain. He felt life rushing out of him. "We must maintain the praise. Sing louder, my warriors of praise! Praise as one! Do not let fear consume you. Praise through the fear! Let the praise stand against all evil. Believe in God's power and protection. Focus your thoughts on God. God is far greater than any power Sivvius can unleash. Again I say, there is power in the praise!"

The seven voices of praise rose in unity and power. Even Michael and Patrick, still on their knees, sang with power and might. Alton felt the tentacles softening again. He felt life pulsing through his body.

"It's working!" shouted Walter. "God's power of protection is incredible!"

"Yes, Walter! God is awesome! Keep praising!"

*   *   *

Within himself, Sivvius was in agony. He felt the madness racing through his mind. He could not believe this incredibly powerful wave of essence death was being halted. Suddenly he felt a speck of goodness deep within himself bubbling up. He thought it was gone, but now he realized it had only been suppressed. Somehow, the pressure of the battle had allowed this good to seep out from the hidden places of his mind. He felt his insanity growing, like an unstoppable plague rushing through his body. He fought with himself to maintain a sense of control.

Sivvius raised his head to the sky and cried out again. "My friends! More! Give me more! All the power you have! I don't care about the cost! Whatever it takes to end this once and for all!" He felt the power building again. He felt the sizzling again, the pulsing. It grew rapidly. He felt it consume his body and mind. It became so intense he began to fear it. He felt like his body was about to explode. He struggled to think. He waved his arms, once again feeling the power pulse through his arms, expanding into his hands. He thrust his hands at them, and as the energy surged out of him, he felt a sudden weakness. A deep weakness. As if part of his life essence had surged out with the power. Then he felt a pulse of energy against his body. It seeped into him. He felt it sucking out his own life. It was as if some of the essence death had bounced back upon him. The madness raced through his mind. It sapped him of strength.

* * *

The latest wave of energy was so strong it knocked Alton to the ground. He felt the tentacles again. Darkness and death pulsed through his body. He knew God was protecting them, but this wave was beyond any other. He could barely think. His body was robbed of all strength. He felt the wave pulsing through his body. Fear consumed his thoughts. And the devastation intensified. His feet began sinking into the ground, the heat seeping through his shoes. Hail pelted his body. Electric balls bounced off his head, burning his hair and sending charges of mind-numbing electricity through his skull. Fire spread across the land as all the beauty around them was consumed by Sivvius's brutal devastation.

The praise continued, but the voices were weaker, fading.

"Oh God, help us!" cried out Alton. "What should we do, Lord? This last wave is just too much. How can we overcome this attack?" Alton pushed past the fear and focused all his thoughts on God. He sensed something.

"Angus, I was just thinking of the Jakes!"

"Are you daft, man? How can you be thinkin' of the Jakes now? We're about to die here!"

"Walter … remember the Jakes? Remember how Angus named them all the same name?"

"Yes, Alton," Walter said, his words barely audible.

"Michael, remember how he called one and they'd all come?"

"Yes, Alton," said Michael. "And remember the neighbor?"

"Yes," said Patrick. "The neighbor was named Jake too! Say his name and the dogs come running!"

"Lots of dogs," said Letter A.

"All at once," said Letter B.

A laugh seeped out of Alton's mouth. He couldn't begin to fathom how, not with all the death and darkness he was feeling. Yet he kept laughing.

"Come here, Jake," laughed A.

"Yeah—come on Jake, one and all," laughed B

"That's it!" said Alton. "Laugh. Forget the fear. Forget the darkness. Stand against it. Resist it. Remember the good, pure humor we had, thanks to Angus. Remember the camaraderie we felt. Laugh together. Let your fear go. Laugh in the face of what is going on around us! Laugh at the fear!"

They were all laughing, even Angus.

"Now, reach out to God! Trust in Him with all that is within you. Now that we are not consumed by fear, our praise can be full and strong. We can sing like never before! Let your joy in God bubble out of you like water from a mountain spring! Let it gush out of you like a massive waterfall over a mighty cliff."

As the praise rose to the heavens, Alton felt the tentacles release their hold. He felt darkness diminishing, light seeping into his body.

"God has shown us a wonderful thing today! He has shown us that laughter is the inverse of fear, and stands against it. Laughing in the face of fear and imminent death, and joining in unity in a pleasant memory, helped us to forget about our terrible situation ... it helped us rise above fear. It enabled us to trust in God and praise Him from the depths of our souls! Now the praise is filling the air, and the essence death has no more power over us. It's gone! One more time I say, there is power in the praise!"

\* \* \*

"Noooo!" screamed Sivvius. "I will not let you win." Sivvius was consumed with rage and madness. Losing the latest round of battle, combined with his agonizing struggle to eliminate the final good in himself, fueled his madness.

"More, my friends! Fill me again! All your power! Through me! Send it all through me!" Sivvius's mind boiled as the power filled him again. It was so strong, he was sure his brain was going to explode. Fear gripped him. Madness wrapped itself around his every fleeting thought. Just as he was about to pass out, he managed to release another wave of essence death, hoping with all that was within him it would be enough to kill them. As it left him, he felt his strength leaving, his body sagging. He stared at Alton, but saw no change in his expression. A wave of energy slammed back into Sivvius. He felt death race through his body. He dropped to his knees.

*   *   *

Alton saw despair and insanity wrestling across Sivvius's face as he watched him mumbling. He knew that somehow, God's protection had caused the essence death to bounce back into Sivvius. Alton feared that Sivvius might die and be eternally lost. Compassion filled Alton's heart. He was about to cry out to Sivvius, but Sivvius raised his head and stared at Alton. Sivvius's eyes were blazing not just with insanity, but also with a strange, new, demented confidence. Alton sensed something terrible … something awful … something the friends from beyond had just revealed to Sivvius.

Sivvius broke his stare, jumped to his feet, and snapped his head toward the sky. "Thank you for your guidance, my friends. Now, I ask, in the name of Satan: send your army of demons to wage war against this pathetic band of seven fools!"

Alton froze.

"Alton!" shouted Walter. "What is he talking about? Can this happen?"

Alton began to feel a strange heaviness in the air.

"Pray, Walter! We must all pray! And sing!"

But they were not singing. Alton knew they felt the strange heaviness as well. It was growing rapidly, and it was so dense and so dark, it was paralyzing.

"Yes!" screamed Sivvius. "My friends, let your demonic army wage their war!"

Alton sensed an utterly evil presence like never before. He felt an evil force pressing against him, fear racing through his mind, consuming his thoughts. He could not see the demons, but he could feel their power. The evil presence was so thick in the air he could almost taste it. Alton dropped to the ground, his knees tingling against the hot, mushy surface. He felt himself losing consciousness. He saw the others on the ground as well, writhing in fear and pain.

"My friends! Fill me with power one more time! Give me one final wave of essence death. These fools are completely vulnerable now. Let us end this now!"

Alton watched Sivvius reaching his hands up into the air, receiving power from his friends, preparing for the final blow. "God! Please help us! We can't stand against this. What should we do? What should I pray for?"

Alton saw Sivvius shaking as the demonic power filled his body.

Alton squeezed his eyes tight, and focused all his senses on God, listening with his mind and spirit. He felt inspiration from God. He knew what to do.

"Lord Jesus," cried out Alton, "please send your angels to fight against the demonic forces from beyond. In your mighty, awesome and perfect name, we ask that you send your mightiest warrior angels."

Alton immediately felt a rush of chills. They were chills of confirmation. He knew God was going to answer his prayer. He sensed in his spirit that God had been preparing the angels for this very moment. He knew the final step was for him to ask. He knew now, more than ever, that God had chosen to use His angels in this final battle. He started to feel a divine presence as he had never felt before. It was driving out the evil presence that had been so thick in the air. The weight upon him was lifting. Light consumed him. He saw joy and wonder on the faces of his friends.

"NOOOOO!" bellowed Sivvius. He waved his arms in the air and snapped them toward Alton. Alton felt only a wisp of air pulse against his body.

"Council of Seven! God has truly sent mighty warrior angels to fight the demons in the spiritual realm around us. The battle is waging now! I sense it in my spirit. I feel it in the air. And the angels of God are winning. The demons can't stand against them. Raise your voices in praise to God! Let us join in the battle with our praise."

"Help me, my friends," screamed Sivvius. "Empower the demons! Give me power!" Sivvius reached his arms up, waved them around, and thrust them toward Alton. Again and again he flailed his arms. His face was fully contorted with insanity and agony.

Alton felt nothing from Sivvius's futile attempts. As the seven continued their praise, he felt divine waves of peace. The waves grew in intensity and frequency, each wave bringing more peace. He sensed the angels were on the verge of victory.

The peace soon became so thick in the air that Alton felt the final wisps of evil dissipating. Then, just as if it had never been there, he felt complete absence of evil. He knew the angels had conquered the demonic forces. He knew even the mighty friends from beyond had been shattered. He knew God had sent and empowered the mightiest of angels to win this final battle with precision and swiftness. He was completely shocked how quickly God and His mighty angels had won. He looked up at Sivvius and saw him drop his arms to his sides and collapse to his knees. He saw complete dejection and agony on his face. Alton could not bear to look. He shifted his gaze away from him.

\* \* \*

Sivvius stayed on his knees, exhausted. "I can't believe what has happened," he whispered to himself. He cried out to his friends from beyond but sensed nothing. They were no longer with him. Any power he had possessed had fled with them. He felt completely alone, utterly dejected, and absolutely powerless. "I never thought it would come to this. I have lost everything. I have risked everything, and lost everything. My whole life ... wasted. All of it over and done with so quickly in this final battle. The fruit of decades of sacrifice ... decades of work ... spoiled forever ... rotten and dead to the core.

"Maybe I should have listened to Alton. This happened because of my choice: I chose evil, and evil cannot stand against God.

"Now I must face the consequences. I have failed my friends from beyond. Because of my failure, they have lost as well. They will torture me forever for this loss. And even worse, I have failed Satan. He will make me pay. He will create a special place in hell for me. He will torment me forever, with the most awful torment imaginable. And I know God will never forgive me for what I have done. A lifetime of harassing His elect and leading countless souls to evil ... how could He ever forgive such a thing? Even if He could, I could not accept it. I would not know how to. My friends may be gone, but evil is still in me. I AM evil. My destiny is set. Oh, what a wretched man I am."

Sivvius felt his body sagging even more. He rocked back and forth in a daze. He felt utter despair. Utter hopelessness. He couldn't analyze or plan or scheme or hardly even think any more. There was nothing left. He was silent, as the magnitude of what had happened resonated throughout his being.

He felt the deepest agony he had ever experienced in his life. For the first time, he realized the magnitude of the terrible evil he had done. He felt just how dark his soul had become. Yet he sensed something else. A small measure of hope, a trace of goodness, still there, not fully extinguished, now aching to be released. But he could not release it, could not bring it out, could not remember what it was like to feel forgiveness. With the small measure of strength left in his body, he managed to whisper something he thought he would never even think.

"Alton ... please ... help me."

# Chapter 32
# Monday, 1:00 p.m.

Alton looked around and was amazed by one thing more than any other: there was complete silence. He could not remember ever experiencing such quiet. There was no wind, no lightning, no cracking earth, and no yells from Sivvius. Just perfect silence. And perfect peace. A thought gently weaved through his mind. He smiled as he let it whisper across his lips: "We won."

Alton stood motionless, bathing in the glorious peace. Then he heard a mild fluttering around him as he noticed leaves growing back on the trees. He watched as the cracks in the ground closed. He watched in awe as the earth around them was miraculously restored. Flowers pushed up from the ground, charred bark regained its original texture, the smell in the air became sweet and fresh and new.

It was all so amazing, yet he knew something even more amazing had just occurred. He looked at Sivvius, with his head still sagging toward the ground.

"Of course I will help you, old friend. I forgive you for all you have done to me. And even after all you have done against God, He will still forgive you. He *can* forgive you, just as completely as He forgives those with the smallest of sins. He truly loves you. That is the power and mystery of His amazing grace. All you need do is cry out to Him. Ask for forgiveness. Seek His son. Become His friend. You can have complete cleansing and freedom through Christ! Then goodness will flow through you again."

Sivvius lifted his head and stared deeply into Alton's eyes. Alton could see the yearning, the searching, the struggling.

"Remember what it was like before you turned to evil? Remember the joyous days of your early youth, when you used to know God? Can you remember now?"

Sivvius remained silent, staring into Alton's eyes ... searching.

"Let go, Sivvius. Let go of the past. Let go of your fear. Let go of your hopelessness. Turn to God and ask for His forgiveness. Accept His son into your heart. Receive a new and fresh way of thinking. It is never too late. Remember Saul. Remember the thief on the cross."

Sivvius bowed his head but remained silent.

"Yes, Sivvius. That's it. Bow your head to God and ask forgiveness. He waits at the door to hear your words."

\* \* \*

Sivvius's thoughts were running wild. Could what Alton has said really be true? Could I really have a second chance? Could God really forgive me for a lifetime of evil? Could I really be saved from this utter hopelessness and agony and fear? Could I really ... have joy again? He felt a glimmer of hope percolating deep within his soul, yet could not let it rise. He could not allow himself to receive forgiveness. It was just too late. He had done too much. He had done far worse than Saul or the thief on the cross. He realized Alton could not help him.

\* \* \*

"Alton," he whispered, "I can't do it. I'm too far gone. I can't talk to God about this."

Alton sighed. He knew there was nothing more he could say to convince him. Sivvius was unable to grasp the power and reality of God's forgiveness and love. A lifetime of evil thoughts had grooved such a pattern in his mind that he couldn't open it to a new way of thinking. He pulled the sprays from his pockets. He knew what must be done. He had considered it for a long time, and the third scroll had confirmed it.

"Sivvius, do not be afraid. I will send you to a place that will enable you to remember what it was like to have joy and wonder. You must see yourself in another way: the way you used to be. You must go to a place where you will remember the good. You must see what you were before Satan wreaked havoc in your life. You must see how he turned you against God. You must see your wrong choices. You must see yourself as God sees you."

Alton looked deeply into Sivvius's eyes as he prepared to spray. He focused intensely on sending only Sivvius, and then sprayed the three sprays upon his own arm.

"Remember that God loves you."

Alton watched Sivvius slowly fade away.

"Goodbye, my old friend," said Alton, tears welling in his eyes.

There was silence ... for a long time. Finally, Walter broke it.

"Where did you send him, Alton?"

"Do you recall what your father said in the third scroll about the time equals mass formula holding great promise?"

"Yes, at least to some extent. But there was a lot going on, so I don't recall everything."

Alton motioned for the others to gather around.

"Walter has asked a great question, and I would like for all of you to hear the answer. The third scroll mentioned that the location-jumping aspect of the formula is very powerful, but that the time-jumping aspect is even more powerful, and would need to be used for a very special good when Sivvius is at his weakest. He mentioned that the only way for Sivvius to repent would be to see himself another way.

"Today I used the sprays for this very special good. I sent him back in time to his childhood. To the time when he was happy, and free, and good. To a time before he turned evil. To a time before his father became abusive and mentally destroyed his mother. I want him to remember just how wonderful things used to be. I think his eyes will be opened when he sees himself the way he was then. And when he sees the trigger point that started his turn away from God, the point where he made the first wrong choice, he will see how Satan used that to pave the way to offer many more opportunities for wrong choices that ultimately led him away from God. This is the only way to help Sivvius overcome the patterns of evil that have been ingrained in his mind. This is the only way for Sivvius to repent and turn to God."

"But how will it work, Alton? Will there be two of him?"

"Yes, Walter, I'm quite sure of it. He will be there in his current state of mind and body, and he will also see himself as a boy."

"I wonder what will happen. Is there not a risk of something getting fouled up in the space-time continuum?"

"There is risk, to be sure. But to reach Sivvius, it will take much. And he must be reached. He must see himself as he was. I believe we'll know if something goes wrong in time. If so, we'll pray, and we'll find a way to mend the fabric of time."

"But what about Sivvius's evil army? What will happen to it, now that Sivvius is gone? And what of all the souls that are part of it … all the souls that are on the path to eternal hell?"

"Sivvius's evil army has been dealt a mighty blow today. With their General of evil gone, and God's healing power upon the earth evident around us, I feel hope that many will turn back to God. It's never too late for them until they die. Just like it's still not too late for Sivvius. As they see the beauty of the earth being restored, they may develop faith in God again. You know human nature, my friend. It's much easier to follow God when everything is going well. But when things get really tough, true character is required, and many fall away. So now that things are going better, perhaps many will realize what they've done and turn back to God.

"Yet it would be naive and unwise of me to think the army will simply dissipate over time and eventually be no more. We'll need to pray for the salvation of lost souls, and especially the Captains. There are many Captains who were personally trained and grown by Sivvius. There are surely some who will be power-hungry and ambitious enough to try to rise to be the new General. One thing we can and should pray for, is that the Captains compete so much against each other in their lustful attempts at more power, they weaken the army from within.

"We may even need to attempt to meet with some of the Captains. We can tell them what mighty acts God has done and how He has defeated Sivvius. If we could get some Captains to repent, or at least one, it could pave the way for massive repentance through the ranks.

"We must also study time equals mass further. The power to send others back in time, as we did with Sivvius, could help them to have a better chance at repentance as well. Just think of the power of this ... to be able to send those that turned away from God to the point when they used to be close to Him, or to the trigger-point in their lives that sent them down the wrong path—whether they had ever known God or not. We'll see how things turn out with Sivvius. We'll learn from that. I speak of many things, though. We'll need to pray about these things, and talk more about these things."

"But what about ... what about my dear Ingrid? I don't know if I can stand another day without the hope of using the sprays to find her. How much longer must I wait? I've thought about trying to find her here in this time, but ... I'm afraid. I'm afraid she'll be with another. I'm afraid after decades of longing for her that if I found her married to another man I'd be crushed and utterly rejected. Hopelessly alone for the rest of my days."

Alton rested a hand upon Walter's shoulder and gave a reassuring squeeze.

"We shall truly make this a top priority, Walter. We can start with developing a plan for how we will help you reach her. The priority has been on using the sprays only for defeating Sivvius, and although we have much to do to reach the many other deceived souls on the earth, your aching for Ingrid is of great importance to me. We shall spend some time each week experimenting with the sprays to help you find her in the past. You *will* find her. Perhaps you will be able to speak with your younger self and encourage him to win her heart. We will find a way.

"For now, let us enjoy this moment of triumph! Sivvius has been defeated, the earth has been restored, and the way has been paved for the salvation of millions of souls! Let us bow our heads in a prayer of thanksgiving to Almighty God."

Alton's heart leapt when he saw the looks of joy as he gathered everyone in a circle. When they finished their prayer, Alton laid out the plans for their next steps.

"My dear friends, with God's help we have truly triumphed. We stuck together and never gave up. And we have all grown closer to God. We have seen the mighty power of His love as it defended us and delivered us into victory. Hats off to each and every one of you for staying the course. Yet as much as I would love for us to take a long vacation, we must not lose the momentum or any ground we have gained. There are many things we need to do—"

"Sorry to interrupt," said Angus, "but did you feel anything strange?"

"I thought it might have just been me that felt it, probably due to exhaustion. What exactly did you feel?"

"Hard to say for sure. It just felt strange."

"I also felt something unusual," said Michael. "What about you guys?" he asked the Letter brothers.

"Yes ... I felt something, but I don't quite know how to describe it," said A.

"Can't describe it," said B.

"Patrick? What about you?"

"Yes," said Patrick. "Something strange. It's almost like I felt lighter for a moment."

"Yes," said Alton. "Lighter, or almost like a feeling of disorientation. Completely different from anything I felt during Sivvius's attacks."

"Uh oh," said Walter."

"What do you mean, uh oh?" barked Angus.

"Well, I did see a little something else in the scroll just as Sivvius was unleashing his final attack. But we were so consumed with the battle, I had no chance to mention it."

"So there were more words?" asked Alton.

"Yes."

"Please tell me! What did they say?"

"Something about how even with Sivvius being fully defeated, there would be some very serious lingering issues we would need to resolve."

"Some issues?"

"Yes ... some things we would need to work out. Some problems caused by Sivvius. Apparently, he got a little carried away with his weather attacks and caused some imbalances in the earth's core. I think the strange sensations we are having may have something to do with that."

"These imbalances, are they—"

"So what're we supposed to do, Walter?" barked Angus as he cut off Alton's question.

"Well, the scroll kind of said that if we didn't work out these issues, things might not go too well."

"Like in what way, you pork shank?"

"It didn't get into too much detail, other than saying if we didn't work them out, the earth might implode."

"Implode?"

"Yeah, you know, like explode but in an inward kind of way?"

"I know what implosion is laddie, but you mean to tell me the scroll said the earth could implode if we didn't work some things out?"

"I'm afraid so."

"Did it give us any hints about how to work them out?"

"Not anything substantial. But it did say we'd better not wait too long …"